Divine Fate

To Pam –
Thank you for your
support and friendship during
this long process!
            much love,
            Audrey

Audrey M. Insoft

First published by Dog Ear Publishing
4010 W. 86th Street, Ste H
Indianapolis, IN 46268
www.dogearpublishing.net

ISBN: 978-1-4575-1329-9

This book is printed on acid-free paper.

Printed in the United States of America

To David,
who gave me wit, wisdom, and the courage to continue

To Alexander,
who gave me inspiration, imagination, and pure joy

Truly, I've experienced Divine Fate.

Author's Note

I met Sandy and Paul Pinkerton in September of 2000 when they facilitated the adoption of my son Alexander. At the time I knew little about them and had few opportunities to socialize with them during my trip to Vietnam. Over the years I gleaned bits and pieces of their story as annual Christmas letters told of adoption trips, news of their growing family, and orphanage projects. Adoption websites provided glowing accounts of their work by appreciative families, and a friend told me about Paul's surprising MIA discovery during an annual Tet (Vietnamese New Year) party. It was through this haphazard information-gathering that I discovered their remarkable story and approached them with the idea of documenting it in a book. Paul readily consented, while Sandy had to be convinced it was a good idea. When you read the book, you'll understand why.

At first glance Paul's story may not appear groundbreaking. Like many young men who entered the Vietnam War, he was scared and uncertain. Like most, he returned home marked by the experience, a changed man. Yet the similarities end there. Unlike others, Paul's experiences gnawed at him after the war and propelled him into action. He had only a high school education, yet soon found himself in a circle of politicians, journalists, and foreign dignitaries. He was a man of limited financial means, yet he self-funded numerous trips across the globe in search of POWs and MIAs. Motivated by guilt, remorse, and regret, Paul based his life's work on seeking redemption from his past.

Sandy was also unrelenting in the search to find meaning in her life. The product of an unhappy childhood, she looked for a place to fit in, to belong, to be loved—a way to erase her family history. It was through this emotional pain that she discovered her passion in life: forming families through adoption. It was from her own heartache that she developed an affinity for special needs children—the children most likely to be rejected, the children most like herself.

Paul and Sandy were adventurers, risk-takers, and pioneers. They pursued their dreams when common sense dictated otherwise. They made choices that most rational people would not consider. They fought for what they believed in, gave up a normal lifestyle, and made huge sacrifices in the process. As a result they have been called heroes, saints, and martyrs. This is but one reason, why I find their story so compelling.

Divine Fate is a story of abandonment and loss, but also one of bravery, resilience, and perseverance. The book documents the Pinkerton's journey through life and how they overcame their past to make more fulfilling futures for themselves.

This is neither a war book nor an adoption book. Yet, set against the backdrop of both the Vietnam War and the adoption world, the reader is taken behind-the-scenes to look at both venues. I was completely captivated by Paul and Sandy's stories; I hope you will be, as well.

Divine Fate is their story, told to me from their viewpoint and perspective. It's an account of their life events as they experienced them, and I interpreted them. I've spent hundreds of hours interviewing them, their families, friends, and coworkers, and conducting extensive research to fill in the blanks. Every attempt has been made to verify the facts and seek the truth.

Even so, keep in mind that Paul and his fellow veterans have stretched their memories back forty years to recall events they've actively tried to forget. A number of people could not be located including: Fran Myers, Scott Collins, Major Cecil Hill, and a few of the veterans mentioned in this book. Others declined interviews including: Karl Campbell, Bobbi Campbell, Martha Pinkerton Maney, Carol Pinkerton Kipphorn, Sister Hai, and the current staff at Lutheran Social Services (LSS) of New England. Despite these shortcomings, I was able to piece together the Pinkerton's story in what I believe is an accurate account of their life history.

Writing this book has been an incredible journey for me. I have a new appreciation for the sacrifices made by the men and women in uniform, both on and off the battlefield. Sadly, many continue to suffer from Post-Traumatic Stress Disorder (PTSD) and the lingering effects of combat. Paul's story wouldn't exist but for the fact that he agonized over his war experiences, using his burden to help the abandoned and forgotten in the world. Many of us have reaped the benefits of his pain through our adoptions.

The issues surrounding POWs and MIAs are extremely complex and I've barely scratched the surface. It's interesting to note that after each major war, civilians and veterans have conducted searches for the missing, which have been successful in some cases. Yet, according to statistics from the Defense Prisoner of War/Missing Personnel Office (DPMO), approximately 73,000 American military personnel still remain unaccounted for from World War II, 8,000 are still missing from the Korean War, and another 1,700 are unaccounted for in Southeast Asia during the Vietnam era. Although Paul's focus eventually changed from searching for MIAs and POWs to helping orphans, he never forgot his original cause.

As a strong advocate of adoption, I'm a lucky recipient of its process. I am eternally grateful to Sandy and Paul, Lutheran Social Services of New England, Adoptions From The Heart, Sister Hai and others, for the significant roles they played in bringing my son into my life. I have the utmost respect for the adoption agencies mentioned in this book. If my assessments seem critical in any way, that is not my intention. International adoption is a complicated process and one that's constantly in flux. Setbacks and mistakes can occur and should be anticipated by prospective adoptive parents. Sadly, as of 2009, there were still 1.4 million orphans living in Vietnam and approximately 44 million orphans worldwide, according to UN statistics. More recent statistics show the numbers of orphans growing exponentially, with new estimates ranging from 143 to 210 million orphans worldwide. Where would these children be without the many adoptive parents, adoption agencies, and facilitators who work together to form families?

But, while I embrace adoption, I refuse to romanticize or sugarcoat it. Like the hidden atrocities of war, international adoption sometimes has a darker side, a side not as beautiful as its children. Some of the orphanage scenes in this book may shock and disturb you—they should! Please keep in mind that what's common, routine, and acceptable behavior in the United States (with regard to children and orphans), is not necessarily practiced or adhered to, in other countries. Orphans are not always treated well and corruption does exist.

Finally, although this book is based on true events, some names and situations have been changed for legal and privacy reasons.

Now ... let me take you on this journey, where events happen for a reason, divine intervention often exists, and lives are forever changed by strange twists of fate. Perhaps yours will be changed as well.

CHAPTER 1

Subhumans

In war, there are no unwounded soldiers.

—José Narosky

Paul Pinkerton watched his friends disappear into the belly of the cavernous plane and desperately wished there was some way to escape. But of course, there wasn't. He'd spent a year preparing for this moment and now, standing in full military dress, laden with combat gear, there was no turning back.

It was late July, 1968. As he nervously paced the tarmac of Peterson Field in Colorado Springs and waited to enter the plane that would take him to Vietnam, he felt more like a frightened and resentful child than the confident Army sergeant he was presumed to be.

Initially he had viewed the war as something to tolerate, a major inconvenience given the fact he was newly married and starting a career as a barber. A few clergy in town had carefully composed letters for their young parishioners in order for them to obtain conscientious objector status, but Paul felt they were all liars and cheats who had deceived both their Government and the God they professed to worship. He wanted no part of it. So, while he didn't much care about flying halfway across the globe to stop the spread of Communism, his sense of duty, responsibility, and patriotism prevailed.

Not that this feeling came easily or naturally. He hated the idea of being plucked from his middle class life and thrust into war in a country he could barely locate on a map. But worse than that, as the date of departure drew near, he became terrified. Dire warnings from basic training replayed in his head—day in and day out—like a long-running, tormenting tape. Although he didn't know much about war or combat, he

1

knew it was inherently dangerous and most likely deadly, and dying at twenty years of age was not in his plans.

An early, fleeting thought of escaping to Canada was not an option. He was much too attached to his parents and siblings to leave them for an indeterminate amount of time. Plus, his father-in-law, a World War II veteran, would never allow his daughter to leave the country dishonorably. Furthermore, desertion was unheard of in his small home town of Manheim, Pennsylvania. It simply wasn't done.

So here he stood, armed with the little Bible his father had given him and a fierce resentment of the U.S. Government for placing him in the unenviable position of going to war. His mind was filled with wild and irrational thoughts of what awaited him in Vietnam. He was certain he'd have to shoot his way off the plane; a strange misconception that had originated during basic training.

Paul's friends didn't share his opinions or his fears. Mild-mannered Mike Hardin, Paul's closest buddy, took a pragmatic approach to military duty. Mike admitted that serving in a war was not something he relished, but felt it was required payment for living the good life in Ohio. As he put it, "Women bear children and men go to war. It's most likely unpleasant, but it's something you accept because you are who you are." Although sad to leave his family and new bride behind, his feelings were tempered by a healthy dose of youthful cockiness and an untested sense of bravery.

Mike and twenty-three-year-old (Everett) Lewis Page stood together on the tarmac laughing and cutting up for the camera as one of their buddies snapped pictures. Lewis regarded his tour as an exotic and exciting adventure. He was the youngest son in a long line of military men and going to war was an expected obligation. He sauntered into the plane on Mike's heels waving a Confederate flag and replacing his military helmet with a Confederate hat; typical accoutrements for a man from Georgia in those days. The two sat together in the back of the aircraft near the cargo area and exchanged small talk during the long flight.

Paul, Mike, and Lewis were all part of a large military organization: the 1st Infantry Brigade, 5th Infantry Division (Mechanized). Their unit was the Headquarters Company of the 1st Infantry Battalion, 61st Infantry (Mechanized) also known as the 1st of the 61st (1/61st), and they were members of a 4.2 mortar platoon—one of the most dangerous occupations in Vietnam.

They had arrived in Fort Carson, Colorado in March under the code name "Project Diamond" to reorganize and train for deployment to Vietnam. During the fifteen-week training course there had been glimmers of hope the deployment wouldn't occur, but it was only political spin. The war continued. Their Division was alerted for riot control duty on April 6 following the April 4 assassination of Dr. Martin Luther King, Jr. Paul,

Mike, and Lewis had stayed in the airport with their uniforms on, but were not called to duty while their sister unit, the 1/11th had been briefly deployed to Chicago. The three men thought that additional rioting might keep them stateside but, when regular training resumed just a week later, it was certain their destiny was Southeast Asia.

Men in other divisions traveled to Vietnam on commercial jets while Paul, Mike, and Lewis flew on the massive C-141A StarLifter. It was the first jet aircraft designed to meet military standards as both a troop and cargo carrier. Although it may have been acceptable for carrying cargo, it was less than luxurious for passengers. The men sat shoulder-to-shoulder in small canvas jump seats that ran lengthwise along the outer edges of the plane facing inward, or in back-to-back seats in the middle of the aircraft, facing outward. A few small windows were located in the back of the plane where cargo and weapons were stored; otherwise the environment was dark and close.

There were no flight attendants. Meal service consisted of warm canteen water and bad C-rations. The uncomfortable conditions rendered it almost impossible to sleep and there was nothing to distract one's thoughts except for mindless chatter or the occasional card game.

Paul didn't enter the plane with his buddies. He was too engrossed in his own anxieties to seek them out, too worried to socialize. His brooding thoughts finally exhausted him and he went to the back of the plane to look for a place to sleep. Unfortunately, the weapons and gear were piled too high to make that a practical plan.

Earlier in July an advance party of 300 had departed for Vietnam. Paul had been given the opportunity to travel in this early group, but had declined, reasoning there was safety in numbers. Later, he would discover this choice was a mistake. So now, he was among the remaining 4,578 troops of the 5th Division departing from Peterson Field between July 22 and July 31.

Paul's plane contained approximately one hundred men; men whose common bond was entering the unknown, soldiers going to war. Although most had briefly considered the possibility of being injured or perhaps even killed, there were other dangers too treacherous to entertain: being held prisoner or declared missing in action, hiding during combat, taking one's own life, becoming a drug user, committing atrocities, or being a victim of friendly fire. The majority of men on any given plane would see the horrible devastation and painful destruction of combat, but no one could know or predict what his own tour of duty might bring.

There was only one certainty: the youth who entered war would leave it forever changed, transformed from innocent, baby-faced boys into soulful men who had seen too much, too early. On this summer day there was barely a hint of what was to come. These were tan, lean, seemingly invincible soldiers who displayed a confidence not borne out of any real expertise or practical experience, but of youthful naivety and ignorance. As Mike admitted later, "We were all too young and dumb to be afraid." All, that is, except for Paul.

As the flight progressed, there were subtle signs of change. Paul dozed off, only to awaken to the sounds of someone retching nearby. A sour smell of vomit filled the air. "Oh man," he thought, "that's just great! All I need is to smell puke for the next twenty hours."

Few, if any, of the men were accustomed to the rigors of international travel; difficult under the best of circumstances, but unbearable when your final destination was a war zone. Some men vomited because of the swinging canvas seats, others because of nerves, and still others because of heavy drinking the night before. But, whatever the reason, Paul thought it was damn disgusting. The only relief came during intermittent refueling stops along the way.

It was midnight when Paul disembarked in Anchorage, Alaska, his first stop. He and the others stepped off the plane to breathe the cold crisp air, smoke endless cigarettes, and refill their canteens. Later, he would look back longingly at that stop in Alaska and remember how peaceful and still the night had been; serenity he could only dream about in Vietnam.

As the hours wore on, the flight became an uncomfortable blur. The mood in the plane, which had started out somewhat pleasant, turned somber as some of the soldiers now felt like cattle heading to the slaughter. They finally reached Tokyo, a hectic hub that soldiers passed in and out of, on their way to Vietnam. As they were herded into a restricted area of the terminal, a soldier on his way home approached Mike.

"Where you guys headed?" he asked sardonically since he already knew the answer.

"Vietnam," Mike replied.

"Well, that's a good place to be *from*! You remember that." The sarcasm of the returning soldier was a jab to Mike's psyche, but he decided to put the clever little phrase in his back pocket for future use.

The last refueling stop was at the tiny island of Guam where endless rows of B-52s sat ready for combat. Later, no one remembered much about Guam, probably because they were too focused on their next stop: Vietnam.

***

The giant aircraft moved into Vietnamese airspace, the foul air electric with the palpable tension of the men inside. Paul's heart pounded wildly. He held his breath and large beads of sweat formed on his forehead. He couldn't see outside, but he felt the wheels touch the runway. His chest tightened like a vise. The back door of the plane opened with a loud bang and before long, heavy equipment began to unload the duffle bags of personal gear and weapons that were strapped onto skids inside.

Vietnam immediately assaulted the senses. Even before the men stepped off the plane they reacted to the intense heat and stench: "God Almighty, it's hot! What the hell? I can't breathe! What *is* that smell?" According to regulation they were required to stay in full military uniform, including their helmets. Paul's heart had slowed to a mere gallop, but his uniform was already drenched with perspiration.

There was a cacophony of noise with planes taking off and landing every two minutes and incoming mortar attacks in the not-too-distant jungle. The DaNang Airport supported massive numbers of commercial aircraft, fighter jets, and helicopters and was purported to be the busiest airport in the world during the peak years of the war.

Paul moved off the plane and stood under one of the cement revetments built to shield fighter jets from rocket attacks. It provided some small respite from the broiling sun, but it was still damn hot. He surveyed the landscape, spotting Monkey Mountain looming high on the horizon, and thought, "Boy, if I ever get out of this hellhole, I'm never coming back!" Vietnam was like nothing he'd ever experienced; run-down and shabby with air so thick and pungent that stinking heat waves radiated from the pavement like low-lying fog. This was not a place he would have chosen to visit in his wildest dreams. But then again, he didn't pick it; the U.S. Government selected it for him.

He looked at the fighter jets coming and going and realized, as he had at Peterson Field, that there was no place to hide. There was only one goal now: survival.

* * *

A convoy of 2-1/2 ton (Deuce-and-a-half) cargo trucks arrived to take the troops to Wunder Beach, located on the South China Sea approximately eighty miles north of DaNang, along Highway 1 in the mid-section of the country. The soldiers grabbed their duffel bags and their "Matty Mattels," a nickname for the lightweight and almost toy-like M-16 assault rifles they carried, and jumped aboard.

The ride gave everyone pause for concern. No one had been issued ammunition, despite the fact that they could hear incoming rocket and mortar attacks in the distance. The Army wisely decided it was too early in the game to supply the troops with bullets. All it would take was for some nervous, over-eager soldier to start shooting and all hell could break loose.

Lewis, who had been told that the Viet Cong wore conical hats and black pajamas, carefully scrutinized the numerous Vietnamese dressed in this outfit, who walked along the road uncomfortably close to their convoy of trucks. Little did he know that almost everyone dressed this way, Viet Cong or not. But that wasn't his only concern.

"What are these for?" Lewis shouted to the driver, pointing to the sandbags lining the bottom of the truck.

"Landmines!" the driver yelled back knowingly.

Lewis bumped along the road in the open-air truck, wishing he hadn't asked. His anxiety increased as the truck stopped for another incoming attack up ahead. Lewis glanced down at his weapons—an empty .45 pistol and an unloaded grenade launcher—and felt like one giant bull's-eye. For some reason, he had been issued those weapons in lieu of an M-16.

Paul was mesmerized by the passing landscape as he took in the unfamiliar sights and noticed the little Vietnamese children darting in and out of view. His reverie was interrupted.

"Hey Pinky!" someone yelled, causing him to look down. Jim Miller, an acquaintance from Manheim, was on the road below pulling security duty for the convoy.

"I'm short! I'm goin' home next week!" Jim called out exuberantly.

"That's great! See ya back in Manheim!" Paul forced a grin.

"Lucky bastard!" he thought, "I should be the one going home. How am I ever going to get through this?" With twelve long months ahead of him, and fear and uncertainty settling into his gut, a year was an eternity.

* * *

Paul's fears were not unfounded. Statistically speaking, he was in one of the worst possible situations, a fact that became known after the war. The Army sustained 66 percent of all war casualties and 1968 and 1969 were the two deadliest years of the war, the time period in which 48 percent of all war casualties occurred. Paul, Mike, and Lewis were classified as E-05 buck sergeants, a group that sustained 9 percent of all Army casualties, while many of their comrades were E-04s, a group that sustained nearly 20 percent of all Army casualties.

Even being in Vietnam for a single day was risky business. An unsubstantiated yet plausible statistic that appears on The Vietnam War Memorial website (The Wall) states that nearly 1,000 men lost their lives on their very first day in Vietnam. Statistics later showed that the majority of all Army deaths during 1967-1972 occurred while a soldier was in his first three months in-country and still new to the job.

* * *

Paul didn't become a statistic on his first day, nor did his friends. They arrived at Wunder Beach unscathed, although somewhat shaken by their harrowing ride in the convoy. Wunder Beach, true to its name, was a beautiful expanse of white sandy beach on the South China Sea that Lewis swore, even put Daytona to shame. And, lucky for them, it was secure.

The downside was that Wunder Beach was open and deserted and undoubtedly the hottest place they'd ever been in their lives. Although they were required to stay in uniform, a few men purposely exposed their bodies and shaved their heads, becoming so badly sunburned they had to be taken out by medevac. This tactic worked once, then word went out that the next person to go on sick call for sunburn would be court-martialled. Most men complied with the regulations, but secretly swam naked in the cool waters of the South China Sea as soon as they had a chance. It was a temptation too great to resist.

Paul and Mike collected junk from the beach and built makeshift shelters with their plastic ponchos to provide shade from the searing heat. There wasn't much to do and they waited listlessly for additional men and equipment to arrive. They were safe, however, and as far as Paul was concerned, that was nothing to complain about. He sadly realized that the men in the advance party had bided their time and were now a month ahead of him in terms of going home. He'd made the wrong decision, but it was too late to change the past. He spent his days writing passionate love letters to his new bride Patricia (omitting that little detail) and more mundane letters to his parents and friends back home.

Once the men received ammunition, they began to defy authority. Desperate to stay cool, they rolled up their sleeves and pant legs, and took off their helmets. The military provided warm beer and soda, which everyone wanted cold, ice cold. Paul and a few other men took the fire extinguishers out of the tanks and armored personnel carriers (APCs) and used them to cool down the drinks, much to the ire of the officers.

Paul didn't care about their anger and thought to himself, "What are you going to do about it? Send me to Vietnam?"

In basic training, officers had held the upper hand, but now they had to tread lightly. They were dealing with armed and volatile men and although rare, it wasn't unheard of for an unpopular officer to be "accidentally" injured or killed.

Lewis had only been at Wunder Beach for four days when he began to have problems of a different sort from the rest of the men. His jaw was swollen, his teeth were throbbing, and he was in excruciating pain.

An officer noticed his bulging cheek. "Page! What the hell's the matter with you?"

"It's my wisdom tooth, sir." The tooth had bothered him prior to leaving Fort Carson, but no one had believed him; they thought he was just trying to get out of duty.

"Well, go see the medic and get it taken care of."

"Yes sir."

The medic, who was not a dentist, referred him on to the Navy hospital in Dong Ha. From there he was airlifted to the USS Sanctuary, a hospital ship stationed off shore. It was Lewis's first time in a helicopter—a ride he wouldn't soon forget. He traveled with an injured soldier and during the flight, the man rolled onto his lap and died.

Lewis arrived at the hospital ship and was placed with another dental patient. Both men underwent surgery. The surgeon, however, pulled not only Lewis's infected tooth, but two healthy wisdom teeth as well. As they recovered, the two patients sat together, cheeks puffed out, laughing and making fun of each other. But their laughter quickly subsided as they took in their surroundings. The hospital was a gruesome place, filled with men who had sustained all types of horrible injuries. Lewis looked at the man on his right and tried to figure out what was wrong with him. As he continued to stare he eventually determined that the man was smoking a cigarette out of his tracheotomy: the oddest sight he'd ever seen. His bravado shaken, he vowed to be diligent when he returned to his unit.

By the time he recovered, the hospital ship was now in DaNang, far south of Wunder Beach, and Lewis wondered how he'd get back to his unit. The Army liaison wasn't able to help, so he and another soldier headed out together and hitched rides where they could find them. They arrived in Dong Ha, which was under attack. Unfortunately, Lewis had not been issued ammunition for his weapons yet. The two frightened soldiers ran through the mortar rounds and caught another ride, this time on a truck headed to Wunder Beach. The other soldier found his unit first, leaving Lewis to go on by himself, alone and unarmed. By the time Lewis arrived at Wunder Beach, everyone was gone.

* * *

Lewis had been listed as MIA and it was by sheer luck that he found Paul and the others ten miles southwest of Wunder Beach, in an area called Landing Zone (LZ) Sharon, so called because helicopters landed there. LZ Sharon was a grim little place; a vacant lot with a few tents slapped on it. However, their stay was short and soon they moved on to an area called Leatherneck Square, a contested area encompassing Con Thien, Gio Linh, Dong Ha, and Cam Lo. As they worked their way north, Paul, Mike, and Lewis eventually ended up at Con Thien, known as A-4 to the military and "Hill of Angels" to the Vietnamese.

Con Thien was a fire support base located so close to the Demilitarized Zone (the DMZ separated the Communist north from the opposing south) that on a clear day you could see the North Vietnamese flag flapping in the breeze. In Paul's estimation it was no place for angels. It was a desolate spot situated on top of a hill, surrounded by brush, overrun with rats, and during the rainy season, knee deep in mud. But, for now, it was home.

The three were greeted by a tough group of Marines, the 3rd Marine Division, whose control they were under, for operational purposes. The Marines wasted no time in assessing the new guys.

"Look at them with their nice green uniforms. Fuckin' candy-asses!"

"Yeah, these boys are all decked out, head to toe. Stupid idiots!"

The Marines mocked the new guys who had not yet learned the nuances of jungle warfare. They quickly taught them survival basics, information the three were more than happy to put into practice: lose the underwear and socks, they only give you a rash; forget the gas mask, you won't need it here; drop the flak jacket, it won't save you; replace that steel pot with a soft hat, or you'll die of the heat. Experience was worth everything.

The Marines had been through hell and it showed. They were a scrappy bunch with their old M-14s, rotted uniforms, and worn-out equipment. Con Thien had been under siege before the 1/61st arrived and most of the Marines were finishing their tours exhausted, disillusioned, and ready to go home. Although they were happy to be replaced, the Marines were highly skeptical of their replacements and their ability to carry on the mission.

Likewise, the 1/61st regarded the Marines with equal parts of respect and disdain. The Marines were tough survivors, but they were sloppy and careless. They left C-rations and food everywhere, attracting the rabbit-size rats that populated the area. They also had a bad habit of discarding ammunition and equipment when and where it suited them, a dangerous practice given the fact the enemy was nearby.

One day the Marines were playing basketball when mortar rounds hit.

"Get inside, get inside," yelled Lewis and Paul as they ran to the bunkers for protection.

"Ah, don't worry about it. The NVA (North Vietnamese Army) don't have powerful mortars like we do," remarked one Marine coolly.

"That's right. Bring it on you bastards! You can't kill me!" boasted another.

They continued to play their game throughout the attack as Paul and Lewis hid in a bunker, flabbergasted at the men's foolish actions. Fortunately, no one was killed.

* * *

Paul's new home was a bunker, a deep hole in the ground, dug out by a bulldozer with an opening for a door. A makeshift floor was constructed of old ammo crates and the roof consisted of a large steel plate with five or six layers of sandbags stacked on top to withstand enemy attacks. Bunks were stacked three high. Paul selected one of the top bunks, using the supports near the roof to store personal items, not yet knowing that this was where the rats ran at night. Paul and Mike shared a bunker with a few others while Lewis shared a bunker with his good friend, William Daniel.

"Pink," as Paul was known, had a small circle of friends. His buddy, Mike Hardin, was a car enthusiast who had attended training with him since 1967. Floyd Rensberger, another close friend, had been with him since boot camp, although they were in different companies now and rarely saw each other. Pink was also friendly with Lewis Page and William Daniel plus Hall, Berry, and Cruz; men whose first names he didn't know. In Vietnam men purposely stayed on a last name basis and kept some emotional distance; that way, there was less to lose.

So far, Paul had not engaged in combat. It was late August and he'd been in Vietnam for a month, a fact he knew by tallying each day he'd survived. He spent his days cleaning up garbage, clearing the brush around the hill, and placing claymore mines around the perimeter to keep out the enemy. He was still scared, but had adopted the attitude of "so far, so good." Lewis, on the other hand, was already experienced in running for his life and had seen the horrors of war. He harbored no illusions about what could happen and went through each day with an underlying sense of foreboding and uneasiness. He feared the others were far too complacent in their false sense of security. He was justified in his worry, because things were about to change.

* * *

It was another sweltering day in Vietnam. Paul and his comrades moved slowly through the jungle, separated by twenty to thirty yards as instructed. Paul was near the front out of everyone else's view. From the rear came a gunshot, a quick staccato that cut the silence of the elephant grass. Adrenaline coursed through his body like a double shot of strong whiskey. More shots rang out. Everyone grabbed his weapon and started shooting, not knowing exactly where or what to shoot—no orders had been given. The wild firing continued until everyone ran out of bullets. Finally there was silence, except for the screams of the wounded. Two Americans had been caught in the crossfire. Another soldier lay dead. The enemy: nonexistent.

In the early days of men's tours, accidents and friendly fire were all too common, driven by raw fear and irrational behavior. Sometimes a soldier tripped and discharged his weapon by accident, or someone got spooked and randomly started shooting. In either case, the results were generally the same. Men ended up injured or dead, as they did on this particular day. It took some time before American soldiers could differentiate between the sounds of an M-16, their standard issue weapon, and an AK-47, the enemy's weapon of choice, being fired.

Paul grabbed his radio and called for a medevac unit to pick up the two wounded as he worked his way over to where the other men had gathered. The crowd wasn't with the wounded; instead they were gawking at the dead body of their comrade lying on the ground. There was an uneasy fascination with the body and a macabre desire to see the damage caused by errant bullets. The dead man wasn't a pretty sight. Repulsed, the men backed away, shocked at how rapidly one could go from a fit and active soldier to a lifeless, bloody mess; a grim reminder that they were, in fact, in a war.

A couple of days later the men were out on patrol and came across a huge hole in the ground. It was three feet wide by ten feet deep, angled at the bottom. One soldier reached for the pin on his hand grenade, eager to toss it down.

"Wait up, wait up," instructed an officer. "Let's see what's down there first. Ramsey, you go down with a flashlight."

The others stood back as Ramsey, a small lithe man, was lowered into the hole. Paul couldn't breathe, certain the hole was connected to an underground tunnel filled with enemy soldiers. But soon Ramsey reappeared, his eyes the size of coat buttons.

"There's a bomb down there, a giant bomb, maybe 1,000 pounds or more! Let's get the hell out of here!" And that's exactly what they did; leaving the bomb for other unsuspecting troops, while silently thanking the cautious officer for saving their lives.

After a week in the bush, Paul returned to base camp. He immediately peeled off his filthy clothes and took a lukewarm shower under the spigot of a fifty-five gallon drum. It was a poor excuse for a hot shower, but a luxury nevertheless. He donned his only clean uniform which was already faded and worn, much like its owner.

Conditions at camp were the same as he had left them. Gook, the dog, secured by trading cigarettes with a Vietnamese local, was playing with Wendy, the resident spider monkey. Mike, Lewis, and Daniel had not been on the mission in the bush with him. Mike was reading a car magazine he'd received in yesterday's mail call, Lewis was sleeping after a ten-hour shift in the Fire Direction Center, and William Daniel was manning the radios, listening for fire missions. All was relatively quiet. Paul sat down and lit up a cigarette, relieved to finally let his body relax. It was short-lived. He was on his third puff when he received new orders.

"Pinkerton, command bunker wants you now. Grab your tools and let's go!"

There was no rest in sight. The lieutenant colonel was extremely proud of the fact that he had Paul as his own personal barber and he often invited other officers and their aides to come for haircuts, keeping Paul busy for hours at a time. Paul was tired but didn't actually mind the inconvenience. It was extra money and something to do during the long hours of boredom that turned his thoughts dark and moody. He pulled out his barbering tools and headed to the bunkers, ready to use his newly-acquired skills on the big brass.

Hours later, his friends saw the tools and begged for haircuts as well. Paul flashed a grin and lit up a cigarette. "Okay, get your money out, and line up!" Not one to turn down his friends, he set up shop as the guys took turns sitting on the ammo can. At $1 a cut, it meant a night of card playing and a few cold beers. Not such a bad deal after all.

* * *

Military organizations are organized hierarchically into groups of descending sizes. The 1st Infantry Brigade, 5th Infantry Division (Mechanized) was broken down into battalions, battalions were broken into companies, companies were divided into platoons, and platoons were further subdivided into squads. Paul, Mike, and Lewis were all members of the 4.2 mortar platoon of the Headquarters Company of the 1/61st Battalion. The 4.2 mortar platoon consisted of four squads, each containing six men, and a Fire Direction Center (FDC), that coordinated the firing of the mortars. Each of the four squads had a huge gun—a 4.2 mortar designed for high angle firing—that was mounted on an M106 mortar carrier, called a track (a vehicle resembling a tank). The guns and the Fire Direction Center (FDC) stayed together and the FDC controlled all four guns.

Lewis Page and William Daniel worked in the FDC. Mike and Paul were both trained as Forward Observers (FOs), but after a short stint, Mike became a gun squad leader. Paul was strictly a Forward Observer, the man who directed and adjusted fire support from mortars. Essentially he was a front line foot soldier.

As an FO, Paul carried the AN/PRC-25 radio, also known as "Prick 25," into the field. Fully loaded with accessories and spare batteries the radio weighed twenty-five pounds and, with its two tall waving antennas, made him a prime target for the enemy. In addition to the radio, Paul carried his water supply, C-rations, an M-16, and personal items, for a total of sixty pounds of gear. Given his heavy load, the heat, and the terrain, he moved slowly. Carrying the radio was a job most men shunned while Paul saw it as an advantage. The troops were unaware of what was going on, but Paul knew exactly what was happening, and knowledge was power. He and the other FOs talked to commanding officers on the radio and on occasion, challenged their authority. He felt a sense of security in knowing the facts so that he could respond accordingly.

Paul was the first line of defense. He called in missions to the FDC providing them with the coordinates of enemy targets. Using topographical maps and a plotting board, the FDC determined the altitude and deflection of the gun sights and calculated the range and direction to the target. The FDC called in the elevation, charge, direction, and deflection to the gun crew who then fired. The FOs observed the round and, if it was off target, provided the necessary adjustments. Once on target, the guns "fired for effect," meaning that all four guns fired together in a pattern. The enemy rarely, if ever, stood a chance against such massive firepower.

Frequently Paul and Mike were loaned out to other units and served as the FO and gun squad leader when and where they were needed. Lewis and Daniel stayed at base camp and only worked for the 1/61st. The four men were not always together as a team and therefore did not have exactly the same experiences, except for the major missions.

* * *

September 4, 1968, was an ugly day in Vietnam, soon to become uglier. The monsoon season had started and torrential rain was pounding the bush. Company A of the 1/61st had gone out early in the day to pick up Marines and bring them back to base. The Marines reported enemy in the area and by 4:00 p.m. heavy fighting ensued. More members of the 1/61st were sent out to help; Paul, Mike, and Lewis were among them.

Company A of the 1/61st was led by Captain Charles E. Vernon, who was known as a gung-ho leader. One of the platoons under Vernon's command had its track stuck in the mud and came under enemy fire. As Vernon rushed toward the battle area to help, he was also ambushed. His track was hit by enemy rockets and he and many of his crew were seriously wounded. Although injured, he continued to fight as the other units of the 1/61st stood their ground.

Paul found himself in the midst of the fighting, calling in fire missions fast and furious. His heart galloped erratically, his eardrums nearly bursting from the noise of gunshots and rockets. There was total chaos with soldiers running, officers shouting orders, men screaming in pain, and blood spewing into the muddy mess. It was terrifying and wildly exhilarating at the same time. The fighting seemed endless, but it lasted less than three hours. When it was over, the carnage was counted: twenty-seven Americans were wounded, including Captain Vernon (who later received the Award of the Distinguished Service Cross for his conduct in battle), and three Americans were dead. Enemy counts were difficult to ascertain because it was nighttime and a typhoon had hit the area during the battle.

The next morning Paul and his fellow officers had the sickening task of conducting body counts, an imprecise science, with body parts strewn here and there or sometimes turned into unidentifiable mush. By the time Paul went out to do his grisly duty, others had already moved in like vultures on road-kill, stealing whatever they could find. Paul moved cautiously, as he examined the enemy up close for the first time. As he made his way up an incline, he was startled to find a dead Vietnamese soldier lying on the ground with half of his head missing. His wallet was open and pictures were strewn nearby.

Paul carefully picked up one of the photos and stared at the smiling faces of the man, his wife, and their small child. He wondered how and when the man's family would find out about their loss, tears welling up in his eyes. His sadness turned to anger when he recalled the words of one of his commanding officers during training: "The Vietnamese are subhumans. They don't feel, they don't cry, they don't have emotions. They're no better than monkeys."

This wasn't supposed to happen, this empathy for the enemy. As if to appease the dead, Paul said to no one in particular, "Damn it, this isn't right. This is really fucked up."

It no longer mattered what he had been conditioned to think. This was a human being lying dead in the mud with a family waiting for him to return. Paul's hands shook as he carefully replaced the pictures inside the dead man's pocket. Everything he had tried to believe was a thinly-veiled sham. Survival would no longer be as simple as dodging bullets. Now it required blocking out the images, the sounds, the smells, and the reality of his experiences. Paul spit the vomit out of his mouth and shouted, "FUCK THE ARMY!" as loud as his voice would carry.

* * *

After the first battle, men came to look at the dead Vietnamese who were lined up in rows like children's action figures. Some took pictures and, on rare occasions, someone desecrated one or more of the bodies by cutting off body parts as souvenirs.

American soldiers who lost close friends went through a period of shock, grief, and anger followed by a gradual hardening, like a callous building on a foot. Men eventually became immune to seeing dead bodies; their reactions changing from one of horrified interest to a crude, raw truth: "Gee, that's too fucking bad, but I'm happy as hell it isn't me."

The September 4 battle, known as Operation Kentucky, was the first of many to come. On September 13, Operation Sullivan, a search and destroy mission into the DMZ was put into place. Paul went on foot, carrying the radio as usual. Mike was with the gun crew in a track and Lewis manned the radios in the FDC. Unlike the September 4 mission which had been relatively short and consisted of men on foot and in tracks, this mission called in air and naval support and lasted over twelve hours.

Paul entered the DMZ right after the B-52s passed through. Smoke was still coming out of the churned up ground and the surrounding trees were shattered. Bullets cracked the overcast sky and the now-familiar con-fusion began. Sporadic firefights continued for hours as Paul alternated between calling in fire missions and calling for medevac units to help the wounded. At one point, with the enemy close by, he instinctively prepared to shoot.

It happened so quickly there was no time to think, only react. A North Vietnamese soldier jumped up right in front of him, startling both of them. For a brief instant they looked into each other's eyes, but Paul acted first, emptying twenty rounds into him, nearly cutting him in half. Paul watched, horrified, as a slow motion scene unfolded in front of him like some bad movie clip. The man stared at him, blinking, coughing, gasping for breath, refusing to die. This was not at all how Paul had imagined killing the enemy. It was not what he had watched so many times in his favorite cowboy shows where death was neat and quick and somehow honorable. This was the real deal with the horrible smells of exploded organs filling his nostrils and the warm blood of the enemy splattered on his hands, face, and uniform.

In the background Paul heard someone yell, "Way to go Pink! You nailed him!" Paul felt nothing. He was numb; his own blood no longer seemed to circulate. A terrible thing had just happened. There was no time for guilt or reflection, however, because he was still in the midst of a fire-fight. He would have time later—a lifetime actually—to remember today.

CHAPTER 2

Homesick

Where we love is home,
Home that our feet may leave,
But not our hearts.

—Oliver Wendell Holmes

E ventually there was time to think and Paul needed time to think. He had just killed a man, face-to-face, looking into his eyes. Yes, it was war and death was to be expected, but to cut down another man in the prime of his life was a terrible burden to bear. Who was he—someone's brother or lover, or worse yet—a husband, a father?

Paul would never forget those eyes; eyes that screamed out in shock, agony, and even, indignation. "Why me and not you?" they asked. Eyes that defiantly said, "I will not die." Yet suddenly, the man was dead and his eyes stared off into nothingness.

Paul grieved and secretly cried. He asked God for forgiveness, for the saving of both of their souls. But mostly he raged. There was something wrong with a system that required one man to kill another. He'd had no grievance with the man. It was simply that this man had stood in the way of his own safety, his own life.

He thought back to the time when his grandfather had died in front of him; the mystery, the sadness, the helplessness he'd felt then, just as he felt it now. Could he have done anything differently? No. There was nothing he could have done differently—either time. He just had to sit with the heavy weight of it and now he didn't even have grandma's shoulder to cry on. Some days he just wanted to be a kid again.

* * *

Paul Neilson Pinkerton was born on July 30, 1947—the second child of Paul Eugene Pinkerton and Deborah Miller Singer. Paul's parents were married on June 2, 1945, and exactly nine months later their first child, a daughter, was born. Approximately eighteen months later, Paul entered this world. Three more children followed in rapid succession, arriving in 1950, 1953, and 1957.

On January 31, 1959, a cold and dreary day in the small Pennsylvania town of Manheim, the sixth and final Pinkerton child was about to be born. Paul's paternal grandmother was babysitting three of Paul's siblings. Eleven-year-old Paul and his five-year-old brother Jim were at the Saturday matinee taking in a cowboy show. As the boys left the theater to walk home late that afternoon, young Paul spotted his parent's '53 Oldsmobile across the street.

"Boys," his father called, motioning them over. "Mommy has to go to the hospital now! I'm taking you over to grandma's house. Get in."

Paul and Jim were excited at this turn of events: a new baby was arriving and they were going to visit "Ma Ma," (pronounced maw maw), the grandmother on their mother's side of the family. She and Grandpa were doting grandparents who had television and real butter, two essentials missing from the more austere Pinkerton household.

Ma Ma, gray hair in a bun and an apron across her broad body, greeted them at the door. Grandpa was dozing on the couch. "Hello boys. Come on in," she said warmly as they raced past her and tore off their jackets. She waved to her daughter, who was already deep in labor, as the car sped out of the driveway.

Paul and Jim were just in time to watch professional wrestling on Channel 10, the boys' favorite. They turned on the TV and flopped into chairs. Grandpa continued to sleep while Ma Ma went back to knitting a sweater for some lucky family member. Shortly after 6:00 p.m. Grandpa stirred and made a deep moaning noise. Ma Ma rose from her chair, sensing something was wrong. She took her husband's hand and calmly asked, "What can I do?" Without opening his eyes, he gurgled, and was gone, peacefully asleep forever. The clock read 6:18 p.m.

Jim stood in the kitchen and watched as his grandmother systematically called the doctor and various family members. Crying, Paul bolted outside and ran in aimless circles. He wondered what to do next, his mind desperately trying to process what had just happened. Ma Ma brought him back inside without saying a word. As they sat on the couch together, she wrapped a protective arm around him. Paul leaned his head back onto her shoulder and they sat silently, tears running down their cheeks.

Eventually the phone rang, breaking the eerie silence in the house. "It's a girl! She was born at 6:17 and we've named her Martha Jean!" Paul's father proudly proclaimed. There was a brief exchange of words and the phone went dead. One life had ended and another had begun, within the space of a minute.

* * *

Paul grew up in a tiny house, originally built as a barn, on West Gramby Street in the heart of downtown Manheim. The house was representative of the Pinkerton family values: close-knit. With three boys in one bedroom and three girls in the other, it was cozy to say the least.

The Pinkerton household was loud and boisterous, filled with the noises of small squabbling siblings and numerous family pets that at any given time included cats, dogs, rabbits, and birds. Money was always short, but the children were blissfully unaware of their parent's financial woes. Earning $54 a week, Paul's father struggled to support his ever-growing family and sometimes their five o'clock supper consisted of nothing more than bowls of oatmeal or crackers with milk, meals the children detested.

Paul's father was a dapper little man standing five feet seven inches tall, with brown hair, dark green eyes, and a mustache. He spent his entire career at Raymark Industries, a company that manufactured asbestos brake linings for cars, where he worked in advertising, purchasing, sales, and other backroom operations. Family was his priority and he poured everything into caring for his wife and children.

Paul's mother, Deborah Singer, was born in 1919, the daughter of Paul Singer and Elsie Miller. She was one of ten children, six of whom survived. The Singer family was a large, well-known clan in Lancaster County, known mainly for their family's size and the fact that they were college-educated professionals, something rare in this blue-collar area.

Paul's mother was a substitute teacher in the elementary school attended by Paul and his siblings; a source of both embarrassment and comfort for them. She held her children to high academic standards although Paul, always an average student, didn't apply himself. He preferred playing outdoors to sitting in a classroom or doing his homework. He particularly hated reading and spelling, subjects he would have failed but for his mother's diligent tutoring.

The Pinkertons were patient, easygoing people who devoted their energies to their children and always put family first. Although loving and caring, they didn't verbalize their feelings. Love for their children was an unspoken assumption and the words "I love you" were superfluous.

Paul's parents came from religious backgrounds and met at the Manheim Zion Lutheran Church. Paul's parents followed suit and baptized Paul and his siblings as Lutherans. Paul sang in the choir and was an acolyte. On any given Sunday you could find the red-haired, green-eyed Pinkerton clan among the congregation. The Pinkertons were God-fearing, sober, conservative Germans; representative of the Manheim population of 5,000 in the 1960s.

Paul had a happy childhood, punctuated by a few unhappy events he would remember forever. As a youngster he attended sleep-away camp, a miserable tear-filled week fraught with loneliness. He tried Boy Scout camp a few years later, but once again realized that homesickness was an "affliction" he suffered. Paul, like his parents, didn't like to wander too far from home.

Growing up, Paul and his siblings spent time with grandparents, aunts, uncles, and cousins in their extended family, but only on the Singer side of the family. The Singers were a gregarious, fun-loving bunch who celebrated holidays, held family reunions, and carefully documented their family history for posterity. Conversely, the Pinkertons had strained family relationships. Paul's favorite Singer was Uncle Jim, a Lutheran minister, who took him on fantasy bear hunts and gave him thrilling car rides during which he appeared to aim for poles or trees, then seemingly returned him to safety at the last possible moment.

* * *

At an early age, Paul discovered the power of politics. He worried about the Cold War with Russia and constantly fretted because his family didn't have a bomb shelter in their basement. This thought plagued him as a child and infuriated him as an adult when he finally realized the truth. Although he vaguely remembered the day President Kennedy was shot, he vividly recalled Kennedy's Bay of Pigs speech in 1961 when he and his father sat in a frigid car in the school parking lot and listened to the entire speech on the car radio, foregoing the wrestling match they had planned to attend. At the time, Paul wasn't exactly sure what all the words meant, but knew that the speech was important. It further reinforced the idea that he needed a bomb shelter in his house.

For Paul, tough lessons about death were gleaned at an early age. At eleven he was an eyewitness to his grandfather's death and, a short time later, one of his uncles suffered a heart attack in the Pinkerton family dining room and subsequently died. He was thirteen when his friend David was killed in a bicycle accident, just one day before he and Paul were to be confirmed together at church. Paul learned that as wonderful as life was, it could quickly be snatched away.

* * *

Paul's parents were entrepreneurial types who found interesting and creative ways to make extra money. They cut down trees from their grandmother's farm and sold them on their front lawn before Christmas and peddled Dutch-made products (underwear and the like) at home parties. The men in the family joked about the noisy, female-only gatherings held in the Pinkerton's parlor, deeming them "hen parties," but appreciated the fact that the parties added cash to the family coffers.

The primary source of extra income came from a boarder who lived in the miniscule bedroom on the first floor next to Paul's parents. Their first boarder was a man named Charlie Rickert, a World War I veteran. Paul remembered him as a very old man who sat on the front stoop and said, "Thank you, thank you ever so much," whenever he or one of his siblings performed a kind deed for him. When Charlie became ill, Paul's mother took care of him. Before he passed away in their home, he gave her three $100 bills for safekeeping until his daughter arrived. Paul's father woke up all the children and gathered them at the kitchen table to examine the money, pessimistically declaring, "You'll probably never see any more of these in your life!"

Paul, like his parents, had a strong work ethic. At an early age he found he could make a quick seventy-five cents babysitting his younger cousins. At fourteen he became interested in cars and fantasized about the car he would buy when he turned sixteen, hoping his parents would chip in for the purchase. Instead, his mother secured a summer job for him at a local farm. So while many of Paul's friends spent that summer having fun and relaxing at the new town pool, Paul sweated and toiled at the farm hauling tobacco, planting corn, and milking cows. He worked six days a week, twelve hours a day and earned $20 a week—money that Mother Pinkerton promptly confiscated for safekeeping.

After two years of working on the farm and one summer working at the local IGA cutting meat and bagging groceries, Paul was finally able to buy his prize: a second-hand red 1960 Chevy Impala with a big engine. The only problem was that he had failed to factor in the cost of insurance and gas, so the sleek, fast car sat dormant in front of the house for a few more months until there was enough money to drive it.

* * *

Paul was a normal teenage boy whose concerns included pimples, hormones, Saturday nights, and cars, not necessarily in that order. He attended Manheim Central High School and had a small group of close friends that included Steve Bucher, Marty Sauble, Jr., and Jimmy Thomas. The boys were an eclectic bunch. Paul was the largest and strongest. Standing six feet two inches tall and weighing over 180 pounds, he was an imposing presence. "Pink" as his friends called him, was amiable and compassionate, a giant teddy bear who went to bat for anyone who needed his help.

Steve Bucher was the smart, good-looking member of the group and the son of a local homebuilder. His mother had earned the reputation for being strict and raising polite boys. Steve was interested in girls, sports, motorcycles, cars, and aviation. His goal was to become a pilot one day.

Jimmy Thomas was a shy farm boy who wore glasses. He had a quiet demeanor, average appearance, and pleasant personality. He was an unassuming guy who naturally fit into their group and enthusiastically participated in all of their various activities: attending wrestling matches, bowling, playing baseball and football, roller skating, watching movies, and drag racing down local Manheim streets.

Marty was deemed the wild one. At five feet six inches tall and barely 125 pounds, he was high-spirited and full of energy, a tough competitor who put the fear the God into anyone who challenged him at touch football. Marty was best known for his high jumping in track (easily jumping well above his height) and for the loud and infectious laughter that flowed out of him easily and sometimes, inappropriately. Marty loved cars. He drove a fast Corvair and true to his passion, worked at Sauder Chevrolet. Marty was shy with the girls, but was considered everyone's best friend; everyone adored fun-loving Marty.

Paul and his friends hung out at the local hamburger joint, the Sweet 'N Hot Stop, nicknamed Curly's for its bald owner Curly Myers. Curly, a married man in his early 30s with two sets of twins, liked to socialize with the boys. Once he even took Steve and Marty along with him to Florida to fish, water ski, and go to the Daytona 500. Curly was indulgent with the youths and stayed open late so they could shoot pool, play pinball, and eat more burgers and fries. Whenever Mrs. Pinkerton worried about Paul's whereabouts, she called Curly first. Curly enjoyed teasing Paul, yelling out in a loud, sing-song voice: "Pinky, your mommy's on the phone!" as Paul, red-faced and embarrassed, dashed for the door.

As a teenager, Paul frequently tested his parent's patience by getting into trouble. Not serious trouble involving alcohol, drugs, or jail time, but simply the growing pains of youth: staying out past his curfew and getting speeding tickets. Once, however, he went too far and his actions landed him on the local news and involved with state troopers. It wasn't a prank that others took lightly.

It was a hot summer night and everyone was a little bored. Paul, Marty, and Steve teamed up with two acquaintances, Sid and his friend. Sid drove and the youths cruised around in his 1947 Plymouth convertible, top down, eating watermelon. Out of the blue someone in the car said, "Hey, let's go buy some eggs and hit road signs!"

"Yeah, that sounds good!" They all agreed to the plan, purchased several dozen eggs at a local farm stand, and headed into the countryside. As they sped along pelting road signs, one of the youths lobbed an egg at an oncoming vehicle, accidentally landing it inside the driver's open window. The irate motorist turned his car around and began chasing them. Unfortunately, the old Plymouth, weighed down by five large boys, couldn't go very fast. Sid pulled into a farm lane and turned off the car lights in an attempt to lose the angry motorist, but the man was gaining on them.

Sid had another plan: "When the 'S' curve comes up, I'll slow down and everybody jump. Find a place to hide and I'll come back for you later. If I put the top up, he won't recognize me and I'll lose him." The sixteen-year-olds found this plan to be logical, so as Sid slowed the car, everyone jumped except for Paul. He had decided to stay behind and sat in the middle of the back seat, holding what remained of the eggs. When Sid saw him still sitting there, he yelled, "Jump, Pink, jump!"

As Sid accelerated, he saw Paul stand up on his trunk and, when he disappeared, assumed Paul had safely jumped like the others. But Paul had landed on the pavement on his head, knocked out cold. The driver of the pursuing car saw the accident and drove off, afraid to get involved. Jerry, a friend of Paul's who happened to be out on his motorcycle, saw the whole incident and stopped to help.

Paul woke up for a brief moment, just long enough to give Jerry his wallet and his watch. "Give these to my parents," he said before passing out again. Jerry went to call the police and within minutes the road was filled with emergency vehicles. Sid drove off while Marty and Steve hid in a swamp, aware they'd have a long walk home if Sid didn't return for them. They didn't know about Paul's accident, but were curious why police cars and emergency vehicles were surrounding the area.

Paul sat up in the ambulance only to hear the paramedic say, "Put your head down. You're hurt pretty badly." The next time he woke up, he was in a hospital bed with a severe concussion, vomiting watermelon. His parents and the police were at his bedside asking plenty of questions. Paul didn't want to get into trouble and was still slightly confused, so he told two or three unlikely stories including a scenario in which he was pushed from the car. State police jumped to the conclusion that the incident was gang related and brought in helicopters to track down the alleged gang members whom they planned to charge with attempted murder.

Steve Bucher arrived at Paul's house three hours later to check on him, unaware of his accident. Mother Pinkerton was less than pleased to see him and held him responsible for Paul's injuries, making Steve's night worse than it already was. Meanwhile, Sid had returned to the scene of the accident to pick up Steve and Marty, but was told by the police to move on, so he drove home and went to bed.

The next day the local radio station ran a story about the incident and incorrectly reported that Paul was not expected to live. The Pinkertons knew the story wasn't true, but poor Jimmy Thomas, who had not participated in the previous night's activities, heard the radio report, dropped everything, and rushed to the hospital.

Paul wasn't dying, but he did have a serious concussion. However, his bigger headache was telling the truth about what had happened. When the facts came out, all the boys received a summons, charging them with littering. Sid, the driver, was allegedly charged with leaving the scene of an accident, reckless endangerment, and other violations. His license was taken away for a year and he received a stiff fine. Ultimately, he decided not to spend a year without a car. Reportedly, he quit school, joined the Navy, and left town.

Paul, Marty, and Steve collectively decided they were not going to pay their fines, pointing to a technicality. The summons incorrectly listed the location where they had pelted the signs with eggs. The Justice of the Peace (JP) in Manheim was a friend of Mother Pinkerton's and urged her to make Paul concede.

"Look, if these boys don't pay, they'll be charged with something more and it'll go on their permanent record. If they pay, this will blow over. They made the state police and helicopters come out, which cost a lot of money. The department isn't too happy with them. Everyone just wants this thing to be over."

As the midnight deadline for paying the fine approached, Mother Pinkerton became increasingly angry with Paul, insisting he do the right thing. Paul, Steve, and Marty finally relented, arriving at the JP's house at 11:45 p.m., just fifteen minutes before the deadline. They knocked and knocked and knocked at the door.

"What is it?" the JP asked, when she saw the boys.

"We came to pay our fine. We have to pay it by midnight." The door opened and a fuming JP and her angry husband, both in pajamas and robes, glared at them.

"You kids have some Goddamn nerve coming here at this hour! We should go back to bed and make you suffer the consequences." For the next few minutes the tirade continued as the JP and her husband made their feelings abundantly clear. Marty found the situation comical and started laughing uproariously. Paul and Steve couldn't help themselves; Marty's laughter was infectious. They began giggling, which made the JP's tirade even louder and longer. But, when all was said and done, the fine was paid and the lesson was learned. From that day forward, everyone referred to their folly as "the egg incident."

**

As high school graduation approached, Paul tried to figure out what to do with his life. College was out of the question. He had no academic desires and good grades and money were both in short supply. Based upon his interests, the guidance counselor suggested two possibilities: become a forest ranger or a meat cutter. Both options required attending schools out of state and Paul had serious doubts about his ability to leave home. In the end, he decided to follow in his father's footsteps and secured a job at Raymark Industries.

Graduation night was a magical evening; a time to celebrate past accomplishments and anticipate a world full of possibilities ahead. For Paul it also marked his first kiss. On graduation night, after the family parties were over, Paul and his buddies went to his friend Mary Ann's house to play spin the bottle, where he shared his first kiss with Mary Ann. By 11:00 p.m. the girl's mother announced that it was time for everyone to go home and Paul and his friends obediently complied.

The next day Paul, Marty, Steve, and Jimmy drove to Wildwood, New Jersey, for a weekend of fun and sun, a graduation gift to themselves. Paul returned home with wonderful memories and a bad case of sun poisoning. Later that week Paul, his sister Carol, and a neighbor girl named Sandy went to the Pensupreme Dairy (nicknamed "The Joint") in a nearby town for milkshakes.

As soon as they left the restaurant, Sandy started in on Paul. "She likes you, she really likes you!"

"Who likes me? What are you talking about?" Paul had been oblivious to the flirting that had taken place.

"That waitress! Didn't you see the way she looked at you?"

"Uh, no ..." Paul unsuccessfully strained his memory to recall what she looked like. Curious, he returned two days later only to find an older woman, clearly not the waitress Sandy had teased him about.

"The last time I was in here I think there was another waitress working ... do you know who she is?" Paul hedged.

"Oh yes, that's Patricia. She has tonight off, but she'll be in tomorrow."

"Okay. I'd like a banana milkshake." Paul decided to come back the following night, more intrigued than ever.

The next night, Paul reappeared and ordered another milkshake. He stared at the pretty, slender woman with the long brown hair, but felt too awkward and embarrassed to say anything as the older waitress whispered in her ear. He left and recounted the story to Steve later that evening. Steve immediately knew who he was talking about. "Oh, that has to be Patricia Schaumberg. Dad just built a new house for her dad, Tom. He's a barber in Lancaster."

Paul and Steve schemed to go to The Joint together and propose a double date to appease Tom, who was known to have strict rules. Patricia greeted Steve and acknowledged Paul, surprised that they knew each other. Introductions were made and a date was planned. Tom sanctioned the carefully orchestrated event, but at the last minute Steve's date cancelled, leaving Paul and Patricia alone at Hershey Park. Paul kissed her in the Mill Chute ride and from there the relationship blossomed. Soon they were going steady.

* * *

After graduation Paul swept floors, the lowest paid job in the factory. Paul easily completed his work in one or two short hours and asked for something else to do, but was simply told to slow down. He spent his remaining time standing around and eating. The job was boring, but it was money.

As Paul's relationship with Patricia progressed, she gently suggested he make a career change and attend barber school, an idea that appealed to him. It would make Tom happy and it would certainly be more exciting than pushing a broom. But there was an added incentive that Paul hadn't considered.

The war was heating up and although Paul and his friends hadn't given much thought to the possibility of being drafted, the political climate was rapidly changing. One day when Paul came home for lunch, his mother handed him an envelope from the U.S. Government. Realizing what it was, his heart sank. Soon after, he enrolled in barber school and applied for a deferment, which he received. For the moment he was safe, and he prayed the war would be over before his deferment expired.

Unable to begin barber school until a new semester started, Paul continued his factory work, graduating to the supply department filling orders. Patricia (Pat) was in her junior year of high school. Marty worked at Sauder Chevrolet and helped with the family farm, Steve assisted his father with carpentry jobs, and Jimmy worked at the New Holland Machine Company. Paul and his friends spent time together, but not as much as before; they were already moving on with their lives.

Early in 1966 Paul started barber school and found it to be easy and enjoyable. After nine months of study and seven months of apprenticeship, he was officially a barber. He graduated from the Harrisburg Barber School in May of 1967. But Uncle Sam, who had been patiently waiting, was now at his doorstep and his second draft notice couldn't be avoided.

In June, when Pat graduated from high school, Paul proposed; a move that Pat's father vehemently objected to. Tom didn't object to Paul per se, but he was a World War II veteran and he knew about war. He worried that his little girl might end up a young widow. Paul felt compelled to get married. If he didn't marry Pat now, he feared he would lose her. Two years were a long time to wait for someone and he didn't want to be one of those guys getting a "Dear John" letter while he was in Vietnam. Pat wanted to get married too. She loved Paul and felt his chances of survival would be substantially improved if they were married.

Wedding plans were hurriedly set in motion before Paul left for Vietnam, although Tom tried everything in his power to dissuade them. He even offered to buy Paul his own barbershop after his tour, if they waited. Nothing worked. Paul and Pat were young, in love, and impetuous. The wedding was on.

Meanwhile everyone in town began receiving draft notices. When Steve received his notice, his mother felt he should become a 1-W (conscientious objector) like his Mennonite cousins, an option he chose not to pursue. Marty, contrary to popular belief, was also drafted, receiving his notice on the same day as Steve. Marty was an only child and an only son, but in order to avoid the draft he needed to be a sole surviving son. That meant that his father or a brother would have preceded him in a military death, which was not the case. Jimmy was drafted, but ultimately failed the physical because of bad eyesight and curvature of the spine, a rejection that left him feeling guilty and depressed.

Paul didn't grow up in a military family and had little knowledge about war. Two of his uncles, Uncle Hoxie and Uncle Bob, had served in the military, but both were strangely tight-lipped about their experiences. Paul had always thought Uncle Hoxie to be a little unusual, behavior he could later attribute to post-traumatic stress disorder (PTSD). For now, Paul was unaware of what he might encounter in training or combat and no one was willing to enlighten him.

Paul was scheduled to report to the Selective Service Office in Lancaster on July 6, 1967, and, as the date approached, he experienced terrible anxiety about leaving home. He begged his parents to drop him off and quickly drive away because he realized how difficult it would be to say goodbye. When the day arrived, his parents reluctantly complied and left Paul standing at the office in a pool of tears.

From Lancaster, Paul and the other men traveled by bus to the military base in Harrisburg for swearing in and physicals. Paul and the others were handed paper cups for urine samples and glass tubes for blood draws. Someone in the group thought the urine should be poured into the glass tube and everyone followed suit. Chaos ensued, followed by abusive screaming by military officers, an orientation to the basic training that was to follow. After these preliminaries Paul flew from Harrisburg to Fort Benning, Georgia, to begin boot camp—otherwise known as hell.

Paul was a heavy smoker like his father and, at a whopping 238 pounds, was out of shape and overweight, conditions that quickly singled him out for enrollment in the fat man's squad. Membership in the squad meant a starvation diet, endless exercise, and no privileges. Paul didn't have downtime like the other men and spent his weekends on guard duty or KP. One night, desperate for food, he ate an entire tube of toothpaste. But, when the nine weeks of training were over, he emerged a trim 195 pounds of muscle and grit, brainwashed and ready to kill.

There was only one redeeming quality about basic training. It was the place where he met Floyd Rensberger, a good friend who remained with him during the rest of his training. When he graduated from boot camp, Paul received his Military Occupational Specialty (MOS). He was an 11C10: 11 meant Infantry, C meant mortars, and 10 signified the rank of a private. From there he was sent to Fort McClelland, Alabama, for Advanced Individual Training (AIT) in mortars, where he arrived the very next day.

Finally out of the fat man's squad, AIT was slightly easier and there were women on base, the WACS (Women's Army Corps), which made for a more interesting environment. Some of the women were gay, some pretended to be gay to ward off the attention of the men, and a few, now realizing they weren't cut out for military duty, purposely tried to get pregnant, their only way out. But Paul's primary focus was on mortar training, fine-tuning the ways in which to kill the enemy. During AIT Paul met Mike Hardin from Ohio, a soldier who would ultimately serve with him in Vietnam.

While Paul learned about mortars, Pat planned their wedding and managed her father, Tom, who showed his displeasure by being difficult at every turn. Her plate was full. In addition to wedding preparations, she attended beauty school at night and worked at Hamilton Watch during the day. (Ironically, Hamilton Watch manufactured timing devices for mortars during the war.)

Steve and Marty were also sent to Fort Benning for basic training but, by the time they arrived, Paul had already moved on to Fort McClelland. Steve and Marty were not together on the huge base, but occasionally saw one another. Both thought basic training was tough, but they handled it well and, unlike Paul, didn't end up in the fat man's squad.

At the end of AIT, Paul learned he was going on to NCO training; training for Non-Commissioned Officers. The Army needed E-05s (also known as buck sergeants) and both Paul and Mike Hardin were selected for advanced training. Between AIT and NCO they received a two-week leave. Paul went home and, halfway through his leave, on November 18, 1967, he married Patricia Schaumberg, the eldest child of Tom and Virginia.

The wedding was a beautiful evening affair attended by Jimmy Thomas and numerous other high school friends. Unfortunately Marty and Steve were still in basic training and couldn't be there. Pat, by now exhausted and emotional, cried through most of the ceremony and Paul worried that she was having second thoughts. In reality, it was sheer exhaustion that brought on the tears and the happy couple spent a few blissful days on a honeymoon in the Poconos.

Paul reluctantly left his bride and returned to Fort Benning for NCO training, which was only tolerable because Mike and Floyd were also there. Normally training to become a buck sergeant was a process that took eight to ten years but, with the Army's need for bodies in Vietnam, Paul's training took a mere ten weeks. Some of the men resented this quick promotion of rank and nicknamed Paul and Mike "shake 'n bakes." Paul was not impressed with his new status and, whenever possible, railed against authority. Unlike the Commissioned Officers, who were there by choice, Paul was there because he'd been drafted. By the end of NCO training in early 1968, Mike and Paul were three-stripe sergeants.

Steve Bucher completed his basic training and moved on to Fort Polk, Louisiana, for Advanced Individual Training. Marty never received orders to leave Fort Benning and was made an instructor. Steve wisely told Marty to take advantage of his good fortune; he could probably spend his entire tour there and avoid Vietnam altogether. But Marty felt left out and unhappy so he volunteered for the 82nd Airborne, making Vietnam a certainty.

In March of 1968, Paul, Mike, Lewis, and Floyd went to Fort Carson, Colorado. The mood was decidedly different there, as men were placed into their companies for Vietnam. Deployment was a given and there was an underlying current of tension in the air. Men increased their cigarette and alcohol consumption and strange events began to occur. The men were anxious about Vietnam and some tried to avoid it at all costs. Allegedly, a couple of men were shot and accidents became more frequent.

Even Mike was involved in an accident while he was at Fort Carson. A nervous soldier by the name of Frank Cates was driving an armored personnel carrier (APC) down a steep embankment as part of a training exercise. Mike was inside. Cates lost control and flipped the APC (or track as it was called), demolishing the vehicle. Fortunately, no one was hurt. When Cates called the accident in on the radio, Lewis was on the other end. Cates said, "We've just flipped the track over, over." Lewis laughed at the absurdity of the message, but the accident was no laughing matter. Cates was taken off track-driving permanently.

Steve came home to Manheim before departing for Vietnam and stopped at Curly's for lunch. Curly, always outspoken, reprimanded him for not going 1-W (conscientious objector). Steve ignored his comments and struck up a conversation with Al Gibble, an older friend from high school who was leaving for Vietnam in a few days. Both men were pumped up and raring to go and promised to look each other up in 'Nam. But before Steve's leave was over, Alvin Gibble came home in a box, the victim of small arms fire. His tour of duty was a short twenty-one days long. By the time Steve left for Vietnam in April, his confidence was waning.

In April the Army gave married men at Fort Carson a perk: they allowed their wives to join them. Paul and Floyd and their wives lived off base in Manitou Springs in the same apartment building. Paul lived on the second floor and Floyd lived directly below him on the first. Chris, Floyd's wife, and Pat became close friends and spent all their time together while their husbands worked at the base; on the weekends the couples went sightseeing together.

Mike and Lewis were single and had their own circle of friends that included: William Daniel, an enlisted man from Texas who collected expensive cars; Leon Berry, who married a bartender before leaving for Vietnam; Henderson, a rodeo champion from out west; and Hall, who was slightly younger than the rest. Paul was in the same unit as these men and enjoyed their company, but naturally preferred to spend his time with his new bride.

By the end of June everyone came home. The men had a short leave before returning to Fort Carson for the last time. Pat and Paul, who had borrowed Tom's car, dropped Mike off in Ohio as the three drove from Colorado to Pennsylvania together. The leave was a blur and soon it was time for Paul to say his final goodbyes to his wife and family, a gut-wrenching experience. Mother Pinkerton hugged and kissed him, shedding big tears of despair. She even proclaimed her love for her eldest son, in uncharacteristic fashion.

Leaving their families behind, the men returned to Fort Carson, spending their final three weeks packing equipment and preparing for Vietnam. Before they left the States, the Company Commander threw a big party for his troops. Paul didn't think going off to war was anything to celebrate, so he refused to attend. Mike, who had just married during his leave, also passed. Lewis went to the party, but was thoroughly disgusted by what transpired. Reportedly, the wife of one of the soldiers from the advance crew was their entertainment. She danced provocatively and supposedly stripped naked by the time the evening was over. Most were shocked at her behavior, although there were those who relished every second, taking pictures, and egging her on. When Paul heard the details of the party, he thought it was a pathetic ending to their time at Fort Carson, but he didn't give it more than a fleeting thought because he was single-mindedly focused on what awaited him in Vietnam.

CHAPTER 3

Letters from Home

Never think that war, no matter how necessary,
Nor how justified, is not a crime.
Ask the infantry and ask the dead.

Ernest Hemingway

Time spent in Vietnam vacillated between short, intense adrenaline bursts of combat and long stretches of tedium and boredom. Paul hated firefights, but craved the powerful chemicals they produced, an extreme rush he was unable to duplicate elsewhere. He filled his days cutting hair and amused himself by stepping outside the bounds of traditional buzz cuts, creating styles like Frank Cates's bird's nest hairdo; a hairdo that resembled a bird's nest sitting atop his head. Paul tried to master a card game named Punk but always lost, much to the delight of his friends. Whenever possible he slept during the heat of the day and spent his nights watching the firework displays of combat, listening to dreamy music on Armed Forces radio, or catching exciting missions on his Prick 25.

Mike read car magazines and built furniture from the pieces of miscellaneous junk lying around the bush. The furniture provided some small measure of comfort and reminded him of home, a place he sorely missed.

Lewis, an artist, painted signs for the firebase and on the tracks. He found an old World War II cookbook and tried to make his C-rations more palatable by experimenting with dishes called Chicken under Bullet and Foxhole Dinner for Two. He didn't enjoy card games, but pulled guard duty so others could play; but for a fee, of course.

Everyone spent time writing letters. Paul and Mike penned love letters to their new brides back home and received heavily perfumed letters in return. Lewis, a bit of a ladies' man, wrote to a number of girlfriends in addition to his sister and parents.

At one point the stress of combat became too much for Lewis as he told his parents the truth of the situation: "Don't believe the papers, because we're getting the punk knocked out of us. We had five dead yesterday ..." His mother wrote back and told him to stop sharing so many grim details and, like a typical mother, gave her son unsolicited advice on a number of other issues.

Lewis responded angrily. "If you can't treat me like an adult, don't bother to write back." But soon he regretted his harsh words and dashed off an apology letter explaining, "You have to understand that I'm seeing a lot of stuff ..." His apology was automatically accepted and mail call continued as usual.

Pat wrote to Paul every day, describing the mundane details of her life, including the "love you, miss you, can't wait to see you" sentiments of a lonely newlywed. Paul's mother watched for the mailman each day, obsessively counting the days between letters, while his father suffered in silence. Mail call was the most important part of everyone's daily routine.

Pat stayed busy and carefully avoided the six o'clock news. Her circle of friends included women from work and school, and Chris Rensberger, Floyd's wife, whom she called frequently. She loved the Pinkertons and relied on them for moral support. The feelings were mutual. Every Sunday she had dinner with them, put puzzles together with Paul's youngest brother, Dave, and talked to the older siblings. She still lived at home with her parents in order to save money while Paul was away.

* * *

The soldiers grasped onto anything resembling normal life where they could find it, often befriending the needy Vietnamese children who looked to them for money, food, and attention. Children were kept out of military areas by perimeter wire, but that didn't stop them. They followed the soldiers everywhere, selling cold beer and soda for a dollar, and hawking whatever else they could find to make money. At first the soldiers balked at their expensive prices, but when their money, doled out in Military Payment Currency, rotted in their pockets, they decided to spend it rather than waste it.

The military rule was "no fraternizing with the locals," but almost everyone held a soft spot for the children who were innocent victims of the war. Paul loved the children because they reminded him of his younger siblings. He befriended a large group of them and they knew that this big American soldier was friend, not foe. He gave them candy and treats, purchased their beer and soda, played games with them, and called the medic over to treat their numerous scrapes and wounds.

Mike and his gun crew handed out C-rations and treats to the kids, although Mike often found himself fraught with guilt and worry after an encounter with the children. One day as he traveled through a village of rice-growers, a small child came up to bargain and sell his wares. The child's father, bent over in a rice paddy, stared enviously as his son made more money in five minutes than he made in a month. The disparity didn't escape Mike's notice. He worried about being disrespectful of the village elders and saw that helping the children on a short-term basis could negatively impact the Vietnamese economy long-term by promoting its reliance on the soldiers. In Vietnam, even good deeds produced conflict; there were no easy solutions in a war zone.

Lewis enjoyed the children and owed them a huge debt of gratitude. More than once they saved his life, warning him of dangers on roads or rivers he was about to traverse. Once, however, he encountered a problem with one of the kids. Lewis and the others were at the river washing out their APCs (tracks) when a group of ragged little children arrived, eager to help. A deal was struck and each child received fifty cents for his work. The soldiers sat back and relaxed as the kids cleaned the vehicles, playing and laughing in the sun. Everyone had a good time until an older boy, who wanted a piece of the action, appeared.

The other kids said, "Go away, we make deal already with soldiers." Angry, the young teen began throwing rocks, narrowly missing one of them.

"You get out of here!" Lewis yelled. The boy pitched another rock into the crowd of children, but was off his mark.

Lewis lifted the lightweight boy up and over his head and threw him into the muddy river. Peals of laughter followed as the boy stomped off, red-faced and humiliated.

Five minutes later the boy reappeared, firing an automatic weapon. The children scattered and the soldiers jumped into their tracks. Lewis's track driver chased the boy over a hill, accidentally flattening a house in his path. Unfortunately, it was the boy's house. When Lewis saw him a few weeks later, the child recognized him and began shouting, cursing, and making obscene gestures at him. Lewis wondered what would become of the boy, a child so hardened by the events in his young life.

In Paul's experience, incidents of children harming soldiers were relatively rare. More common were incidents of soldiers abusing children. He witnessed several abusive situations, events that disturbed him more deeply than the carnage of combat. One day an officer decided to make an example out of a young boy who was at the perimeter wire talking with the soldiers. The officer took the boy, who was only eight or nine, blindfolded him, tied his hands, and forced him to sit on a hill in the blazing sun for hours on end. The terrified boy cried nonstop. Eventually the smug officer set him free, confident that he had made his point, despite angry protests from Paul and others.

Enraged, Paul wrote to Pat about the incident and asked her for the address of a Pennsylvania senator to report the abuse. Mysteriously, Pat never received his letter. As time passed, Paul lost sight of his request and eventually dropped the issue, but his anger didn't subside. He told Mike, "It's no wonder there are snipers out here. If someone did that to my kid, I'd shoot somebody too."

* * *

September continued to be a terrible month. There had already been two major operations and the month wasn't over yet. Paul went on a mission near the DMZ, on loan to another unit. It was early afternoon and an air strike had been called in, with suspected enemy in the area. A spotter plane, a small piper cub, was sent in first to mark the designated area with phosphorous, making it easier for the B-52s to hit their target.

Paul watched as the piper cub swooped in at treetop level and shot two phosphorous rockets off one wing. The pilot banked the wrong way (on the heavy side with the remaining rockets) and as he turned away, the plane flipped over and crashed into the hilltop. On the radio Paul heard, "On your feet, let's go! We need to secure the area." The plane contained maps and other classified information that had to be retrieved. Paul and the others sprinted to the crash site.

The plane was mangled, but the men managed to lift up the wings, revealing the pilot's dangling leg. Paul and the others worked together, pushing and pulling the plane until the pilot could be unstrapped and taken out of his seat. What they discovered was a headless pile of limp flesh, every bone in his body broken. Paul was accustomed to the gore of combat, but this was more than he could stomach. Within minutes an ashen soldier came running in from the perimeter, holding the helmet containing the pilot's head. His eyes were wide open, staring from the beyond. They wrapped the body in a poncho and a chopper came in to take away the pilot's remains. The medic shook his head, "Christ, what a way to send someone home to his family!" Paul, who felt nauseous and faint, couldn't agree more.

It was almost dark. The men set up a makeshift camp and stayed in the area until the next morning. At dawn it was time to move again. In characteristic jungle pattern, they spread out so the enemy could see only one person at a time. They had just walked a short distance when a single shot rang out. Someone called for the medic, but there was no answer. The medic had taken a bullet to the back, blowing open his entire chest. The men looked at each other, recalling his words from the previous day. Now they had to send his broken and mangled body back to his family.

In two short days, two more men had died. Paul had been in Vietnam for less than sixty days, but it already seemed like a lifetime.

By the end of the week emotions were running high and physical endurance was running low. The men were exhausted from a week on patrol and their feet were wet, sore, and bloody. As they approached an area of rice paddies, an officer flying overhead in a helicopter informed them of enemies nearby. Reportedly, he commanded them to run across the open rice paddies to secure the hilltop on the other side. The company commander disagreed. "What's the importance of the hilltop? Why can't you call in artillery? You can level it in two minutes. Just call in artillery."

The officer supposedly responded, "No, I want everyone to get online. I'm willing to expend 10 percent of the men to do this."

"I don't think they're going to go. I don't think I can force this one."

Paul and those with radios heard the heated conversation and chimed in, "No, we're not doing it. It's suicide to run across an open rice paddy. We're not doing this. We won't go."

Paul thought, "Oh sure, this asshole wants to see some action; he's safe and sound up in his helicopter! Damned if I'm doing this."

The officer shot back, "What do you mean you're not going to do it? You'll do it or you'll be court-martialled. If you refuse orders in a combat situation, I can have you all shot!"

There were approximately 300 men on the ground and the men with radios started to mutiny. "Fuck you. We don't care about your rank. We're not doing this! We're not dying for something this stupid. Fuck you! Fuck the Army!"

"I'll have you shot, do you understand?" the officer screamed.

Paul's heart rate went into overdrive. "Holy shit, he's not giving up!"

Someone on a radio supposedly said, "Fine. If you make us do this, the survivors will shoot you! You have to land your helicopter eventually and when you do, you're a dead man! You won't make it through the day, I guarantee it!"

For an exciting thirty minutes the tense exchange continued until finally, the officer backed down and everyone went back to base camp. Paul was afraid of possible repercussions, but nothing happened. They had disobeyed orders and survived yet another day. For Paul, it didn't get any better than that.

***

Paul returned to base camp only to discover that his friends had been going through their own version of hell. Lewis, Mike, Berry, Hall, and some of the others had remained at Con Thien while he was out on patrol. The 4.2 mortars (guns) had been taken out of the tracks and placed in pits for harassing and interdicting (H & I) fire during the night.

This meant that random ambush targets were fired upon every night to keep the enemy off balance and away from the soldiers' area of operations.

A 4.2 mortar round came in a two-foot canister with tape around it, about six to seven inches from its end. At the end of the canister was the mortar round which looked like a stem sticking out with charges stuck on it. The charges were square and yellow and looked like slices of Swiss cheese with holes in the center. To prepare for each night's H & I fire, targets were plotted during the day as the gun crew received the direction and elevation of the guns, the targets, and the number of charges. The soldiers took the instructions, prepared the charges, and wrote the information in chalk on the barrels. All the canisters came fully loaded with charges, but some rounds didn't require the full load, so they pulled off the extra charges and discarded them in a pile on the ground.

As nightfall came, Lewis was manning the FDC, calling out the rounds to be fired while Leon Berry stood with a flashlight cutting the charges on the rounds, checking the markings on the barrels. Hall was on the radio communicating with Lewis. Lewis called out a round, expecting confirmation, when he heard a blood-curdling scream from Hall. He rushed out of the FDC and saw thirty-foot flames shooting out of the pit. A spark had ignited the charges on the ground.

Leon Berry ran around wildly, his skin blistering from the waist up. "Pour water on me! Pour water on me!" He flopped down on a sandbank as Lewis dumped water from a shell canister onto his back, peeling his skin like an onion. The flashlight in his hand had melted, his fingers virtually burned right into it.

Hall, who had been in the middle of the explosion, was still on fire as he ran through barbed wire, unaware of what he was doing. Mike and Henderson grabbed him and rolled him in the dirt to extinguish the flames; attempting to not injure him further. Men standing nearby were also burned in the accident, but not as severely as Hall and Berry who were closest to the charges. Helicopters medevac'd the men out, taking them first to a hospital ship off shore, and then either to the United States or Japan. No one knew for sure, because the men were never heard from again.

One of the sergeants, who had been asleep during the accident, came out of his bunker as the helicopters took off. When he heard the details of the fire, he allegedly remarked, "What a stupid thing to do! They should have covered up those charges."

Lewis, shaken, vehemently defended his friends. "You're a sergeant. Where were you? When guns are firing, it's your responsibility to be out with the crew. You should have been out here with them."

"They knew what they were doing. Don't try to blame me for their accident. They were just too stupid to cover up the charges."

"Shut up you asshole! They're probably dead and it's your fault. Sleep on that!" Lewis stormed off, sickened by the man's lack of concern.

Lewis took Berry's flashlight back to his bunker and stored it away for safekeeping. Days later he took it from its hiding place and gently touched the object, wondering if his friend had survived. Eventually he discarded the item to erase the painful memory from his mind, but the experience was as permanently etched in his brain as the fingers on the flashlight.

* * *

Frank Cates, the man who had flipped the track during training in Fort Carson, was an assistant gunner in Vietnam, an assignment that was short-lived. Because of his nervous nature and his tendency to fall apart during combat, his fellow soldiers requested that he be placed elsewhere, fearing he would put them in harm's way. The First Sergeant agreed and made him his jeep driver, a decision he soon regretted.

One day as the First Sergeant stood in his jeep giving orders, Cates popped the clutch, throwing the sergeant out of the vehicle and breaking his arm. The incident earned him the title "Killer Cates." He was once again reassigned, this time to latrine and KP duties. He was miserable. He was generally good-natured about the teasing of others, even about the bird's nest hairdo that Paul had given him, but he found his current duties and the subsequent jokes about them degrading and insufferable.

Lewis took pity on him and went to the First Sergeant. "Top, I'd like to have Cates back in the platoon. I could use some help and I've got things for him to do."

"Well, okay you can have him back, but keep him away from me and make sure he doesn't put anyone else in danger."

From then on, Cates considered Lewis his best buddy and a ritual developed between the two. Lewis pulled ten-hour shifts in the FDC, frequently at night, and during his shift Cates checked in with him. "Would you like some coffee?"

"Sure." Cates ran off to make coffee.

"Would you like a cigarette?"

"Yeah." Cates ran off to find a cigarette.

"Would you like to play rummy?"

"Sure, deal the cards." And so it continued. Over time Lewis came to know and respect this unusual person and eventually discovered the reasons behind the man's behavior. Cates had volunteered to serve in the Regular Army, apparently to save his younger brother (who was drafted) from being sent into combat in Vietnam. He had completed one tour in Vietnam, but had extended his tour in two, six-month increments to keep his brother out of harm's way.

In a letter to his sister, Annie, Lewis wrote: "One of the guys who is on his second tour is shell shocked. When he was here before, he and his buddy were in a hole together. They changed places just as a mortar round came in. It hit his buddy and killed him. It seems to have had a great effect on Cates. We all try to take care of him; he wants to be part of a group so badly. We try to imagine what he was like before, or what we would be like, under the same conditions." To Lewis, Killer Cates was a hero and one of the best. And although Mike, Paul, and the others couldn't see it yet, there were glimpses of Killer Cates in all of them.

* * *

Steve Bucher, Paul's high school friend from Manheim, arrived in Vietnam in April of 1968 and was assigned to the 199th Light Infantry Brigade located in an area around Saigon. His platoon conducted area sweeps during the day and ambushes at night. Like Paul, Steve carried the radio and quickly discovered that he was the enemy's prime target, but unlike Paul, he passed the honor along as quickly as he could when new replacements came on board.

After three months he went on R&R and, when he returned, his buddies were either dead or in a hospital in Japan, the result of an ambush during his absence. Steve was reassigned to LRRPS (Long Range Reconnaissance Patrols) and was dropped off in remote sites to spy on the enemy. Three months later he was assigned to U.S. Army Headquarters in Long Binh where he sat safely inside writing manuals.

Marty had arrived in Vietnam on May 30 as part of Delta Company, 2nd 505th Infantry Battalion, 3rd Brigade, 82nd Airborne Division, located in Phu Bai, which was north of DaNang and south of Con Thien. Later, he moved closer to Saigon.

Paul and his circle of high school friends stayed in touch by mail. Jimmy wrote letters to Marty, Steve, and Paul to provide details from home and the three wrote to each other within Vietnam. All of Marty's letters contained basically the same news: sketchy details about combat, extensive information about hot, fast cars, and the promise to "get together when we get home and raise some hell, and not just a little bit either!" Letters were always signed with the standard FTA or Fuck the Army closing, every man's current sentiment.

On two separate occasions Paul and Steve had an opportunity to get together, meeting for quick nights of drinking and commiserating. Neither were big drinkers, preferring instead to keep their wits about them, but meeting a dear friend in a war zone called for something out of the ordinary.

* * *

Paul and Lewis had similar habits. Both enjoyed the occasional beer and both smoked cigarettes. Mike had neither vice. Lewis, not a smoker before his tour, started smoking as a result of one of his duties: handing out rations of cigarettes to the men. Smoking was a source of jokes among the soldiers. During the late 1960s tobacco companies began posting warnings on the packages: "Cigarette smoking may be hazardous to your health..." sparking the men to come up with their own slogans: "Mortar attacks may be hazardous to your health!" "Being in Vietnam may be harmful to your health," and "If the cigarettes don't kill you, the bullets sure as hell will!"

Cigarette smoking and a couple of beers were mild compared to the pursuits of some. Morphine was repeatedly stolen out of the medic's bag and heroin was easy to obtain. The children sold pot and secured whatever else the men wanted for a price. In Vietnam no one cared too much and, as a result, a soldier's conduct often devolved to two basic rules: show up and shoot. Everything else was superfluous.

Paul gave marijuana a try twice, but found neither time enjoyable. He worried that he might wander off and become lost so he put Mike on high alert, asking him to watch out for him. Mike agreed, and safely tucked Pinky into bed during his two forays into pot smoking. Lewis also tried pot. He sampled it during his R&R and became violently ill from the strong and unfamiliar smoke; he never touched it again.

The soldiers knew they could negotiate with the children for whatever goods and services they wanted, but the children frequently outsmarted the soldiers, getting the better end of the bargain. The men witnessed Sergeant Goth, a career soldier, approach a child at the wire. "I want Four Roses Whiskey. Can you get it for me?"

"Yeah."

"How much?"

"Ten dollar."

"Okay. Be here tomorrow night."

"No problem. I get it. Four Roses. Tomorrow night."

The next night the child appeared with a paper bag. Sergeant Goth handed the child $10 and the child thrust the bag into his hands and quickly ran away. Goth took the bottle out of the bag and let loose with a line of expletives. He held up a crusty old bottle filled with beer on which a crude label with four red roses had been applied. The soldiers watching the exchange had a good laugh, not only because the child had tricked the sergeant, but because there was no love lost between career soldiers and draftees, who had somewhat different value systems.

Draftees, for the most part, did not want to be in Vietnam. Their primary goal was to go home unscathed. However, the lifers or career soldiers sometimes needed to create, or become involved with, dangerous situations in order to obtain the ribbons and medals required for advancement. While the overwhelming majority of lifers were legitimately brave and heroic men who fought valiantly and protected their men, there were the occasional few who appeared to sacrifice their men to earn these coveted ribbons. Still others felt justified in obtaining medals or ribbons for the silliest things, like getting dirt in their ears or sustaining tiny surface wounds.

Paul ironically noted that some of the officers who had been the most demanding of him in the States were the first ones to fall apart during combat. Others seemed to disappear after arriving in Vietnam, staying far in the background, leaving him or Mike to serve as the highest ranking NCOs in charge; a responsibility neither man desired.

However, there was one lifer who stood out among the others. Second Lieutenant David Merrell, a recon platoon leader, was by all accounts highly respected and admired. He treated his men as equals, genuinely cared about their physical and mental well-being, and held them to high moral standards. Mike became friends with Merrell and witnessed an incident that won his respect for the man.

After one of the firefights, Vietnamese bodies were gathered and stored by the bunkers. A few men decided it would be a good photo opportunity and posed with the dead. Merrell came over and quickly put an end to the show, reminding them that these were people, not lions shot on safari. His point was well-taken.

* * *

September had been a difficult month that included two major battles, the fire accident, and unbearable weather conditions. October continued to test the men's mettle.

On October 23, Operation Rich was put into effect, an operation that placed Paul and his friends deep into the DMZ in a dismounted operation (not in their tracks). They left Con Thien in the darkness of night and moved north across the Ben Hai River, turning east, then south, heading straight into enemy forces. It was the first true Combined Arms Operation in which the Navy, Air Force, Marines, and Army all worked together.

The battle lasted five long days and, when it was over, there were 308 enemy forces killed and a large but unknown number wounded. Only sixteen Americans were wounded and eight were killed, including Second Lieutenant David Merrell and his radio operator, PFC Thomas Ray.

Second Lieutenant Merrell was killed late in the day, too late to remove his body from the area. At base camp the men reportedly held a wake, placing Merrell's body in a poncho on the ground, for a viewing of sorts. All night the men circled the poncho, paying their respects. Paul found it to be a strange yet comforting act, as he joined the parade of mourners and pondered his own fate. Mike mourned the death of his friend in private, incapable of viewing the body of his buddy lying motionless on the ground.

Paul was more than familiar with the sight of dead bodies by now. As a front line NCO, he still conducted body counts of dead Vietnamese, seeing firsthand the devastation his fire missions created. However, it was one thing to count the bodies of the NVA, but quite another to find a small child's leg painted onto a tree or a woman's torso stuck in the jungle mud; the results of civilians coming too close to the battlefield. It was during those times that Paul felt the blood drain out of his head, his breath sucked away. Everything went still and quiet as he struggled to make peace with himself, his shame and guilt unbearable. Sometimes he turned to his little Bible in supplication or sometimes his raw anger boiled over as he loudly exclaimed, "Fuck the Army! Fuck this place!" But mostly, he tried to forget.

* * *

By November Paul had been in Vietnam for four months and felt like an old man, not the twenty-one-year-old that he was. The more he experienced, the angrier he became. He continually questioned why he was there and what real purpose the war served. As far as he could tell, nothing was being accomplished except for killing and wounding Vietnamese people, destroying their land, and corrupting their children. Was he really saving anyone from Communism? Both Paul and Lewis wrote home and cynically reported that the soldiers turned young girls into prostitutes, and little boys into smokers and potty-mouthed cursers who picked up the GI language and used it at every opportunity. In Paul's mind, it was a sad state of affairs.

More infuriating incidents occurred and he wrote home again in search of a senator who might listen to his reports of abuse. One day orders came down to enter a free fire zone, an area in which anything that moves is a legitimate target, be it animal or human. Flyers had gone out in advance warning the local Vietnamese to leave; everything in the zone was now free game. Paul and his friends entered the zone and, within a very short time, encountered a group of elderly Vietnamese. No one picked up his weapon, despite orders. None of the men was willing to shoot a group of harmless senior citizens who were apparently on their way home. But now, they had the uneasy task of deciding what to do with them.

"Let's take them back to camp and let the colonel deal with it," someone suggested. They all agreed and gently herded the group of confused Vietnamese back to base camp.

Initially, the colonel was angry; orders were orders, after all. However, he had no intention of shooting them either. Instead he decided to humiliate them; giving the appearance that he had captured them. As Paul and the others looked on, they felt angry about the degrading scene unfolding before them, but were greatly relieved that nothing worse had taken place. The frightened seniors were quickly released and it was just another day in the war.

*** ***

On another occasion, Paul witnessed a tanker from another unit trying to solicit a young girl for sex. When she refused him, the tanker decided to scare her by throwing an incendiary grenade (used to burn holes in metal) in her direction. However, his aim was poor and the grenade ricocheted off a tree, hitting her and splitting her head wide open. Afraid of what he had done, he and his friends drove off, leaving the girl to bleed to death. Paul and his comrades rushed to her side and called for a chopper. Paul didn't hear what happened to her in the end. All he knew was that he was going to flood some senator's office with letters and somebody better have some answers because he was mad, damn fighting mad.

Unfortunately, Paul often witnessed acts of cruelty during the war and didn't see the flip side of things. Behind-the-scenes, large numbers of soldiers throughout the country gave freely of their time, energy, and talents by distributing food, clothing, and medicine to those in need; spending time in orphanages caring for infants; and making a positive difference wherever they could.

In November, Paul and his friends had a break from firefights and spent time helping the South Vietnamese people in what was termed civic action operations, a formalized program of help. Medical and dental care was provided for the locals and large amounts of clothing, school supplies, and necessities were distributed. Voluntary contributions were collected from the troops for a children's hospital and for widows. Many of the soldiers felt that they were finally doing something that made sense—helping people instead of killing them.

Around the same time everyone was allowed R&R. Paul flew to Bangkok with his friend Floyd, relishing the chance to escape the chaos of the war and simply relax. Floyd liked to drink and spent much of his time getting drunk. He and Paul visited strip clubs and bars in the evening and went sightseeing during the day. The time passed all too quickly and soon they were back in Vietnam.

By the time Thanksgiving rolled around, they were back at Wunder Beach to help the locals relocate their village. New homes were built and the old village was leveled and destroyed in an attempt to keep out the

Viet Cong. There didn't seem to be much point to it but, for now, it was their job and it was better than being in firefights.

Bored, Paul and his friend went to the shore one day with tin cans and a pile of ammunition. They threw the cans into the water and, when the waves carried them far out to sea, they shot at them, using up as much ammo as they could. Before long, a helicopter flew in and landed on the beach right next to them.

"Who's in charge here?" demanded the commanding officer as he stepped out of the chopper.

Paul knew he was the higher ranking of the two, so he replied, "Me, sir."

"Well, what the hell are you doing?"

"Uh, I guess just using up ammo and shooting tin cans, sir."

"You guess? You guess? I almost called an air strike on you. We thought we were receiving hostile fire from this beach, you dumb ass! You're lucky you're standing here right now. We almost killed you! I should court-martial you!"

"I'm sorry, sir." Paul was nervous. The ever-present threat of a court-martial was no laughing matter.

"Well, you better be! Don't ever let me catch you doing anything this stupid again or your ass is mine!" With that he stormed off and the chopper disappeared.

"Whew! That was close. We won't do that again!" Paul said to his friend, wiping the sweat from his brow.

Thanksgiving came and went without fanfare. The men received a hot meal and a few people had the opportunity to call home. Paul was not one of them. In December Paul, Mike, Lewis, and a few others were sent to the Ba Long Valley to build a road. They were a small group, consisting of about twenty Army troops and twenty Marines. It was a dangerous place for so few men to work. They were in the middle of the jungle in hilly terrain, making them sitting ducks for the North Vietnamese Army (NVA). The work was hard and treacherous and, with the pouring rain and muddy conditions, heavy equipment kept sliding off the sides of the ridiculously steep and winding road.

After a couple of weeks of backbreaking labor the men were given the order to destroy the road they had just built. They wondered about the purpose of their work and if the people in charge knew what they were doing. As they left the area, they crossed the river and set up camp for the night. Paul woke up the next morning and felt something wet and sticky on his leg. He looked down to see his entire pant leg covered in blood.

"Oh my God, I've been shot!" he thought. He cautiously pulled up his pant leg but, instead of finding a bullet wound, discovered a huge leech, swollen with blood that he had knocked open during the night. Disgusted, he pulled it off and washed his leg in the river. The leech left a permanent scar that looked like an incision, but Paul considered himself lucky. Leeches were common and some men found them in areas of their bodies where no worm should dare to go.

* * *

By the time they returned to Con Thien it was Christmas. Packages from home flooded in with treats and small Styrofoam Christmas trees. Generally, anyone who had a family received some sort of package and Paul pitied those who didn't. It was bad enough to be in this Godforsaken place, but to not hear from your family during the holidays was unthinkable.

There were plenty of Christmas trees to go around so Mike and Paul gave theirs to a couple of Vietnamese children who delighted in this strange custom. Lewis received a knock-off Zippo lighter in his Salvation Army package and, not needing it, gave it to one of the children. The child, overwhelmed by the gift, gave Lewis his one and only toy in return: a C-ration can rigged with a wire and pebble which served as a noise-maker. Lewis had tears in his eyes as he accepted the gift from this poverty-stricken child.

* * *

As the Pinkertons and Schaumbergs celebrated Christmas, Paul's absence was painfully obvious. The only good news was that he had been in Vietnam for six months and half of his tour of duty was over. Time moved slowly, but at least there was an end in sight. For Paul, things were changing as the Army implemented a strategy known as an infusion program. A large number of troops were going home, which created huge gaps in some of the units. Rather than bring in all new and green replacements, seasoned and trained troops from within Vietnam were transferred into those units to ensure they weren't compromised in strength, integrity, or expertise. Paul was being infused (or transferred) in January, which meant he'd leave his existing unit and join an entirely different one, near Saigon. Paul didn't regard this as good news. Things had calmed down in Con Thien and a known commodity was better than an unknown one. He trusted his fellow soldiers and had several friends within the 1/61st. As January loomed ahead, Paul became increasingly anxious about his upcoming move.

Meanwhile letters continued to flow back and forth between Jimmy Thomas and the gang. Marty had two interesting pieces of news. First, he had found a friend who promised to set him up as a race car driver after the war, a thrilling proposition for this car-crazed youth. Second, he was getting an early out by giving up his December R&R and extending his

tour by a few days. Jimmy knew that Steve had landed a good job writing
manuals and Paul was hanging in there as well. He relished the day when
his buddies would return home and they could all hang out at Curly's
again.

* * *

It was almost midnight when the phone jarred the silence in the
Pinkerton household. Dave woke up and listened to his mother answer
the phone in the hallway outside his bedroom. In a distressed voice she
exclaimed, "Oh no!" A couple minutes later she hung up the phone crying. His parent's voices were muted so Dave had to strain to hear the conversation, but he thought he heard his mother say that Marty Sauble had
been killed. The next morning when Dave woke up, everything was back
to normal and there was no mention of Marty. His mother didn't say a
word, so Dave assumed it had all been just a bad dream.

Steve Bucher returned from a pleasant R&R in Australia with a pile
of letters awaiting him. He picked up Marty's first, hoping he was in an
area where they could meet; he missed his buddy's good spirits and laughter. Marty had the usual news: cars, combat, and the desire to get together
soon, signed with his typical FTA closing. The next letter was from Steve's
mother, informing him of Marty's death from a friendly fire accident.
Steve threw down the letter and cursed, feeling angrier than he'd ever felt
in his life. This reaction was quickly followed by intense grief at the loss
of his good friend.

Mail call came and Paul received his usual stack of letters from Pat
and home. He flipped through the envelopes and saw one from his local
pastor, Raymond Foellner. Immediately he knew there was bad news, a
premonition that became a reality as soon as he saw Marty's picture on a
newspaper clipping enclosed with the letter. Pastor Foellner wrote: "I
regret that I did not personally know Martin Sauble. Your mother told me
of the very close friendship which has arisen between the two of you.
Paul, I am not going to attempt to give a hint or suggestion as to why it
happened to anyone, let alone a fine friend such as he was to you … " followed by comforting words of faith, words that were painfully useless at
that particular moment.

After mail call Paul disappeared into his bunker. The other men, sensing something was wrong with Pink, respectfully stayed away. From outside they heard the sobs, the terrible mournful wails of their distraught
comrade. No one spoke of the incident. In Vietnam you knew enough to
leave others to their grief—it came so insidiously to all of them. Martin G.
Sauble, Jr. was killed on New Year's Eve as a result of friendly fire, less
than one month after his 21st birthday.

* * *

By the middle of January it was time for Paul to leave the 5th Division to join up with the 1st Division in a town named Di Anh in the Song Be Province near Saigon. He and half the troops were infused to other areas. Paul was given his orders and told he had five days to arrive. How he got to his destination was his problem; no transportation was provided. Paul hitchhiked his way primarily by plane, catching a flight from Dong Ha to DaNang and DaNang to areas south. As he moved south, he carried his paperwork with him, carefully ripping out the pages indicating his R&R in Bangkok so that he could secure another one in a couple of months. Paul figured it was the least the Army owed him at this point.

In his new division, the Headquarters Company of the 1st of the 11th, 1st Infantry Division, Paul became a squad leader, responsible for a group of men. It was an unfamiliar and uncomfortable position; a job he wasn't trained to do. He worried about putting the men in danger and verbalized his fears to whoever would listen. Eventually he was put back into a mortar platoon.

In the South there were no NVA to contend with, only Viet Cong who often appeared as friends during the day and enemies at night. Paul felt uneasy with his new environment and wished he were back with his friends. However, things back at Con Thien had changed too. Lewis went home in February and Daniel, a true lifer, reenlisted. Mike, who had several more months of duty, encountered some of the worst fighting yet and lived in constant fear for his life.

Just as Paul settled into his new unit, everything changed for the worse. Lieutenant M arrived as a new platoon leader. He had red hair, a feisty personality, and an appetite for action, any action. He carried a loaded .45 and spent most of his day fantasizing about the enemy, twirling and fast drawing his pistol like a Western cowboy. Paul and the other men were afraid of him and worried about his attitude. One day he came to Paul with a proposition.

"I'm organizing a LRRP with a few of us. I want you to go as the forward observer; we'll go out for a couple of weeks and gather information about the enemy. It'll be great!"

"Shit no, I'm not going!"

"What do you mean you're not going? You're going."

"No, I'm not. I'm not trained for LRRP and I'm not doing it."

"The hell you aren't! Are you planning to disobey my orders in a combat situation? I could have you shot for that."

"Fuck you! I'll go back to the main base and protest this. I'm not going!"

"Well you can't go back to base. You're coming with me and that's it!"

Paul knew that going on a LRRP was certain death. He hadn't been trained in LRRP and the patrol, by its very nature, was extremely dangerous. It entailed a small group of men going out in the bush, far removed from everyone, purposely seeking out the enemy. It sounded like suicide to him. He was only a few months short of going home and didn't plan to get killed engaging in such a risky endeavor.

Later that week as he worked outside the bunkers clearing rocks with a pick, he took a long, hard look at the sharp instrument in his hands, squeezed his eyes almost shut, and slammed the pick on top of his boot as hard as he could. He achieved the desired result: his foot throbbed in pain and bled profusely. He limped in and was promptly taken to the main base camp for medical attention.

The x-ray revealed no broken bones. He received stitches and a bandage. Paul requested an appointment with the Inspector General. He told him about Lieutenant M and warned the IG, "Please do something about him before he gets a lot of guys killed ... or gets himself fragged."

The Inspector General smiled wryly, reportedly saying, "You don't have to worry about him. There's a helicopter bringing him in right now. He shot himself with his .45. You can go back now sergeant, you'll be okay."

* * *

Paul continued to write home daily, but was finally able to put his stationary away and talk to Pat in person. In May, they met in Hawaii for his second R&R. It was the most incredible feeling in the world and Paul savored every second. They spent a glorious week together, filled with intimacy, sightseeing, and sheer relaxation. Ironically, Floyd Rensberger and his wife Chris were also in Hawaii, staying in the same hotel. When the two couples ran into each other, the women were wearing identical dresses, causing exclamations of surprise and hoots of laughter. R&R couldn't have been better except for the fact that it ended much too quickly and Paul had to return to Vietnam. Saying goodbye a second time around seemed even more torturous than the first. Pat thought it was difficult too, but felt confident that her husband would come home safely in two short months.

When Paul first entered Vietnam, he was given his DEROS or Date of Expected Return from Overseas. Paul finally closed in on this date, joining the much-coveted short timer's club, men nearing the end of their tours. With approximately two months to go, Paul ticked off the remaining days in a calendar he held close to his heart. With each passing day he became more wary of his surroundings and unusually paranoid about his survival. It wasn't uncommon for men to go through their entire tour in

Vietnam only to be shot a week or two before departure. He was determined not to let that happen.

Every afternoon the helicopter landed with the mailbag, Paul's favorite time of day. One afternoon his name was included in the list of men being taken to the rear for out-processing. The pilot said, "You have ten minutes. Grab your gear and let's go!" Paul scooped up his things and said short goodbyes to his friends, promising to write when he got home. He jumped in the helicopter and off he went.

At the processing station there were tents with wooden floors and bunks with real sheets and mattresses. With the exception of R&R, it was the first time in a year he had slept in a real bed. But the first thing he did was take an extremely long, hot shower, change into fresh clothing, and splash huge quantities of someone's leftover 4711 Cologne all over himself in an attempt to eliminate the jungle stench that permeated his being.

The next day he underwent a physical exam and his duffel bag was inspected. The military checked for items that needed to be returned. Paul had bargained for a knife early on and wanted to keep it for the memories it held, but it was confiscated. The officer inspecting his possessions also came across his barbering tools.

"What's this stuff?"

"My barbering tools."

"Do you have a barber's license?"

"Yes."

"Show it to me."

"I don't have it here! It's at home, for crying out loud!"

"Then I have to take the tools."

"Fine!" Paul was pissed off that the Army had to fuck him over, even on his last day in Vietnam, but then a wicked smile crossed his face. He looked at the officer and thought, "No, I get the last laugh because I'm going home and you're not!"

The next morning Paul boarded a plane from Saigon to DaNang. In DaNang he walked across the tarmac, crossing paths with the new arrivals. Paul was so jubilant his feet barely touched the pavement; an adrenaline rush kept him at a nervous high. He boarded the TWA plane without looking back and took an empty seat. As the plane soared into the air, Paul held his breath, still waiting for something horrific to happen. When the pilot finally announced they had cleared Vietnamese airspace, the men inside the plane erupted into whoops, cheers, screams, and applause. They were survivors and they were going home! Paul thought to himself, "I made it! It's over! I can forget about it and get on with my life!" Little did he know—that would be impossible.

CHAPTER 4

Abandonment

You don't choose your family.
They are God's gift to you,
As you are to them.

Desmond Tutu

T he mid-1960s were an important time for Paul Pinkerton. In fact, 1965 was the year in which he: graduated from high school, turned eighteen, met Pat Schaumberg, and received his draft notice. Ultimately, those events led to his career as a barber, his marriage, and his service in Vietnam. But, unknown to Paul, there was a young child, living only forty miles away in another Pennsylvania town, whose life would also be significantly altered by the events that occurred in 1965. This woman would someday become his wife …

* * *

It was a cold February night in 1965 and trouble was brewing in the old farmhouse. Blanche and Senter were babysitting as usual and they were fed up with the situation. They loved and pitied their nieces—ten-year-old Bobbi and five-year-old Sandy—and helped the girls' mother, Hazel, when they could, but they had reached their limit. Hazel, Blanche's younger sister, was selfish and narcissistic; a woman who shirked her parental responsibilities and passed her children off to Blanche and her longtime companion, Senter, as easily as some people gave away unwanted pets.

Today would be different. Before Hazel arrived, Blanche braced herself for confrontation.

"Are the girls ready to go?" Hazel asked, as she breezed in the door.

"Hazel, I've had it! This can't continue. I'm tired of these kids going back and forth all the time. You're always coming and going with the girls and it has to stop!" Blanche's voice rose to an angry crescendo.

"What are you talking about?" Hazel demanded defensively.

"Damn it! You know what I'm talking about, don't play stupid with me. They come and go from this house every week. You drop them off and leave them for days at a time. You say you'll pick them up, but then you don't. This is it. We've had enough of your nonsense!" Blanche roared.

"How dare you, you bitch!" screamed Hazel.

"You listen to me." Blanche moved close to Hazel, wagging a large index finger in her face. "I'm telling you right now, either leave them with us or take them. Or leave one and take the other, but you need to decide now. We're not having the kids shuttling back and forth like this for one more day! Decide now!"

"Don't you tell me what to do!" yelled Hazel as she gave Blanche a shove.

Blanche, a broad-shouldered woman, stood her ground. She pushed her sister in return, shifting the weight on Hazel's high heels, sending her sprawling backwards onto the floor. Hazel jumped up, red-faced, ready to fight.

Bobbi, the older of the two, understood the ramifications of the exchange and interjected herself into the mix. "Mommy, take me home. I don't want to stay here!"

Hazel screamed, "See what you've done? Bobbi's upset!"

Blanche laughed sarcastically, "See what I've done? You fool! Take care of your own children for a change!"

The fighting and arguing, pushing and shoving continued well into the night, becoming louder and more raucous by the minute. Sandy cowered in the corner, her big brown eyes filling with tears. Senter picked her up and gently placed her in his oversized lap, uncomfortable that she had to witness the scuffle.

The fighting escalated to a breaking point. Hazel caved first. "All right! All right! I'll take Bobbi and you keep Sandy. Come on Bobbi, let's get out of here!"

Sandy jumped out of Senter's lap and ran to her mother. "No, Mommy, no! Take me too, take me too." Sandy grabbed onto her mother's legs, attempting to stop her. "Please take me too!"

Hazel roughly shook off Sandy's tight grasp and dropped her to the floor. "No! You're staying here and Bobbi's coming with me!"

Sandy screamed and tackled her mother's left thigh, grabbing on as Hazel moved towards the door. Her mother dragged her across the kitchen floor with each labored step.

"Please Mommy, please, take me too, take me too!" begged the desperate and confused child.

"No!" Hazel forcefully pushed Sandy out of the way, and hurried out the door with Bobbi.

Blanche followed her into the freezing night air. "I'm telling you Hazel, that's it. We'll raise Sandy as our own, but from now on we're making all the decisions about her. You remember that!" Hazel didn't respond. Ignoring Blanche, she slipped into her car, her thoughts already focused elsewhere.

Sandy stood dejected in the middle of the kitchen, sobbing and shaking. At five-years-old she already realized that her mother didn't want her and perhaps never had. Car doors slammed loudly as the hollow sound of abandonment enveloped the house like a shroud.

Later that evening Sandy begged Blanche to let her talk to Bobbi. When the phone was finally handed over, she implored her sister to reconsider her choice. "Please come back and stay with me. You're my sister. I love you. Come back!"

"No, Sandy, I'm not coming back. I'm with Mommy and this is where I want to be. I'll see you sometime." Sandy was left with nothing but a dial tone.

It was months before Sandy saw either her mother or her sister again.

* * *

William Senter Robinson was born in 1909 in Mountain City, Tennessee, the son of a poor and uneducated farmer. Senter, as he was known, left Tennessee when he was sixteen and moved to Avondale, Pennsylvania, where he secured a truck-driving job at a mushroom cannery. Like his father, he loved the outdoors and he eventually purchased a large dairy farm outside Oxford, in Southern Chester County. In 1933, he married Ruth Thompson, who bore him two sons: Howard and William, who was nicknamed Donald. Ruth was only thirty-two when she died of breast cancer, leaving Senter alone to raise their two young boys.

From that point on, Senter's life became somewhat of a mystery. During a party or social engagement he met Blanche Fletcher, a young divorced woman with a penchant for cigarettes and strong coffee. In 1950, Blanche moved to the farm to live with Senter, marking the beginning of a bizarre relationship for this pair. Senter felt it was a mortal sin to remarry, citing the Bible as his defense, so he refused to marry her. Yet, openly having a lover in the 1950s was generally unacceptable behavior too. Senter's solution to his dilemma was reportedly to force Blanche into hiding—treating her like a leper and shielding her very existence from the outside world.

For seven long years, Blanche led a secretive and miserable life. She worked on the farm, milked cows, and fed animals, but whenever a visitor arrived, she hid in the cobweb-filled attic or cold basement until the person finally left. She was the surrogate mother to Senter's two teenage sons who called her Maggie. The boys hated and resented her; first, because she wasn't their mother and second, because she was in charge of ensuring that their homework and chores were done. All around, it was a difficult life for Blanche who became lonely, depressed, and frustrated. She discovered, during those long hours of hiding, that the pain of her existence could be eased somewhat by a bottle of liquor and she became a heavy drinker. But, inexplicably, she didn't leave. Perhaps it was because she truly loved Senter and his boys or perhaps she simply didn't have the resources to venture off on her own. No one knew for sure. But Blanche's life changed suddenly the day her brother-in-law, Romeo Shoun, came to the farm to visit Senter and she was unable to take cover quickly enough. Their secret exposed, she never hid again.

When the Robinson boys reached adulthood, they both purchased farms. Howard became a schoolteacher and taught in the local Oxford school system in addition to running his farm, which was located just two miles from Senter's farm. Donald purchased a large farm that adjoined his father's property and the two worked side-by-side sharing cows, machinery, headaches, and profits.

Both Donald and Howard married and each had five children. Some of the children were close in age to Sandy and became her playmates, children with whom she shared holidays and family gatherings. As a little girl, Sandy enjoyed these friendships, but as she grew older it was obvious that her dark Hispanic looks and questionable lineage would keep her from truly becoming a part of this extended family.

* * *

The two little girls, Bobbi and Sandy, sat huddled together in the church pew at the Beulah Baptist Church. Sandy looked around and noticed that the other children sat with their parents while her parents, Hazel and J.C. Campbell, were visibly absent. Hazel preferred to drop her girls off at the church steps and collect them later, much later, when church services and Baptist hospitality were long over. Bobbi, the older sister, quietly slipped a wallet from her purse, a wallet she had found in her mother's car. She angrily rifled through it, looking at its contents: money, a couple of old photos, and a driver's license of a man who clearly was not J.C. Sandy peered cautiously at the picture on the license, thinking the face looked vaguely familiar. It was a handsome face with jet black hair, dark eyes, and a seductive smile. Only later did it occur to her that the face looked much like her own.

* * *

Cecil and Bertha Fletcher, like the Robinson's, lived in Mountain City. They were also poor, uneducated people who raised their four children (Ruth, Hazel, Blanche, and Kermit) in the backwoods of rural Tennessee. As teenagers, the children left Tennessee and moved to Pennsylvania to pursue better lives as farmers or factory workers in the numerous mushroom canneries that dominated Southern Chester County at the time.

Blanche left Tennessee at sixteen. She married, but divorced a few years later when her marriage devolved into an unhappy, abusive relationship. She never had children, but whether it was due to her inability to bear a child or because she didn't want to subject a child to her unhealthy environment, was not known. Blanche was a striking woman; not striking for her beauty so much as for her large and imposing frame. She stood nearly six feet tall, weighed 170 pounds, and had large hands and feet. As a young woman, she took great pains with her appearance. She wore stylish clothing, fixed her hair, and carefully applied her makeup, all of which may have appealed to Senter, the widower with the two young children. When the two first met, Senter was forty and Blanche, a mere twenty-four.

Hazel remained in Tennessee and married J.C. Campbell when she was sixteen. A year later their first child, Karl, was born. It was a horrific home birth that deterred Hazel from having additional children for nearly a decade. Hazel and J.C. lived with the elder Fletchers until they also moved to Pennsylvania. Although Hazel was madly in love with J.C., her feelings were never reciprocated and, despite the fact that J.C. was a womanizer and a drinker, Hazel stayed with him for a tumultuous twenty-five years.

Ten years after Karl was born, Hazel gave birth to Barbara, or Bobbi, as she was called. By the time Bobbi was born, J.C. had engaged in a number of extramarital affairs of which Hazel was painfully aware. Her heart broken, she decided to make herself available to other men should the opportunity arise.

Hazel, an attractive woman, was smaller in stature than her sister, Blanche, and meticulous about her appearance. She wore beautiful clothes, bright red lipstick, and a tight-fitting girdle to rein in her pear shape. With her dark hair and pale white skin, men took notice and soon, Hazel achieved her goal of finding a lover.

Hazel had no formal education, but was a shrewd and intelligent businesswoman. She worked at a local cannery and quickly moved up the ranks to a high-level management position, wielding her authority with cold and calculating moves. Many hated her, most feared her, and all knew her as a tough and formidable manager who fired her employees as effortlessly as she applied her ruby-red lipstick. It was through her position that she met fellow employee Angel Silva, a dark and exotic Puerto Rican who stole, and ultimately, broke her heart.

Angel, like J.C., was a womanizer and a drinker, but with his handsome good looks, his seductive charm, and his seemingly generous nature, many women couldn't resist him. Hazel was one of those women. A steamy love affair ensued. Hazel loved him and hoped to be the future Mrs. Silva, a dream that never came to fruition.

Angel was a gambler who had saved enough of his winnings to leave Puerto Rico. He came to Pennsylvania, without his wife, to work in the mushroom industry. He returned to Puerto Rico once a year, just long enough to impregnate her during each visit. In four short years, four children were born. When he earned enough money, he brought his wife and children to the States.

* * *

In 1959, Karl was fifteen and old enough for Hazel to ignore. Bobbi was five and had just started kindergarten. On October 21, Sandra Gail Campbell was born, the result of Hazel's love affair. The birth dismayed Hazel, who considered all of her children major inconveniences in her life. She continued her affair with Angel and spent as much time with him as she could. She hoped to win him over, particularly since she had produced his child, a child who looked exactly like him.

Baby Sandy was just five weeks old the first time Hazel dropped her and Bobbi with Blanche overnight, presumably to work late at the office. It was the beginning of a pattern that continued for years. Hazel called Blanche and asked if the girls could spend the night. Blanche agreed. But when the next day arrived, Hazel made up excuses to delay pickup for another day or sometimes two or three, stretching the girls' welcome, and Blanche's patience. Over time, Blanche and Senter took care of the girls on the weekends and sometimes mid-week, while Hazel pursued Angel. The routine continued until Blanche and Senter reached their breaking point in 1965, on the night when Hazel relinquished Sandy to Blanche forever.

When Blanche and Senter took over as Sandy's parents, Blanche was thirty-nine and Senter was fifty-five. Raising a young child was not something they had bargained for at this stage in their lives, but they resigned themselves to their new roles. Blanche, who had a serious drinking problem, straightened herself out, ending her addiction to alcohol. Senter was not a traditional father to Sandy, but he treated her kindly and accepted her into his home.

Sandy struggled to have a normal childhood. On one hand, she had Senter's grandchildren as playmates, a number of relatives with whom she celebrated holidays, a farm full of animals, and acres of land to enjoy. She rode her bike, took swimming lessons, and attended school like any other child. Blanche and Senter loved her, although their parenting methods were often unconventional and inconsistent.

Yet, more often than not, Sandy's childhood was marked with pain. Hazel, who had so easily handed her over to Blanche, was unwilling to give up control. Hazel and Blanche fought over her constantly, disagreeing over both small and large details of her upbringing. Hazel insisted on taking Sandy to parent-teacher conferences and doctor visits, maintaining the illusion of the doting and caring mother. However, she never—not even once—told Sandy that she loved her. Sandy grew up unloved and unwanted with the painful memory of her abandonment never far from her thoughts.

Blanche frequently and openly told Sandy she loved her, while Senter was more secretive. He preferred to take Sandy out for a walk in a field or for a ride in the car, out of Blanche's earshot, to tell Sandy that he loved her and that she reminded him of Ruth, his wife who had died.

In some ways, Senter was a kind and charitable person. He often took food and milk to the poor and elderly in the community. Every Christmas he hung up an enormous stocking for Sandy that he filled with treats and toys, and each Easter he ensured that Blanche bought her a beautiful new outfit. Yet, he was also stingy with his family, both emotionally and financially.

Money matters between Senter and Blanche were strange, like much of their relationship. Senter gave Blanche, the woman with whom he shared his bed, a paycheck. Sandy grew up with clothes on her back, food, shelter, and medical care, but little else. Money was tight for Blanche and Senter, and Hazel rarely stepped in to contribute to her daughter's financial needs. J.C., who was generally kind to Sandy and had given her his surname, refused to provide for her. She was, after all, not his child. Furthermore, Angel, who had four other children to support, couldn't help either.

Blanche assumed sole responsibility for Sandy's discipline and swore her to secrecy whenever a problem arose. Senter never felt the need to share this parental responsibility, nor did he inquire about Sandy's behavior or the ways in which Blanche dealt with conflicts. Blanche's disciplinary methods were often weak and ineffectual, and she gave Sandy few parental guidelines or restrictions.

Sandy's most joyful times occurred when she was very young and still relatively carefree; childhood days spent riding her bike, swinging on the swing that Senter built for her, and playing with relatives. She loved Christmas. It was a time when Hazel swooped in with an armload of presents (but still no love), Blanche cooked fabulous holiday meals, and Senter filled her door-sized stocking with toys and treats. But, as she grew older, she was more aware of her situation and with each passing year, became increasingly unhappy and conflicted.

* * *

Blanche and Senter expected a great deal of Sandy at an early age. Work was not optional and, as a part of their family, she was required to do her share. When she was eight, she mowed the huge farmyard lawn, and by the age of ten, she was up at four o'clock each morning to milk cows with Blanche. Sandy became the master of the herd as she kept track of breeding schedules, sick cows that required medicines, and other bovine details. It was a huge responsibility for such a little girl, but one she proudly accepted.

Not that there was much choice. Blanche and Senter were her parents and she wanted to please them. Furthermore, there was nowhere else for her to go. Hazel had made it abundantly clear she didn't want her. Aunt Ruth (Blanche and Hazel's sister) and Uncle Romeo were raising their own children, and Uncle Kermit (their brother) was frequently in trouble with the law. So, Sandy stayed at the farm.

Senter maintained a large dairy farm that encompassed 100 acres and included a three-story stone house, a huge modern barn, and several other buildings. To Sandy it was a beautiful and idyllic setting and, as a small child, it seemed enormous. The farm contained its share of dogs, cats, horses, and dairy cows, all animals that she loved. The barn, which was new and immaculate, was Senter's pride and joy. It was frequently inspected and had to be constantly maintained. By contrast, the house was a wreck. It was old, ramshackle, and in need of major repairs. The linoleum had potholes, the wallpaper was torn, and large portions of the house were simply sealed off and never used. Furthermore, Blanche was a terrible housekeeper who left the dishes unwashed, the beds unmade, and the laundry undone.

Like the house, Blanche was rundown too. Long ago she had traded her fashionable attire for overalls and boots, and she sometimes went a couple of days without combing her hair. She had turned into a farmer and saw no shame in it. She was a big strapping woman who milked cows, threw hay bales, and worked harder than most men in the area. When she wasn't in the barn, she could be found sitting among piles of clutter at the kitchen table, chain-smoking cigarettes, and drinking large cups of coffee.

Senter was a larger-than-life figure who stood six feet tall and weighed 250 pounds. His big barrel chest and strong muscles were maintained by backbreaking farm labor and nightly chin-ups. He pretty much had every-thing he wanted in life: a farm he loved, two dutiful sons, a companion to live out his days, and a little girl who worshipped him. For a man from backwoods Tennessee, it was a rich, full life.

By 1968, when Sandy was eight-years-old, Hazel's life had changed. Karl had married and started his own family. Bobbi was a teenager and no longer of much concern to Hazel. As a youngster, Bobbi had been shuffled from relative to relative so that Hazel could pursue her affair with Angel but, now that Bobbi was older, she was basically on her own. Hazel and J.C. had finally called it quits and J.C. had moved out. Angel was still in the picture, but Hazel had grown weary of his lies. Angel's oldest son was serving in the Vietnam War and Angel promised that when his son returned, Hazel would be the next Mrs. Silva. It was an empty promise and Hazel knew it. With her heart broken yet again, she began a series of affairs, marriages, and divorces that spanned a number of years. Hazel, successful at work, failed miserably in her relationships with men and even her own children.

* * *

As a teenager, Sandy became increasingly discontented. The farmhouse was an embarrassment and, with the exception of two close friends, she couldn't bring anyone home. Her best friend, Donna Culberson, was a classmate who shared a common bond: they both had dysfunctional households. Donna's parents were alcoholics and when Sandy went to Donna's house, she avoided them. Similarly, when Donna came to Sandy's house, she overlooked the constant clutter of junk, the dirty dishes in the sink, and the rundown condition of the house. But neither Donna nor Sandy spent much time in each others' homes, preferring instead to hang out at the mall or the hamburger joint or just cruise in the car, like normal teenagers.

Sandy didn't look like anyone else in the family and searched for answers to her identity. Unfortunately, no one was talking. Hazel insisted that Sandy's father was J.C. Campbell, her ex-husband, and she never wavered from her story. Blanche was sworn to secrecy. Sandy had waist long, jet-black wavy hair, dark eyes, and olive skin, in sharp contrast to Hazel's and J.C.'s fair skin types. Where she obtained her looks was a question that would remain unanswered for years to come.

Sandy's other close friend was her boyfriend, Steven Lang, nicknamed Little Skippy. Little Skippy also had a dysfunctional background, a common theme in her early friendships. Sandy and Steven went on dates and Senter took a particular liking for the boy; so much so, that soon Little Skippy was living on the farm with everyone's blessing.

With graduation approaching, Sandy wasn't sure what to do with her life. She had briefly worked in healthcare at a nursing home, but her training had consisted of changing bedpans and other unpleasant tasks, so she didn't pursue that option. When Steven proposed, she began preparing for her wedding which would take place just three months after her graduation, on September 24, 1977.

Like everything else, the wedding became a bone of contention for Blanche and Hazel. Hazel insisted that she was the mother of the bride. It was her name that appeared on the wedding program and it was Hazel, not Blanche, who sat in the front row of the church to watch her daughter marry. Blanche took a back seat, or pew, as the case might be.

The wedding was an elaborate affair with 300 guests and a huge wedding party. The reception was held at a hall with a live band. Sandy was beautiful in her Southern Belle dress; her long wavy tresses cascading down her slender silhouette. Out of love for her daughter, Blanche catered the entire wedding and prepared all the food herself, an amazing feat.

Unfortunately, the beautiful bride and handsome groom had about as much staying power as the plastic figures adorning the top of the cake, and their marriage was doomed for disaster. They were two children from difficult backgrounds trying to play house. Sandy, although skilled in farm chores, didn't know how to cook, clean, or even make a bed. Blanche had failed to teach her basic life skills. Steven was wild and irresponsible. He couldn't hold down a job and, with his newfound freedom as an adult, he allegedly started to party and see other girls. Within a year, the newlyweds went their separate ways.

At eighteen, Sandy went to work for Hazel at the mushroom cannery, returning to the farm each day to help Blanche milk cows. Hazel had given up her house because she had remarried; Sandy purchased it and moved in, with Hazel's blessing. Hazel, unlike Blanche, was a fanatic about cleanliness. She was a meticulous housekeeper who kept her laundry current and ironed everything, right down to her sheets and pajamas. With Hazel's help, Sandy learned the skills needed to maintain a proper household.

Sandy hoped that by working with her mother at the cannery she might develop the close mother-daughter relationship she had lacked as a child, but Hazel remained cold and distant towards her. They ate lunch together, but only spoke to each other as employer and employee. Sandy was disappointed and rejected once again. Furthermore, she couldn't make friends with her co-workers because everyone knew she was Hazel's daughter and, fearing Hazel, they kept her at bay.

One day a delivery man came to Hazel's office. Sandy was eating her lunch at her mother's desk; Hazel had stepped out for a few minutes. Sandy and the man exchanged pleasantries, then the delivery man whispered, "Oh, how do you stand working for that old bitch?"

"You know, I have to. She's my mother."

"What! She's your mother? Oh my God, you're kidding me!"

"No, she's my mother."

"I'm so sorry. I didn't mean to call her a bitch …" the man back-ped-dled as fast as he could go.

"It's okay, really it is." Sandy already knew that the factory workers and delivery people hated her. Her mother was unduly nasty and ran a tight ship, but it was what management wanted and how Hazel secured her hefty promotions.

***

Although she worked with Hazel, Sandy regularly returned to the farm to help Blanche and Senter. One day she went over early, but missed Senter because he had already left. It was not an unusual occurrence. He owned two other farms that he rented. He frequently went to check on the farms and talk to his tenants, Mr. Hahn and Mr. Windell. However, by the time Sandy and Blanche were ready to milk cows late in the afternoon, neither had seen Senter the entire day, giving both cause for concern.

"Have you seen daddy?" asked Sandy.

"No, honey, I don't know where he is. He hasn't been home all day and I'm worried about him."

"You start milking and I'll run over to the Windell place." Sandy drove to the other farm and searched for her father, to no avail. Then she went to the Hahn farm and still could not find Senter. As she drove home, she felt an impending sense of doom.

"Mommy, I can't find him anywhere. Let me look around here." Sandy checked in with her mother and hurried away to search further.

She headed out of the barn, down the barn bridge, and over the hill, and spotted the sickening sight of tractor wheels up in the air. The tractor was upside down with Senter pinned beneath it. Sandy, crying and screaming, ran as fast as her legs could carry her.

"Daddy! Daddy!" The sight of her father trapped under the tractor was almost more than she could bear and, by the time she reached him, she was hysterical. As she approached the tractor she was relieved to see he was still alive, although seriously injured.

"Sandy, stop crying right now! You can't help me if you're crying. Get your wits about you!" Despite his pain, Senter was still a commanding presence.

"Okay, okay, what should I do?" Sandy tried to pull herself together.

"Turn the key. The tractor's been running for hours and diesel fuel's spilled all over me. Turn off the tractor!" Sandy obeyed, realizing Senter was lucky the tractor hadn't burst into flames.

"What do you want me to do? We need to get help!" Sandy saw her father's arm crushed under the steering column of the tractor and felt helpless.

"Run up to the house and get Donald. He'll need his front-end loader to get this tractor off of me."

Sandy raced to the barn at lightning speed. "Mommy, Mommy, call an ambulance! Daddy's pinned under a tractor! Donald needs his front-loader. Quick!"

Senter had been trapped under the tractor for more than eight hours. He'd been clearing boulders from the land, when the unsteady tractor had overturned. His injuries were serious, and he spent the next two years in and out of the hospital to repair his crushed arm and hand. He never fully recovered and ended up selling his cows to Donald, forcing him into an early retirement.

For Sandy, it was a day she never forgot. Like her own abandonment, she realized how the entire course of one's life could change in just a matter of minutes.

CHAPTER 5

Adjustment

You gain strength, courage, and confidence
By every experience in which
You really stop to look fear in the face.
You are able to say to yourself
I lived through this horror.
I can take the next things that come along.

Eleanor Roosevelt

P aul returned from Vietnam to a grand celebration. His father hung a "Welcome Home Paul!" banner from roof to basement outside his house, Mother Pinkerton cooked an elaborate dinner, and all the relatives came to greet him. It was a day filled with hugs, kisses, tears, laughter, and a collective sigh of relief. There was just one problem: it was only one short day in the life of Paul Pinkerton.

The next day was business as usual. Pat returned to her job, Paul's parents took the banner down from the side of their home, and life moved on for everyone but Paul, who sat home alone thinking, "Now what?" It was June of 1969 and barbers were becoming passé, replaced instead by hair stylists in chic salons. Paul rejected the idea of working in a fancy salon, making vain men more beautiful. After enduring combat, it seemed like frivolous and meaningless work, so he gave up on the one career he'd been formally trained to do. The decision of what to do with his life weighed heavily upon him as it had during high school.

Listless and bored, he spent the next few days pacing around the small cottage Pat had rented for the two of them. Coming home was proving to be a huge letdown. He walked down to the feed store one afternoon just to clear his head. He'd gone there as a child to buy pellets for his pet rabbit and he wanted to return, if only to inhale the fresh, sweet smells that had seemed so comforting to him in the past.

The secretary immediately recognized him from church. "Paul, you're home from Vietnam! When did you get back?"

"Just the other day ... I'm home and looking for work."

"I'm sure we could find something for you. Let me get Hank and see what he has available." She disappeared into a back room, talked to the owner, and the two came back to the sales area.

"So, you're looking for work. Did you ever drive a truck?" Hank asked.

"Oh, yeah, I drove everything in the service," Paul fibbed. He had occasionally driven the armored personnel carrier just for fun, but technically had never driven a truck.

"We have a driver who wants to get off the road to spend more time with his family. Are you interested?"

"Sure."

"Come by tomorrow at nine, and Henry will show you the ropes."

"Great!" Paul was happy he had someplace to go the next day. He didn't really care what the job entailed; he just needed to be busy.

* * *

Initially, Paul's family didn't perceive any major changes in his personality when he came home. He seemed a little older, a little more mature (which also came with being married), and perhaps, a bit more reserved. Everyone tread lightly, afraid to ask him about his experiences in Vietnam for fear it would upset him or bring back unpleasant memories. They were curious, but mainly they just wanted to forget about the war. Paul was safe and although the war continued, they no longer had a personal stake in it.

Paul was unable to initiate conversations about the war. He felt that unless you'd been there, you just couldn't comprehend what it was like. It was something akin to describing the color red to a blind person. No matter how hard the person tried to grasp the concept, it probably couldn't come close to the real thing. But deep down he was desperate to talk about his experiences, baffled that no one asked him about his year in hell. Apparently, no one cared enough to find out. His family held back. They thought that if Paul wanted to talk about the war, he should be the first one to bring it up. This frustrating, elusive dance continued for years.

Paul talked to Pat occasionally, but felt she placated him and downplayed his experiences. Once, when he poured his heart out to her and told her about shooting the NVA soldier, her response was, "If you hadn't

shot him, he would have shot you. It's war. You did what you had to do."
Her black and white analysis was no consolation for him. He needed to
grieve and rage and come to terms with what had happened. In his mind
he had done terrible things for which there was no forgiveness. He
couldn't forgive himself, and he was pretty sure God had not absolved
him either. Furthermore, he refused to exculpate the Government for placing him in a position where it was necessary to commit acts of violence
against other human beings. But, instead of talking, he kept his thoughts
bottled up, with the pressure building inside him.

Virginia, Pat's mother, asked him to speak about his year in Vietnam
at a women's church group. Paul declined. He felt the experiences were
too raw to verbalize in front of a group of women he hardly knew, but he
did offer to write his thoughts down on paper. Virginia agreed and took
Paul's notes to the meeting, not bothering to read them in advance. Imagine her surprise when she read, "We turned all the young girls into prostitutes and taught five-year-old boys how to smoke. I think that was
wrong, but that was our major accomplishment in Vietnam." The church
ladies were aghast. Not only was Paul un-American in his rhetoric, he was
crass to boot. Paul didn't care. In his mind it was the truth, if anyone
cared to listen.

The majority of the time Paul was the same old Paul: happy-go-lucky,
easygoing, and fun to be around. It was Pat who witnessed the dark times
when Paul was caught up in his own moody thoughts, unable to articulate
what was bothering him.

He scared her on more than one occasion when he said, "You'll know
when I need help; I won't. I think I'm okay, but if you see that I need help,
just promise me one thing: if I need to see a counselor or psychiatrist,
make sure he's a Vietnam vet because if not, he won't understand me."

Pat promised, but thought to herself, "That's not going to happen. He
better hold it together because finding a psychiatrist who's also a Vietnam
vet will be close to impossible!"

On the surface, Paul's life looked pretty normal. He and Pat settled
into a routine and were gainfully employed. They spent Saturday nights
with friends at Hershey Bear hockey games, they went to church each
Sunday, and they spent Sunday afternoons with either the Pinkertons or
the Schaumbergs. From Paul's perspective, things were okay, but they just
weren't the same. When he let his mind wander, he thought about the kids
back at the wire, the buddies he'd left behind, and the dark secrets he carried deep within his soul. He couldn't watch the evening news without
becoming angry and cynical. He knew the real situation in Vietnam and
he couldn't believe the spin the politicians and reporters put on their
analysis of the war—it made his blood boil.

Just becoming a civilian again was a major adjustment. Soldiers in Vietnam did almost anything they wanted, but back in the States there were confining rules and regulations at every turn. If you drove ten miles over the speed limit, you received a traffic violation, which Paul soon discovered. Only a week earlier he had carried a loaded gun, drove vehicles when and where it suited him, drank beer, cursed plenty, and slept during the day. Now he was back in polite society, with a wife and boss to please, and financial obligations to meet. At times he felt overwhelmed but, more often than not, he felt angry and powerless. The Government had spent over a year preparing him to kill and fight, but not one minute teaching him how to return to society. He felt used, like a one-night stand. The Government had taken what it wanted from him; now it wanted nothing more to do with him. He was alone in his struggle.

***

The old Manheim gang wasn't the same either. Fun-loving Marty was gone. Steve had been home for about six months when he became gravely ill with a fever that spiked to 106 degrees. The doctors had a difficult time diagnosing his illness, but finally determined that he had contracted malaria in Vietnam and it was just now manifesting itself. He was placed in a veteran's hospital to recuperate and felt extremely fortunate when he saw the men around him who were in much worse shape than he was.

Steve returned home to a less than stellar reception. Shortly after he came home from Vietnam, he went into Curly's for lunch. Curly, who was vehemently opposed to the war, gruffly served him his pizza and told him, "Eat up and get out. We don't need your kind in here." Steve was shocked! Curly was his friend and this had been his hangout. It wasn't as if he had enlisted for the war, he had been drafted.

Then Steve went to join the VFW (Veterans of Foreign Wars) and was turned away. In its eyes, the Vietnam War was a conflict, not a war, so technically he wasn't eligible to join.* He was furious. Later the VFW changed its position, but it was too late for Steve who never forgot—or forgave—the incident. All around, there seemed to be a general lack of respect for Vietnam vets. He had been through as much as anyone and, like many, had suffered in silence. There was one thing his experiences taught him: never watch war movies again.

Steve stayed in Manheim for less than a year before moving away permanently. Manheim felt confining now, too small and too conservative. He obtained his pilot's license and moved to Pittsburgh, where he met his future wife. He remained there for two years and then moved on to Cleveland, where he stayed for the next twelve.

While Steve and the others were in Vietnam, Jimmy had acquired a new group of friends, some of whom were bad influences on him. His life had turned in the wrong direction. He suffered from feelings of guilt that he hadn't served his country like his buddies and his relationships with Paul and Steve became strained; their outlook on life now so different.

Paul's Vietnam buddies were also in transition. Mike Hardin returned home to his life in Ohio where, unknown to Paul, he suffered from nightmares and mild depression, typical symptoms of Post-Traumatic Stress Disorder (PTSD). Mike desperately wanted to talk to his father, his closest friend and confidant, about his experiences. However, his father advised him to put it behind him and move on, which he tried to do without much success. Even the birth of his daughter, Margaret, was a reminder of Vietnam. She was born on the second anniversary of Operation Rich, the operation in which he lost his good friend, David Merrell.

Mike, like Steve, didn't feel respected as a veteran either. People gave him disgruntled looks over the Army fatigues he wore and stereotyped him as a drug user and trained killer. It was all very disconcerting for someone who had served his country honorably and received the Bronze Star for his bravery. Even his employer penalized him for the time he'd spent in Vietnam by decreasing his pension benefits. Coming home was no great shakes.

As soon as Lewis returned home, he took a three-hour bath, a feeble attempt to cleanse both his body and his spirit. He went back to college and roomed with a former Marine who had also served in Vietnam. One day as they walked across campus, a car backfired and both of them instinctively fell to the ground, much to the amusement of their fellow students. Lewis, like Paul, thought about his buddies back in 'Nam and went to Fort Benning to obtain supplies for them. The guys in the mortar platoon needed aiming lights for night use and firing fans to correct the drift of the mortars—items they could never obtain in the field. He couldn't believe the Army had left the men so vulnerable and he knew the items could mean the difference between life and death for his fellow soldiers.

Lewis, like the others, experienced difficulties returning to society. He suffered from insomnia, the sound of helicopters made him queasy, and his speech was peppered with four-letter words. He took a girlfriend to see the movie, "The Green Berets," but they left long before it finished. The fact that people cheered when an enemy soldier was impaled made him sick to his stomach. Didn't they understand the tragedy of it all? Lewis kept his feelings to himself, hoping his memories could be pushed so far back in his mind that they would eventually disappear. Like everyone else, he was wrong.

Lewis's biggest shock came in 1971, a few years after his return, when he rode in a parade car in Atlanta. He put his uniform back on and proudly sat beside his girlfriend, who was in the USO (United Service Organizations). As the car moved down the street, people rushed up screaming "baby killer" and "murderer" at him. He never donned his uniform again.

* * *

Many men who returned from Vietnam drove fast cars or motorcycles or pursued dangerous sports like parachute jumping or mountain climbing. Whether this was a subconscious death wish or not, no one knew for sure. For many, it was simply the desire to feel once again the intoxicating rush of adrenaline they'd become addicted to during the war. For others, it was the feeling of being invincible; if they made it through Vietnam, they could make it through anything. Unfortunately, that was not always the case.

Paul's good friend, Floyd Rensberger, returned home shortly after Paul in July of 1969. Floyd had only been home for a week when he went drinking with an old friend in his hometown of Syracuse, Indiana. Floyd was speeding down the road with his friend next to him when he collided with another car. The resulting crash killed Floyd, his friend, and the driver of the other car, a professor from Michigan. The professor's wife sustained serious injuries. Floyd's death was a huge blow to Paul, who couldn't believe he'd lost another close friend. He and Pat didn't make it to the funeral, but flew to Indiana a short time later to see Chris, Floyd's widow. It was an excruciatingly painful experience and Paul blamed his friend's death on the war. For years Pat and Chris stayed in touch until one day, all communications abruptly ceased. Pat later heard that Chris had remarried and surmised that Chris wanted to cut off all past associations to Floyd. Pat understood the rationale, but never forgot her good friend.

Paul had his own brushes with death. One night he, Steve, and Jimmy went out drinking, one of those rare occasions when he left Pat to go out with the guys. Steve was driving his brand-new 1969 Chevy with Paul at his side. Jimmy sat in the back seat. As they headed home they passed through Eltonsville. Steve slowed down for the ninety-degree turn in the center of town, but a speeding car driving in the opposite direction came around the turn in his lane and forced him off the road. Steve hit a wall, flipped the car on its top, and was thrown halfway out of the vehicle.

Paul and Jimmy were trapped inside the car; rescuers used the jaws-of-life to extricate them. Both ended up with concussions and cuts and spent the night in a local hospital. When a nurse told Jimmy there were only two of them in the hospital, he feared Steve was dead, but Steve had walked away from the accident without serious injury. Fortunately, a bystander who witnessed the incident told police that the accident was the fault of the other driver—a lucky break for Steve, who avoided the breathalyzer test that evening.

On another occasion, Paul was involved in a motorcycle accident. But between his injuries and the sight of his mangled helmet, he was scared enough to put his bike up for sale.

* * *

Paul and Pat lived in their little cottage for a year then moved to a bigger apartment. Pat was a hairdresser and Paul continued to work for Agway as a truck driver. He enjoyed being his own boss as he traveled on the open road. He let his hair grow long and wore an arm patch that read, "If you're not part of the solution, you're part of the problem." No one commented on it, but he sensed uneasiness on the part of his clients when he made deliveries. Eventually he changed his image, cut his hair short, and wore a dress shirt and tie to work; easily becoming the best-dressed truck driver that Agway employed. He noticed that his clients—who were scattered throughout Pennsylvania, Maryland, and Delaware—suddenly treated him with more respect.

Occasionally Paul and Pat talked about having children, but it was still early in their marriage. They were essentially newlyweds (having spent a year apart) and they enjoyed their freedom as a young, married couple. There was plenty of time to start a family. Plus, Paul's older sister, Carol, had given birth to her first child while Paul was in Vietnam. The elder Pinkertons were busy fawning over their first grandchild and, consequently, weren't pressuring Paul or anyone else for another grandchild just yet.

But while Pat was content to postpone having children, there was one obligation that couldn't wait any longer: visiting Marty's parents. Every time she mentioned it, Paul made up excuses, procrastinating to the point where it was now an embarrassing situation. He had been back from Vietnam for almost a year and still had not stopped by to see the Saubles.

"Paul, this Sunday is Mother's Day. I called Jane and Martin and told them we'd come by in the afternoon ... then we're going to my mother's for dinner," announced Pat.

"Aw, geez ..." Paul knew this was it. He was on the hook and there was no way out. When Mother's Day came, they picked up a rose plant and headed to the farm. Once there, he felt uncomfortable and awkward even though the Saubles were lovely and gracious and thrilled that he had finally come for a visit. Paul didn't know what to say, he was afraid he'd break down in tears, and he felt guilty for being alive when Marty wasn't. The visit was sheer torture. He never mustered the emotional stamina to visit again and always felt guilty and inadequate about his inability to do so. It was a situation he'd regret for years to come.

Steve paid the Saubles a visit as soon as he returned home but, unlike Paul, felt much more at ease, perhaps because he had spent more time with them as a youth. At one point he asked to use their bathroom, which was upstairs. Entering the second floor hallway, he passed Marty's old bedroom. He was surprised to see that the room was a shrine, maintained the way Marty had left it, with shoes at the end of the bed and clothes in an open closet, as if he would return home any day. Steve involuntarily shuddered as he hurried along, aware of Marty's ghostly presence. He made a mental note never to use the bathroom again.

Mrs. Sauble had written to Marty every day, without fail, while he was in Vietnam. She confided to Paul's mother that during the first year after his death, she had cried nearly non-stop, devastated by the loss of her only child. But, surprisingly, she wasn't angry with the Government or upset about the war. She was simply filled with overwhelming grief. Mr. Sauble shared Paul's sentiments that both that the war and Marty's death had been senseless. However, he didn't harbor any feelings of ill-will towards the man who had accidentally shot his son. It was a given that in wartime, bad things happened.

***

After a couple of years, Paul and Pat decided to buy a house. It seemed like a waste of money to pay rent so, with a little help from Tom, Pat's father, they purchased a small house in Lititz, just a few miles from Manheim. Pat set up shop in her new house as a one-woman styling salon. Paul continued his work as a truck driver, but also looked at ways to supplement their income. His grandmother had grown African violets, which he loved, so he decided to build a greenhouse on the back of their home and sell plants and flowers on the side. He also built and sold picnic tables on the front lawn with the help of another veteran, Marlin King. Paul, like his parents, had an entrepreneurial spirit.

Soon Paul was consumed with the greenhouse, fussing over his plants to the exclusion of everything else. Pat viewed Paul's behavior as his version of therapy. She was a little concerned about his obsessive nature, but figured the greenhouse was better than alcohol or drugs, so she didn't discourage him. Life continued on and it seemed like they were working more and enjoying life less. Discussions about children became infrequent and Paul felt an empty hole widen in his heart. He loved children, and felt sad that he didn't have a family already. However, he kept those thoughts to himself. From Pat's perspective, there was simply no time to fit children into their busy schedule and she preferred to spend the little free time she had alone with Paul.

Paul resigned himself to his current situation, but he held onto his anger over the war. One night in 1978 while watching the evening news, a story caught his attention. There was a segment about protesters who had chained themselves to the White House fence, proclaiming the Government didn't care about prisoners of war (POWs) and men still missing in action (MIAs) in Vietnam. Paul was shocked. Why hadn't he heard about this before? He was irate and thought of little else for days. It was bad enough that the Government had let him down, but to leave people behind? That was unconscionable!

He became more vocal about his feelings and for weeks Paul ranted and raved about the Government's failings, driving his family and friends crazy in the process. Finally, someone said to him, "If you're so damned concerned about it, get off your ass and do something, or else shut up!" It was the impetus he needed. He made some phone calls and found a local POW/MIA group in Harrisburg.

The next Sunday he attended a memorial service and balloon release. There were 119 men from Pennsylvania still missing in Vietnam, so the group symbolically released 119 helium balloons into the sky. Paul openly wept—his anger and frustration bubbling to the surface. Other men at the release took notice and later, at the picnic lunch, they took him aside to talk about his feelings. It was an amazing day. Suddenly he didn't feel alone anymore. There were other men who felt exactly the same way that he did.

For the next two years, Paul threw himself into the POW/MIA cause with a vengeance. He attended memorial services, balloon releases, picnics, and parades, and became an active part of the Harrisburg contingency. Pat frequently joined him, supporting him in whatever manner she could. Paul's family sometimes thought he got a little carried away, but if it was part of his healing, who were they to say it was wrong? Pat's father, on the other hand, did not like Paul's involvement but, for the most part, kept his mouth shut.

In general, there was rivalry between the World War II and the Vietnam veterans. The WWII men viewed Vietnam vets as cry babies and whiners and conversely, the Vietnam vets viewed the old-timers as unsympathetic and entitled. The Vietnam vets had suffered as much, or more, than the WWII vets but, instead of coming home to parades and free cups of coffee, they were despised and hated. The two groups didn't see eye-to-eye and probably never would. Paul and Tom handily avoided most conversations about the war knowing that if they started a dialogue, it would become an ugly exchange.

By 1978 Paul was tired of driving a truck and was looking for other work. His situation at Agway had changed and he no longer had the freedom or the overtime he desired. He loved his greenhouse and thought he could do well in the plant business. By coincidence, a greenhouse in Manheim came up for sale. He decided to pursue it.

"Pat, I think this is a great opportunity. I want to make an offer on it. What do you think?"

Paul wanted to act immediately. Partially this spontaneity was inherent in his personality and partially it was a leftover combat-related reaction to act first and think later. No one in the Pinkerton family had owned his own business before, but Paul was willing to try—and risk—anything. Pat was not so impetuous.

"I think it's a good opportunity too, but are you sure? It's a big operation. Running it won't be the same as the two of us working on our little greenhouse out back. This is a major commitment, and I'd have to give up my salon." Pat wasn't 100 percent convinced it was a good idea, plus she enjoyed being a hairdresser.

"Let's talk to your dad and see what he thinks, okay?" Paul queried.

"I guess that would be all right," Pat replied.

Tom was discouraging. "The greenhouse business is a bad business to be in. My friends had a greenhouse and they had a tough time of it. Don't get involved."

Paul didn't take Tom's advice to heart and continued to pursue the purchase until everyone got on board. Now he just needed to convince the owner.

Paul went to the greenhouse to make an offer, but another party from out-of-state was already there, cash in hand. Paul felt certain it was a done deal and that he had missed his opportunity. Stalling, he spoke to the owner at length and learned that the man was retiring, but still wanted to keep a hand in the business. Paul convinced him that he would need his help. He could stay on for awhile as the boss without being the owner. The owner was sure that he would be pushed out immediately if he sold to the out-of-state couple, so he accepted Paul's offer on the spot. On September 1, 1978, Paul and Pat became the proud owners of a greenhouse.

The next two years brought hard times. When they purchased the greenhouse, the price of oil was sixty cents a gallon, but by 1979 it had almost doubled. Making ends meet was a constant challenge and the couple worked day and night to keep the business alive. They managed to stay afloat only by using every trick imaginable.

The commute from Lititz to Manheim became impractical because the plants required constant care and tending so they built a house on the greenhouse property the following year. Around the same time, Pat decided to pursue floral design with the hope that flower arrangements might increase their income and generate interest in the business. They drove to Cleveland for a three-week crash course in design and stopped to visit Steve Bucher and his new wife, Wanda, along the way. Although it was a pleasant visit, Paul felt oddly estranged from his friend. Their lives had taken vastly different paths. Paul saw Steve as a wealthy and sophisticated man who had left Manheim far behind, while he was still the same small town boy struggling to make ends meet.

While Pat was in Cleveland, Paul returned home and secretly built her a flower shop. She was thrilled by the surprise. Now she had her own space in which to practice her new profession. Pat quickly became successful and discovered she loved floral design even more than hairdressing. But the work was hard, the hours were long, and even Hershey Bear hockey games with friends had fallen by the wayside.

Paul didn't mind. He was consumed with two things: the greenhouse and the POW/MIA issue. He sold flowers and plants in Manheim and had a wholesale operation that encompassed Pennsylvania, Maryland, and Delaware. He spent much of his time on the road driving a fourteen-foot refrigerator truck to deliver flowers to forty-five retail shops, logging 1,000 miles per week. In keeping with his cause, he placed a huge banner on the side of the truck that read: "Abandoned and Forgotten – 2,372 Americans Missing in Vietnam. Call this number: xxx-xxx-xxxx." The phone number was the White House comment line. He encouraged everyone to call and voice their opinions about missing Americans. He didn't know how effective it was, but displaying the banner made him feel better.

During his involvement in the cause he met the Smith family, from Bellefonte, Pennsylvania. The Smith's son was missing and they were convinced he was somewhere in Laos or in Vietnam, near the Laotian border. They were the only MIA family that Paul knew personally and for years he wore Smith's MIA bracelet, imprinted with his name and the date he went missing. The idea behind the bracelet was simple: if the person's remains were returned, you sent the bracelet back to the family. Paul wore the bracelet for years and never took it off, treating it with the same respect as his wedding band.

Over time, Paul became dissatisfied with his participation in local POW/MIA events and searched for something with more substance. He and Pat made the two-hour drive down to D.C. to visit the newly-built Vietnam War Memorial and, by chance, encountered a POW/MIA group handing out information and collecting money for the cause. Paul was excited; this was the opportunity he'd dreamed about. He wanted to be in a decision-making group and felt that if he aligned himself with people in Washington he might have access to politicians and others who could make a real difference. Maybe he could even help the Smith family who, by now, were so fed up with what they perceived as the Government's apathy, they talked about assembling a private search party to look for their son themselves.

Throughout the 1980s Paul spent every weekend in Washington and most of the time Pat went with him, which was purely an act of love on her part. She was interested in the cause, but didn't share his anger or passion. The men at The Wall were generally unpleasant to her. They sent her out for sandwiches or excluded her altogether. She got the message and eventually spent her days at museums while Paul collected signatures, sold POW paraphernalia, or simply chatted with people walking by the memorial.

As the years passed, Paul slowly became disillusioned with his efforts. He met a few politicians, but dealt with their resistance at every turn. One particular event infuriated him even further and turned him off the D.C. cause permanently. On Memorial Day there was a huge rally at The Wall with a number of prominent speakers. One speaker was raising money to send volunteers to Vietnam to look for MIAs. Paul volunteered and offered to pay his own way, but was told by the man that his commitment to the cause had been insufficient and he didn't deserve to go. Meanwhile, total strangers had signed up to go. Paul was infuriated and confronted the fundraiser later in the day. Allegedly, the person laughed in his face and said, "Oh, none of those people are actually going. That was just to get the crowd stirred up to raise more money." It was the last time he attended a rally in D.C., and he left the event flashing with anger.

Paul felt that he'd made a huge commitment to the people in D.C. and they had let him down. And now he had a bigger issue to contend with: his marriage. Paul had spent time, money, and energy on his causes, to the detriment of his marriage. Over the past few years, his relationship with Pat had deteriorated; they were growing further apart.

From Paul's perspective, they had different values and needs and their marriage was already beyond repair. He wanted a family and wanted to work on POW/MIA issues. Pat optimistically thought that everything in the marriage could be resolved if only they could spend more time together.

She truly felt their marriage was relatively normal given all that she and Paul had been through: his tour in Vietnam, the ups and downs with the greenhouse, Paul's intensity over the POW/MIA cause, and years of constant, grueling work. Their marriage wasn't 100 percent, but whose was? They were doing as well as could be expected and she loved Paul unquestionably.

But Paul, unhappy and dissatisfied, assumed that Pat felt the same way that he did—that their marriage had disintegrated to a partnership of convenience, not love. He still loved her as a friend, but no longer viewed her as a romantic partner or wife. The real problem was that neither one talked to the other.

In 1988, Paul and Pat took separate vacations. She went to the beach for a week with her friends and he went to the Republican National Convention in New Orleans. Paul felt badly that they were going their separate ways, but Pat felt that he had followed his own path for years, dropping his responsibilities and attending POW events whenever he wanted, as she picked up the slack.

Paul cut off most of his associations with the POW/MIA group in D.C., but still participated in local and national activities on occasion, as he turned his focus to his next step: returning to Vietnam. Somehow, some way, he had to go back to investigate the real story about POWs and MIAs. There was only one problem—he had no idea how to get there.

* Author's Note: Officially, Vietnam veterans have been eligible for membership in the VFW—according to the organization's by-laws—since July 1, 1958. However, in rare instances (like Steve Bucher's), some members of the VFW chose to go against stated VFW policy, and denied membership to Vietnam vets. The VFW has worked diligently to rectify this unfortunate situation.

CHAPTER 6

Adversity

*We would never learn to be brave and patient
If there were only joy in the world.*

Helen Keller

S andy was lonely and unhappy. She and longtime friend Donna Culberson worked for Hazel at the mushroom cannery, but she didn't enjoy the work or being bossed around by her mother, who remained cold and aloof. She spent less time at the farm these days because there were no cows to milk and Blanche was busy nursing Senter back to health. And although Steven was long gone, he had refused to grant her a divorce, making the dissolution of their marriage a constant power struggle.

Sandy was plenty familiar with power struggles. They had been a recurring theme throughout her life. Blanche and Hazel continued to fight over her even more viciously than before and Sandy knew that if she visited one, she had to visit the other. On Mother's Day she gave gifts to both Mommy Hazel and Mommy Blanche, but learned the sisters kept score, necessitating the purchase of identical gifts. At one point Hazel even accused Blanche of stealing Sandy away from her, but Blanche quickly and appropriately set the record straight.

Late in 1979, Sandy met fellow employee, Richard Simpson. Richard, like Sandy, was in need of companionship and love. The two gravitated towards each other and soon became friends. Shortly after they met, Richard's brother started working for a moving company, making significant amounts of money. Richard, slightly envious of his brother's newfound success, left the cannery and joined him in hopes of increasing both his salary and his freedom. He asked Sandy to accompany him.

Sandy, fed up with Blanche and Hazel's constant bickering over her, felt this was the escape she'd been seeking. She quit her job and hit the road with Richard. They joined a major moving company and made short-haul moves, going as far west as Ohio, south to Florida, and up the east coast to Maine. Richard drove the truck and moved heavy boxes and furniture while she completed inventories, kept logbooks, and packed up entire households.

Sandy enjoyed meeting clients, traveling to new places, and working independently. The job was exciting and fun, and she and Richard worked well as a team. Their relationship progressed. Richard convinced Steven to sign divorce papers and release Sandy from her long-standing marriage. He became her new-found hero and she repaid her debt to him by accepting his marriage proposal.

The divorce from Steven was finalized in 1981 and in October of 1982, Sandy became Mrs. Richard Simpson. Unlike her first wedding, Sandy planned a small, unassuming ceremony at a wedding chapel with a handful of people in attendance. And, unlike before when Hazel had dominated the scene, she made sure that this time around, Blanche and Senter held their rightful places as her parents.

Soon after they married, they switched to a different moving company based in Richmond, Virginia. The agency convinced them that Sandy should learn how to drive an eighteen-wheeler so they could make long-haul trips out west, a considerably more lucrative venture. They accepted the challenge and within a short period of time, Sandy sat behind the wheel of a big rig and drove across the country. This was more fun than she'd ever imagined and her horizons opened up to places like California, Oregon, and Texas. Between jobs they visited places of interest and explored the countryside, a new adventure for both of them.

Life was good with one exception: Sandy desperately wanted to have a baby. Richard wasn't particularly interested in children, but reluctantly went along with the idea as the couple tried to conceive. Sandy became pregnant, but the pregnancy quickly ended in a miscarriage. Over the next few months she spent time in doctor's offices, undergoing numerous tests and procedures, trying to determine the cause of her problem.

* * *

Between road trips, Sandy and Richard came home to rest. One summer day in 1986, Sandy visited Hazel as she often did when she was off the road. During a polite, but strained conversation, Hazel suddenly excused herself to go to the bathroom. When she returned, she said, "Oh my goodness, I've started my period!" Sandy's eyebrows shot up in surprise. Hazel was sixty at the time and long past menopause.

Because of her own female problems, Sandy expressed her concern. "Mommy, I think you better go to a doctor right away and have that checked out."

Hazel wisely followed her advice. She went to the doctor the following week and was diagnosed with cervical cancer. Sandy immediately stopped working so she could spend time with Hazel while Richard continued long-haul moves by himself, respecting Sandy's need to be with her mother.

Hazel checked into a local hospital and underwent radiation treatment, but it failed to stave off the cancer. Knowing that her cancer was already out of control, Hazel went to another hospital for the sole purpose of managing her pain. Eventually she returned home to die.

Hazel's current husband, Ray, helped with her care, but it was Sandy who came every day bearing gifts, food, and most of all, love. Hazel, although thankful for Sandy's presence, wanted Karl and Bobbi to visit her. At one point Hazel, frustrated and angry, pounded her fists on the bed and moaned, "I know Bobbi's not going to come. Why won't she come? I know she's not coming!"

"It's okay Mommy. It's okay. I'm here with you." Sandy understood that Hazel's impending death was just too difficult for Bobbi or Karl to handle emotionally. Their childhoods, like hers, had also been turbulent and unstable.

For the first time in her life, Hazel looked at Sandy and realized what her daughter meant to her. "I know I never told you Sandy, but I'm so happy I have you. I love you."

Tears streamed down Sandy's face—bittersweet tears. It had taken a lifetime to hear those words, but now it was too late. Her mother was dying. Over the next few months Sandy and Hazel grew closer, finally having the mother-daughter relationship they had never enjoyed, as Sandy felt the pressure of time closing in on her.

She begged Hazel for information about her birthfather, but Hazel wouldn't budge, not even as she neared death. Sandy had heard the name "Angel" bandied about numerous times before and asked Hazel point-blank if he was her father.

"No Sandy, he's not your father. He was just a family friend." Sandy felt it was a lie, but couldn't force the truth out of her. Sandy was hurt and disappointed, knowing that her mother couldn't be honest, even during her last days on earth.

Hazel, weak and frail, was unable to eat and was in constant pain. A visiting nurse, Ray, and Sandy all tried to make her comfortable. Sandy bathed her, changed her sheets, and provided love and support. She rarely left her bedside, desperate to salvage the little time she had left.

Hazel died at 2 a.m. on Christmas morning, just six months after she was diagnosed with cancer. Sandy held her hand and watched her take her last labored breaths. When her mother finally slipped away, Sandy threw herself on the bed, crying and screaming uncontrollably, consumed with unbearable grief. She couldn't believe that Hazel—the mother who finally loved her—was gone.

* * *

Hazel's death was only part of Sandy's terrible despair. The doctor's final verdict regarding her miscarriage was that she could not have children and, just one week prior to Hazel's death, she underwent surgery. She was devastated.

Sandy, who was not physically or emotionally healed, assumed total responsibility for planning Hazel's funeral and, when it was over, sank into a deep depression. Karl and Bobbi dealt with their grief privately, in their own ways. Even in their sorrow, the siblings were incapable of supporting one another; the family was divided once again.

Despite all the pain, life marched on and Sandy and Richard continued to move clients across the country. Sandy's heart wasn't in it. She was still physically weak from her surgery and emotionally drained from grieving two major losses in her life. But, as Richard predicted, their income increased exponentially and they discussed the possibility of building their own home. The little house in Oxford suddenly seemed small and claustrophobic and it was a constant and painful reminder of Hazel. It was time to move.

Sandy casually mentioned their plans to Senter. "I think we're going to buy a piece of land in Quarryville. We looked at it the other day."

"Quarryville! Why do you want to go to Quarryville? It's so far away. I want my family close to me." Senter was adamantly opposed to the idea of Sandy moving to Quarryville even though it was only fourteen miles away.

"Daddy, it's only a few minutes away and the price is right. We can't afford land in Oxford. It's way too expensive."

"No, I want my children here." Senter liked having Donald, Howard, and Sandy close by, as they'd always been.

"Well, Daddy, I don't know what else to do. We can't afford to build here."

Senter pointed to the land across the road from his farm. "I'm gonna give you that piece of land over there. You can buy it from me for a dollar."

"Don't tease me." Sandy knew the land he was pointing to was a huge twelve-acre lot.

"No, honey, I'm serious. Give me a dollar." Sandy looked at his dead-pan face, realized he wasn't joking, and pulled a dollar bill out of her purse. Handing it to him, she became an instant landowner.

Senter looked at her shrewdly, "I have a feeling that if somethin' happens to me, those boys are gonna give you a hard time. I want to know that you're okay. You build a house over there."

Sandy hugged and kissed him, reeling from what had just transpired.

* * *

Over time Sandy discovered that Richard, like Steven, had some problems. They built a beautiful house on the large plot across from Senter's farm and, at Richard's urging, furnished it with expensive antiques. He insisted on white carpeting throughout and forced Sandy to vacuum it each and every day. He wanted perfection and nothing less would suffice. The house was a showplace and, although Sandy had honed her house-keeping skills to the point where she maintained it immaculately, the constant pressure of perfection was draining and tiresome.

Sandy didn't want a perfect house. She wanted a baby, and probably more than one. Her thoughts turned to adoption. It was a topic she had broached several times with Richard, but his response had always been less than enthusiastic. He really didn't want a child and, now that they couldn't have their own biological children, the idea of adopting appealed to him even less. Sandy was disappointed and heartbroken. She knew what she wanted and she wouldn't be happy until she had a baby.

Just as Richard demanded perfection in his household, he became more difficult in other ways too. He was often grouchy and moody. When he was off the road, he drank too much, a pattern that turned from occasional to more frequent use. However, that was only when he was home. When he was on the road, he was focused and motivated, sober and alert.

Work continued to take center stage and they changed moving companies yet again, switching this time to a big company in Washington D.C., an elite firm with Government accounts. They moved FBI and CIA employees which required them to undergo background checks and fingerprinting.

Sandy and Richard worked like a well-oiled machine. They were efficient and professional and never argued over responsibilities. But, for Sandy, the work was difficult and exhausting; it no longer held the appeal it once had. They drove non-stop twenty-four-hours a day, sometimes seven days a week. Sandy usually drove for six or eight hours straight before collapsing into the bed in the back of the truck to sleep. Physically, it was hard, hard work. Sandy, who only weighed 115 pounds, helped Richard unload the truck when hired hands couldn't be found. Sometimes they moved people during the holidays and spent Thanksgiving or Easter on the road rather than with their own family.

There were days when Sandy daydreamed about having the lifestyle of other women who wore pretty dresses, shopped at malls, and had their nails done. Instead she lifted heavy furniture, worked in an industry dominated by men (which meant listening to their crude language and off-color jokes), and drove an eighteen-wheeler across the country. She was just one of the guys, a role she didn't always relish. But, the couple actually had a huge advantage, because they were the only husband and wife team working at the agency. In fact, Sandy was the first woman the agency had ever hired.

In January of 1989 when the senior George Bush took office, their moving company was contacted; furniture not needed in the White House would be moved to Kennebunkport, Maine. Sandy and Richard were given the job, much to the chagrin of their fellow workers who had seniority. But the reason the job fell to them was quite simply, Sandy. Mrs. Bush was home alone and the company didn't want her to feel uncomfortable with a group of big, burly men entering her house. A woman's presence was needed to soften the rough edges of the situation.

On moving day, Sandy went into the family residence to speak to Mrs. Bush alone. Dressed in a comfortable pair of sweatpants, Mrs. Bush greeted her warmly and the two women talked for a considerable length of time. Then Sandy got down to business as she professionally questioned her about the details of the move and completed the required paperwork. It was Sandy's shining moment. The men had to wait by the truck until she allowed them to enter the home. For once, she ran the show.

The move went smoothly. At one point Mrs. Bush picked up a carton of her personal belongings and carried it to the truck. One of the men unwisely objected, "Oh no ma'am. Please, we'll carry that for you."

Mrs. Bush allegedly retorted, "Oh no you won't!" as she marched right past him. The men were quickly reminded that the lady of this house, the First Lady, was not going to be told what to do.

Shortly before the move was finished, Mrs. Bush suddenly disappeared. She returned wearing a beautiful dress and her characteristic pearls. She graciously offered to pose with Sandy and Richard and at the appointed time, good-naturedly stepped outside into the freezing cold for a photograph. It was a great day for Sandy, making all of her hard work slightly more palatable. Not only did she have center stage, she also had a personal chat with the new First Lady.

* * *

At the age of twenty-seven, Sandy still didn't know who her birthfather was or where he could be found. With Hazel gone, she relentlessly searched for answers. One day when Senter was out of the house, Sandy implored Blanche to tell her the truth.

"Please tell me about my birthfather. You must know something. Please tell me. I have to know who he is."

"No, Sandy. I don't want any trouble. Let it go."

But Sandy couldn't let it go. She needed to know where she came from, why she looked the way she did, what her biological father was like, why he had abandoned her, and answers to a multitude of important questions. It was her life and she had a right to know the details of it. She wouldn't be swayed. Every chance she had she hounded Blanche for information until finally, Blanche relented.

Sandy was careful to ask Blanche about her biological father only when Senter, her real daddy, was away from the house. The last thing she wanted to do was to hurt her father—the man who had raised her as his own, loved her, and been so kind to her. It was on one quiet day in the old farmhouse when Blanche, worn down and exasperated, finally told Sandy the truth: Angel was her father.

It all started to come together in Sandy's mind. As a child, she remembered seeing the strange man with Hazel; the wallet that she and Bobbi had rummaged through in church; the name she had heard repeatedly as a youngster. Her initial reaction was anger. Hazel had lied to her over and over again, even on her death bed. But her anger was quickly replaced with excitement. Now that she knew who he was, she had to meet him.

* * *

Angel Silva was born in Puerto Rico to parents of meager financial means and little education. When he was a young boy, his father died, leaving him, three young siblings, and his mother, alone. As the oldest child, Angel was expected to support his family. Eventually his mother remarried and produced two more children. Angel grew up in a tough and abusive environment, providing the training ground for his future parenting skills.

Angel was a handsome man with dark skin, dark eyes, and a feral sex appeal that women couldn't resist. He was a drinker, a gambler, and a womanizer with charming ways and a generous nature. At an early age he married a beautiful, gentle woman named Ramona, who worked as a local seamstress. Angel struggled to support his new wife. Word on the street was that wages were better in the States so, as soon as he won enough money on the poker table, Angel left Ramona behind and moved to Pennsylvania to work in the burgeoning mushroom industry.

In the States, Angel quickly acquired a girlfriend nicknamed Miss Louise, but returned to Puerto Rico each year to visit Ramona. After four short years, four children were born: Angel, Hector, Sandra, and Raymond. Ramona knew about Angel's dalliances and was angry with him but, with four small children, she was not in a position to leave. Eventually Angel moved his entire family to Pennsylvania and Ramona began to work at the mushroom cannery as well—that was when the real trouble began.

Sandra Silva, Angel's daughter, was about seven-years-old when she heard the name "Hazel" used in her home. Hazel had been the source of many arguments between her mother and father. Since Ramona worked at the cannery she knew all about Angel's love affair with Hazel, but when she caught wind of Hazel's pregnancy, all hell broke loose. It was the final blow. Ramona had suffered through all of Angel's affairs and skirt-chasing antics, but a pregnancy ... well, that was just too much to bear.

Once, when Sandra was twelve-years-old, she stopped by the cannery after school to visit her mother. As they talked about her school day, Hazel suddenly appeared with four-year-old Sandy. Sandra was shocked as she looked at herself in miniature. The little girl had her face, her hair, her eyes, her complexion, and even her name! Ramona ran out of the room, muttering, "I can't believe it! She looks just like Sandra at that age!" Sandra understood that this little girl was Angel's love child and instantly hated the girl and her mother. She didn't hate them for who they were so much as for what they represented: her father's decadent and selfish lifestyle, and her mother's pain and humiliation.

Angel was a terrible father to his four children. He was absent much of the time and when he was home, he was verbally and physically abusive. He was compulsive about drinking, gambling, and engaging in sex. The drinking eventually caught up with him and he spent time in and out of hospitals and rehab centers. Doctors warned him that if he didn't stop, the booze would kill him. The words didn't have much impact on Angel; the only thing that sobered him up was when Ramona became ill. She had Alzheimer's disease and Angel had to look after her. He stopped drinking and cared for her at home until it became too difficult; then he placed her in a nursing home. She remained there until she died thirteen years later. By the time Sandy found Angel, he was a sober man.

* * *

Through conversations with Blanche, Sandy discovered that Angel lived only a short distance away, fifteen miles, in fact. She was shocked to discover that he had been living nearby, her entire life. Armed with his name and general location, she found his phone number. Shaking, she picked up the phone and dialed.

"Hello, may I speak to Angel Silva, please?"

"I'm Angel. Who is this?"

"My name is Sandra Campbell and I understand that you worked with my mother at the cannery. She said that you were a friend of hers for many years."

There was a pause and Angel asked, "What's your mother's name?" He knew the answer, but he wanted to be absolutely sure.

"Hazel. Hazel Campbell. Did you know her?"

"Oh my God, you're my daughter!" Angel shouted.

Sandy was shocked. She wasn't sure that Angel even knew about her. The conversation continued briefly and the two agreed to meet the next day at the McDonald's in Kennett Square. Sandy told Angel she would carry a brightly colored purse so he could identify her. It was their private signal.

Angel jumped on the phone and immediately called his other daughter, Sandra.

"Guess who I got a phone call from today? You'll never believe it!"

"Gloria?" Gloria was one of the relatives they spoke to infrequently. Angel played the guessing game for a few minutes until he couldn't contain himself. "No! It was your sister!"

"My sister? I don't have a sister!"

"Yes you do. Don't you remember Hazel?"

"Oh, right." Sandra, who had finally forgotten about Hazel and the little girl who looked so much like her, felt a visceral anger rising within her core.

"Come with me and meet her!" Angel was like a small child with a new puppy, bubbling over with excitement.

"No, Dad. I'm not coming. I don't want to meet her and I don't think you should either. You've never been in touch with her, so why see her now? What does she want from you—money? I don't think you should go."

"Well, I'm going!"

"All right then. Go see her!" Sandra slammed the phone down, furious with her father. How could he betray her mother again? Her poor mother had suffered enough because of Hazel and her daughter, and now she was in a nursing home dying from a terminal illness. How could he do this to her?

* * *

The next day Angel and Sandy met. Angel, wary of Sandy's intentions, wore tattered clothing and hadn't shaved or showered. Sandy was shocked by his appearance, but knew that the small, dark man was her father. Likewise, there was no doubt in Angel's mind that this was his daughter; he didn't need a colored purse to pick her out in the crowd. The two had a guarded conversation with each evading questions and lying about details of their lives. It would take time for Sandy to trust this man who had abandoned her, and Angel was unsure of Sandy's intentions. Was it money she wanted? She certainly wouldn't get it from him!

At one point in the conversation Sandy couldn't control her curiosity. "If you knew about me, how come you never tried to see me or contact me?"

"Oh, but I did. When you were little, I came to the farmhouse one night. I had some friends with me and I guess we'd been out drinking or something. That old man came out with a shotgun and told me to leave and never come back! So I left. I wasn't about to get shot!"

"Well, if Daddy hadn't scared you off with the shotgun, what were you planning to do?"

"I was going to take you to Puerto Rico and have some of my relatives raise you."

"What?" Sandy shivered involuntarily.

"Yeah, well it didn't happen."

Sandy couldn't believe her ears. She was afraid to imagine what her life might have been like had she been kidnapped and moved to Puerto Rico. She shuddered to think of such a thing. Thank God for Senter and his shotgun!

As they parted ways Angel promised to call, which he did a few days later. It was the beginning of their relationship and the start of a honeymoon period for the two. Sandy was thrilled to finally find her biological father and Angel immediately called his sons and told them the exciting news about their sister. Their friendship began with phone calls, but soon progressed to lunches and barbeques with both Angel and his sons. Sandra kept her distance, still suspicious of her half-sister and her motives. It would be a long time before Sandy and Sandra would meet face-to-face.

* * *

Although Sandy didn't enjoy maintaining Richard's perfect house, she enjoyed living in close proximity to Blanche and Senter and, when she wasn't on the road, she saw them every day. It was 1990. Senter was over eighty-years-old and Blanche was sixty-five. Senter had never regained his full strength after the tractor accident and even hale and hardy Blanche showed signs of aging. Sandy helped them with household chores and errands, always the dutiful and loving daughter.

Sandy kept Angel a secret because she didn't want to hurt Senter, who was, after all, her real father and irreplaceable. Senter began complaining about stomach pains; Sandy noticed him gulping down antacids and other over-the-counter medications. She worried, but couldn't convince him to see a doctor.

His health steadily deteriorated. His pain worsened, he lost weight, and eventually he couldn't eat solid foods. Senter had stomach cancer. Sandy felt he had known all along but had resisted doctors and hospitals, deciding they were his last resort.

Sandy felt her life whirling out of control again. She was still mourning Hazel and her own inability to have children; she was spending more and more time with Senter, who was sick and dying; and she was dealing with Richard's anger. Although Richard had been sympathetic when she stopped working to be with Hazel, he was now fed up with her family obligations and wanted her back on the truck.

Furthermore, Sandy's honeymoon period with Angel was coming to an end. Angel, she discovered, was not the man she had imagined. When she finally met her half-sister, Sandra, the woman angrily remarked, "He will *never* be a father to you!" The statement rang true as Sandy grew closer to Angel and saw that Angel, like Hazel, was selfish and often incapable of love. Sandy slumped into a depression. Donna worried about Sandy's physical and mental well-being but, unfortunately, there was no end to the misery in sight.

CHAPTER 7

Discovery

All men should strive
To learn before they die
What they are running from, and to, and why.

James Thurber

*I*n 1989, twenty years after his return from the war, Paul was unequivocally convinced there were American POWs being held in Vietnam
and he was determined to search for them. There was just one stumbling
block—he didn't know how to get back into the country. He went to what
he considered the source and dialed the Vietnam Mission to the United
Nations in New York.

"I'm trying to find out how to obtain a visa for Vietnam. Can you tell
me what the procedure is?"

"What's your purpose in going?" When Paul paused too long, the
man allegedly continued, "If it's for business, I'd advise you to forget it.
We've had a trade embargo with Vietnam since the war and it's still quite
difficult to conduct any type of business there."

"I'm not going for business. I just want to tour the country." Paul
didn't think it was prudent to reveal the real reason for his trip.

"Where are you staying? What are your travel dates?"

"I'm not sure yet ..." Paul hadn't anticipated so many questions.

"Well, you need to have specific travel plans in order to obtain a visa.
Call back when you do."

Paul called the U.N. every few days. Each time he spoke to a different
person, but each time he heard the same message: you need a plan if you
want to travel in Vietnam. He pulled out his pen and paper and wrote to
various Congressmen hoping one could pave his way, but didn't receive

any responses in return. Frustrated, he wasn't quite sure what he should do next.

Then, one morning in July, as he settled into his favorite chair with the local Sunday paper, an article jumped out at him. It was the story of Earl and Pat Martin from Ephrata, Pennsylvania, who headed up the Asia program of the Mennonite Central Committee (MCC). They had recently been in Quang Ngai, Vietnam, to celebrate their son Minh's sixteenth birthday. Paul thought, "If they managed to get in, I can too!" Using directory assistance, he tracked them down and, by late afternoon, arrived at their doorstep.

Pat and Earl Martin had fascinating life histories. Both were Mennonites who had volunteered to work in Vietnam with the MCC in the mid 1960s. (The MCC is a worldwide ministry of churches, whose broad priorities include providing disaster relief, developing sustainable communities, and promoting justice and peace.) Earl had been sent to Quang Ngai, 500 miles north of Saigon, to help dislocated farmers who had left their homes because of the fighting during the war. Pat and Earl had both worked in refugee camps providing food, clothing, shelter, and vocational training for the Vietnamese. While there, the two met and married. In 1969 they came back to the States, but returned to Vietnam in 1973 for their second assignment: dealing with unexploded mines, bombs, and grenades left lying in the fields. It was during this time that their second child, Minh, was born. Pat and the children fled Vietnam in March of 1975, prior to the collapse of Saigon. Earl was among a handful of Americans who decided to stay on after the Communist takeover, experiencing a few harrowing moments in the process. He left in July of 1975 and later wrote a book about his experiences.

Paul drove up to their home in his greenhouse panel truck that displayed his POW rhetoric on the side. When Earl saw the truck, he became leery of his visitor. Earl wasn't convinced there were POWs being held against their will in Vietnam and was afraid that Paul might be some kind of right-wing ideologue who'd try to push his political agenda on him. Earl's fears were soon allayed when he and Pat engaged Paul in conversation. It became apparent to Earl that Paul was simply a guy searching for the truth; a man who had a deep humanitarian concern, not only for American victims of the war, but for the Vietnamese as well. Pat also found Paul to be open and sincere, and the three talked from mid-afternoon well into the evening.

For Paul, the conversation with the Martins was both a wonderful education and a solution to his problem. Paul learned that the way to enter Vietnam was to obtain a visa through the Embassy in Bangkok—there was no Embassy in Vietnam at the time. More importantly, Earl told Paul to get in touch with his friend, Don Luce, who headed up the Asia

Resource Center. Don had a long history of working in Vietnam begin-ning in the 1950s, and Don and Earl had worked at companion organi-zations in Washington, D.C. Currently, Don was running informational tours to Vietnam, and his next tour was leaving in a few months.

Paul raced home, called Don, and introduced himself. Don didn't waste any time considering his request. "I have a tour going in January. There's one seat left if you want it. The tour runs for two weeks and costs $900, which covers airfare, food, hotels, and sightseeing. I'm making hotel reservations now, so let me know in the next day or two if you're interested."

Paul didn't hesitate. "I'm in. Sign me up!" Don added his name to the group roster.

As the date approached, Paul found he had ambivalent feelings about the trip. Although he was exhilarated with the prospects of searching for POWs in Vietnam, he was also more than a little apprehensive. What would it be like to return to the place that had haunted him for so long? He felt nearly as much anxiety as he'd experienced twenty years earlier standing on the tarmac at Peterson Field and wished he'd asked Luce a few more questions before he'd signed on to go.

The members of the Harrisburg POW/MIA group admired Paul for his courage, but also worried about his safety and well-being. What would he encounter in Vietnam? Surely the enemy hadn't forgiven Amer-icans for the war. Would he become just another statistic?

There was no doubt in Pat's mind that Paul was going on the trip despite his reservations. He'd struggled with his past and now he had a chance to confront his demons face-to-face. The benefits of the trip seemed to far outweigh the risks so she encouraged him to go.

On the evening of January 23, 1990, Pat and a huge entourage of the POW/MIA contingency accompanied Paul to the Harrisburg Airport and made quite a scene at the terminal. Most people cried and some were hys-terical. There were more than enough hugs and kisses to go around, and it seemed to Paul that he was going off to war for a second tour of duty. It was a short, yet horrible, goodbye that he later described as a real bitch.

* * *

There were eighteen people in Luce's tour group. The plan was for everyone to meet in San Francisco, but how they arrived there was up to each individual. Paul checked into the Harrisburg Airport and discovered that one of the tour members, a young college student named Bill, was also on his flight. They spent the entire flight talking and, by the time they landed, Paul characterized him as a spoiled rich kid whose sole purpose in traveling to Vietnam was to have an adventurous winter break. He'd cho-sen Vietnam over Vail because it sounded more exotic. Paul was angry that the trip meant so little to him; Bill's motivation paled in comparison to his more serious pursuits of looking for POWs and healing his emotional wounds. Still, it was nice to have a companion, so Paul agreed to share a room with him.

The group met in California and flew together to Bangkok, where they stayed for a number of days. Paul was anxious to move on to Vietnam, but this was part of the process, so he bided his time until the Vietnamese visas were issued. Don had his own agenda for the trip. In addition to educating his group about Vietnam, he worked with a Thai organization called Empower, which focused on AIDS prevention and education. Don took them to a hospital to hear a lecture about AIDS and escorted them to several sleazy bars to hand out condoms and flyers to prostitutes and their clients. Paul thought this was a good idea while some of the others, like his young friend Bill, were less than enthusiastic about the activity.

One of the older members of the group casually approached him. "Hi. My name's Steve. You're Paul, right? If you don't mind me asking, why are you on this trip?"

"Yes, I'm Paul, Paul Pinkerton. I'm a Vietnam vet and I believe there are prisoners still being held in Vietnam. I plan to look for them and find some evidence I can bring back to our Government."

"Well, that's quite an undertaking, but I don't think there are any prisoners left in Vietnam. The war's been over for fifteen years. I'm sure they're all either dead or released by now."

"I don't agree. I have addresses of places where I think men are being held captive and I intend to find them!" Paul had strong convictions about his position and a sincere desire to help the soldiers who'd been left behind.

They spent four days sightseeing in Bangkok before finally flying into Hanoi. Paul wept as he entered Vietnamese airspace; so many memories flooded his mind. The ride from the airport into Hanoi was surreal. It was the Vietnamese New Year (known as Tet) and people were celebrating in the streets. Children ran everywhere and it reminded him of the kids he had befriended at the wire. His senses went on overload as he took in the loud snaps of firecrackers, the gaudy colors of the decorations, the swarms of people, and the aromatic smells of Vietnamese food.

The groups' arrival at the hotel caught the attention of a Japanese film crew, who were in Vietnam to produce a documentary promoting tourism. They talked to several people in the group, but were particularly interested in Paul, the Vietnam veteran who had returned. Paul told them about his quest to find POWs and the film crew eagerly asked if they could follow him around, anxious to capture some exciting moments on tape.

On Monday, Luce scheduled a meeting with various Vietnamese officials, one of whom was the head of the Women's Union. Paul listened politely but realized they had vastly different viewpoints. He knew he was obliged to attend the meeting as part of the tour, but he didn't have to agree with her opinions. The film crew wasn't allowed into the meeting, so they remained at the hotel and bided their time until the group returned.

When Paul came back, he was introduced to their interpreter, a former NVA soldier who had fought at Quang Tri during the same time he'd been there. They wired Paul with a microphone and headed out; Paul directed them to the locations he wanted to explore. Luce, unaware of his adventure, thought he had gone out sightseeing. Their first stop was at the famed Hanoi Hilton. As Paul and the interpreter walked around the perimeter, it was clear it had been vacated of prisoners long ago. Paul was disappointed, but not unduly surprised.

The second stop was at 17 Ly Nam De Street, an address frequently mentioned at POW meetings as a location where prisoners were still being held. As they approached the street, the interpreter suddenly became agitated. He told the crew it was a bad idea to come here and expressed concern over their safety. Paul was anxious too. The area seemed desolate and appeared to be a military compound of some sort. One of the buildings was boarded up, surrounded by a wall covered with broken glass. The entrance was enveloped in barbed wire. Paul's heart beat erratically. He had been told this was a sewing factory, but clearly it wasn't. Maybe there were prisoners here!

The film crew piled out of the car and started to set up their cameras. The interpreter stayed in the car with his window rolled down, while Paul and a photographer walked to the entrance and cautiously knocked on the front door. A man in uniform answered. He shouted in Vietnamese and the interpreter ran over to hear what he was saying. The two men had a short, heated conversation in Vietnamese, and then the uniformed man slammed the door in his face. The interpreter ran back and yelled in Japanese at the film crew who gathered up their gear and threw it into the car. Paul didn't know what was happening but, judging from the terrified looks on everyone's faces, knew it wasn't good. He followed suit and jumped in the car.

As they sped away, Paul asked what had happened, but no one would answer him. They dropped him at his hotel without explanation. Stunned, he thought, "What the hell was that all about?" Paul was now unequivocally convinced there were POWs at the site, although there was no way to prove it. He also realized it would be dangerous to pursue the location further. He never saw the film crew again.

Unknown to Paul, the site had been used to house POWs (and possibly store remains) years earlier. The compound had been the family residence of a French military officer during the French era in Vietnam, and was later taken over by the People's Army of Vietnam (PAVN). From 1967 to 1973 the compound had housed POWs, but was returned to the PAVN and used as their motion picture department after 1973. A jail down the street, at 4 Ly Nam De Street, had also housed POWs until 1970. It was torn down in 1990 (after Paul's visit), and replaced with a multi-story apartment building to house members of the PAVN and their families. Although the site looked desolate, it was actually being used for various purposes. During Paul's visit, there were no prisoners being held at the compound, but some of the original buildings were being used as offices. They were later destroyed or renovated.

The reason for the uniformed man's demeanor had nothing to do with hiding prisoners, but everything to do with military protocol. The location was a military installation and they didn't welcome unscheduled visits by foreigners—especially those bearing cameras. Any filming at the location would have required advance permission from the Vietnamese Government. The uniformed officer at the door was most likely worried that someone in authority would find out about the visitors, and he wanted them gone before there were any repercussions from his superiors.

Shaken, Paul felt he needed to talk to someone. He went to Luce, who was more than a little angry with him.

"You can't be doing things like this! I'm responsible for you while we're here. I didn't know you were going off to places like that by yourself! Why didn't you tell me?"

"Sorry. I didn't think it would be a problem."

"Well, next time let me know before you go off searching for POWs! You could get us into serious trouble with the Vietnamese Government. I'd like to go home at the end of this trip, how about you?" Don was furious. Paul felt like a child being scolded by an angry parent, but Don's point was well-taken. Who knew what the Government might do? He made a mental note to proceed more cautiously in the future.

Back at the hotel, Paul encountered a group of nine boisterous veterans who had returned to Vietnam to party and have a good time. They made fun of him for wearing his POW bracelet and criticized him for being part of the POW/MIA movement. Paul felt they were hypocrites because they wore their Army gear and flaunted the fact that they were veterans. When Paul left them, he felt embarrassed and angry. "No wonder vets have such a bad rap; these guys are real assholes," he muttered to himself.

Paul spent the next three days in Hanoi sightseeing, attending meetings, and interacting with the locals. Don's meetings became much more interesting. Paul met the Vietnamese Minister of Commerce, and a person who held a position equivalent to the American Secretary of State. They both fascinated him. But, as the time in Hanoi drew to a close, he couldn't stop thinking about 17 Ly Nam De Street and tried to figure out a way to return. He continually asked the drivers of cyclos (a three-wheeled, rickshaw-type bicycle, used to carry passengers) to take him there, but they repeatedly refused. He finally gave up, deciding his efforts were futile, the endeavor too risky.

Paul enjoyed talking to the locals, continually amazed at their lack of animosity. One day he struck up a conversation with a sixty-year-old cyclo driver who was hanging out by his hotel. The man noticed Paul's T-shirt and pointed to his own shirt, which had clearly come from America. He pulled out an old paper bag from under his seat which contained a photograph of an American tourist, and proudly said in broken English, "This my friend in USA."

Paul wrote in his journal, "Here was a man, working for pennies a day, whose greatest treasures in life came from the very people who bombed the shit out of him." To Paul, it was inconceivable that the Vietnamese people didn't hate Americans. Nearly everyone back home hated vets, why didn't they?

On Friday, the group left Hanoi and flew to DaNang. Paul choked up as they landed. The airport looked exactly as it had during the war and, in some odd sense, he felt like he was coming home. They drove three hours from DaNang to Hue and Paul realized he had traveled the road before; some areas appeared frighteningly familiar. Both in DaNang and in Hue he was approached by Vietnamese locals selling dog tags. He wrote down the names to check against his list of POWs and MIAs, but guessed they were probably the black market tags he had been warned about previously.

During the war all soldiers were issued dog tags, which had to be replaced when they became illegible or lost. Replacement tags, which sometimes had printing errors, were just discarded—sometimes carelessly thrown in the trash. The Vietnamese collected lost and discarded tags and later sold them to unsuspecting Americans who thought they belonged to POWs or MIAs. Dog tags appeared everywhere in Vietnam after the war. Paul knew this, and was wary of the merchandise.

He spent the weekend sightseeing around DaNang and Nha Trang. Walking on the beach with others from the group, he spotted a man who was missing his leg and part of his arm. As the man approached, Paul asked the group's interpreter to ask him what had happened. The conversation revealed that the man was a North Vietnamese Army veteran who had fought in the war for nine years. He'd lost not only limbs, but his entire family and home, as well. Through the interpreter Paul learned that the man had fought near Con Thien and Paul wondered if he'd been the one responsible for the man's injuries.

The man politely asked him, "How do you like Vietnam?"

Paul responded enthusiastically. "I really like it here. The people are so friendly. I enjoy your country." Eventually the man questioned him about the war and Paul squirmed with discomfort over this touchy subject. By now, a curious crowd had gathered as the two veterans talked back and forth through the interpreter.

The man looked Paul in the eye and said gently, "Twenty years ago we were soldiers and we did what we had to do—terrible things that our Governments made us do. But now, we are no longer soldiers and we must love each other."

"Yes, you're right," Paul was able to choke out through the lump that had formed in his throat. The two men shook hands and parted.

The exchange over, Paul left the group and sprinted back to his hotel where he let out a sob the minute he slammed his door shut. Paul thought, "Here's a man who's lost everything, talking about forgiveness and love. I can't comprehend it. Compared to him, I lost nothing. I came home to my house, my wife, my family, and my possessions, yet I can't forgive anybody!" Paul thought about the conversation over and over, trying to make sense of it in his mind.

* * *

For Paul, the trip was an endless series of discoveries and mysteries. The people were unexpectedly gracious and kind, some of the scenery was gorgeous, and the abject poverty was overwhelming. Paul handed out pocket change and candy to children wherever he went and found their appreciation overly-effusive, as if he had handed out $100 bills to each and every one of them.

Signs of the war continually shocked him. From the emotional site of the My Lai Massacre to the intricate and ingenuous Cu Chi Tunnels, he realized how lucky he was to be alive. But, more than that, the sites told of the suffering of the Vietnamese people. He spent many nights awake, distressed. He saw the defoliated land in the countryside, the numerous Vietnamese locals missing limbs from landmines, and the jars of deformed babies in the hospitals, a result of Agent Orange. The North Vietnamese had won the war, but at what price?

On the POW front, the results were inconclusive. He had received a few leads, but they had never materialized into anything concrete. He was disappointed. As he continued to question the English-speaking locals, no one had seen or heard anything out of the ordinary. He was beginning to doubt whether there really were POWs in Vietnam. It appeared, like others had tried to tell him, that it was much too difficult to hide them within

Vietnam. If they existed, they had perhaps been moved to nearby Cambodia or Laos where they would be less conspicuous. Still, he wasn't ready to give up just yet.

As the trip drew to a close, the group spent the remainder of their time in Saigon. Paul walked the streets and stopped now and then to sit in the small cafes for a beer or a strong coffee; he wished he could share the experience with Pat. He had called her a couple of times to check in with her. He genuinely missed her and couldn't wait to tell her all about the trip. But mostly, he wanted her to love Vietnam as much as he did because—with or without her—he was coming back.

The time spent in Saigon was magical. Don was well-connected and one night the group was invited to a reception at City Hall hosted by the mayor himself, a heady experience for Paul and the others. On another occasion, they were invited to a dinner hosted by Don's friend, a wealthy individual who owned a beautiful home with a lavish courtyard, overflowing with orchids. It was another evening when Paul wished Pat was by his side.

Before leaving the city, Paul made a point to visit the famed Rex Hotel in downtown Saigon, where reporters and high-ranking military officials had held court during the war. It was a well-known site and Paul wasn't about to miss it. Outside the hotel, a chubby little shoeshine boy of eleven or twelve caught his attention.

"Hi! What's your name?" Paul asked.

"Spanky."

Paul laughed. Clearly Spanky wasn't his Vietnamese name, but the child did resemble Spanky from the show "Spanky and Our Gang (The Little Rascals)."

"Shine shoes mister?" Spanky asked.

Paul didn't need a shoeshine, but he wasn't going to turn down the child. He sat on a stool and let Spanky work his wonders. Paul handed him ten dollars, more than five times the price of a shoeshine. When Spanky realized he didn't want change, he broke into a big grin. Paul left feeling happy, as did Spanky, who wondered about the big, rich American who gave him so much money.

Eventually it was time to leave. The tour group flew to Bangkok, but only long enough to process out and head for the States. Paul left Asia with a firm resolve to return as soon as possible. He discovered that he loved this country and its people, but was also disappointed because he had not fulfilled his mission of finding POWs.

Despite his earlier reprimand, he and Don became friends and spent many nights engaged in lively discussions and arguments on a wide range of topics. Don didn't always agree with Paul, particularly on the issue of POWs, but he respected his viewpoint. Don found Paul to be a very likeable guy who was sincere in his efforts to help others. He also appreciated his help on the trip, because Paul frequently came to the aid of an older member of their group who needed assistance.

Paul learned that Don had a long, rich history of working in Vietnam that began in the 1950s when he worked with the International Voluntary Services organization, a Peace Corps type of group. Later, as an interpreter, Don reported on the stories of torture in the Tiger Cages at the Con Son Island prison, a major story that splashed across the pages of *Life Magazine*. Don went on to work with the Indochina Mobile Education Project and traveled throughout the United States speaking on issues related to Vietnam, Cambodia, and Thailand.

Paul was somewhat in awe of Don's broad-based experience and his intimate knowledge of Vietnam. Plus, Don listened to Paul's many opinions respectfully and with an open mind. The two agreed to stay in touch once they returned to the States, and Paul felt it was more than just lip service on Don's part.

Paul came home with Vietnam in his blood. He couldn't think or talk of anything else. He told Pat about his adventures, anxious to share every detail. She was happy he had arrived home safely and for many weeks noticed that he seemed happier than she'd seen him for years. Perhaps it was the cure he'd needed all along.

The members of the POW/MIA group were eager to hear his findings and he became the featured speaker at their meetings. Another man who was often present at the meetings was Ron (Ronald) Murray, a serious individual who read dark poetry from a book of war poems he had published.

Paul didn't know much about Ron until he met him at one of the group's monthly meetings at a steakhouse in Hershey. Ron was sitting several seats away at a big round table when someone asked Paul a question about Manheim. Ron's ears perked up.

"Paul, are you from Manheim?" asked Ron.

"Yes," Paul responded.

"Did you know Marty Sauble?" continued Ron.

"Yeah, Marty was a good friend of mine, my best friend actually. How do you know him?" Paul was curious.

"I served in Vietnam with him; I was his sergeant. Yeah, that Marty was quite a guy! He was a damn good soldier. If he hadn't died, he would have received the Purple Heart. I'm sure of it."

"Yeah, Marty was a great guy. I can't believe he's gone," Paul remarked sadly.

"I was with him when he died." Ron's voice became low and soft. "I feel responsible for his death."

Paul felt the wind knocked out of him. Was this the guy who'd shot Marty? There was silence at the table among those who overheard the exchange; no one was quite sure what to make of the conversation. The members of the POW/MIA group wondered about Ron and, for years, rumors circulated that he was the one who had accidentally shot Marty. Only a handful of people, including the elder Saubles, knew for sure.

* * *

Unexpectedly, Don called Paul and asked him to serve on the Board of Directors of the Asia Resource Center, to provide a veteran's point of view. Don felt that Paul was insightful about the problems that ARC was trying to resolve, and knew that Paul was anxious to help. Paul was ecstatic. Not only would serving on the board give him the opportunity to travel back to Vietnam, it signified that an organization valued his opinions. It would also give him direct access to politicians and people of influence. His dreams were coming true.

In July of 1990 Don, Paul, Bob Kane, and Mark Bonacci traveled to Vietnam to make two documentary films. One film, requested by the University of New York in Buffalo, centered on the art of block printing, a form of painting. The other, a film called "Lament of a Warrior's Wife," focused on Vietnamese MIAs.

However, this trip, unlike the previous one, did not go smoothly. In fact, just about everything went wrong. Paul became ill soon after he arrived, suffering from a cold, sunburn, ringworm, and an upset stomach. The men were supposed to meet Don in Saigon, but Don wasn't there. He'd been called to Hanoi by the Ministry of Foreign Affairs. He'd left word at the hotel, but the staff didn't pass along his message or even tell the men that he had been there, even though his suitcase was still at the front desk. Eventually Don called to check on things and by chance, Mark overheard his voice on the other end of the line.

Once they met up, there were other issues with which to contend. The weather was unbearably hot and humid and permissions for filming were slow in coming, causing them to waste a considerable amount of time. And, although the accommodations on the first trip weren't lavish, the accommodations on this trip were downright crude.

However, the trip proved invaluable and Paul learned a great deal from being a part of the filming process. The statistics in the film (provided by both Senator Kennedy's Subcommittee and the Vietnamese Government) were startling. He was shocked to learn that there were: 300,000 Vietnamese MIAs, one million Vietnamese affected by Agent Orange, one million dead, another million disabled, one and a half million Vietnamese who were wounded, and 370,000 orphans. As Paul had personally witnessed, Vietnam was a country devastated in just about every possible way; and now, it was economically isolated from the rest of the world.

Paul had no experience in filming documentaries, but joked that he was the guy who lugged the heavy stuff around. As they traveled through the countryside, he once again spoke to the locals. By the end of the trip he was leaning towards the conclusion that POWs were not currently being held in Vietnam. The risks were much too great and there was no place to hide them. The locals knew everything and were willing to talk for a price.

He spent more days in Vietnam than originally planned, simply because of the numerous problems and delays, which didn't please Pat who had filled in for him at the greenhouse. However, Paul seemed at peace and perhaps that was worth her effort. The trip was a success and the two documentaries were produced. The film on Vietnamese MIAs was shown on a limited basis on PBS stations in the United States, but didn't receive the broader network showing they had envisioned. Paul was proud to be a part of such an amazing process, even if he was only the guy who carried the heavy equipment.

He dreamed that Pat would love Vietnam as much as he did and made plans to take her there. Vietnam was now an integral part of his life and he wanted to share it with her. Plus, he had a vision for the future: he hoped to move to Vietnam someday. Of course, this wasn't an idea he had yet disclosed. Instead, it was a plan he swirled around in his head like the last dregs of beer in a glass.

Don and Paul stayed in touch and, before long, Don told Paul he was planning another January trip, similar to the one he had led the previous year. Paul didn't hesitate. He told Don he was coming on the trip and bringing Pat. He broke the news to her with a big grin on his face, waiting for her reaction. She consented, although not as enthusiastically as he had hoped for.

January arrived quickly and soon they were on their way to Vietnam. During the flight, Pat had more than a few complaints. The long trip was extremely uncomfortable in coach seats and her legs hurt. Paul was sympathetic to her plight, but hoped this wasn't a sign of things to come. Traveling in Vietnam was akin to roughing it, and he worried about how well she would fare. The itinerary for this trip was much the same as the first, beginning in Bangkok, flying to Hanoi, and working their way south to Saigon.

Pat enjoyed herself, but she didn't share his excitement or passion for Vietnam. She had little tolerance for the heat and humidity, she disliked the spicy food, and she thought that, in general, everything could stand a good coat of paint. Quite simply, her interests were different than his. Paul tried to be patient with her. He wasn't searching for POWs on this trip and just wanted to show her a good time. She thought the experience was okay, but she decided the trip was a one-time deal; she had no desire to return. Paul was deeply disappointed but never verbalized his feelings. Instead, he turned his attention to his next trip because, by now, he was having a love affair with Vietnam and he couldn't get enough of the place he had once feared and dreaded.

CHAPTER 8

Hope

*Most of the important things in the world
Have been accomplished by people
Who have kept on trying when there seemed
To be no hope at all.*

Dale Carnegie

C hristmas was rapidly approaching but, instead of feeling festive, Sandy was depressed. The holidays were a constant reminder of Hazel's death. Plus, there was only one gift she wanted, and it was highly unlikely she would receive it for Christmas or any other day of the year. For what her heart craved most wasn't a possession, but a child; she desperately wanted a baby. She talked about adoption incessantly, but Richard had little interest in becoming a parent.

Then, just days before Christmas, he relented. Partly it was to make her happy and partly it was to silence her. He was tired of her continuous babbling about babies and knew she wouldn't stop until he caved in and said yes. Before he had a chance to change his mind, she hurried him down to the Pearl S. Buck Foundation in a nearby town, where they filled out an adoption application with the agency's Welcome Home Social Services division. It was December 20, 1992.

The agency offered a program in El Salvador that promised a baby quickly (in approximately six months) and required only two or three days of travel in-country. Sandy knew that Richard wouldn't travel to El Salvador so she planned to ask her half-sister, Sandra, to accompany her. Their relationship had now progressed to the point where asking her for help was no longer out of the question.

Once Christmas was over, Sandy and Richard attended group sessions at the agency to prepare for their home study. A home study is a comprehensive look at all aspects of a prospective adoptive parent's life including: their finances, family backgrounds, mental and physical health, parenting style, the condition of their home, references, and extensive background checks. No stone is left unturned. Sandy worried whether everything would pass muster, since she seemed to have more than her fair share of skeletons jangling around in the family closet.

She had ample reason to worry. The social worker called the day before their visit and announced, "I'll be arriving at your home at nine and I'll be there until four. I'm a vegetarian, so please prepare something light and appropriate for lunch."

Sandy, put off by the woman's attitude, thought, "Wow, you plan to be here all day? What could we possibly talk about for that long?" She cleaned the house, picked up clutter, and fussed over the special lunch, feeling more than a little anxious about the social worker's visit.

The woman arrived on schedule and was more intimidating in person than over the phone. Sandy's vision of a warm and helpful social worker was quickly replaced by one of a stern drill sergeant. She interviewed Richard and Sandy separately before she asked them questions together as a couple, allegedly interrogating them for hours on end about every aspect of their lives. She searched through their house like an amateur sleuth, probing the attic, the basement, the garage, the closets, and even under the sinks. Nothing was overlooked.

As the day progressed, Sandy thought to herself, "This can't really be happening! This is totally ridiculous! Why did we have to get *her*?"

The social worker prefaced her long list of questions by saying, "I have a number of questions I need to ask you and you must answer all of them." Reportedly, she fired off a barrage of questions that Sandy deemed insulting and embarrassing. Sandy, determined to pass this hurdle, looked her straight in the eye and answered every single one, while seething with rage inside. What right did this woman have to ask such personal and intimate questions? And more importantly, what did they have to do with adopting and parenting a child? Did this woman really need to know if she and Richard had engaged in premarital sex? By the end of the day, Richard was ready to throw in the towel. "Look, Sandy, if this is what we have to go through, I'm done!"

Sandy, too, felt beaten and demoralized. She couldn't believe what had transpired. She became even angrier when she compared notes with the other women in her group, whose experiences had been vastly different from her own. Their visits were completed in one quick hour and they had been asked basic questions, not the intrusive ones that she had been required to answer. She felt violated and exposed. Why was her luck always so bad?

As weeks turned into months, Sandy wondered why their home study wasn't completed. She called the social worker numerous times, but the answer was always the same: "I'm working on it." The other social workers finished their reports. In fact, everyone else in the group completed their home studies, received referrals (were matched with their babies), traveled to El Salvador, and were already home with their babies. Only Sandy and Richard continued to wait, frustrated and angry.

Sandy stepped up the frequency of her calls, determined to find out the cause of the delay. Finally, at the end of May, the report was finished. But, in the meantime, El Salvador had closed for adoption. Sandy was livid. She called the agency looking for restitution, but they suggested she pick another program; a task more easily said than done.

Most of the agency's programs took several months or years to complete and required extensive travel, so she ruled them out. The Korean program didn't take too long and appeared to be her next best option, but she was told that there were only ten Korean children available. Five children were already matched and the other five were special needs children. Sandy knew Richard would never agree to a special needs child and, as a first-time mother, she wasn't sure she was up to the task either. Realizing that she was out of options, she said, "Okay, fine. Just forget about it." She was done. Maybe this was a sign from God that, like Hazel, she really wasn't meant to be a mother.

* * *

By now, Senter was very ill. Although he remained at home, he was in tremendous pain. He spent his days confined to bed watching preachers on television, growing more religious by the day. He refused to leave the farm because it was the one place he loved. He was also old-fashioned. In backwoods Tennessee you kept an infirm relative at home, with the family gathered around, until he died in his own bed. Senter fully expected this was how his life would end.

Poor Blanche had her hands full. Senter, angry and combative, lashed out at her in pain and frustration. Plus, his second-floor bedroom required that she trudge up and down the stairs several times a day, toting trays of pureed food or water or medicine. Although she was patient, eventually she reached her limit. She called Sandy for help.

Sandy was more than willing to come to Blanche's aid. She took charge of their household: she bought their groceries, washed their laundry, cleaned their house, and ran their errands. She helped with Senter's care and calmed him down. Although Senter raged at Blanche, he never raised his voice to her, Daddy's little girl. She spent every free moment with him, knowing from past experience, there wasn't much time left.

One day while Sandy was in the drugstore buying his medications, the lady behind the counter struck up a conversation with her. The woman, Mrs. Duncan, knew of Sandy's desire to have a child.

"How's your adoption going?" she asked.

"It's not. I've given up. Nothing worked; it's not going to happen. I'm really upset, but it just didn't work out." Sandy, still bitter from the experience, didn't elaborate.

"Well, my son's girlfriend is pregnant. He's only nineteen and she's seventeen and they're way too young to have a baby. They don't have jobs or money or anything. I don't know how in the world they're going to have this child. Maybe you should talk to them."

Sandy was wary. "I don't know ..."

"Let me talk to them, and next time you're in the store, come by and see me. I'll let you know what they think."

"Okay." Sandy was apprehensive, but encouraged by the news. She rushed home with Senter's medication and told Mommy Blanche about her encounter.

"Oh honey, don't do that. Don't get involved. You'll be disappointed again if they change their minds or something happens. Don't do it."

Later, when Sandy talked to Richard, he had a similar reaction. "Forget it. You're just asking for trouble. You don't have time for a baby anyway; you're spending all your time across the street. Forget about having a kid." Richard was done.

Sandy knew they were probably right, but couldn't let go of this last glimmer of hope. She couldn't get the conversation with Mrs. Duncan out of her head. After mulling it over, she went to the minister at her church and asked for his opinion. He said, "No, Sandy. It's too risky. Don't get involved. You're setting yourself up for a big letdown. Find another way to have a child."

If only she could! But, by now, the possibility of becoming a mother had taken on a life of its own, propelled by its own volition. She approached Mrs. Duncan and inquired about the situation again, and Mrs. Duncan indicated the couple wanted to meet her. The next week she secretly met with Mary and Doug, the young, pregnant couple. She liked them immediately, but carefully steered clear of any adoption talk. Instead she inquired about Mary's health. "Have you seen a doctor yet?"

"No, I don't have any money to see a doctor."

"Let me see if I can get you into a clinic or something. Maybe you can apply for public assistance. Who's going to pay for the child's birth?"

"I don't know." It was clear the young girl didn't know what to do or where to turn for help. Sandy decided that Mary and her baby deserved better, regardless of whether the outcome worked to her advantage.

Sandy helped them and soon Mary received prenatal care at a clinic. Meanwhile, Richard complained more and more. Not only was Sandy spending her days at her father's bedside, now she was also investing time and money helping this unknown couple. Their arguments escalated until finally Sandy said, "Just meet them once and you'll understand why I'm doing this. Just once, okay?"

Richard sullenly agreed and Sandy invited the young couple to their house for a cookout the next weekend. Richard, like Sandy, instantly liked them. Doug was intelligent, articulate, extroverted, and musically talented, while Mary was sweet and demure. The two couples had fun and it was the first of many visits.

As their friendship developed, Sandy and Richard finally broached the topic of adoption. Mary and Doug decided they wanted them to adopt their baby and eventually verbalized their feelings. But, by now, Sandy was skeptical. With each passing month, she felt her chances of actually adopting the baby were decreasing. She resigned herself to the possibility that the adoption would never occur. She also knew that the couple, although young and struggling, would make good parents.

On more than one occasion, Sandy told Mary: "I know you're telling us right now that you want us to have your child. But, after you carry this baby for nine long months and go through labor and childbirth, you might change your mind. If you do, it's okay. Really it is. This is your baby. I don't want you to feel any pressure. You make the decision and whatever that decision is, it's okay. I'll just be glad I was able to help you in some way." And Sandy truly meant it. She couldn't imagine a worse scenario than receiving a baby the parents wanted to keep.

* * *

Senter went from bad to worse. The visiting nurse who helped with his care insisted he go to the hospital. He was in terrible shape: dehydrated, unable to eat, and in constant pain. Surgeons approached Blanche and Sandy and recommended he undergo exploratory surgery. Senter reluctantly agreed, knowing it was a last ditch effort. They opened him up and discovered it was too late. His cancer was rampant; there was nothing they could do.

Emotionally and physically drained, Blanche was distraught at the prospect of losing the man she had loved for forty-three years. As Senter's condition worsened, she never left his side, almost requiring medical treatment herself. One day Sandy when came to visit, she discovered that Blanche had been up all night with him. Her face was drawn and pale, with dark, puffy circles drooping to her cheekbones. Sandy insisted she go home. "Mommy, I'm taking you home right now. You need to rest. Go lie down for a few hours, and I'll come back for you later." Blanche, too tired to argue, nodded her head in resignation.

Sandy drove Blanche home and went back to the hospital. Within ten minutes of her return, Senter died. Sandy couldn't believe it. Her daddy, the man she loved and respected, was gone. First there was Hazel, and now, Senter. She didn't know how she would survive this latest blow.

Blanche did not take the news well. Not only was she a grieving widow, she was also mad as hell. She blamed Sandy for her unthinkable sin: not being at Senter's side when he died. For a woman from Tennessee this was an unimaginable burden to bear. You stayed with your loved one until they died—period. She had violated the unwritten code of the family and it took a long time before she came to terms with that fact or forgave Sandy for it.

Senter was interred at the Beulah Baptist Church, the same church that Sandy had attended as a child. He was buried next to his wife, Ruth, a slap in the face for Blanche, who had spent the majority of her life with him. It was the sign of things to come.

* * *

It was the summer of 1993 and Sandy felt like she was drowning in an enormous sea of stress. Senter had just died, Mary was seven months pregnant, Angel continued to pursue a strained father-daughter relationship with her, and Richard's mother just discovered she had cancer. Then the final blow was delivered. Allegedly, when the family gathered for the reading of Senter's will, they discovered that only Donald and Howard had been included; Senter had left nothing for Sandy or Blanche.

Sandy was dumbstruck. It wasn't money she wanted, but rather, the recognition that she'd been an important part of Senter's family and his life. Instead, she was left out, forgotten, summarily dismissed. She had never fit in anywhere. When Hazel didn't want her, she had struggled to fit in with the Robinsons. Clearly, the message was that she had not succeeded. But, worse than that, Blanche, who had devoted her life to Senter, who had stayed at his bedside day and night, providing the most intimate aspects of his care, had also been rejected. How could this happen?

Sandy began to doubt Senter's love for both herself and Blanche. Over the years, her father had taken her aside on hundreds of occasions telling her privately how much she meant to him and how much he loved her. Had it all been a lie? Senter, always mysterious, was still an enigma from the grave.

Blanche was sixty-eight when Senter died. Where was she to go? What was she to do? She had lived at the farm for over four decades and had devoted her life to him. Sandy encouraged her to hire a lawyer and fight. Surely there was something that could be done. Blanche refused to believe that the sons would make her leave the farm, but supposedly they felt it was their right to do whatever they wanted. But, when all was said and done, Blanche prevailed. Legally, she was considered Senter's common law wife and she inherited everything.

However, Blanche was willing to share. She gave the sons tractors and cars, farm equipment, and personal possessions. All she really wanted was to live out her days in the old farmhouse and, in the end, she got her wish.

* * *

Through all of her adversity, Sandy had three positives working for her: friends, religion, and hope. Although she was depressed and overwhelmed by the events that continually swirled through her life like summer tornadoes in Kansas, she still had hope. She had hope that she'd eventually adopt a baby, hope that her life would straighten out, and hope that somewhere, sometime, someplace, she would finally fit into a family.

The recurring theme in her life was: "Why was I born? Why was I put on this earth? No one wants me and I don't belong. Why am I here?" Over and over she implored God to answer her questions, but so far He had remained mute. It was her dream that one day it would all be made clear to her.

As Mary's due date approached, Sandy became increasingly uneasy about the birth. She really didn't know if Mary and Doug planned to give them the baby, who was now known to be a girl. She felt so uncertain about the possibility of motherhood she refused to buy any baby items. There would be no crib, no baby clothes, and no diapers in her home until she actually had the baby in hand. There was no sense in creating more pain. In all probability, it simply wasn't going to happen.

Richard's mother died in the middle of August; one more blow to the fragile household. The funeral was held on August 16, and the next morning she and Richard slept late, exhausted from the upheaval of back-to-back family tragedies. A ringing phone awoke them. Sandy answered, only to hear Mary's panicked voice on the other end of the line. "I have to go to the hospital—now!"

"Okay, I'll be right there!" Sandy jumped to her feet. "Richard, get up. You need to come to the hospital with me. Mary's having the baby!"

"No, I'm too tired. Besides, what am I going to do except sit around and wait. You go."

"No, I need you to be with me. I don't want to be there alone."

"Oh, all right, I'll go." Richard grumbled all the way to the hospital.

They arrived at the maternity ward to find Mary in bad shape. Her doctor had prescribed bed rest weeks earlier, but she hadn't listened and now her blood pressure was at a dangerously high level. The doctor induced labor to set the birth into motion; she had to have the baby today.

Everyone was ill-prepared. Sandy and Richard were dazed by the rapid-fire events unfolding around them, and Mary and Doug felt scared and uncertain.

Doug, a musician, thought Mary needed music to get through her labor and sent Sandy out to look for Mary's favorite tunes. She came back with music by Pink Floyd, which Mary focused on between contractions. During the early part of the labor, Sandy and Mary talked about the baby's name. In the end, Mary abdicated the decision to Sandy, who chose the name Hannah Elizabeth. Hannah was from the Bible, and Elizabeth was the name of Richard's baby sister who had died.

Richard fidgeted in the waiting room while Sandy stayed with Mary to offer support and encouragement throughout her labor and birth. When the baby was finally delivered at ten o'clock that night, Sandy ran out of the room, overcome with emotion.

"Richard, she's beautiful!

"What do you think will happen?"

"I have no idea. I don't know what they plan to do."

Later, Sandy saw Doug with a nurse in the hallway. The baby was swaddled and they were wheeling her up to the nursery. They stopped so that Richard could take a peek. The couple left the hospital not knowing if they were Hannah's parents or not.

The next day Sandy sat by the phone waiting for it to ring. When it didn't, she knew that Mary had changed her mind. A few tears slipped down her cheeks as she thought about the pink, pudgy baby and the future she had fantasized about for so long. Late in the afternoon, the ringing phone disturbed her thoughts. It was Mary, sounding hurt. "Why aren't you here? I thought you'd come."

"I thought you'd want to spend time with Hannah. You need to spend time with your baby, alone."

"No, I want you to come. Please come."

"I can't. I'm not a relative. They told me yesterday that only relatives are allowed to visit."

"It's okay. I told them you're my mother. Come over."

"You told them I'm your mother?" Sandy was incredulous. "Okay, I'm coming!" She dashed to her car and drove well over the speed limit during the hour-long drive to the hospital. A nurse was just bringing Hannah into Mary's room to be fed. Mary said to her, "Give the baby to my mom. She'll feed her."

Sandy gulped. Here she was, pretending to be Mary's mother, but she had rarely fed or even held a baby before. She looked to the nurse for help, "I don't think I'm very good at this, uh, anymore. Could you please show me how to do it?" Sandy flushed red.

The nurse gave Sandy a quick lesson in holding, feeding, and subsequently, diapering the baby. As Hannah snuggled into her, she felt pangs of need and desire stabbing her heart like hot pokers. But then, as she looked at the faces of Mary and Doug and saw the tears in their eyes, she felt guilty and terrible. She was split in two; the situation was untenable.

The next day was even more confusing and troubling. Mary called early in the morning and told her she could bring her family to see the baby. Sandy gathered her entourage: Richard, Blanche, half-sister Sandra, and Sandra's daughter, Kelly. Doug's extended family was there too. Everyone took turns holding the baby, as they tried to make uncomfortable small talk. Meanwhile, no one knew who Hannah was going home with the next day when Mary was released from the hospital.

Everyone finally left the hospital room and Sandy hung back. She sat next to Mary on the bed and looked into her sad eyes, "I can see how much you love her and I know how hard this is. She's your baby, not mine. If you think you want to keep her, then you should keep her. I won't be angry and I won't feel bad. I'll just feel really happy that I was able to help you and that you made the right decision for yourself. Whatever you decide is okay, but I need to know. So please ... just tell me."

Mary sobbed and choked, her words tumbling out, "Sandy, if it was anyone else I'd probably change my mind, but I want you to have her."

"Are you sure? Are you absolutely sure?"

"Yes, I'm sure." The two sat for a long time, holding hands, both weeping for different reasons. An underlying sadness pervaded the decision. It wasn't exactly how Sandy had pictured becoming a mother.

The next morning Sandy rushed out to buy a few basic items, then she and Richard hurried to the hospital to bring baby Hannah home. They arrived at the hospital only to find Mary and Doug still there; none of their family members had thought to pick them up or be there for support. Richard and Sandy had no choice but to offer them a ride, an awkward and unfortunate situation at best. The four adults and baby Hannah drove off together. Richard dropped the couple off at Mrs. Duncan's house. Sandy felt sick to her stomach as Mary and Doug stepped out of the car; tears streaming down their faces, staring back at the baby they were leaving behind. She prayed they wouldn't regret their decision.

* * *

The first weeks were a huge adjustment. Sandy was a nervous first-time mother and Richard was a little jealous. He didn't like competing with an infant for Sandy's attention and affection. Fortunately, Hannah was a healthy, happy baby who was easy to care for and nurture. Sandy fell in love with her the instant they were home and she eventually settled into the natural rhythm of motherhood. Being a parent was everything she had hoped for and more. She was filled with joy, and life now seemed to take on a bigger purpose. The depression that had clouded her existence for so long disappeared, like a balloon escaping from a child's fist into the sky.

In fact, most things in Sandy's life had turned around. Blanche, who had the farm back after settling her battles with the boys, was happy to be a grandmother and supported Sandy in her new role as a mother. Angel planned to take her to Puerto Rico to meet his extended family, and all of his children, including Sandra, now accepted her as part of the family. There was just one problem: Richard.

Richard resented the time Sandy spent with Senter while he was ill and dying, then he resented the time she spent with Mary and Doug, and now he resented the baby. He wanted his old life back, moving furniture, with Sandy by his side. He didn't understand that her maternal instincts had kicked into gear and she no longer wanted to drive a truck across the country. She wanted to be home with her new love, Hannah.

The couple's arguments escalated, they were fighting all the time. It wouldn't be long before one more event pushed them even further into crisis. But, for now, Sandy had a beautiful baby girl who brought new hope into her life and that was all she needed.

CHAPTER 9

The Find

One does not discover new lands
Without consenting to lose sight of the shore,
For a very long time.

André Gide

Paul wore Lewis Smith's MIA bracelet as a daily reminder of things gone awry, not only with the war, but the world at large. Lewis P. Smith II, a twenty-five-year-old Major in the Air Force, had been missing since May 30, 1968, shot down in the Saravane Province of Laos. Now, twenty-three years later, Lewis was still missing, declared dead by the military over a decade ago. His parents, Earl and Betty Smith of Bellefonte, Pennsylvania, still held onto the hope that their son was alive, as evidenced by the presence of his overflowing Christmas stocking still hanging on their mantel. More than anything else, they desired closure. They planned to travel to Laos to find some answers if they could obtain permission for the trip from the U.S. and Laotian governments. Paul was determined to take them not only into Laos, but to the crash site as well.

When Paul decided to do something he was stubborn and unrelenting—unwilling to let go, until all possible options had been exhausted. He'd adopted a new philosophy after the war that he occasionally stated aloud for others: "If the consequences of chasing my dreams or pursuing my goals aren't certain death, then I'm going for it!" This "Damn the torpedoes, full speed ahead" approach was one he held onto tenaciously. Helping Betty and Earl was one of his goals, and one way or another he planned to take them to Laos before they were too old and infirm to travel there.

For Paul, going to Laos was no big deal. He'd traveled to Vietnam three times already and considered himself a seasoned traveler as he became more confident and comfortable with each subsequent visit. He also felt that he'd be able to help the Smith family through his connections with the Asia Resource Center (ARC).

In late spring of 1991 Paul approached Roger Rumpf, who had replaced Don Luce as the new Director of ARC. Roger and his wife, Jacqui, had a long history of working and living in Laos beginning in 1978. They were representatives of the American Friends Service Committee (AFSC) for three countries of Indochina: Cambodia, Vietnam, and Laos.

The AFSC is a Quaker organization, and although Roger and Jacqui were not Quakers, they embraced its religious practices of working towards social justice and peace. During the war, the AFSC provided humanitarian relief to both sides. After the war, the AFSC, like the Mennonites, worked on specific projects related to unexploded ordinances and Agent Orange and, more broadly, issues surrounding reconstruction, reconciliation, and healing.

Roger knew that Paul was very concerned about the MIA issue and was sincere in his desire to help the Smith family. He introduced him to Linthong Phetsavan, a Laotian Charge d'Affaire in Washington, D.C., who was one of his personal friends. Mr. Phetsavan was sympathetic to Paul's cause, but was concerned over the Smith's safety in traveling to this remote and treacherous area of his country. He advised Paul and Roger to meet with U.S. officials to receive their approval first, before he would sanction the trip. They set up meetings with Scot Marciel, Laos Desk Officer at the State Department, and Ann Mills Griffiths, Executive Director of the National League of Families of American Prisoners and Missing in Southeast Asia.

Ann listened to Paul state his case, but said she felt the trip wasn't a good idea for the Smiths because of their ages (both were in their 70s). She also felt that families, as a whole, were better served by government-to-government negotiations. Paul bristled at her comments.

Paul interpreted her statements to mean that he had overstepped his bounds, an unacceptable viewpoint in his eyes. For him, and particularly for this issue, there *were* no bounds! He felt that the U.S., Laotian, and Vietnamese Governments weren't doing enough about MIAs and he surmised that Ann didn't want the publicity or embarrassment should he be successful during his trip.

Ann had been in her position at the League since 1978 and had vast experience in working with the Lao and visiting crash sites. She knew the complexity of the issues that surrounded admitting the Smiths into Laos and, in particular, allowing them near the crash site. Roger too, felt that as well-intentioned as Paul was, he was naïve in his understanding of the physical and political ramifications of his efforts.

First, there were the practical issues. The crash site was in a remote jungle with rugged terrain. Most likely, a helicopter would be needed to transport the Smiths into the area. Furthermore, crash sites often had to be cleared of land mines and unexploded ordinances, and checked for Agent Orange before they were approached. Roger, unlike the U.S. Government, had neither the funds nor the technology to accomplish those tasks. Even under the best of circumstances, jungle crash sites could be filled with unseen dangers, such as poisonous snakes and insects, and hidden ravines. How would people in their 70s be able to manage? What if they were injured? And, what would happen if, on the rare chance everything worked out well, they actually made it to the crash site? They weren't forensic anthropologists and poking around a site could disturb or destroy any evidence that remained. Both Ann and Roger knew these facts and had serious reservations about allowing the Smiths anywhere near the site.

In fact, Roger had specifically warned Paul not to promise the Smiths that they could go to the actual site. He felt that the better approach was to take the Smiths into Laos to see the countryside so they could get a sense for what might have happened to their son. He would encourage them to meet the Lao people, whom he felt would be open to talking with them and, if the Smiths were lucky, they might even stumble across someone with pertinent information. Paul agreed, but still secretly planned to go to the actual crash site if he could manage it.

Politically, the issues surrounding the trip were also complicated. Laos is a land-locked, undeveloped country with a long history of being used, and sometimes abused, by surrounding countries. The Lao were sensitive and suspicious about questions pertaining to POWs and MIAs, and diplomatic issues with the U.S. had often been strained. Both Ann and Roger had spent many years building relationships with the Lao; they knew the importance of both cooperation and government negotiations. Ann feared that the Lao might perceive the Smith case as a substitute for broader-based negotiations and she needed their cooperation on a much larger scale.

But while Ann and Roger had their concerns about the trip, they admired Paul for his efforts and, of course, had compassion and sympathy for the Smiths. Who knew better than Ann the heartbreak and anguish of the families of MIAs? Ann's own brother had been listed as MIA in 1966 while on a night mission over North Vietnam and had never been recovered. Roger felt that there were few obstacles that Paul couldn't overcome and was amazed at the amount of time, money, and emotional commitment he gave to his various causes. He felt that even if you didn't agree on everything, you still had to honor people like Paul for their will-ingness to go the extra mile. Paul's transformation from a soldier to a per-sonal crusader had been quite remarkable in Roger's eyes.

Back and forth negotiations continued for weeks until Paul and Roger again held court with Mr. Phetsavan at his Laos Embassy office in Wash-ington, D.C. However, Phetsavan was still conflicted about signing off on the trip. The two men tried everything in their power to convince him oth-erwise. Phetsavan, sensing desperation, decided to use it to his personal advantage.

"I'm concerned about that tree," he said coyly, pointing to a large oak tree outside his embassy window. "It looks like it's going to fall over. What do you think?"

"I have a chainsaw. Maybe I can come back and cut it down," Roger volunteered. As friends, he and Phetsavan had often done favors for each other. "Paul, do you have a chainsaw?"

"Yeah, I do. I can help, but that's a big tree ..." Paul wasn't keen on the idea of taking down a huge tree, but if that's what it took to win the man's favor, so be it. Paul and Roger agreed to return the following Sun-day to cut down the mighty oak as Paul wondered how he had been talked into the job.

Early Sunday morning Paul went over to the greenhouse with Pat. A large flower shipment had arrived and he had to unpack the flowers and put them in water before he left for Washington. The boxes were tied tightly with twine and, as he sliced through the tough threads with a box cutter, he slipped and stabbed himself in the arm.

"Damn it!" Paul exclaimed, looking down at the deep slice in his flesh. It was bleeding profusely and, despite his efforts, showed no signs of stopping. "Pat, can you drive me down to the hospital? My arm's bleeding like crazy and I can't seem to get it stopped. I might need stitches!"

"Let's go. You need to take care of that before you leave for D.C." When they arrived at the hospital, the doctor questioned Paul about his injury.

"Oh, it's just a self-inflicted wound," Paul joked, as the doctor gave him four stitches. "Can you hurry up? I need to get down to the Laos Embassy in D.C. to cut down a tree for the ambassador this afternoon."

The doctor didn't believe him and was seconds away from calling in the police to find out who had stabbed him. He pulled Pat aside and ques-tioned her to see if she could verify his unlikely story. Paul, realizing the doctor's suspicions, chuckled to himself; his explanation did sound a bit like he was ready for the psych ward. Pat assured the doctor that his stab wound was accidental and the doctor reluctantly released him.

Paul met Roger in D.C., and the two spent the afternoon taking down the massive tree and hauling the wood to Roger's house for his fireplace. Paul ripped out one of his stitches during the course of the day, but felt it was a small price to pay if he could get the Smiths into Laos.

The next few months were exciting ones; Paul felt optimistic. The trip was taking on a life of its own and the proposed entourage was growing bigger by the day. Not only were the Smiths, Roger, and Paul planning on going, now the press was getting involved. Barbara Brueggebors, a long-time friend of the Smiths and a journalist, planned to accompany them on the trip on behalf of her newspaper *The Centre Daily Times* of State College, Pennsylvania. Another journalist, Romayne Naylor, of *The Keystone Gazette* in Bellefonte, also planned to join them. Stories about the proposed trip hit the local papers and even the Associated Press picked up the story. Soon Betty and Earl received calls and support from MIA families across the country.

Paul and Roger continued to meet with Government officials as the circle of influence widened to include Charles Trowbridge at the Department of Internal Affairs and Carl Ford in Intelligence at the Pentagon under Secretary of Defense Dick Cheney. More interest was generated in the press and Paul allegedly spoke to Ti-Hua Chang at CBS News and Sylvia Chase from PrimeTime. Even 60 Minutes expressed some interest in the story. Phetsavan invited Paul and Pat to a political dinner where they rubbed elbows with more than a few famous politicians. Paul, now elevated to celebrity status, fielded questions from the press and discussed the proposed trip with high-ranking Government officials.

The trip was tentatively scheduled for January 20. In early November, the Smiths met with Griffiths and Phetsavan to seal the deal. Everyone filled out visa applications. The hope was that Jacqui, Roger's wife, could facilitate the issuance of the visas through the proper channels in Laos, where she was currently residing. The Smiths needed money for the trip so Paul enlisted the aid of the Centre County Veterans Council to start fundraising, even though it was slightly premature and the trip had not been officially sanctioned yet.

Preparations were moving along nicely but, just when everything looked like it was a go, the trip was abruptly cancelled. In one of the meetings Roger attended without Paul, access to Laos was denied, with the age and health of the Smiths cited as the reason.

Everyone was disappointed, but most of all Paul, who refused to let go of the plan. He decided he'd go on his own. He reasoned that he was younger and stronger than the Smiths, and he knew exactly where to look based upon maps he had seen of the crash site. Betty and Earl gave him their travel fund along with their blessing. If they couldn't go, at least Paul could represent them. Pat was highly skeptical of the journey and worried for his safety. Traveling to a remote jungle, in an area where Laotians didn't want Americans poking around, didn't seem like such a good idea. What was he getting himself into this time?

* * *

The previous January when Paul and Pat traveled to Vietnam with Don Luce, they became friendly with a man named Scott Collins. Scott was a young firefighter from the northwest who liked Vietnam and expressed an interest in returning one day. Paul decided to ask Scott to accompany him on this trip to Laos. He reasoned that Scott's presence might allay some of Pat's fears and provide backup should he need it. Scott jumped at the chance. After a brief discussion, the two men picked a travel date in June, just a few short months away.

As the travel date approached, Paul's vision for the trip became broader than simply searching for Lewis Smith's remains. He decided to go to Hanoi first to meet with American officials to question them about MIAs. He and Scott flew into Vietnam and went to an office called the Joint Task Force-Full Accounting (JTF-FA, which had previously been the U.S. MIA Office); whose mission was to work with Vietnamese officials to seek out information related to American MIAs. Paul felt it was important to go on record with them and make it clear that he and Scott were in Vietnam and Laos to find MIAs and to look for Smith's remains. It was a cover-your-ass move that might be necessary should anything adverse happen to them during their travels.

When Paul arrived at the JTF-FA office, he spoke with one of the staff members, Robert J. Destatte. It was unusual for Americans to come looking for remains and Destatte thought that Paul was wise to check in with him. Destatte admired him for his efforts, but cautioned him to be careful. Destatte knew from personal experience that Paul could potentially encounter some unsavory characters and put himself in danger. Plus, he wanted to be very clear that he was in no way encouraging or asking Paul and Scott to do this work; they were doing it on their own initiative. There were strict rules at the JTF-FA, against employing U.S. citizens to collect information on MIAs without written permission and advance coordination with those in authority. If Paul were to run afoul of local authorities and indicate he was working with Destatte (or for the U.S. Government) there was the possibility he could be perceived as a spy and treated as such. Destatte's advice was sound, but Paul didn't give it much credence.

Paul and Scott spent a couple of days in Hanoi before heading south to Saigon. They sifted through flea markets on the streets of Hanoi and searched for dog tags and other clues that might lead to missing Americans.

Everywhere they went Paul asked the Vietnamese locals: "Do you know anything about missing Americans?" The answer was always "no," and the search in Hanoi came up empty.

Three days later they arrived in Nha Trang, a city north of Saigon, where the pair conducted more sidewalk searches. Paul repeated his standard question and heard negative responses in return until one day, a cyclo driver whispered back, "Yes, I know about missing soldiers." Nearly breathless, Paul pressed the man for more details.

The cyclo driver knew a family in town who had information, and perhaps proof, of MIAs. The three planned to meet the next day, Tuesday, June 16, 1992. Paul was too excited to sleep and spent a long and restless night. When morning finally arrived, the cyclo driver took Paul and Scott to his friend's house deep inside the city limits.

The tiny house was down a narrow little back alley in Nha Trang. Although Paul and Scott tried to keep a low profile, they were unsuccessful. Curious neighbors spotted them and pointed and shouted at the pair. American tourists were an unusual sight in Vietnam in 1992 and virtually nonexistent in this secluded neighborhood. The locals wanted to know why they were here and, more importantly, why they were meeting with their neighbors.

The Vietnamese family consisted of elderly parents and their English-speaking son, who did all the talking. He nervously showed Paul and Scott dog tag rubbings and photos of dog tags and an ID card. He explained that a helicopter had crashed years earlier, and he had gone to the site in 1978 to retrieve the items. The family also claimed to have a map.

Paul's excitement was tempered with skepticism about the items in their possession. "Photos and rubbings aren't enough proof. I need to see the actual items, the real dog tags and the real ID card."

As the men talked, nosy neighbors kept coming to the door to find out what was happening. After thirty minutes the family felt too threatened to continue the conversation, fearful that the police might show up at any moment. Private individuals were strongly encouraged to turn over war-related items (like dog tags) to the Government. Those who didn't relinquish the items were generally looking for financial gain from tourists, like Paul. Sometimes the police used this knowledge against these collectors by claiming they were having unauthorized contact with foreigners and threatening them with jail time if they didn't pay a fine.

The young man, although nervous, was eager to convince Paul that he had legitimate artifacts. "It's only 8:30 now. Let's meet at the beach at 11:00 and I'll bring you the items. The driver will take you there." Paul, Scott, and the cyclo driver left the house as discreetly and quickly as possible as curious neighbors continued to gawk.

At the appointed time the driver took them to a remote beach area where they met the family once again. The young man handed Paul a paper bag full of items that included the dog tag of a man named Ronald Stanton, a burned ID card of Charles Deitsch, a plastic plaque inscribed "Radio Call 619053," one bone fragment of a human jaw with seven teeth, and a bone fragment that appeared to be part of a human skull. There was also a slip of paper with the name "Humphrey, William C., Jr." written on it. Paul became nervous when he saw the items; they certainly appeared real, but there was only one way to be sure.

"I need to take these with me so I can examine them. I'd like to take them back to my hotel."

Surprisingly, the family consented. Paul left them and spent the afternoon alone in his hotel room, investigating the items. First, he pulled out a camera and took pictures of the evidence, carefully documenting what he had received. He grabbed his official list of missing Americans and checked the dog tag against it, finding that Ronald Stanton was on the list, missing since October 20, 1968. Next he checked the ID card of Charles Deitsch and was surprised to find that he, too, went missing on the same date. Paul reasoned that if the men had been lost in a helicopter crash, as stated, there may have been additional men aboard. Humphrey wasn't listed as an MIA or POW.

Paul patiently went through his list of over 2,000 names, checking for more men missing on October 20. When he completed his task, he added three more names: Jerry G. Bridges, Henry C. Knight, and Charles H. Meldahl. For Paul, it all made sense; a helicopter crew generally included a pilot, a co-pilot, a door gunner, an engineer, and a crew chief—a total of five men. A shiver ran down his back as he looked at the bones lying on his nightstand, wondering who they belonged to.

The air inside the room became still and close; the four drab walls transformed from a dreary hotel room into a tomb for the missing soldiers. Ghostly images played in his mind as he carefully replaced the bones and personal effects back into the lowly paper bag. He stared at the hotel furniture where he had so casually placed the men's remains and felt irreverent. Shaking it off, he picked up the phone, dialed the JTF-FA office in Hanoi, and asked for Destatte. The voice on the other end reported that he was out of the office and wouldn't return until four o'clock. Damn!

The hours moved slowly as Paul checked and rechecked the information. He wondered about the men's families. From surveying the list, he knew the men came from various parts of the country: Ohio, Tennessee, California, Washington, and Florida. What kind of hell had their families been living? Had they given up hope or were they, like the Smiths, still seeking closure and peace?

* * *

It was October 20, 1968. A typhoon had moved into the area and the weather was, according to one of the men, stinking. The members of the 243rd Assault Support Helicopter Company were stationed at Dong Ba Thien in South Vietnam. Three aircraft were scheduled for resupply missions that day, flying from Dong Ba Thien to Ban Me Thout in the Central Highlands. The first chopper to depart was known as Freight Train 053, headed up by none other than Charles (Pappy) Deitsch, a fifty-six-year-old warrant officer and seasoned pilot who had flown in both World War II and the Korean War. Pappy was a colorful character with a reputation known throughout the region. It was said that all Pappy had to do was show up, give a whistle, and the aircraft would come and strap itself to his ass. Pappy was quite a guy, one who took his men under his wing, so to speak, and treated them like his own family.

Pappy was the aircraft commander of the Chinook helicopter that day, with Henry (Hank) Knight as his pilot, Jerry Bridges as flight engineer, Charles Meldahl as crew chief, and Ronald Stanton as door gunner. Meldahl wasn't supposed to fly with Pappy that day, but felt uneasy about his original assignment and traded spots with his childhood friend, Brian Main, who was on one of the other two choppers.

At 7:00 a.m. Pappy headed out first, five minutes ahead of the other two aircraft. The second helicopter contained Tony Alvardo, as aircraft commander, Jon Beckenhauer as his pilot, and three other crew members. Likewise, the third aircraft contained a flight crew of five, one presumably being Brian Main.

Pappy flew out into the rain and low lying clouds and called to the others to "go up feet wet," which meant to go up the shoreline for the first twenty miles before turning inland over the mountains. Tony, Jon, and their crew were only ten miles into the mission when the tower called to inform them that the mission had been cancelled because of the terrible weather conditions. They were told to turn back. The crews of the second and third aircrafts did as they were told and returned safely. Both the tower and Tony repeatedly called Pappy but, between his altitude and transmission interference due to the mountainous terrain, the messages were never delivered. No one worried; Pappy knew what he was doing. He was due at his location at 8:00 a.m.

Hours passed and still no one heard from Pappy. He couldn't be reached. Now it was time for worry. A broadcast went out to everyone in the area but, because of the typhoon, it was much too dangerous to send out a search party. Three long days passed before the search began. For two weeks they looked for the helicopter to no avail. The terrain where the chopper was thought to have crashed was rugged with thick jungle canopies making it virtually impossible to find the aircraft. Finally, everyone reluctantly gave up the search. Pilots flying in the area continued to *look for the aircraft during each and every flight, hoping to spot some sign of Pappy and his crew, but were never successful. It was the only crew from the 243rd ever to be lost and not recovered.*

* * *

At 4:05 Paul called the JTF-FA office again and finally reached Destatte. Paul recapped what had happened and discovered, much to his surprise, that Destatte's office had received information on the case before. Starting in 1979, dog tag information was received for one or more of the crew members under a case file called REFNO (Reference Number) 1306. Destatte did a quick search and confirmed that all five men went missing on the same day as a result of a Chinook helicopter crash. Destatte was scheduled to travel to Saigon on other business anyway, so he agreed to meet Paul later in the week to see the items in person.

Paul and Scott were excited about these latest developments and decided to leave Nha Trang that evening. Neither was familiar with the train scheduling, so they went to the station to pre-purchase tickets and obtain the timetable for Saigon. When they left the hotel, the cyclo driver was sitting outside.

"Where are you going?" he asked.

"We need to go to the train station," Paul said. The cyclo driver drove them to the station and waited outside as they purchased tickets and grabbed schedules. Paul and Scott rushed along; they didn't have much time to return to the hotel, pack up their belongings, and return to the train station to catch the next train, which was leaving at six o'clock. When they came out of the hotel for the last time, both the cyclo driver and the young man who gave them the items were waiting.

The young man spotted their suitcases and angrily demanded, "I want the items back; they belong to my family." Paul ignored him as he and Scott loaded their luggage and jumped into the small cyclo. The man moved closer to Paul in a threatening manner. Paul looked him in the eye.

"The items belong to the United States Government. You can't have them back." Paul sensed trouble. "Let's go," he said to the driver, hurrying him on to the station.

The cyclo driver pedaled away quickly, but the young man jumped on his bicycle, caught up to them, and yelled at Paul and Scott to stop and return the items from the crash site. They created a scene as they moved down the streets of Nha Trang, the young man pedaling his bicycle only feet from the cyclo, shouting at them the entire time. To appease him, Paul said, "I'll give you the items at the train station."

At the station, Scott and Paul jumped out of the cyclo and grabbed their belongings as the young man lunged at them. The cyclo driver yelled at Paul, "Give him his stuff! Give it back!" Paul and Scott ran towards the platform with their suitcases in hand as the Vietnamese men followed in hot pursuit. The train pulled in and, when the doors opened, the two jumped in, leaving the cyclo driver and young man standing on the platform still screaming at them to surrender the items.

"Whew!" Paul panted. "That was close!" Unfortunately, it wouldn't be his last encounter with the angry pair.

* * *

Paul and Scott spent a couple of days in Saigon before Destatte's arrival. They walked around flea markets and continued to search for clues. Again, they came up short. They stayed in a small, uncomfortable hotel downtown near the Rex and Paul paid a visit to Spanky, the chubby little shoeshine boy he had befriended during his earlier visits to Vietnam.

Spanky was happy to see this big American man who mysteriously appeared every few months. By now, Spanky had mastered enough English to carry on a conversation and was clever enough to beg him for money. Paul, who had a soft spot in his heart for this engaging little boy, found it impossible to refuse his requests for cash. Spanky had lost his father at an early age and, as the eldest son, was now responsible for supporting his mother and siblings. Paul took pity on him, aware of Spanky's terrible burden. What Paul didn't know was that Spanky wasn't just dependent upon him for funds, he already considered him his surrogate father.

At 7:30 on Friday morning, Paul, Scott, and Destatte met in the lobby of the Rex Hotel. After a brief conversation, Destatte decided they should retreat to the privacy of Paul's hotel room at the 69 Hotel so he could take pictures of the items and catalogue them, just as Paul had done in his room in Nha Trang. Destatte methodically photographed the items and promised to return after he researched the information. Paul and Scott waited anxiously.

Destatte returned with amazing news: the radio call number on the plaque was in fact the call number of a missing Chinook—the items could be real! Paul and Scott were jubilant at the news, but Destatte wasn't finished. "I have to give the bones to the Vietnamese officials for checking. If they're identified as Caucasian remains, they'll be sent to the Central Identification Lab in Hawaii for DNA testing. The other items will also be sent to the Lab and once everything is processed, the personal items will be returned to the families."

The official turnover occurred the next day at 10:00 a.m. at the Casavina Hotel in downtown Saigon where Destatte's Vietnamese contact, Sr. Colonel Tran Bien, and his security officer took possession of the evidence. A formal receipt was drawn up and was signed by both Destatte and the Vietnamese officials. Although Paul's name was mentioned on the receipt, he was not allowed to sign the papers and Scott's name was omitted entirely. Paul questioned why.

"It's standard Government procedure to have the names of private citizens either not included or 'redacted' from official reports and documents," replied Destatte.

Paul was angry. He felt that the Government wanted to save face and avoid embarrassment over their failures rather than admit that private citizens were doing a better job at finding missing Americans than they were. He wanted the victim's families to know the real story, which might provide the impetus for others to search for their loved ones. Plus, he wouldn't mind the praise and publicity either.

"Don't black out my name on the report. The families have a right to know what really happened here. I'm going to follow up on this issue and if you don't notify them within a reasonable amount of time, I'll do it for you!" Paul no longer trusted Destatte or the U.S. Government to do the right thing. It seemed like a cover-up and he wasn't going to let that happen.

Paul continued, "When are you going to excavate the crash site? I'd like to be part of the excavation team."

"First we have to make sure the information is valid by having everything thoroughly examined and right now we're not 100 percent sure where the site's located. I have to be honest with you; it's highly unlikely you'd be allowed to join the crew. Excavations are often grueling operations in remote areas; only highly trained professionals are qualified and fit enough to do the work. You have to understand that the people who go out to do these operations are young and healthy and accustomed to living under extremely difficult circumstances in the field ... I'm sorry." Destatte was trying to let him down easy.

Paul fumed silently. He had heard this all before, but as it related to the elder Smiths, not himself.

Destatte understood Paul's feelings. After all, he had gone to considerable lengths to acquire the information and had exposed himself to danger. It was only natural that he would want to receive some recognition for his efforts. But Destatte also felt that Paul was mistaken in his mistrust of the Government and its inability to follow up with the families. He felt confident that ultimately everything would fall into place and Paul would be satisfied with the end results.

For the next day or two, the three men stayed in Saigon. Destatte had additional work, but spent some time with Paul and Scott. He took them to the best pho (soup) shop in Saigon and showed them his favorite bookstores. For Destatte, it was a show of good faith and for Paul and Scott it provided a little respite from the excitement they'd experienced during the last two weeks, before they went on to Laos to look for Smith's remains.

* * *

With the thrill of his discovery rapidly fading, Paul had to focus on the real reason for his trip: to explore the area in Laos where Lewis Smith had been shot down and, if possible, recover his remains. Paul knew from reading the final report that Smith's dog tags were found in Mukdahan, Thailand, by a logger working in the area. He planned to travel to Mukdahan first and then cross the border into Laos. Since he had to go to Thailand anyway, he decided to start his journey in Bangkok at the U.S. Embassy to follow up on whether they had done anything yet about his discovery in Nha Trang.

When he arrived at the Embassy, he asked to speak with someone in the POW/MIA office. Allegedly, Major Cecil Hill was sent to the lobby and invited him in for lunch. Over a cafeteria lunch, Paul questioned Hill about specifics in the final report on Lewis Smith and asked for information about his discovery related to Freight Train 053. As the conversation wore on, Paul noticed a distinct change in Hill. Initially he had been pleasant enough, but soon Hill nervously scanned the cafeteria, clearly uneasy with his civilian guest. At one point, he interrupted Paul and supposedly said, "You know my boss wouldn't be happy if he knew I was talking to you. He's an old player and wants things done according to the 'Government way' of doing things. I don't have any information I can give you about either issue." Paul thanked him for lunch and left, disappointed in what he saw as the Government's unwillingness to let civilians help.

Paul and Scott traveled to northern Thailand to cross the Mekong River into Laos. As he stood on the riverbank, Paul saw the area he planned to explore just one short mile away on the other side. As the two prepared to enter a boat, they were told they couldn't go into Laos without visas. This was something they hadn't anticipated; Paul groaned in frustration. Obtaining visas entailed an eight hour bus ride back to Bangkok, a plane ride to Hanoi; retracing all their steps. Funds were running low, as was their stamina, so they called it quits and returned to Bangkok.

Paul was determined to talk to Hill again and returned to the Embassy. This time Hill didn't let him inside the property. Standing on opposite sides of the gate, the two men exchanged pleasantries, but nothing more. Paul left discouraged and angry. It was Thursday, June 25, and he and Scott were scheduled to fly home on Monday. With only one chance left, Paul returned to the Embassy the next day.

This time Hill allowed Paul inside the gate, but not inside the Embassy. They sat on a bench outside and Paul expressed his concern for the family who had turned over the remains. Would the Vietnamese

Government punish them? After all, it was highly frowned upon to be in possession of such items. Hill assured him that there had been no repercussions. Then Hill allegedly said, "The information you turned over has reached us. I have a report on my desk with your name in it. Frankly, I have to tell you that people here aren't very happy about it. Not happy at all."

"Well, that's just too damn bad isn't it?" Paul retorted. "When I get back to the States, I'm following this case and, if families aren't notified, I plan to contact them myself."

Hill had no comment, but ended the meeting and walked across the courtyard. Paul watched as he disappeared inside the building and then stood for several minutes observing the foot traffic coming and going from the Embassy. He saw hoards of tourists entering the Embassy and thought, "They're letting everyone in but me. They won't even let me past the front gate because I did their job for them and everyone here knows it! What unbelievable bullshit!" Paul stormed off and on Monday, he and Scott flew home.

* * *

Paul returned home to a few unpleasant surprises. First, Betty and Earl were angry that he had not succeeded and demanded their money back, money that would take months to repay. Pat, while interested in his discovery, was running out of patience. While he was away she'd split her time between the flower shop, the greenhouse, and the road; managing employees and completing Paul's truck route, virtually on her own. She was exhausted and slightly resentful. It was not the homecoming he had anticipated.

Unknown to Paul, a forensic team, comprised of both U.S. and Vietnamese members, met in late July to examine the remains he had turned over to Destatte and Sr. Colonel Bien. They determined that the remains were Asian (Mongoloid) and left them in the care of the Vietnamese. The dog tag and the ID card were forwarded to the Central Identification Laboratory in Hawaii (CILHI), the largest forensic anthropology lab in the world, and the site where other evidence pertaining to REFNO 1306 was being collected and examined.

Paul turned his attention to the families of the missing crew members. He remembered that Ronald Stanton, the door gunner, was from Massillon, Ohio, the location nearest him. Since he knew that local groups often supported POW/MIA families, he contacted Massillon's veteran's group and discovered that Ronald's sister, Bettie, had attended several meetings. He struck up a conversation with one of the veterans and pumped him for information. First, he wanted to know how to contact Bettie and then he asked if she had heard anything about her brother recently. The answer to the second question was no. Paul was furious. Just as he had feared, the Government had not followed-up with the families; the task would be up to him.

He swung into action. During the first week of September, he contacted Bettie and as many family members of the crew as he could find. Then he contacted Senator John Kerry's Select Committee on POW/MIA Affairs and the Defense Department to find out more about the case and inform them of his discovery. Two weeks later, he told his story to the Harrisburg TV station (CBS21) while a sister station in Cleveland (WJW Fox 8) broadcast Bettie Stanton in Ohio. The local press was on hand, and soon stories appeared in the *Akron Beacon Journal* in Ohio.

At some point that fall Bettie received Ronald's dog tag, although it was not entirely clear how, or from whom, she received it. The most common story was that she had been too distraught to open any mail from the U.S. Government and numerous certified letters had piled up on her kitchen counter. Apparently, she had signed for the letters, but never had the heart to open them. The letters told of the discovery of her brother's dog tag and asked her what to do with it. Finally, a friend was allowed to open her mail and made the shocking discovery, at which point Bettie requested that the dog tag be sent to her.

Paul's primary purpose in notifying the families, the media, and Governmental agencies was to precipitate some action. He was dissatisfied with the Government's lack of urgency and felt that families and the press could put pressure on them to expedite the excavation of the site and resolve the case. It was a noble idea, but somewhat unrealistic. At that point in time, reports, artifacts, and remains for REFNO 1306 were still coming into CILHI, and the exact coordinates of the crash site were still undetermined.

In July of 1993, Pat and Paul traveled to Massillon to meet Bettie for the first time. The press was in attendance again and Bettie indicated that she felt her brother was still alive. Paul told her he planned to return to Vietnam to run a counter-scam on the Vietnamese family members who had given him the remains. He planned to offer them money (but not deliver), in order to gain access to the crash site. During the visit, Paul also met with the Western Stark County Chapter of the Vietnam Veterans of America, to motivate them to conduct their own searches for MIAs.

Paul's discovery gave the MIA families hope that the case would soon be resolved. But for Paul, there was no closure in sight. He worried about his failure in Laos. He had disappointed both the Smith family and himself. Furthermore, he continued to harbor the idea that the family in Vietnam who had turned over the remains had more information than they were letting on, perhaps about other MIAs, and most certainly about the crash site. He went back to work, feverishly trying to pay off his debt to the Smith family, while keeping his goal in sight: to return to Vietnam as quickly as possible.

CHAPTER 10

True Love

There is only one happiness in life,
To love and be loved.

George Sand

Sandy

I t was a day full of possibilities. The weather was as crisp as a Macintosh apple, the sun shimmered in the brilliant blue sky, and peachy hues of autumn dotted the landscape. Richard pulled his cherry red 1929 Ford out of the garage and honked the horn playfully to attract Sandy's attention. "Let's go for a ride! C'mon, get in!"

Sandy stood on the sidewalk with two-month-old Hannah in her arms and hesitated. The old car wasn't equipped with safety features to accommodate an infant car seat. "I don't feel comfortable putting Hannah in the back of that car; there's no way to strap in her car seat. You go ... we'll just stay home."

"Come on. Don't be such a killjoy. Let's go!"

"No, it's too dangerous." Sandy headed for the front door of the house with the baby, trying to avoid another fight.

"Fine, be that way, you bitch!" Richard yelled as he sped off, jealousy rearing its ugly head once again.

Sandy spent the day playing with Hannah, happy with her decision. Richard found some friends, went out drinking, and eventually ended up in Maryland.

Late in the afternoon the phone rang. "Mrs. Simpson?"

"Yes?"

"Your husband's been in a car accident. He's at Johns Hopkins in Baltimore in critical condition." The police officer from the scene solemnly relayed the bad news.

"What? Are you kidding me?" Sandy clenched her fist around the phone.

"No ma'am. I'm sorry."

She jumped in the car, dropped Hannah off with Blanche, and flew down the highway to Baltimore. Richard was in the intensive care unit with a myriad of tubes and machines attached to his body; barely recognizable as the man who'd left their driveway earlier that morning. His lung was punctured, his ribs were fractured, his spleen was injured, and the skin on his face and arms had been ripped away from his flesh. Sandy was pretty sure he would die. But miraculously Richard pulled through the first day. Then he lived through the second, and the third, and after a week, he showed limited but steady improvement.

When his condition stabilized, Sandy returned home to retrieve Hannah, despite protests from Richard, who begged her not to leave his bedside. For the next few weeks Sandy and Hannah shuttled back and forth between Pennsylvania and Maryland.

Eventually Richard was released from the hospital, but returned a short time later when his spleen ruptured as a result of his earlier injuries. Sandy was at her wit's end. Her life was like a stack of children's building blocks, wobbling unsteadily as each new block of misery was precariously piled on. Even the slightest shift was sure to send her over the edge.

Richard spent nearly four months in and out of hospitals until he finally returned to their home across the street from Blanche and the farm.

The accident and recovery took its toll in more ways than one. During the long months of recuperation no one worked. The bills piled up, as did the frustrations and anger. Sandy and Richard fought constantly and no matter how hard Sandy tried to appease him, nothing was ever right in his eyes. He resumed trucking, another source of friction between the two. Richard insisted that Sandy and Hannah accompany him on a long-haul trip to Florida. Sandy conceded, but after the grueling trip with an infant, she called it quits. It was no longer practical or desirable to continue trucking; the road was simply no place for a baby.

In January, Richard was home between long-haul jobs. Sandy was with Hannah in the kitchen, which was located on the main floor of their split-level home. Richard was downstairs watching television. The phone rang and Sandy answered.

"Hello?"

"Hi sweetie, it's mommy. What are you doing?" Blanche asked.

"I'm just making some bottles for Hannah. Richard's home and we're having a quiet day," Sandy replied.

"Can I ask you for a favor, dear? Would you mind picking up my medicines at the drugstore?" Blanche frequently asked Sandy for help.

"Sure, I'll go in a few minutes." Sandy never refused her mother's requests because now Blanche was fighting cancer. She bundled Hannah in a warm coat and hat and yelled to Richard on her way out the door, "We're going to the drugstore ... be right back!"

When Sandy and Hannah returned, both the house and Richard were fuming; Sandy had forgotten the boiling bottles on the stove and the entire house had filled with black, acrid smoke. His perfect house had been defiled and Richard was furious. Sandy called a friend in the fire restoration business to clean up the mess and they spent the weekend with half-brother, Raymond. But the damage took more than two days to repair, so they flew to Puerto Rico to stay in the house that Sandy and her half-sister, Sandra, jointly owned. When they returned to Pennsylvania, the physical environment was back to normal, but Richard was more volatile than ever.

Richard's anger had increased over time and Donna worried for her friend's safety. On one occasion she even saw Sandy with numerous bruises; bruises that Sandy explained away as a fall down the stairs. Donna wasn't so sure.

* * *

Before Hannah's birth, Angel urged Sandy to travel to Puerto Rico with him to meet the other relatives and connect with her Puerto Rican roots. Sandy agreed to the trip, partly out of curiosity and partly because now that Senter was gone, she no longer felt that spending time with Angel was disrespectful of him. With the bitter disappointment of the failed El Salvador adoption still fresh in her mind, she packed her bags.

Much to her delight, she had a wonderful time. The relatives greeted her with open arms and treated her like royalty. She enjoyed the balmy weather, spicy food, and flamboyant culture of the island and felt relaxed in this place where her dark hair and eyes, were no longer an oddity. For the first time in her life, she settled comfortably into her own olive skin. But then, there was a surprise. While visiting relatives, one of them pulled out a photo album containing pictures of her as a young child.

"Where did you get those?" she demanded.

"Your mother sent them to us," replied Angel's half-sister, Theresa.

"Hazel?" Sandy was taken aback. Why had she done such a thing? It was another unanswered question to add to the long list of puzzles that comprised her baffling and complicated life.

Sandy returned to Puerto Rico a short time later with her sister-in-law, Karen, a trip that proved both uncomfortable and humiliating. Angel was an older man in poor physical health with emphysema and bad teeth. Yet he still fancied himself a young Don Juan and flirted with every pretty girl that crossed his path. He even made a pass at Karen, which completely mortified Sandy.

"Dad! Why in the world did you do that? How could you embarrass me like that? She's my sister-in-law, for God's sake!"

"I don't know ... she's good looking!" Angel grinned sheepishly.

"Stop it! Give it up! You're too old and too sick for young girls. It's disgusting." Sandy thought back to Sandra's comment that Angel would never be a father to her and silently concurred, ashamed of his lewd behavior.

Later in the trip, Angel insisted that Sandy and Sandra take a look at a new housing development on the island. As the two half-sisters admired a cluster of pretty homes, Angel turned to them and said, "See that one over there? I'm buying it for you two."

"Dad, I don't know what to say. Why?" Sandy was in disbelief.

"I have a lot of Pampers to replace, you know." It was Angel's way of expressing his guilt for not providing financial support for Sandy when she was a child.

"What about the boys? Are you buying them a house too?" asked Sandra.

"No, the boys can take care of themselves. This is just for you and Sandy." Angel's philosophy, which he shared freely, was that women were weak and inferior beings, incapable of taking care of themselves; they needed his help.

Sandy and Sandra thanked Angel for his generosity, but when the boys heard the news they were jealous and hurt. Now the tables were turned and it was the boys, not Sandra, who resented and mistrusted Sandy. Accepting the house was a decision Sandy soon lived to regret.

Initially, the boys had embraced Sandy while Sandra had kept her distance. Sandra, who grew up hearing about Sandy and Hazel, hated both of them and had to be won over by Sandy. Her turning point came when the entire family visited Ramona, Angel's wife, who suffered with Alzheimer's.

Ramona didn't seem to remember Sandy. It didn't matter to Sandy; it was confession time. When everyone left the room, she sat alone with Ramona and held her hand. "I'm Sandy, Hazel's daughter. You might not remember, but Hazel had an affair with Angel and I'm their child. I'm so sorry for the pain and hurt and embarrassment I've caused you. I know you've had a hard life with Angel. I'm sure his affair with my mother was devastating and one more blow to suffer. I'm so sorry. My mother's no longer alive, but if she were, she'd apologize too. I just wanted you to know that."

Ramona sat silent and expressionless, perhaps comprehending some
of it or perhaps none at all. For Sandy, it wasn't important. These were
words that needed to be spoken. Sandra, who was secretly listening at the
door, stood quietly with tears streaking her makeup, astounded that
Sandy had the selfless compassion to apologize to her mother even though
she was blameless. It was a turning point in their relationship. Sandra
never again questioned Sandy's motives.

* * *

A week or two after returning home from the hospital with newborn
Hannah Sandy heard the sad news that Mary was not doing well emotionally after relinquishing her baby. Sandy felt terrible but didn't know
what she should do. As the source of the woman's pain, she was clearly
not the person to comfort her. A couple months later Mary called and
requested an opportunity to see Hannah.

Mary and Doug arrived at the Simpson home and spent an hour playing with Hannah while exchanging awkward small talk with Sandy and
Richard. Sandy felt a huge knot tighten in her stomach. She realized that
at any given moment she could lose her daughter forever.

Two or three months later Mary asked to see Hannah again. Sandy
consented, knowing that the possibility of losing her child was becoming
more certain with each subsequent visit. Until the actual adoption papers
were signed, there were no guarantees or certainty. She and Richard had
tried to expedite the court date to finalize the adoption, but things were
moving slowly and their day in court was still months away. Meanwhile,
Sandy couldn't fathom the thought of losing Hannah and used every possible strategy to block it out of her mind.

* * *

Paul

By now Paul was well-known by the circle of veterans who attended
events in the surrounding area. Most admired his courage in returning to
Vietnam and many knew him as the guy who could get in and out of the
country whenever he wanted; a skill set that most vets lacked. They often
looked to him for information or support as they contemplated making
their own journeys back.

One night the phone rang just as Paul sat down for dinner.

"Hello, Paul?"

"Yes?"

"Hi. My name's Robert. I'm a vet too, and I hear you've been back to
Vietnam several times. I'd like you to join my group. I have a bunch of
guys assembled to go back in a couple of months to rescue POWs. I'd like

you to head up one of my rescue teams! Can we talk? Maybe we can meet tomorrow?" The man exuded energy through the phone lines.

"Yes, of course," Paul answered, intrigued. They decided to meet in Allentown the next day. Paul hung up the phone exhilarated at the prospect of this news. If there was a rescue to be made, by God, he was going to be a part of it!

Paul rushed through his flower deliveries to get to the end of the day when he could find out about the POWs. He arrived in Allentown and sat across from Robert in a diner, cup of coffee in hand.

"So what's this about rescuing POWs? Where are they? What's your rescue plan?" Paul didn't waste any time.

"I believe some POWs are being held in a cave in downtown DaNang. We plan to approach the shore by boat and shoot anyone on the beach. Then we'll throw tear gas into the cave, smoke out the captors, rescue the POWs, and leave by boat to a waiting ship, where we'll sail away."

Paul's smile faded. "Have you been to DaNang lately?"

"No," the man admitted.

"Well, you can't walk onto shore or into the city with weapons! And you can't just go around shooting people and using tear gas! The war is over. What are you thinking about?" Paul refrained from continuing with the words "dumb ass."

"No, really I think it's the only way we'll be successful with the rescue. I'm sure we can pull this off!" Robert was convinced of the viability of his plan.

"You're going to end up dead or spend the rest of your life in a Vietnamese jail, period. Your plan is never going to work."

"I've got guys ready, willing, and able to go!"

"Who plans to go with you? Can I see the list?" Paul realized that Robert wasn't rational and worried for the safety of his recruits. He planned to contact each and every one of them. "Let me give them a call so they know how to obtain their visas, okay?" Paul hurriedly copied the list.

"Sure! Are you coming with us?"

"No. You need to re-think your plan."

That night Paul called the other men and explained the situation. They all agreed the plan had serious flaws; no one was willing to risk being jailed or killed in Vietnam. The trip was cancelled. But one man, Guy Van Schaemelhout, desperately wanted to go and asked Paul when he planned to return to Vietnam. It was the excuse Paul needed. He decided to assemble his own group of veterans to go to Vietnam, both to heal their emotional scars and to search for POWs. He eagerly began to plan his next adventure.

* * *

It was a typical workday for Paul. He arose early and spent eight hours on the road completing truck deliveries to floral shops throughout the region. He joked with shop owners along the way, but never lingered long, knowing he had to keep moving in order to finish his run. When the deliveries were done, he returned to downtown Manheim to do more work and see what was happening at the greenhouse. His sister Martha (Marty) was there and they argued for a few minutes. He and Marty didn't always see eye-to-eye and power struggles frequently ensued. Paul shrugged off their latest disagreement and headed home. The lights in the house were dim, with only the glow of the television illuminating the living room.

"Hi! I'm home!" Paul called out to Pat.

"Hi." Pat, who was exhausted, didn't move from her spot on the couch in front of the television.

Paul walked to the kitchen where dinner was prepared but now cold on the stove. Too tired to heat it up, he put some food on a plate, and joined Pat on the couch as he silently ate his dinner, half-focused on the television screen in front of him. Finished, he moved to the kitchen and cleaned up the dishes.

"I'm going to bed, I'm really tired," Paul remarked to Pat.

"Me too."

The television went dead, the lights went out, and the two collapsed into bed, backs facing, with no more words passing between them. Paul fell asleep wondering how he'd break the news to Pat about his next trip.

* * *

Sandy

Sandy was a typical first-time mother—nervous and a little unsure of herself. She worried she wouldn't hear Hannah's cries during the night, she worried she wasn't doing everything by the book, and she worried over Hannah's general health and well-being. But mostly she worried about the possibility of losing her daughter. So even as she settled into her new role as a mother, making the necessary adjustments to her lifestyle and routines, she often felt more like a babysitter than a parent, knowing that at any given moment Hannah could be snatched away, leaving her childless once again.

As time wore on, she relaxed a bit and felt happier than she had ever felt before. Motherhood suited her and she was a natural at it, unlike Hazel who resented parenting and all of its trappings. Sandy's evolution manifested itself outwardly, as she cut her waist-long, dark hair into a short, sassy hairdo, symbolically taking the weight of the world off her shoulders.

But things certainly weren't perfect either. Richard was often angry with her, Angel was not the father she had imagined, and Blanche was battling cancer, setting the stage for more loss and devastation. Blanche's breast cancer, which had been in remission for several years, had returned after Senter's death and her battles over the farm. Sandy juggled her life between Hannah, Mommy Blanche, and Richard, trying to give each the attention they deserved.

***

Paul

Paul finally broke the news to Pat. She accepted it with graceful resignation, while knowing full well, the extra burden of work it would entail. Cognizant of her concerns, Paul reasoned that helping veterans was more important than her workload.

Three veterans signed on for the trip. Guy Van Schaemelhout, who planned to storm the beach at DaNang with Robert, was from New Mexico. The other two, Terry Derr and Charlie Humm, were veterans from Pennsylvania who knew Paul on a limited basis from his POW/MIA activities in the Harrisburg area. Terry wanted to pursue the POW/MIA issue a little further, while Charlie was fulfilling a promise he'd made to himself in 1966 to return to Vietnam someday, regardless of who won the war.

Copying Don Luce, Paul crafted a trip that began in Bangkok and ended in Saigon. Paul, Charlie, and Terry flew from Harrisburg to Detroit, then on to Tokyo. They planned to meet Guy in Tokyo and fly as a group to Bangkok, but they arrived late and missed their connection. Guy flew to Bangkok alone while the others spent the night in Japan. Paul repeatedly tried to call Guy in Bangkok, but he couldn't reach him. He started to panic when they finally arrived in Thailand and Guy was nowhere to be found. The three men dumped their luggage at the hotel and aimlessly walked the streets, searching for him. Before too long, they spotted a man with a dark complexion and a do-rag on his head and all said simultaneously, "That's gotta be Guy!"

Guy spotted the three Americans and rushed over to them.

"Where the hell have you've been?" demanded Paul, both relieved and angry. "I called the hotel several times, but you weren't there!"

"I didn't come all the way to Bangkok to sit in my room!" Guy laughed.

The men spent a couple of days in Thailand and took Paul's suggestion to have some custom clothing made by his tailor in Bangkok. Before too long, an agitated Guy pulled Paul aside and expressed his concern over a personal matter.

"Paul, I don't know what to do. I didn't bring enough of my medications with me and they won't last the entire trip." Guy, it turned out, was on several prescription medications for anxiety and depression, conditions he'd suffered since the war.

Paul stated the obvious. "You won't be able to get any of those drugs here. Maybe you should consider flying home early. Or I suppose you could take a chance and see how you do without the pills, but that's pretty dangerous. Since you have your medicine for most of the trip, why don't you relax for now, and we'll figure it out later. Don't worry." Paul was a calming presence and Guy took his advice.

The group then flew to Hanoi and spent a few days there. Paul took them to war museums and the famed Hanoi Hilton. Curious, they tried to slip in through the front door, but were stopped by security. Paul also looked up Destatte, his contact at the JTF-FA office—the man to whom he had turned over the evidence from Freight Train 053. Paul was disappointed to learn there were no new leads on POWs or MIAs. Finally, they boarded an overnight train and traveled fourteen hours to Hue (pronounced "way"). The ride was long and uncomfortable in their sleeper car but was also an education. As the men talked to Vietnamese civilians and NVA veterans, they were shocked by their kind reception. There seemed to be no bitterness, hatred, or animosity towards the Americans, but rather a feeling that each side had done what was necessary and now it was time to move on from the past.

Supposedly Guy had been stationed near Hue during the war, so visiting the area proved especially meaningful for him. Guy, who was Paul's main concern, had a wonderful time. Having forgotten about his medication worries, he was the life of the party, laughing and joking continuously. After hearing more of his story, Paul cynically thought, "This poor guy doesn't need all that medication. The VA (the U.S. Department of Veterans Affairs) should pay for veterans to return to Vietnam, instead of drugging them up for the rest of their lives!"

In Hue, Paul secured a van with a driver and the men worked their way south to DaNang, with frequent stops along the way. Paul showed them a number of historical sites and introduced them to his Vietnamese friends as Guy recorded the majority of the trip on his camcorder.

For Paul, each trip to Vietnam was personally cathartic, but there were two specific goals for this journey. One was to show the men a good time; the second goal was to meet with the family who had turned over the remains to him back in 1990. He had a nagging feeling that they had additional information. Determined to see them again, he orchestrated the trip so they made a stop in Nha Trang.

Once there, Paul contacted the cyclo driver and asked him to set up a meeting with the English-speaking son from the family. He wanted to get his hands on the maps and photographs the son claimed he possessed during their last meeting. The man agreed, and they planned a dinner meeting at a restaurant in a secluded section of town.

It was dark when Paul and his three companions arrived at the restaurant, located on a small island, accessible only by a foot bridge. The shabby cafe was noisy and filled with people—Vietnamese people. Everyone stared as the four American men entered the restaurant. They were ushered to a table where the young man and several of his friends sat waiting, wearing both smiles and ominous dark glasses on their faces. Everyone was courteous and pleasant. Introductions were made and meals were ordered.

Suddenly the meeting took an ugly turn as the discussion focused on their previous meeting.

"You stole my items and I want them back!" the young man stated loudly.

"I didn't steal them. They belong to the U.S. Government and ultimately to the families of the missing men. You can't have them back," Paul replied. He remained outwardly composed as he worried about the man's demeanor.

"I'm not taking 'no' for an answer. Look, I have more things," the man said displaying a map, pictures, and some written notes to entice him. "Either give me the items back or pay me 10,000 U.S. dollars!" By now, the man was shouting in English and repeating everything rapidly in Vietnamese. Everyone in the restaurant was silent as they listened to the commotion. Some Vietnamese shook their heads in agreement while others edged closer to Paul's table.

Guy, who had his camcorder along, turned it on under the table to record the conversation. One of the Vietnamese men spotted the blinking red light and cursed under his breath.

Paul thought fast, sensing the impending danger. It was fight or flight time. He and his friends could easily overcome the lightweight Vietnamese men at the table, but they couldn't take on the entire restaurant. He also knew that with $6,000 in his pocket (all the money needed for the remainder of the trip), he was in a precarious position. The other three men were also carrying large sums of money, which they had hidden in their pockets and socks.

The food arrived and the men started eating. The Vietnamese man said, "Your meal costs $200; you need to pay now!"

"I'm not paying $200 for four meals!" Paul knew that $200 would cover the tab for virtually everyone in the restaurant and he wasn't about to be scammed.

Choosing flight, he stood up, grabbed his plate, and threw it upside down on the table. "Come on guys, we're out of here! Let's go!" He rushed his companions out of the restaurant where they jumped into waiting cyclos and sped off across the bridge.

Leaving the restaurant behind, it dawned on Paul that perhaps it was the cyclo drivers who had set them up, arranging this meal at a secluded restaurant where they could easily be assaulted. He questioned them about their involvement, but they repeatedly denied any wrongdoing.

Paul had a sick feeling in his stomach as he thought about how the meeting might have ended. He had been naïve to think the young man would turn over additional information or items without asking for payment. His companions experienced both the fear and excitement that he felt, but relaxed once they returned to the hotel, confident that the danger was over. But Paul spent a sleepless night, worried that the Vietnamese men might come after them. Early the next morning, he hustled them out of Nha Trang as he kept a watchful eye out for the cyclo drivers. It had been a mistake to come here and he regretted it but, for the other men, it was an exhilarating adventure they would never forget.

From Nha Trang they traveled south, stopping in Dalat in the Central Highlands for a day or two. It was hard to believe that they had already been in Vietnam for three weeks; time passed so quickly.

When they arrived in Saigon, Paul finally let down his guard. They were closing in on the end of the trip and for the most part, he had accomplished his goal of showing the men a good time, while helping them relive their pasts. They took a side trip to Vung Tau where Charlie had been stationed. Although Charlie was happy to see the area without dodging bullets, he was somewhat let down as he realized it was a different Vietnam than the one he had experienced. Guy was the biggest success story of them all. He no longer seemed to need his medication and was visibly changed from the man who had first entered Vietnam. However, by the end of the trip, he gave Paul pause for concern again.

"I'm really worried about going home," he confided.

"Why? Didn't you have a good time?"

"Yeah, that's the problem. None of my friends will believe I had a good time here. They don't understand why I even came on this trip," he stated.

"That's crazy! Stop associating with those people," advised Paul.

"I can't. They're my friends. I can't just run away from them," rationalized Guy.

"Well, they don't sound like such great friends to me," Paul snapped. He genuinely cared about Guy, and the idea that his friends were unkind to him made Paul mad. He secretly hoped Guy would stand up to his friends when he returned home.

* * *

During one of their last nights in Vietnam, Paul's personality as a prankster and practical joker came alive, much to the delight of his traveling companions. They went to dinner, had a couple of beers, walked to the downtown area, and ended in front of the Opera House. Around 11:00 p.m. the square emptied and the motorcycle girls (a.k.a., prostitutes) arrived. After summing up the Americans, they approached. "You want to party?" asked one girl.

"Sure—how much?" Paul had no intention of engaging the prostitutes, but decided to play along.

"Fifty dollars," the girl was quick to answer.

"Oh," said Paul in a disappointed voice. "I want a $100 girl. I had a $50 girl once and I wasn't happy. I want a $100 girl." The girls looked at each other with confused faces as the men snickered in the background. After a few minutes of back and forth discussion in Vietnamese one of the girls said, "Okay, $100."

"Oh no," said Paul. "You already said you're only worth $50." The girls, insulted and perplexed, rode off in a huff as the men howled with laughter at Paul's antics. More girls showed up, girls who knew enough to say they were $100 girls, but now Paul wanted $200 girls, and so it went until the girls left the men alone. The guys, still chuckling over the evenings' pranks, returned to their hotel with one more story to add to their repertoire.

When Paul returned home, the giggles were over. Pat, overworked and tired, was unhappy about this month-long trip and more than a little concerned about the money he'd spent. Paul's trips were expensive and every dollar spent in Vietnam was money they didn't spend as a couple. Eventually, things went back to normal which, for Paul, meant a marriage of convenience. He loved Pat as one loved a dear friend, but the passion, the romance, and even the close communication between a husband and wife were long gone. Paul yearned for more, much more. He didn't express his feelings, but the one thing he wanted more than anything else in the world was a child.

Charlie and Terry resumed their lives; the unanswered questions or nagging thoughts of Vietnam that had hung in their minds like cobwebs, now resolved. None of the men had much contact after the trip except for Terry and Guy, who had formed a close friendship during their travels. Terry loved Guy's hilarious sense of humor and his passion for his camcorder. Guy sent reels and reels of footage from the trip to Terry, which Terry eventually edited down to a short VHS tape.

But aside from the jokes, Terry was genuinely worried about Guy, who suffered from PTSD and depression and had trouble navigating veteran's organizations to get the assistance he needed. After the trip the two men spoke every week for over a year. At one point, when Terry didn't hear from Guy for over two weeks, he called his home to find out what was wrong. Sadly, he discovered that Guy had committed suicide, leaving a wife and two children behind. He was only forty-two-years-old.

When Paul heard the news, he blamed himself for not doing more to help Guy. Paul looked at Guy as another casualty of war, sending him into a tailspin of anger and frustration that rivaled the fury he had felt during the war.

* * *

Sandy

It was a cold, snowy day in February when the phone broke the silence in Sandy's house.

"Hi Sandy, it's Vicki! How are you? How's Hannah?"

"Hi. I'm fine. Hannah's great, getting bigger by the day. What's up?"

"I was wondering if you could come down to the flower shop next week to help out on Valentine's Day. We'll be swamped and I could really use another pair of hands."

"But I don't know anything about flowers ... I don't think I'd be much help," Sandy confessed.

"You don't have to do any designing. Just put roses in boxes and ring up the sales. You can bring Hannah along to play with Brandon. Please, please?"

"Okay, I guess I can do that."

"Great! Thanks, Sandy, I really appreciate it."

Vicki was a Robinson. Donald and Howard Robinson, Senter's sons, each had five children. One of Donald's sons, Daniel Robinson, was married to Vicki. Although there was bad blood between Sandy and Senter's sons, Daniel had never shared his father's negative feelings toward Sandy; he simply regarded her as his aunt. Daniel and Vicki had helped Sandy after Richard's accident and were in frequent contact with her. Now it was Vicki who needed help, and Sandy was happy to reciprocate.

The next week Sandy arrived at the flower shop as scheduled. Hannah and Vicki's son, Brandon, played and slept in a playpen while Sandy, Vicki, and the other workers frantically filled orders and moved people out of the shop as quickly as possible. In the morning, before the real rush began, a deliveryman showed up.

"Hi, Vicki. I've got a boatload of flowers for you today!" teased Paul.

"Great! We're going to need all of them. Or should I say, we *better* need all of them. Today's the busiest day of the year—I hope sales are good. Bring 'em in," Vicki laughed.

Sandy stopped what she was doing to look at the man. He was large and muscular with huge hands, long hair, and a bushy beard that flowed from a pleasant, smiling face. "He looks like a mountain man; he's handsome," she thought.

Similarly, Paul noticed Sandy's short dark hair and olive complexion and thought, "I haven't seen her before. What a nice smile." Paul took a second to move to the playpen where he made cooing noises at the two babies and tickled them under their chins. Then he returned to his truck and unloaded the flowers. Within thirty minutes he moved on to his next shop. It was a crazy day and he had to keep a steady pace in order to fit in everyone.

Two weeks later, Vicki called Sandy again.

"Sandy, I could use some permanent help at the shop. Can you come in and help me out? I can't pay you much, but I'll teach you floral design and Hannah can play with Brandon while we work. What do you say?"

"As long as I can bring Hannah, I'll do it." She and Richard needed the extra money, and bringing Hannah along was a necessity.

"Great! Come on Monday and we'll get started. See you at 9:00!" Vicki was thrilled to have Sandy's help and Sandy was happy to be employed by her friend.

On Monday Paul stopped by again. Sandy stared at him, thought he looked vaguely familiar, but couldn't place where she had seen him before. Although he had the same physique as the bearded man she had seen on Valentine's Day, this man wore a crew cut and was clean shaven.

"Oh my God! What happened to you?" Vicki asked dramatically.

"I thought I'd clean up a little bit so I'd be more presentable and maybe even look a little younger. It's always good to look younger, right?" Paul joked.

"I guess, but you don't look like the same guy!" Vicki teased. "Sandy, this is Paul. Go out to the truck with him and pick out some flowers."

Sandy obediently followed Paul to the truck but, when she saw the large assortment of flowers, she didn't have a clue what to do. "What does Vicki usually buy?" she asked Paul timidly.

"She doesn't buy all that much," Paul said ruefully.

Sandy thought, "Well, golly day, that's not very helpful."

"I don't even know what this stuff is. Could you tell me the names of the flowers and help me pick out some things?"

"Sure." Paul patiently went through the flowers one-by-one. He named them, described them, and selected the ones he thought would meet Vicki's approval. "These should work, but let's make sure she wants them before I leave."

Vicki signed off on the flowers and Paul thought, as he left in his truck, "I need to stop by Vicki's more often!"

As soon as he left, Vicki started in on Sandy. "Did you see the way he looked at you? He was checking you out!"

"Oh please," Sandy shrugged, secretly hoping it was true.

The next time Paul came to Vicki's shop, Sandy wasn't there. Vicki said to Paul, "You know, I think Sandy has a little crush on you! She asked about you and mentioned your name several times!"

Paul's face reddened and he didn't respond, but Vicki noticed that in the weeks that followed his trips to the shop became a little more frequent.

On the next visit Vicki sent Sandy out to the truck by herself while Paul stayed in the shop and talked to her. Vicki motioned to the playpen where Hannah and Brandon played. "That's Sandy's little girl, Hannah."

"Really?" Paul's interest was piqued.

"Yes, she's adopted."

"Adopted? That's interesting." Paul was curious. "I better go out to the truck and help her. She doesn't know all the flowers yet."

Inside the truck Paul asked Sandy about Hannah. Sandy answered his questions and confessed that she was terribly unhappy in her marriage. Paul confided in Sandy that similarly, he had considered his marriage over some time ago. By the end of their conversation, Paul boldly asked Sandy an unusual question: "Do you date?"

"No I don't date! I'm still with Richard and I have a baby. I don't date."

"Well, would you like to come out to eat sometime?"

"I don't know." Sandy looked down at the floor, embarrassed.

"You do eat right?" Paul joked.

Sandy laughed, the tension broken. "Yes, I eat! I'd have to bring the baby though."

"Of course, I want you to bring her. What are you doing Sunday? Would you like to go for a drive down to Philly with me? I have to take a load of flowers down. You and Hannah could ride along and we could get something to eat along the way. I'll pick you up here and bring you back to the flower shop."

"Yeah, that would be nice," she said softly.

* * *

Sandy and Paul

Sunday was a warm, sunny day with a magnificent blue sky. Paul felt a happiness he hadn't felt for years. He realized as he chatted with Sandy and played with Hannah that he was falling in love with both of them. The feeling was like airing out a stuffy house after a long, hard winter. Suddenly everything felt new and fresh and alive. The conversation and laughter flowed easily and Paul felt an immediate connection to Sandy, which only highlighted his strained relationship with Pat.

The three stopped for breakfast and Paul was amused as Hannah ate his pancakes in addition to her own hearty meal. They delivered the flowers and stopped for ice cream on the return trip home. Paul was reluctant to let the day end. "It's so beautiful today. Would you like to go to the park for a little while?"

"Sure, that'd be nice. I can put Hannah in the stroller."

The three drove to Elk Neck State Park where they took a walk and enjoyed the balmy weather. Sandy watched Paul fawn over Hannah, marveling at how kind and gentle he was to her, a sharp contrast to Richard's impatience and jealousy. Hannah became fussy at one point and needed a diaper change. As Sandy reached into her bag for supplies, Paul stopped her.

"Let me change her diaper."

"Really? You want to change a dirty diaper? Why?"

"I've never done it before and I'd really like to try."

"Okay," Sandy was surprised by his request. She handed over the supplies and watched as Paul accomplished the task slowly, but efficiently.

The discussion naturally turned to children and Paul confessed that he had always wanted children, but it had never worked out in his current situation.

"How long have you been married?" Sandy inquired casually.

"Twenty-seven years," Paul stated, matter-of-factly.

Sandy's mouth dropped open and no words came out. She thought to herself, "Sandy, this is ridiculous! You've really done it this time; falling in love with a guy who's been married for twenty-seven years. He'll never leave his wife, this will never work."

Paul, unaware of her change in mood, walked over to a little area where pebbles were scattered on the ground. He picked one up and placed it in his pocket, making a point to look into Sandy's big brown eyes. "I'm going to keep this in my pocket and every time I touch it, I'll remember how special today was." Sandy picked up a pebble, too, and dropped it into her pocket as tears stung the corners of her eyes.

* * *

Their relationship heated up quickly. Paul called the flower shop constantly and talked to Sandy as she worked. He changed his route so that Vicki's shop was the last stop of the day. Vicki, intent on enabling the affair, gave them their space, often leaving the shop early so the two could sit and talk. Their phone conversations continued during Paul's ninety-minute ride home to Manheim. By necessity, the couple limited their contact to the flower shop.

One day, aware that Paul would make the last stop of the day at her shop, Vicki devised a plan. "Sandy, I'm going home early tonight and I'm taking the kids with me."

"What do you mean you're taking the kids with you?"

"I'll take Hannah to my house and feed her dinner with Brandon so you and Paul can have some time together," she winked, a knowing glint in her eye.

"Are you sure? Thanks Vicki!" Later, she and Paul took advantage of the child-free evening and unleashed their pent-up passion in Robinson's Flowers and Gifts. Going forward, they carefully carved out time to talk and, on rare occasions, stole more intimate moments together. Their spouses, Pat and Richard, were none the wiser.

While Richard was on the road Sandy hatched an escape plan and moved a few valuable possessions to Blanche's home across the street. She waited patiently for the court date. On May 30, 1994, she and Richard officially adopted Hannah. One week later, she left him. Richard was away on a long-haul trip when Sandy methodically packed her remaining belongings, wrote a Dear John letter, and left the pristine house for the last time.

She and Hannah arrived at Blanche's house to find Aunt Ruth visiting. Sandy asked Aunt Ruth, known as Nanny, if she could stay at her house for awhile. Nanny agreed and Blanche promised to keep quiet, should Richard come searching for her.

Richard returned home and was both furious and desperate as he looked all over town for his family. Sandy called Vicki to inquire about Richard and Vicki was irate. "I can't believe you did it this way! He's a mess. He's calling everyone trying to find you. This isn't right. You should at least call him and let him know that you and Hannah are okay. The man's going to kill himself!"

Sandy appeased Vicki but didn't call Richard. She knew better than anyone that he was fine despite his theatrical performance. She left Nanny's house and stayed with Vicki and Daniel for a brief period during which Vicki convinced her to face her husband in person. Sandy rehearsed her speech in advance.

"Richard, you can take the house and everything in it. It was never really my house anyway; it was yours. I never wanted a perfect house, but you did, so take it. All I want is Hannah."

"Fine," Richard stormed, "but I don't want you living over at that farm. That pigsty isn't fit for anyone to live in!"

Sandy agreed to Richard's terms. She wouldn't live with Blanche even though she knew she should because Blanche was becoming sicker by the day and clearly needed her help. However, Sandy feared that if she went against Richard's wishes he would take Hannah away from her. She lived with Vicki and Daniel just long enough to find her own apartment, carefully avoiding Richard's request for her new address. By the time he found her and showed up at her apartment, he already had a girlfriend.

* * *

Paul

Paul's little brother, Dave, had sensed Paul's unhappiness for awhile but had simply attributed it to his obsession with Vietnam. So, for Dave, it came as a total shock when Paul took him aside to share his dilemma over how to leave Pat. The brothers sat in Paul's truck outside Dave's house as Paul poured out his heart and told his brother about his love for Sandy and Hannah and his desire to leave his wife.

Dave was angry, and blamed Sandy for stealing his brother away from the sister-in-law that he loved. But, clearly, Paul was in pain so he tried not to judge him too harshly. However, things seemed pretty clear-cut. If you were already seeing someone else, you obviously didn't want to be with your wife. For Paul, it wasn't that simple and the ambivalence was ripping him apart. There was only one thing to do: go to Vietnam to clear his head. He and Terry Derr packed up one more time to search for POWs.

It was June when the two men left for Asia. For Paul, the trip was an escape from his problems and for Terry it was a chance to continue the adventures of the previous trip. However, this journey proved uneventful; it provided no opportunities to find POWs or MIAs and, with Guy gone, it was downright boring. Paul and Terry shared a room, which proved awkward when Sandy called unexpectedly one night. As Terry questioned Paul about the mysterious caller, Paul confessed, reminding him that although he was running from the truth, there was no escaping it.

On the flight home Paul flew standby into Detroit, ending up with a one day layover in Michigan. He called Sandy and asked her to join him. She took him up on the offer and boarded a plane with Hannah. They spent a luxurious twenty-four hours together, enjoying each others' company without looking over their shoulders. But, when it was time to leave, Paul flew to Harrisburg and Sandy and Hannah flew to Philly. It was back to hiding.

* * *

It was summer and the height of wedding season. So, when the phone rang yet one more time that morning, Pat thought nothing of it except to speculate about which frantic bride was calling this time. She expected to hear an inquiry about wedding flowers but, instead, was asked an unthinkable question: "Do you know that your husband is having an affair?"

Stunned, she was unable to speak. It was too late anyway; the line went dead. Pat's knees were weak, her face pale, as she rushed out of the shop. She paused only long enough to call out to a worker that she was leaving for an emergency.

She drove home, frantic to reach Paul. She dialed and dialed and dialed his number, becoming more agitated with each attempt, mouthing to herself, "Pick up your fucking phone!" When he finally answered, the words tumbled out of her. She expected to hear Paul crack a joke and say, "That's ridiculous!" but instead there was a long pause, followed by his somber voice responding: "I'll be right home."

CHAPTER 11

New Beginnings

What we call the beginning is often the end.
And to make an end is to make a beginning.
The end is where we start from.

T.S. Eliot

The intricate charade unraveled. When Pat confronted Paul about the mysterious phone call, he admitted the truth, packed a small suitcase, and moved out of the house. She was devastated. Blindsided in the relationship, she was unaware of the depths of his unhappiness. After the initial shock wore off, she became angry. The news was a punch to the gut, but she wasn't going down without a fight. Surely their marriage could be saved.

Paul left the house and drove straight to Sandy's apartment to tell her the news. Sandy grew apprehensive. Who was this caller, and why would she betray their secret? Did she need to fear for her safety? The couple, guilty and remorseful, decided that for the immediate future, they should lie low.

Sandy felt terrible as she reflected on her actions. Was she no better than Hazel with her numerous love affairs and tragic consequences? Just as Hazel never meant to cause Ramona pain, Sandy never intended to cause Pat's heartache. But the truth of the matter was that, when you had an affair, someone was bound to get hurt. Sandy had to live with that fact.

Pat sought individual counseling, hoping that some intervention might repair the damage. Paul went to counseling too, but more for triage than to salvage the marriage which he already deemed too far gone. He went to his Uncle Jim, the kindly Lutheran minister, who became his confidante and advisor in the months to come.

Sandy and Paul were torn with ambivalence. They were in love, but knew their actions were morally lacking. They struggled with their consciences, but couldn't resist the urge to see each other. As the months wore on, their situation became more status quo and they continued their affair, now liberated from the burden of discovery.

Despite her love for Paul, Sandy had a secret reservation about him that had nothing to do with Pat—but everything to do with Vietnam. Paul talked incessantly about his love for the country and its people and his burning desire to return. Sandy felt that perhaps there was more to him than met the eye. She feared he had another family in Vietnam that necessitated his frequent trips abroad.

But Paul wasn't going anywhere for the foreseeable future. It was autumn of 1994 and there was an overwhelming amount of work at the greenhouse. His pocketbook had suffered from his previous trips; it was time to hone his efforts and make as much money as possible. Aside from his work, he spent every waking moment with Sandy and Hannah. He drove fifty miles down to Nottingham each evening, shared dinner with them, put Hannah to bed, and spent time with Sandy, before returning to the greenhouse each night. It was exhausting but blissful.

Proud of his new family, Paul introduced Sandy and Hannah to his siblings. These first visits were awkward and tension-filled exchanges, as family members sought to find out more about this interloper whom they felt could never replace Pat. For Sandy, the encounters reinforced her feelings of inadequacy and her sense of not belonging. She had never been a Campbell or a Robinson, and it was becoming clear that she wouldn't be accepted into the Pinkerton clan either. Paul had good intentions in arranging these gatherings, but the end results left him disappointed and often angry.

Meanwhile, Pat searched for ways to get Paul back so they could work on their marriage. She begged him to come to a counseling session with her therapist. After repeated requests, he finally caved in to the pressure.

The therapist had conducted several sessions alone with Pat, so she went straight to what she perceived to be the crux of the matter.

"Pat tells me that you go to Vietnam frequently. Do you think you can stop doing this little POW thing of yours?"

"No I can't. It's very important to me." Paul felt his blood pressure rising.

"Pat doesn't want to go to Vietnam, and it sounds like you're not willing to give up these trips. How about a compromise? Maybe you can communicate by phone and mail while you're out of the country and still maintain your marriage. How does that sound?"

Paul cringed. The therapist wanted them to be pen pals?

"No," Paul replied, "I don't think that's fair to either one of us. I want to be with someone who shares my views on life. Pat and I don't want the same things anymore."

"Well, you think about it and we'll see what happens," the therapist soothed.

Pat was quiet during the session as she anxiously listened to Paul's answers and watched his facial expressions and body language. The next day when they spoke, she definitively knew the outcome as Paul angrily expressed his feelings about the therapist and their session together.

"I don't like her or her suggestions. I'm not going back to see her again," Paul snapped, still feeling hurt over the therapist's demeaning assessment of his trips to Vietnam.

"Well ... okay then." Pat resigned herself to the sad truth that their marriage was over. Her husband had fallen in love with someone else and there was no competing with this woman and her daughter. Perhaps it was time to move on.

* * *

It was December of 1994 and changes were coming. Sandy's divorce from Richard was finally official, putting to bed the final chapter in that book of misery. She still saw him because of his relationship with Hannah, but no longer had to endure his anger or his need for perfection.

Although Sandy relied upon Paul for love and emotional support, she was, in reality, a struggling, single mother solely responsible for herself and Hannah. Mentally and physically she was exhausted from the events of the past two years. Mommy Blanche was becoming sicker by the day and it was clear that the cancer cells, not Blanche, would ultimately prevail. Sandy was constantly torn between her obligations to her mother and her daughter but, in the end, decided it was Hannah who needed her more.

Doctors told Sandy that Blanche had only a short time to live. Reluctantly, she placed her mother into a nursing home with help from her longtime friend, Donna Culberson, who worked in an elder care facility. Together they secured a pleasant room for Blanche and filled out all the requisite paperwork.

The nursing home was close to Sandy's apartment, which allowed her to see Blanche every day. However, the visits weren't enough in her mother's eyes and her numerous comments only added to Sandy's guilt. Blanche felt justified in complaining; this wasn't how dying parents were treated back home in Tennessee. Like Senter, she expected to live out her days in the farmhouse with her family gathered around her. The only problem was that Sandy was essentially her only family, and Sandy didn't have the time, stamina, or emotional fortitude to devote to Blanche full-time. She was at her breaking point on a number of different levels.

Blanche reprimanded her daily: "Why did you put me in a place like this? Why are you treating me this way? You didn't treat Daddy this way. Why don't you take care of me? Back home, we took care of our parents. I don't understand why you can't take care of me." Blanche went on and on. Sandy felt terrible, but decided there was nothing more she could do.

Blanche didn't die as quickly as the doctors predicted, but Ramona, Angel's wife, did. Ramona, plagued by Alzheimer's, died on Christmas Day, a reminder to Sandy of Hazel's death years earlier, on the same exact day.

* * *

Prior to Christmas, Sandy spent a day alone with Hannah, taking a break from her busy holiday preparations. Hannah was sound asleep as Sandy flipped through TV channels looking for some entertainment. An old movie, *It's a Wonderful Life,* caught her attention and she settled in to watch. As the story unfolded, Sandy identified with George Bailey. She wondered why she had been born and thought, "Yes, the world would be a better place without me."

She didn't fit in anywhere. She had spent much of her life unloved and unwanted and now she was disappointing her own dying mother too. Sandy, like George, had contemplated suicide more than once. Not that she'd ever acted on her desperation, but suicide was never completely out of the realm of possibilities during those dark days following the deaths of Hazel and Senter, after the botched adoption proceedings, and during the times when Richard had mistreated her.

Tears splashed freely down Sandy's face as the movie progressed, the pile of used tissues collecting at her feet like multiplying rabbits. By the time the movie ended it suddenly dawned on her that her purpose in life was to be a mother. She was put on this earth to be Hannah's mother—it was crystal clear why she had been born! She felt almost giddy with the revelation and thought perhaps her life's mission was not only to be a good mother for Hannah, but perhaps other children as well.

* * *

Paul loved and respected Uncle Jim, the gentle man who had spent so much time with him as a youth, but on this particular occasion he strongly disagreed with him. When Paul told Jim about his upcoming trip to Vietnam with Sandy, Jim felt the trip wasn't a good idea. The divorce wasn't final and Jim believed that taking a girlfriend on a trip might complicate divorce proceedings. Paul argued with him and ultimately decided to take Sandy to Asia, with or without Jim's blessing.

Paul's trip to Vietnam had been set in motion a few months earlier. At one of the POW meetings he'd attended, he'd met a man who was a member of the Special Forces in Vietnam. The man was now a farmer in southern Lancaster County, and had organized a group of farmers to work out a milk deal with the Vietnamese. The plan was to sell powdered milk in Vietnam, use the profits to buy cheap Vietnamese goods, and then sell the goods in the States for a profit. The farmers had previously struck a similar deal with the Soviets and wanted to expand the business model to other countries. When the farmers approached Paul with their scheme, he agreed to negotiate with the Vietnamese, if the farmers paid airfare and lodging for himself and Sandy. A deal was made and a trip to Vietnam was scheduled for August of 1995.

Sandy was excited about the trip, but still had lingering doubts about Paul. Although chances were slim he had another family abroad, she still considered that a possibility. She also had concerns about how she and Hannah would fare as international travelers. Hannah was barely a toddler and they were traveling to a third world country. But she had little time to dwell on her fears, because Blanche suddenly took a turn for the worse.

As April of 1995 arrived, it was clear that Blanche was dying and Sandy spent every waking moment at her bedside. Blanche died on April 11, her long battle with cancer over. Sandy felt more alone than she had ever felt in her adult life. This was it. Blanche had been her last real connection to her childhood. She was the loving mother who had raised and nurtured her, and now she was gone.

In robot-like devotion Sandy made all the funeral arrangements, including picking out a headstone and designing the floral arrangements. The days that followed were tear-stained blurs of pain and sorrow, that even Paul couldn't ease, mixed with nagging guilt over denying Mommy Blanche her final request to stay at home. And, although Sandy still had Angel, she felt that for all intents and purposes, she was now an orphan.

* * *

Despite Sandy's grief, the trip to Vietnam was just four months away and eventually she had to prepare for it. Around the same time, a Connecticut man, John Steele, was also gearing up for a trip to Vietnam. He and his wife, Jane, were adopting a Vietnamese child. John planned to travel solo; Jane would stay behind to care for their son. During this trip, Paul and Sandy would eventually cross paths with John Steele. For John, it would be a random encounter with friendly and interesting Americans, while for Sandy and Paul this chance meeting would alter the course of their lives.

When Mary Steele experienced a difficult pregnancy and childbirth, and subsequent problems, doctors advised her and her husband, John, to settle for one child and stop pressing their luck. But that advice didn't sit well with this Connecticut couple, who had their hearts set on two children. So, as their biological son grew older, they opened themselves up to the possibility of adoption. Through the advice of a neighbor they checked out a local adoption agency, but for various reasons, didn't engage their services. A short time later they heard of another adoption agency through a different friend. This agency was Lutheran Social Services (LSS) of New England.

By sheer coincidence, when the Steeles called the agency, Elizabeth (Liz) Kendrick, who had joined LSS around 1990 as their Coordinator of International Adoption, was trying to place a Vietnamese child, who had come to the agency's attention in a rather circuitous manner. Liz had received a call from an American man, trying to help a Vietnamese lawyer in Ho Chi Minh City, out of a strange predicament.

Apparently, the Vietnamese lawyer and businessman, who had lived and studied in Connecticut, had been trying to help an American female friend adopt a Vietnamese child. He'd located an abandoned child in Vietnam who was available for adoption and he was named the child's temporary guardian until the adoption took place. But then, shortly after he was appointed the child's guardian, the woman supposedly changed her mind, and switched to a more secure and established adoption program in China. The Vietnamese lawyer was left with a baby in hand, but no adoptive parent. Panicked, he placed a call to another American friend to find out what he should do. In turn, this American friend sought the advice of LSS of New England.

The lawyer, who had no real interest in facilitating this particular adoption, or subsequent adoptions, enlisted the help of his legal assistant, a young woman known as Miss Kim. With his guidance, she would be able to carry out the steps necessary to successfully facilitate the adoption. Miss Kim was a highly motivated, single woman in her twenties who was eager for the additional job responsibilities and more than capable of executing them.

However, Vietnamese adoption was in its infancy in the early 1990s with only a few adoptive parents and a handful of adoption agencies completing adoptions. Therefore, it was with a huge leap of faith on both sides that the Steele family accepted the referral of the Vietnamese child, and Lutheran Social Services of New England facilitated their first Vietnamese adoption, with Miss Kim's help.

The paperwork for the Steele's adoption took a mere three months to complete. In August of 1995 John Steele flew to the other side of the world to adopt his baby boy, who was now nearly two and living in foster care. His wife, Jane, remained at home with the couple's seven-year-old son.

Upon his arrival in Vietnam, John was greeted by Miss Kim, a beautiful, slender Vietnamese woman with long, jet-black hair. John, who was not a world traveler, had tried to educate himself about Vietnam prior to the trip, but quickly discovered that reading and living are two vastly different experiences. None of his reading materials had adequately prepared him for the abject poverty or cultural differences that he encountered. Miss Kim proved to be invaluable, as did her employer's business acquaintance, Mr. Michael, a Chinese-American man from Phoenix who was staying in the same hotel as John. The three spent countless hours together, sightseeing, conversing, and dining, while Miss Kim walked John step-by-step through the adoption process.

The adoption took three weeks to complete. During the first week John traveled to the foster home every day for short visits with his son, whom he and Jane had renamed Alex. The second week, the foster family delivered baby Alex to his hotel so he could spend more time with him. During the third week, he spent full days and nights with his son as they began to bond with one another.

For the most part, the trip went smoothly, but it wasn't without its pitfalls either. The baby, at twenty-one months, was fearful of John and let his feelings be known through occasional loud outbursts. An active little toddler, Alex, had to be constantly and diligently watched. John, who was unaccustomed to the tropical heat, suffered heat stroke at the zoo. And, like most travelers in Vietnam, he ended up with a severe case of diarrhea that lasted for several days. The end of the trip was the most difficult, however. With Miss Kim's work completed, John was on his own to navigate a day and night in Bangkok to complete the adoption process. This included a medical exam for the baby and an Embassy visit for himself. Then he had to make the long journey home with an unhappy baby who wasn't yet comfortable with this strange man who had plucked him out of his homeland.

* * *

In the late 1980s Pat moved her flower shop from the greenhouse property to a better location in Manheim, to capitalize on foot traffic. Paul transformed what had been Pat's old flower shop into his new home and that was where he had been living since the fateful day of the mysterious phone call. Following their disappointing therapy session, he and Pat saw each other infrequently, and then, only when necessary for business.

Paul eventually planned to marry Sandy and adopt Hannah, but first he needed to put the past behind him. The initial step in that process was to start divorce proceedings. He went to the flower shop and formally told Pat he wanted a divorce.

Fuming, she replied, "If you want it, you go get it!" Still angry and hurt, she felt that it was Paul, not she, who had ended their marriage and therefore, it was his responsibility to take the necessary steps to make the dissolution of their marriage official.

Paul went to an expensive divorce lawyer in Lancaster and quickly discovered that ending a marriage was a costly proposition. Given his upcoming trip to Vietnam, he didn't want to spend so much money so he returned to the shop, handed Pat the paperwork, and asked her to finish what he had started. She was infuriated, but her anger was the impetus she needed. As soon as he left the building, she picked up the phone and dialed another attorney.

Paul, against his uncle's wishes and perhaps even his own better judgment, took Sandy and Hannah to Vietnam with him in August of 1995. Sandy, although still grieving Blanche, anticipated the trip as an adventure and a much-needed diversion from the drama of the past few months.

Pat, unaware of the trip, was once again caught off guard. A month after contacting her lawyer, a draft of the divorce decree was ready so she went to the greenhouse to give the papers to Paul for his approval. She walked in and saw Paul's sister, Marty, busy at work.

"Hi, Mart, where's Paul?"

"What do you mean, where's Paul?" Martha asked, dumbfounded.

"Well, just that—is he out on the road or what?" she asked, annoyed.

"He went to Vietnam with Sandy." The news fell from her mouth like a rock hitting pavement. Martha flushed red; she was embarrassed for Pat and angry with her brother.

"What? I don't believe it!" Pat stormed. It was the final straw. After a few minutes of commiserating with Martha, who shared her disapproval, she went home, stuffed the remainder of his belongings in suitcases, returned to his little house on the greenhouse property, and dumped them inside the front door. Truly, their marriage was over.

* * *

Paul, Sandy, and Hannah flew in coach from Philadelphia to Los Angeles and Los Angeles to Bangkok. The twenty-plus hours in flight provided plenty of time to talk. Paul asked Sandy about her expectations of the trip and shared his own ideas about the places he wanted to show her. Hannah, at nearly two, was an easy baby who spent most of the flight sleeping, eating, and playing, giving them ample opportunity to plan an agenda.

Paul had become so comfortable going in and out of Thailand that he hadn't bothered with hotel reservations, but he quickly realized they needed lodging as soon as they arrived in Bangkok. Although the milk farmers were footing the bill, the budget was lean so they ended up at a dumpy little place on Sukhumvit Road in the heart of Bangkok, oddly named the Miami Hotel. He had stayed there, years earlier, with his group of veterans. However, Sandy didn't care about her meager surroundings as long as she was in Paul's company.

In Bangkok they went sightseeing and shopping and, after three short days, they flew on to Vietnam. When they arrived in Saigon, Sandy wondered why she had agreed to the trip. The airport was a shack and the plane landed in the middle of the tarmac. As she descended the steps holding Hannah, the overwhelming heat and stench of Vietnam hit her squarely in the face. Moving through the airport proved to be an impossible task. Throngs of noisy Vietnamese people pushed and shoved and encroached upon them as they made their way to a taxi.

Sandy breathed a sigh of relief when they finally got in the taxi, only to look down and see the road whizzing by through a huge hole in the floor. Paul watched her reactions carefully and smiled to himself as he recognized both her shock and curiosity at this strange new land. He had visited here so often that little surprised him now, but still, it was nice to see Vietnam through fresh eyes.

Paul crafted the trip to include some of his favorite spots as he moved from Saigon to Hanoi and back. As a representative for the Pennsylvania farmers, his primary focus was to talk to people with whom he might forge a milk deal. Paul found that Hannah was his calling card. Sweet little Hannah, with her ivory skin, curly blond hair, and cherubic appearance was doll-like to the Vietnamese and they were captivated by her. As Paul approached various groups the workers came out, scooped her up, and took her away to play. Paul heard her giggling in delight in the background as the men invited him in to talk business.

Unfortunately, the trade embargo placed on Vietnam after the War had not yet been lifted, so Paul found it difficult to negotiate any deals, even with Hannah's help. Furthermore, the Vietnamese Government regulated the milk industry; all milk in Vietnam went through VinaMilk, the Government-owned milk provider. Paul continued to negotiate, but he soon found his efforts futile.

Sandy found Paul to be a wonderful traveling companion. He was eager to please her and took Hannah's schedules and limitations into consideration when planning their activities. Sandy was surprised to find a man who was more concerned with her needs instead of his own. It was the first time in any of her relationships that she had been given priority and she reveled in the attention and consideration she received from him.

But Paul's considerate nature wasn't the only thing that struck her. Everywhere she looked there were children—dirty, filthy, street children—

who seemed to have no home or parents. Sandy commented more than once that she wanted to pick them all up and give them a decent meal and a bath. How sad it was that no one seemed to care about these ragged, yet beautiful little waifs. Sandy became preoccupied with them, first hounding Paul for information, and then starting a dialogue about adoption.

One day, when the three were in a taxi, the adoption discussion started again. The driver, who knew English, turned to Sandy and asked, "Would you like to visit an orphanage?" She couldn't believe her good fortune.

The driver traveled out into the country and soon they were on dirt roads, in the middle of nowhere. Paul had a sense of dread as they drove farther out into the wilderness until suddenly, they arrived. Two Catholic nuns greeted them at the door and brought them inside to what proved to be a house of horrors. Some of the babies were lying naked on the floor and a few had unusually small heads, a condition known as microcephaly. When a baby defecated, a garden hose was brought out and the surrounding area and babies were crudely hosed down.

Sandy overlooked the filth and held baby after baby in an effort to provide some measure of comfort for these neglected souls. Paul questioned the Sisters about adoption, but the nuns refused to answer, clearly in fear of their orphanage director who hovered over them. He didn't understand English and felt threatened by this American couple. When Paul took his camera out to record the event, the director kicked them out. Apparently, he assumed that Paul was documenting the deplorable conditions to make him look bad or to report him to the authorities.

They left the orphanage, but the images continued to haunt them. On the trip back to Hanoi Sandy announced that she planned to adopt a Vietnamese child. Paul wasn't surprised with her proclamation and suggested they go to the American Embassy in Hanoi to research adoption procedures. After all, they were here, why not investigate?

At the Embassy, Paul took a chance and asked for Scot Marciel, the man whom he had met at the State Department when he tried to get the Smith family into Laos. Paul was told that Scot was out to lunch but would return within the hour. Paul and Sandy ate lunch nearby and returned to the Embassy doorstep exactly one hour later, anxious to meet with Marciel.

The guard instructed Paul and Sandy to wait outside the building, which infuriated Paul. During his many trips to Vietnam he had frequented other embassies and talked to officials about the POW/MIA issue and how they, as our allies, dealt with the situation. Both the British and Australian Embassies had invited him in, provided him with refreshments, and treated him cordially. Yet here, at his own American Embassy, he was banished to the street. He waited on the sidewalk in the heat until he saw

Scot enter the building with a group of people.

"I just saw Mr. Marciel come in. Could you please tell him I'm here and that I'd like to talk to him?" Paul said to the guard.

"What's your name again?" the guard asked dismissively. After a brief exchange, the guard told the three to sit in the lobby and within a few minutes Scot arrived.

"I can't let you in. What do you want?" Scot asked.

"We're thinking about doing an adoption in Vietnam and we don't know the procedures. Do you have any information? Can you tell us what to do?"

"We have a big problem down in Saigon today. I don't have time to deal with this kind of stuff. I'm sorry, but I can't help you. I'm really busy." Scot, a political-economic officer at the Embassy at the time, was already on his feet walking away as Paul opened his mouth to respond.

Paul turned to Sandy with cynicism, "That was really helpful wasn't it? We'll have to find another way."

* * *

Sandy was in Vietnam during the same time as John Steele and like him, her first trip to Vietnam was also proving to be less than ideal. Paul had wisely advised her to bring her own set of silverware to avoid the filthy chopsticks offered by restaurants and street vendors, but even with the best of precautions, she became quite ill and spent a few days retching over a toilet bowl. Paul was sick too. As they took turns vomiting, Sandy said to him with sheer disgust, "Why do you come here? We're sick as dogs and this isn't any fun at all."

"Oh, I get sick every trip. It's part of the Vietnamese experience!" Paul joked, half seriously. He had, in fact, become sick on nearly every journey, but had grown accustomed to it over the years.

While they were still in Hanoi Hannah celebrated her second birthday. They went to a nearby bakery and purchased a teddy bear cake, a terrible tasting concoction that bore little resemblance to pastry. As they walked back, Hannah saw some children on a side street and ran over to play with them. Before Sandy could catch her, she fell into a gutter filled with raw sewage. Paul and Sandy grabbed for the baby wipes and furiously cleaned her hands, panicked because she was a thumb-sucker. They raced back to the hotel and bathed her top to bottom, while they held her fingers out of her mouth. It was a close call!

The three travelers left Hanoi and worked their way south to Saigon, stopping at several locations along the way. Their first stop was unexpected, but one Sandy insisted they make. She knew that Paul had taken veterans back to heal their emotional scars, but was surprised to learn he had never returned to Con Thien himself. Although he claimed he never felt it was necessary, she disagreed, and found a driver to take them there.

The route was familiar and it didn't take much searching for Paul to find his unit's location. The hilltop—once barren, rat-infested, and surrounded by claymore mines—was now a lush, green peanut field. He stood on top of the hill, one eye closed, as he lined up a distant mountain to determine exactly where his bunker had once stood. The memories came flooding back: his fear, the stress, the constant barrage of noise and death and destruction. He remembered Merrell's wake, the day he received the letter about Marty, the day he shot the NVA soldier—all memories of horrible days he had tried so diligently to forget. He turned his back to Sandy so she wouldn't see him cry. It was so quiet now, so peaceful; not a soul was in sight except for the ghosts who hovered silently over this sacred ground.

Paul walked quietly among the plants, taking in his surroundings and reflecting on the past. One might almost think his experiences had never happened, but there were signs, small insignificant reminders of what had taken place here, like the C-ration bag tucked among the peanuts and the rusted beer can jutting from the soil. He paced the rows remembering so many details in a time that seemed like yesterday, but also a million lifetimes ago. Odd, how the mind fooled one.

Sandy didn't say a word but eventually came over and hugged him, a long embrace that allowed him to finally break down into great, gulping sobs. As he composed himself, he gently disentangled himself from her embrace, wiped his eyes, and swept his gaze across the entire hill. "We'd better go. Thank you for today. I didn't realize how much I needed to do this. I needed to come back …" his voice trailed off, once again overcome with emotion. It was a day he would always remember with gratitude.

* * *

They stopped in Hue for a few days and Paul rented a hotel room on the third floor with a small balcony where the couple enjoyed their morning coffee. One morning as they sipped their coffee, they heard the door slam behind them. Hannah shut the door and inadvertently locked them out!

"Hannah, open the door!" they both screamed. Hannah, who thought it was a game, giggled in glee and refused to comply. The more they begged, the harder she laughed. Paul, in his underwear, and Sandy, in a revealing nightgown, weren't quite sure how they would get out of this embarrassing situation until Paul spotted the air conditioning unit jammed into the wall. "I wonder if that's fastened," he said to Sandy. As he jiggled it, he discovered it was loose; he managed to push it into the room and crawl in after it, followed by Sandy.

One day Sandy inadvertently left her pocketbook hanging on the back of Hannah's stroller and later discovered that she had been the victim of a pickpocket. In Saigon, the streets were filled with young "postcard children," children whose parents forced them to take to the streets to sell postcards in order to supplement or, in some cases, provide the family income. The children, desperate for money, often resorted to stealing.

Sandy befriended some of these children and became attached to an eight-year-old girl named Ha, a tiny little girl in a frilly dress who couldn't speak English. Although the girl claimed to be eight, she appeared to be more like a five-year-old because of severe malnutrition. Around her neck hung a card indicating she had a heart condition and needed money. Sandy and Paul both gave her money, but later discovered that it was Spanky who had written the erroneous sign.

Sandy finally met the infamous Spanky, who still worked downtown by the Rex Hotel, and she, like Paul, found him irresistible. Spanky asked Paul to fund his latest venture and she saw Paul hand over a wad of bills to the boy. By now Sandy was confident that Paul didn't have a wife in Vietnam, but felt that Spanky was his adopted son, whether he knew it or not.

Before leaving Saigon, Sandy went shopping downtown and by chance wandered into a shop called Hoang Silk on Dong Khoi Street. The shop's owner, Vo Ngoc Huyhn Hoa (known as Miss Hoa), was surprised to see Sandy and her daughter enter her store; very few Americans traveled in Vietnam at the time. Sandy was equally surprised to find that the beautiful twenty-seven-year-old behind the counter was an enterprising businesswoman. Sandy was impressed with the merchandise which included colorful ao dais (the traditional Vietnamese costume), pajamas and robes, and bolts of silk used for custom-made clothing. Sandy ordered clothing for herself and Hannah which they picked up before they left town. Both parties made a lasting impression on each other; Miss Hoa wondered why this American family had come to Vietnam, and Sandy was curious about the life of the shy, yet warm Miss Hoa.

After a month, the trip came to an end. Through Sandy's urging the three arrived at the airport early and were first in line at the ticket counter. Eventually more people arrived and a line formed behind them. When the ticket agent arrived, a Vietnamese woman and an American man with a toddler cut the line in front of Sandy and Paul.

Paul was irate. "Do you believe that? I'm going to tell him that the people behind us were all in *front* of him. He's got some nerve!"

"Oh, don't worry about it. Who cares if we're first or second in line? Let them go ahead of us. Look at them ... do you think he's adopting that child?" Sandy carefully scrutinized the American man and the Vietnamese child.

"I don't know," Paul replied. "The embargo was just lifted. I guess it's possible."

"I'm going to find out!" Sandy declared. She waited for the trespassers to check in and noticed that only the man and the child held reservations; the Vietnamese woman, wearing a puffy pink dress, stood off to the side.

"Excuse me, sir, but I'd like to know if you're adopting that child," Sandy blurted out.

Surprised, the man replied, "Yes, I adopted him. I'm John Steele, by the way." He extended his hand for Sandy to shake.

"I'm sorry. I'm Sandy and this is my daughter, Hannah. This is my fiancé, Paul Pinkerton. Can I ask you about your adoption? How did you do that? I've been trying to find out how to adopt a child here," Sandy rambled excitedly.

"I completed the adoption with help from Miss Kim," the man replied motioning to his Vietnamese companion. He introduced Miss Kim to Sandy and Paul and, after a short conversation, they exchanged contact information. Soon it was time for farewells and boarding. Miss Kim waved goodbye and good luck to the man and his child. The three adults and two toddlers boarded the plane, but weren't seated close enough to each other to continue the dialogue.

When they landed in Bangkok and disembarked, it appeared that John Steele needed some assistance. He was crouched over baby Alex in the terminal building, changing his diaper, while struggling to keep an eye on his pile of luggage and baby gear.

"Would you like some help?" offered Sandy, who was happy she spotted him.

"I think I could use a hand with this luggage … and I need to get a cab outside. If you could help me, that would be terrific," said John.

They moved through the airport, secured a taxi for John, and agreed to meet at his hotel to continue their conversation. Several hours later, over cups of coffee, they compared notes on their children, Paul talked about his Vietnam experiences, and John explained how Miss Kim had helped him with his son's adoption.

Flying home, Sandy was ecstatic. The chance encounter with John Steele and Miss Kim had been sheer luck and she knew it. Now she had a plan for the future.

John, on the other hand, had a nightmarish flight home with a child who cried incessantly, threw up all over him, and screamed in agony because of an inner ear problem. Once home, the family had a short, but difficult adjustment period before things turned around, making the flight a distant bad memory and good fodder for jokes about parenthood.

* * *

When Paul returned to his little apartment at the greenhouse, he was greeted with stacked suitcases by the door. He didn't know what had transpired during his absence, but when Pat appeared at his doorstep a few hours later, with divorce papers in hand, he realized that she had found out about the trip and was angry enough to finish the process he had begun. Jetlagged and weary, he was surprised at her timing and thought it was more than a little callous. However, Pat was unaware of his schedule; it was purely coincidental that she caught him just hours after he had landed.

Paul signed the papers and by the next month, September, their divorce was final. For both parties it was a sad time; the ending of twenty-seven years of marriage was no cause for celebration. Pat moved on and surrounded herself with family, friends, and work. Paul had Sandy and Hannah to turn to, but still harbored the sadness, remorse, and guilt that accompanied the actions leading to his divorce.

Meanwhile, Sandy became single-mindedly focused on learning how to adopt a Vietnamese child. She called Miss Kim repeatedly, but was stymied by both the poor telephone service to Asia and Kim's command of the English language. After numerous frustrating phone calls, she tried one last time. The static on the phone line was terrible, but somehow she managed to communicate well enough to ask Miss Kim an important question: "If I come back to Vietnam, will you meet with me?"

"Yes, I meet you. You call when arrive."

It was the impetus Sandy needed; she and Paul began planning another trip to Vietnam in November, only a couple months away. In the interim, there were other matters for Sandy to address. The first, although not unexpected, was what to do with the farm. With Senter and Blanche gone, the farm was hers. Although she yearned to keep both the farm and her childhood memories intact, it wasn't practical. In the end she decided to do what Senter had often suggested: sell the farm to the Amish people next door. They had frequently inquired about whether they could purchase the Robinson farm for their sons, and it was one of her daddy's final requests. Sandy was happy to honor it.

More surprising was the unexpected news that she had inherited money from a family member in Tennessee. Apparently, someone willed money to Senter, which ultimately was passed down to her. This new infusion of cash gave Paul the incentive to mention an idea he had toyed with since the trip. Why not buy novelty items in Vietnam (pictures, lacquerware pieces, carvings, etc.) and sell them at the Boston Gift Show? The idea had some merit but, in Sandy's mind, her sole purpose in returning to Vietnam was to meet with Miss Kim.

* * *

Miss Kim was successful in her first adoption with the Steele family. She had learned the process and had formed alliances with both Government officials and Sister Hai, the director of the Tam Binh Orphanage (also known as Mam Non 2), in Ho Chi Minh City. Although baby Alex had lived in foster care, he had also spent time in the orphanage. Vietnamese rules mandated that adoptions be completed in conjunction with an orphanage. From its perspective, Lutheran Social Services saw this favorable outcome as a possible opportunity to pursue Vietnam as a venue for international adoption, but proceeded cautiously before inviting families to participate in this new and untested program. Lutheran's ambivalence resolved itself when one of its staff members decided to adopt from Vietnam, again with the aid of Miss Kim. When everything ran smoothly, the agency decided a Vietnamese program was viable, and they formed an alliance with her.

Lutheran Social Services had first approached Miss Kim's employer to seek a partnership with him, but he had maintained his stance that he was not interested in adoptions. However, he gave them permission to continue their work with Miss Kim, since he was not averse to having her do the legwork for him. Liz Kendrick provided guidance to families on paperwork requirements and travel arrangements, while Miss Kim facilitated the adoption process in Vietnam. Miss Kim accompanied families from appointment to appointment, acted as their tour guide, and graciously invited them to her home for dinner.

John Steele attended information and travel meetings with prospective adoptive families and brought real-life experience to the table with his pictures, his stories, and sometimes his baby—the coveted end result. Quickly, Lutheran's Vietnam program took on a life of its own as word spread in the local community and families became interested in this new venue. Globally, adoption by U.S. citizens took off in record numbers in several countries such as Korea, China, Romania, and Eastern bloc countries. The mid-1990s became a very busy time in international adoption, not only for LSS, but for other adoption agencies as well, who sought to expand their programs in additional countries.

* * *

With the Boston Gift Show just four short months away, Paul was hard at work. He registered for the show, researched the type of displays needed, and built fancy wallpapered panels and pedestals for his booth. Estimating the amount and type of goods to buy, he set forth a plan for the rapidly approaching trip.

Meanwhile, Sandy's sole agenda for the trip was to meet Miss Kim and find out how to complete a Vietnamese adoption. She didn't care about the Gift Show even though she had agreed to participate.

Paul, Sandy, and Hannah finally arrived in Vietnam and spent several days buying Vietnamese products. They went to Marble Mountain in DaNang to get the best deal on marble carvings, and traveled to other areas to buy the goods at their source, which lowered the prices considerably. Sandy grew impatient and insisted they visit Miss Kim the next morning.

Early in the day they traveled by cyclo to an outlying district where Miss Kim's house was located. The house was down a very narrow side street and neighbors came out to stare as the two Caucasians and the little blonde girl approached their neighbor's door. They had not called in advance and Miss Kim and her family weren't prepared for the visitors. Miss Kim's mother answered the door and ushered them into the living room. Miss Kim was upstairs getting dressed. After greetings were exchanged, her mother left the room to inform her daughter of her unexpected guests.

Sandy and Paul waited on the couch and noticed that the glass top coffee table contained pictures of beaming adoptive families and their Vietnamese babies. Paul stared at the pictures and made a pronouncement: "Maybe the reason we're in Vietnam is not for the Boston Gift Show at all, but for something else. I have the feeling that the whole purpose of this trip is going to take place in the next few minutes."

"Then why spend all this money on gifts?" Sandy asked, exasperated.

The discussion ended abruptly as Miss Kim, hair still wet, entered the room. She vaguely recognized them, but was surprised to find these strangers in her living room. Sandy came right to the point of their visit. Miss Kim listened and agreed to work with her. Then they reviewed all the required paperwork: birth certificates, police clearance, home study, and so forth.

Referring to the pictures on the coffee table, Paul asked, "Who are you working with?" He assumed she was working with an American agency.

"Lutheran Social Services."

"Will they be angry if you work with us? We're not associated with them."

"I do as I please. They don't own me. I work with whoever I want," Miss Kim declared somewhat defiantly.

"Good!" replied Paul. Miss Kim then gave them a large stack of paper—sample documents to use as models.

"You give me call when ready," Miss Kim stated.

Sandy couldn't wait to get home to work on the adoption and spent much of the plane ride home reviewing the materials. As she flipped through the papers she thought to herself, "This looks like what I did for Hannah's adoption—heck, I can do this!" She was certain the process would be fairly straightforward and simple.

CHAPTER 12

Adoption

A baby is God's opinion
That the world should go on.

Carl Sandburg

The Boston Gift Show was a disaster. Paul and Sandy spent a week in Massachusetts with 300 pounds of Vietnamese artifacts only to discover they had miscalculated nearly every aspect of the event. It was the wrong venue for their goods, they were placed in an obscure corner of the room, and they didn't have a catalog to hand out to potential buyers. In the end, they made three sales and never received payment for any of them. It was a tough lesson in merchandising, but one Paul made light of by joking that they now had a lifetime supply of wedding gifts.

The Gift Show debacle was the least of Sandy's worries. Her primary concern was tackling the mountain of adoption paperwork as a single parent. Despite her earlier optimism, most of the paperwork was new and unfamiliar and there was no one to ask for assistance. Paul made suggestions, but could offer little substantial help.

One of the biggest hurdles was finding an adoption agency to complete her home study. Although she vividly recalled the frustrating experience with the social worker from Welcome House, she called the agency again, praying for a different person this time. They turned her down cold. In fact, every adoption agency had the same response: "No. We can't do *just* a home study; you need to be involved in one of our international programs."

In desperation, she flipped through the phone book and randomly called every adoption agency within driving distance. By chance, she contacted Adoptions From The Heart (AFTH) in Lancaster. A social worker named Fran Myers was sympathetic to her plight and promised to check with Maxine Chalker, Founder and Executive Director, to see if Adoptions From The Heart could accommodate her. Fran called back two days later with affirmative news.

Prior to her home visit, Sandy attended group sessions with other adoptive families, an eye-opening experience. As families introduced themselves and stated the country of their adoption, she was surprised to hear, "China, China, China, China, China." When it was her turn, she confidently stated, "Vietnam." There was an audible murmur in the room as people exclaimed over her country of choice. The meeting over, Fran approached her.

"You're adopting from Vietnam ... on your own? How are you doing that?"

"I have a contact in Vietnam. A woman named Miss Kim is helping me."

"Maxine might want to talk with you. She's expressed some interest in starting a program in Vietnam. Let me check with her."

"Okay, but I'd have to talk to Miss Kim. I don't know ..." Sandy's only concern at the moment was her own adoption.

Life was hectic enough; Sandy didn't need to add on any more layers of complexity. She worked part-time in a fitness club daycare facility, and helped Vicki at the flower shop on an ad hoc basis. Hannah, at nearly three years old, was a bundle of toddlerhood rebellion that tested not only her patience, but her parenting skills as well. She had just settled into a new home in Mount Joy, purchased with money from the sale of the farm—a practical move given the fact she was expanding her family. Plus, the house was just five minutes from Manheim, which eliminated Paul's long commute. Sandwiched into her schedule was the never-ending adoption paperwork which was confusing, time-consuming, and tedious. However, it wasn't long before Maxine expressed an interest in meeting her.

***

Maxine Chalker was a self-made success story. Born and raised in the Philadelphia area as the adopted child of an upper-middle-class family, she married at twenty, had a daughter at twenty-six, and was divorced by twenty-eight. Maxine, intelligent and industrious, earned her Bachelor and Master's degrees in social work, graduating with honors. She worked as a social worker for a short time before opening her own adoption agency in 1984 in the basement of her home, as an advocate for open adoption. (In general, an open adoption is one in which birthparents and adoptive parents have some knowledge about one another and adopted children have the potential to develop a relationship with their birth family.) By the time Maxine met Sandy and Paul in 1996, she was running a successful agency with several branch offices. She was licensed in three states and had international programs in both China and Guatemala. She had also remarried and was raising stepchildren in addition to her daughter.

When they met, everything seemed to click. Maxine was open and receptive to Sandy's plan to adopt, and was eager to learn more about Vietnamese adoption. She also liked that fact that Paul was a vet and had a prior connection to Vietnam. The couple maintained contact with Maxine through phone calls and visits and Sandy provided periodic progress reports to both Maxine and Fran. Satisfied that Sandy was capable of completing her adoption, Maxine eventually decided to take on both Sandy and Paul as adoption facilitators, realizing the two were a package deal.

At this point, no formal contracts or financial agreements had been drawn up, only the verbal promise that if Sandy was successful with her own adoption, Maxine would bring Sandy and Paul on as independent facilitators. Initially, Sandy didn't give much thought to the prospects of a new job, but felt the pressure building when Maxine unexpectedly said, "You know, I think I'll start promoting this program."

"But I haven't traveled yet," Sandy protested.

"I have faith in you."

"But what if I go and things don't work out?"

"I'm planning to promote the program," Maxine allegedly stated, making it clear her decision wasn't up for discussion.

By September of 1996 Sandy's home study was done and the dossier of paperwork was finally completed, the accumulation of a year's worth of work. Sandy was proud of her accomplishments and relieved that this phase of the process was over. Meanwhile, families who had signed on for the Vietnam program were becoming anxious for advice and guidance. Eventually, Fran asked Sandy to conduct an information meeting. As the date of the meeting approached, Sandy became increasingly nervous. She wasn't a public speaker and certainly didn't feel confident talking about a process that hadn't occurred yet. However, she had little choice but to comply with Fran's request and the evening meeting went off as scheduled in January of 1997.

From Sandy's perspective, the evening was a total fiasco. Unable to answer the majority of questions, she resorted to a tight smile and a pat answer: "I'm going soon. I'll have the answers when I come back!" Paul chimed in to offer advice about traveling within Vietnam, but was also at a loss over details of the actual adoption, which Sandy had yet to experience. After the meeting Fran pulled Sandy aside.

"Um, Sandy ... since we're giving these meetings at the agency, you might want to wear a nice suit and a pair of heels next time." Sandy was mortified, but realized Fran was right. She made a mental note to go shopping for business attire before her next presentation.

Later, as Sandy and Paul recapped the evening, Sandy verbalized her doubts.

"I felt really uncomfortable tonight. I couldn't answer half of the families' questions and they need answers! Fran told me I wasn't dressed properly, and she was right. But I'm just not an office type of person. I never have been and I never will be. I'd rather be out on the road trucking again, being my own boss. Maybe this is all one big mistake ..."

"Sandy, don't worry so much. Just finish the adoption and everything else will fall into place. It'll be fine."

"I hope so ..." Sandy was unconvinced, suddenly overwhelmed by the huge responsibility she had assumed. She looked into the eyes of the prospective parents and fully understood their hopes, dreams, fears, and anxieties, because they were, after all, her own. She resolved to connect parents to their Vietnamese children. Beyond that, nothing else really mattered.

* * *

Meanwhile Miss Kim was busy connecting families with children but with less emotional stake in the process, since her interest was primarily financial. She worked part-time for her employer, the lawyer, and spent the rest of her time engaged by Lutheran Social Services of New England (LSS), facilitating adoptions. Lutheran had successfully marketed their program and families were traveling to Vietnam every month or two to adopt children with Kim's assistance. John Steele, their first adoptive parent, helped with travel and information meetings and Liz Kendrick managed the Vietnam program, in addition to a number of other international programs. All in all, the Vietnam adoption program at LSS was running smoothly and was becoming a popular option for prospective adoptive parents.

Miss Kim, a petite and attractive woman, could be seen zipping about the streets of Saigon on her motor scooter as she moved from hospital to orphanage to governmental agencies to coordinate the adoption process. Lutheran didn't have an American presence in-country and relied heavily upon her skills, acumen, and contacts. Kim enjoyed the work and frequently entertained American families in her mother's home, an added bonus for these early groups. In addition to facilitating adoptions, she also acted as tour guide, concierge, and general troubleshooter when needed.

Sandy continued her communications with Miss Kim, worried that Kim would forget about her. With her paperwork completed, she was anxious to be matched with a child, and she needed to lay the ground-work to establish a working relationship with Kim.

* * *

From the time she was eighteen, Vietnam had been an amazing thread running through the tapestry of Loretta Hackman's life. In 1975 she grad-uated from high school in Mobile, Alabama, the same year that Saigon fell. Following graduation she worked with a Catholic priest to find fos-ter families for Vietnamese refugees arriving in the area. Through her work and subsequent friendships with the Vietnamese, she grew to appre-ciate them as patient, tolerant, big picture people—people she loved and admired. Working with the refugees was a wonderful life experience that Loretta had always cherished.

Years later, married and living in Pennsylvania, Loretta struggled with infertility and sought the aid of Catholic Social Services in Philadelphia to adopt a Caucasian infant. After years of waiting and unusual twists of fate, Loretta and her husband, Tom, eventually adopted a Vietnamese toddler in the United States, a little girl they named Emily. Tom, an only child, was perfectly content to parent just one child while Loretta, who had many siblings, was not. She returned to Catholic Social Services and spoke with her caseworker, Sister Marita, about the possibility of adopt-ing another child, this time perhaps from Korea or China.

Sister Marita was blunt. "Loretta, Asian is not Asian is not Asian. If you have it in your heart to seek out a child who has as many connections as possible to your daughter, that would be a wonderful gift for both chil-dren. But you'll need to travel to Vietnam this time." Loretta took her advice and sought out adoption agencies with programs in South Viet-nam. In the process, she discovered Adoptions From The Heart in the Philadelphia area.

By chance, Loretta and Tom attended the first information meeting that Sandy conducted, but interpreted its outcome much differently than Sandy. The Hackmans felt a great deal of comfort with both Sandy and Paul and appreciated their honest, informative, and practical advice. They knew the adoption was a little risky. Vietnam was a new and untested program for the agency, but they were willing to take a chance on it any-way.

Another couple in the Pennsylvania area had a similar story. Jan Bye and her husband, Paul Dickerson, were never meant to have babies or, at least, that was Jan's belief after her failed pregnancy attempts. In 1990, they adopted a baby boy domestically whom they named Sawyer. But, like the Hackmans, they wanted more than one child. Initially they went down the path of adopting from China through Adoptions From The Heart, an agency they located through careful research and recommendations from friends. But mid-stream in the process, a key Chinese official died and his successor changed the rules for foreign adoptions. The Chinese Government decided to enforce the one-child rule for foreign adoptions as well as Chinese births, leaving the Bye-Dickersons with a dilemma, because they already had Sawyer. When AFTH suggested they switch to the Vietnam program, they readily agreed.

A glitch in the mail prevented the Bye-Dickersons from attending Sandy's information meeting, but they spoke with the Pinkertons at length over the phone. Like the Hackmans, they felt at ease with Sandy and Paul. Neither Jan nor Paul was overly concerned by the fact the program was new and unproven. Jan, a campus minister at Shippensburg University, and Tom, a psychologist, both approached life as an adventure and trusted in a power greater than themselves.

The Hackmans and the Bye-Dickersons were slated as the first two families to adopt from Vietnam, with three additional families in the pipeline. Sandy and Paul planned to carry the dossiers (paperwork) of the five families into Vietnam and file them with the Government to set in motion their adoption processes. But, before anything could happen with the other families, Sandy needed to complete her own adoption first.

* * *

Sandy became impatient as she waited for news about a baby, virtually suspended in adoption limbo. In June of 1997, Sandy and Paul finally received the phone call they had waited for, so anxiously. Miss Kim had a child for them: a little boy named Le Xuan Hung, who was born on November 11, 1996 and was now seven months old. They were overcome with joy—a baby boy! There was no medical report, but Miss Kim indicated the baby was healthy so Sandy immediately accepted the referral (match). A picture arrived a short time later and they instantly fell in love with their infant son. Several more weeks passed before they were granted adoption and travel dates, and were on their way.

In 1997 there were still limited numbers of Americans traveling to Vietnam. There were random journalists writing articles and books, a few social organizations providing humanitarian aid, and expatriates drumming up business in a new Vietnamese economy. But for the vast majority of Americans, Vietnam was still a country that represented pain, heartache, and political mistakes. Those who ventured there in the mid to late 1990s were pioneers of sorts, especially those adopting children.

Paul and Sandy hardly considered themselves pioneers. Paul had returned to Vietnam countless times and Sandy had accompanied him twice. She knew exactly what to expect: bad food and water, unsanitary conditions, a crude infrastructure, and abject poverty. Even three-year-old

Hannah had some inkling of this place and knew she would be the object of admiration and attention of these strange, yet kind, people.

Paul, Sandy, and Hannah flew into Thailand a full week ahead of schedule, purposely allowing time to recover from jetlag and shop for baby supplies before receiving Le Xuan Hung. It seemed a more appealing option than carrying endless amounts of baby gear on the plane like a couple of mountain Sherpa. They spent a day in Bangkok where they checked their adoption paperwork with the appropriate officials and obtained something called a Blue Book, for reference. Then they flew on to Saigon.

It was past midnight when they arrived in Vietnam. Paul hadn't bothered with hotel reservations and planned to stay at his old standby, the 69 Hotel. They navigated the crush of people at the airport, juggled their baggage and a sleeping Hannah, and finally reached a taxi. When they arrived at the hotel, both were dismayed to see that it was closed for renovation. The driver suggested a mini-hotel, the Vinh Thinh (pronounced "vin tin") in District 1. It was a dreary, claustrophobic little place with a broken elevator, inconsistent air conditioning, and no restaurant, but at $12 a night at 1:30 in the morning, it would suffice.

The next morning, not even Sandy's jetlag could stop her excitement. "Let's give Miss Kim a call to let her know we're in town," she bubbled.

"No, let's go buy baby stuff. Call her later." They hadn't shopped in Bangkok as they had planned.

"We'll have plenty of time to shop. I'm going to call her ... maybe we can go to the orphanage."

"Okay. Do what you want." Paul knew it was pointless to argue with Sandy when she had her sights on a baby.

As Sandy made the call, Paul watched her face dance in animation. Something big was in the works.

"Guess what? Miss Kim said we can go to the orphanage to see the baby! She's picking us up in twenty minutes!"

They scurried to get ready and rushed down the four narrow flights of stairs to the street. Traffic was noisy, chaotic, and dangerous. Motorbikes, precariously balancing people and cargo, darted in and out of traffic at lightning speeds; bicycles flew past, cyclos lumbered by, and cars swerved this way and that, all honking continuously. It was only 9:30 in the morning, but the air was already stifling. They were sweating by the time they entered Miss Kim's car.

Tam Binh Orphanage was on the outskirts of town in the Tam Binh District, approximately forty minutes away. Miss Kim bobbed and weaved through the streets while Sandy closed her eyes, certain a collision was imminent. Vietnamese traffic still scared her. They traveled over the Saigon River on dirt roads until they reached the orphanage hidden behind imposing front gates and barbed wire. A guard came to inspect the car and, recognizing Miss Kim, granted her entrance.

They parked and walked to the back building where the babies were housed. Hannah bounced along and chattered about meeting her new baby brother while Sandy took in the gardens and statues that lined the walk. The orphanage director, a short, plump Catholic nun named Sister Hai (short for Sister Huynh Thi Kim Hai) greeted them at the door with a broad and inviting smile and ushered them into the room where baby Le Xuan Hung was staying.

Miss Kim said, "I speak with Sister Hai. You like to hold baby, Miss Sandy?"

"Oh yes!" This was the moment Sandy had waited for, her eyes clouding with mist as Miss Kim handed her the baby. Looking down at him, Sandy was taken aback. The baby was tiny and frail, not as robust as he had appeared in his picture. He had pustules and sores on his hands and feet; his skin was raw and red. She closed her eyes to savor the moment, thinking not of his poor physical condition, but rather the deep love she felt for both of her children and the gratitude she held for her new life with Paul.

Caught up in the moment, she temporarily forgot about the rest of her family. Hannah was busy exploring, curious about this roomful of babies, while Paul stood to the side, tears raining down his face in a monsoon torrent, openly sobbing. When Sandy handed him the baby, his hands trembled.

Paul looked down at Le Xuan Hung and saw not his son, but combat scenes flashing rapid-fire before his eyes: a child's arm pasted on a tree branch, a severed baby's head, a little hand lying alone in the dirt; sickening results of the devastation he had created. It was almost thirty years since his tour of duty had ended, but the wounds were as fresh as the day they were made, now running with tears rather than blood. The war had tainted everything and he had dragged his heavy burden of guilt around like an old Vietnamese woman carrying her produce in steel pots suspended on the ends of a bamboo pole; the weight of it almost too much to bear.

This was a life-altering moment. This was the moment when years of guilt might be taken away, the horrible wrongs of the past forgiven. This was his moment of redemption. Paul felt his debt to the Vietnamese people could never be completely erased, but perhaps this one small act of love was the beginning of the salvation he'd been seeking. Like Sandy, he was unwilling to let go and stood awhile longer holding his son, openly crying, suspended in time.

From outside the door, Sister Hai and Miss Kim observed this American couple, both uncomfortable with the display of raw emotions roiling around the room. It wasn't customary for the Vietnamese people to show their feelings in public; in fact, it was frowned upon. Americans, with their odd customs and strange behaviors, were still a mystery to them. Miss Kim entered loudly to make her presence known.

"You want to take him home?" she asked.

"Yes, of course!" Sandy, oblivious to her lack of supplies, didn't hesitate. "Yes, we'll take him home. Has he been fed?"

"Not yet. I get a bottle and you feed, okay?"

When Miss Kim and Sister Hai disappeared, Sandy turned to Paul. "I want to take his clothes off."

"Why?"

"I don't know. I just need to ..." As Sandy stripped him naked she discovered a huge, ugly scar on his belly. It was obvious that the crude incision was from some type of surgery. Sandy called over one of the caregivers. "What is this?"

The caregiver shook her head and called over Sister Hai, who had just returned to the room.

"What is this?" Sandy demanded to know.

"I've never seen." Sister Hai looked perplexed and played dumb.

"Could you please find out ... now? I need to know what this is." Sandy was frustrated by Sister Hai's presumed ignorance.

"You're upset. Are you taking him?" Miss Kim joined the conversation, worried the adoption was falling through.

"Of course I'm taking him. He's my son and I love him. But I need to know why he has this scar."

"Okay, Miss Sandy, we find out. Here, feed him." Miss Kim handed her a prepared bottle and an extra can of formula. Sandy sat on the cold tile floor, the only place available, and fed her baby while she made quick mental notes about his condition: can't hold up head or sit by himself; far behind developmentally; skin raw and bleeding with pustules; large, uneven scar.

"This baby's in trouble. He's going to need more than just love," she thought sadly.

* * *

It was late afternoon by the time they returned to the hotel room. Hot, sweaty, and exhausted, they dragged themselves up the numerous flights of stairs to their cramped and stuffy quarters. They had stopped to buy diapers, formula, and baby clothes and were finally back, feeling spent. Hannah, already bored by her baby brother, was misbehaving. She resented the fact that he was getting more than his fair share of attention. Paul flipped on the air conditioning as high as it would go and the baby started coughing.

"What's wrong with him?" Sandy asked Paul, shooting him a concerned frown.

"I don't know. Maybe he's overheated. Let's give him a bath to cool him down and feed him. He'll probably go to sleep," Paul suggested.

Sandy called down to the front desk for a thermos of boiling water for the formula and ran water in the little bathroom sink for a bath. Together she and Paul gave the baby a bath as Hannah peered at her new brother. Sandy diapered him and dressed him in his new clothing. There was a knock at the door and the thermos was delivered.

"Thank you. Do you have a crib?"

"No, no crib."

Sandy looked around the room at the queen size bed she shared with Paul and the single bed for Hannah. Unconcerned, she pushed the two bamboo chairs in the room together and piled sheets on top to serve as a crude bassinette. She had already learned that in Vietnam, one often had to improvise. She prepared a bottle, but the baby wouldn't eat. He continued to cough and wheeze and was, by now, completely congested. She looked at Paul, her eyes filled with fear.

"Let's get him over here by the air conditioner. Maybe the cool air will ease his breathing."

Hannah was tired, becoming crankier with each passing minute. Sandy fed her and put her to sleep. Paul held the baby who gasped for breath and grew worse by the minute. When Hannah was finally asleep, Sandy lost control.

"Paul, I think he's dying! What's wrong with him? He's only been with us a few hours and he's dying! What should we do?" Sandy sat on the bed and cried, feeling completely powerless.

"Calm down Sandy. He's not going to die. We won't let him die. Everything will be fine." Paul put on a strong front with his reassuring confidence, but felt the same sense of fear and panic. "Shit," he thought, "this can't be happening. What the hell is wrong with him?"

Paul turned the baby face down over his broad lap and started gently and rhythmically patting the baby's upper back near his lungs. The baby calmed down a bit and appeared to breathe more easily. Periodically he coughed, and a thick glob of foul mucus oozed from his mouth, providing a bit of relief. Eventually he slept, only to wake again. He struggled for breath, coughed, and wheezed, his tiny lungs straining for air. Paul stayed up all night and patted his back, determined to keep him alive. Sandy alternated between tears and prayers as she watched her son fight for his life. Hannah slept peacefully, oblivious to the crisis taking place near her bedside.

When dawn came, Sandy ran to the lobby. "We need a doctor! We need someone right away. My baby is very sick. We need a doctor now!" She repeated her request over and over, half-crazed.

The hotel manager spoke to his workers in Vietnamese until finally an answer was forthcoming. "We get doctor for you soon." Paul and Sandy paced around the small room while Hannah acted out, convinced that having a baby brother, especially a sick one, was no fun. "Take him back! I don't want him! He's sick. Get a healthy baby!"

Finally the doctor arrived. He listened to the baby's chest for only a moment and pronounced, "Pneumonia." Sandy and Paul looked at each other, both thinking the same thing: "Why would the orphanage release a sick baby? Why didn't they tell us? Surely they must have known the child was ill?" But those were questions for later.

The doctor pointed to the air conditioning unit. "Off! Need hot air. Keep him by window. Turn on hot shower and put in bathroom. No cold air." The doctor proceeded to give the baby a shot of some unknown substance and promised to come back the next day.

With the AC off, the baby started to breathe more easily. Paul felt enormously guilty for turning it on in the first place, but Sandy knew that it was only through his efforts that the baby had survived the night. By now, they were exhausted and famished so Sandy went out alone, only to discover that the nearest market was over ten blocks away in a rather unseemly area. She bought French bread, fruit, snacks, and milk, and avoided all prepared foods. She had learned the hard way that food was frequently contaminated and she couldn't afford to become ill during this trip. If necessary, she would survive on bread and bottled water.

When she returned, the staff was playing with her daughter in the lobby. Although Hannah was difficult for Sandy and Paul to handle, she was delightful with the Vietnamese. With her pudgy little body, curly golden locks, and porcelain white skin, they couldn't resist her. The staff decided to give Sandy and Paul a break and provide Hannah the attention she craved. Meanwhile the baby was breathing better, but his pustules were getting worse.

* * *

Each day the doctor came with another shot of antibiotics and the same advice: "Keep him hot," and each day the baby improved slightly, while his rash spread. Whatever it was, it was becoming more pronounced and Le Xuan Hung looked terrible.

"Doctor, what is this? What should we do?" Sandy pointed to the open sores and pustules on his hands and feet that the baby continually clawed.

"It's the itchies. Have no remedy, but American doctor, he know what to do."

"Great," thought Sandy, "he's miserable and there's nothing I can do for him."

The week dragged by slowly. Every day was the same: a visit from the doctor, a temper tantrum (or two) from Hannah, and a trip to the market. Sandy continued to press Miss Kim for answers about the baby's health while Kim danced around the issues, revealing only that the baby had surgery for obstructed bowels and should never become constipated. Miss Kim, like the doctor, called his rash "the itchies," but had no solution for his problem.

When it was time for the signing ceremony (the actual adoption), Miss Kim escorted Sandy to the Ministry of Justice where Sister Hai sat at her side as she signed the papers to become a mother for a second time. What should have been a joyous occasion was simply a solemn and formal ceremony and, when it was over, Sandy felt deflated.

Sandy wasn't alone in her adoption on July 2, 1997. Two couples from Lutheran Social Services also adopted babies with Miss Kim's help. Miss Kim had previously introduced the couples, but Sandy and Paul hadn't spent any time with them. They were too consumed with their baby's medical issues to think of much else. One couple, Mary and Tom Fulton of Connecticut, adopted a baby girl while the other couple, from New England, adopted a boy. As Le Xuan Hung's condition improved, the couples eventually shared dinners, stories of Vietnam, and their woes with one another.

* * *

With the signing ceremony over, it was time to file paperwork to complete the adoption process. In 1997 there was no U.S. Embassy in Saigon and everything was routed through the U.S. Embassy in Thailand. Sandy and the two other couples prepared their paperwork and sent their packages via Federal Express to the U.S. Embassy in Bangkok. They waited anxiously for the Embassy to fax them a Letter of Confirmation (LOC) stating that the paperwork was in order and they could travel to Thailand for the final interview before heading home with their babies.

Mary and Tom Fulton and the other couple received their LOCs within two days and prepared to leave Vietnam. Sandy didn't receive hers and called the Embassy to find out why. An Embassy official by the name of Mark answered the phone and a terse conversation ensued. After introductions were made, Sandy asked why she hadn't received her LOC and what was causing the delay.

"Because your child's paperwork is not complete and it is not correct," he allegedly responded.

"Can you please tell me what's wrong with it?" Sandy asked politely.

"No, I cannot. I am not your counselor, I am not your adoption agency, I am not your attorney, and I cannot help you."

"Can't you just tell me what's wrong?" Sandy pleaded.

"No. Goodbye."

Sandy wanted to scream and beat her fists into a punching bag, but she decided to take some action instead. She called the two families and asked to see their paperwork to compare notes. The families relented and sat nearby as Sandy pored over their papers line-by-line to see how hers differed. There was only one minor difference: Le Xuan Hung's birth-mother's name was listed on his birth certificate. No big deal.

The Fultons and the other adoptive couple flew home, leaving Sandy and Paul alone and confused. Every day Sandy called Mark at the Embassy, and became angrier and more desperate with each call.

"Please, I'm begging you. My son is very ill and we need to get back to the States. I don't understand what's wrong. I don't know what you want. Can't you just tell me?"

"No, I can't. I'm sorry that your son is sick, but that's not my problem." The man supposedly wouldn't budge as the daily phone calls turned into ugly pissing contests. The more Sandy begged the harder Mark dug in his heels, refusing to help her. Finally, one day, the exasperated man gave them the clue they had been searching for.

"Don't you have a Blue Book? Don't you know what the definition of an orphan is? Read the definition of an orphan. You need a relinquishment paper from the birthmother. She needs to release her parental rights to you in writing."

"How in the world am I ever going to find his birthmother in a city of eight million people?"

"I don't know. That's your problem, not mine," he retorted as he slammed the phone down. He was losing patience with this pesky American woman.

Sandy was a wreck. She wasn't eating or sleeping and she'd lost fifteen pounds. She alternated between two states: jittery and angry, or weepy and depressed. Everything got on her nerves, especially Hannah who had turned into a little witch. Hannah's whining for attention and constant complaining about her baby brother only added to Sandy's stress. Every day Hannah screamed the same mantra: "I don't like that baby! That baby's sick. Take him back. Why do you want him? We're not going to keep him are we? He's sick and I was here first. Don't you love me anymore? Take him back!" Sandy's nerves were gone; she was ready to snap.

Miss Kim, who knew something of Sandy and Paul's problems, added to the mix. One day she called Sandy. "I don't think we should work together. You take paperwork back." Sandy had given her the five dossiers from the adoptive families when they arrived, but now Kim had changed her mind. She was concerned over the problems that Sandy was having, but did not fully understand what they were.

"No, you can't. The families are counting on us. The agency is counting on us. When I figure it out, I'll come back with the families. I'll help them through the adoption process and you won't have to do anything. Please, just keep the dossiers. I promise this will all work out."   After much cajoling, Kim reluctantly agreed to keep the paperwork of the five families in the works.

Sandy and Paul had been reluctant to involve Sister Hai since they thought they had the situation under control, but finally decided they were past due in enlisting her aid. Meanwhile, Sister Hai had heard of their problems through Kim. By the time Sandy arrived at the orphanage, Sister Hai was picking up the phone to call her.

Sandy rushed into the orphanage and requested a closed door meeting with Sister Hai. Once inside, she fell to her knees and begged her for help: "Sister Hai, I need your help—I have a huge problem. Please help me. I've been working with the Embassy in Bangkok, but they haven't given me my LOC. They said the paperwork is wrong and I don't know what to do and …" Sandy burst into tears before she could finish her rambling sentences.

A little smile formed on Sister Hai's lips. "It will be okay. I think I have what you need," she said as she retrieved a document typed on orphanage letterhead.

"Oh my God! How …?" Sandy was speechless.

"I heard of the problems. Everything should be fine."

"Thank you, thank you! How can I ever thank you enough?"

Sandy hugged Sister Hai and felt a small, quick hug in return. "Go. Take your son home now!" Sister Hai beamed.

On the taxi ride back to the hotel, Sandy replayed the absurd scene in her head and thought to herself, "Oh my God! I just begged a Catholic nun for help, on my hands and knees. I can't believe I actually did that!"

She ran into the hotel lobby and asked to use their fax machine to zip the paper over to Thailand. Within minutes the phone rang in their hotel room. "Yes, that's exactly what I needed. Come to Bangkok on Wednesday and I'll see you at two o'clock." The line went dead as Mark abruptly hung up the phone.

Sandy raised her fist, "When I see you in person, I'm gonna let you have it!" But, of course, that was only wishful thinking on her part. He still held the power and she wouldn't dream of jeopardizing the last step in the process.

* * *

With the trip coming to a close, there were two pieces of unfinished business. One was to decide whether or not they actually wanted to become adoption facilitators given all that had transpired in the last three weeks. For Sandy, there was no choice.

"We have to come back. If families have as much trouble as we did, they're not going to do this. They'll go home and say it was the worst experience of their lives. They'll say it was extremely hard and they didn't know what to do or where to go or anything. Miss Kim couldn't help us, who will help them? We have to do it—not for the agency or ourselves—but for the children. These kids deserve to be adopted and families deserve to come and have an easy adoption experience." Paul agreed without hesitation.

"Let's get moving because we need to find a better hotel and places for families to shop and sightsee and eat. Just because we didn't get to do anything fun, doesn't mean they won't be able to have a good time. We need to make arrangements so families go home loving Vietnam." To this suggestion Paul more reluctantly consented, unwilling to spend his days looking at hotel rooms and restaurants. However, Sandy dragged him around downtown Saigon, where they checked out hotels, jotted down names of shops and restaurants, and looked into possible sightseeing tours. By the time they left Vietnam, they had a laundry list of places that families could explore.

The second order of business was strictly a social matter. The doctor, who had treated their son over the past weeks, invited them to his home for dinner. He was thrilled that Sandy and Paul had adopted the child and were taking him to America to live a wonderful and presumably, privileged life. Sandy and Paul, grateful for his help, couldn't refuse his kind invitation. On the night of the engagement the doctor sent a driver for them.

They had no idea where the doctor lived, except that he had mentioned he lived in District 7. The drive was long and dark and it started to rain. The driver finally came to a stop and a Vietnamese woman, holding an umbrella, opened the car door. She said, "We're going to walk up this path." Sandy noticed that all the houses in the area were shacks and as they followed her, people opened their doors to stare. The dirt path was endless and steep and as they walked farther away from the car, Sandy felt uneasy. Walking single file, she looked back at Paul as if to say, "Where is she taking us? Are you sure this is safe? Are we being led into some kind of ambush?"

They walked and walked and walked and eventually crossed a shaky board bridge over a creek, risky business given the fact they were both carrying children. Just as Sandy was about to turn around and make a run for it, she saw a beautiful, grand house on the hill ahead of them, lights blazing.

"Come in," the doctor shouted as he opened his front door and saw them.

Inside, Sandy and Paul were shocked to see that the doctor had invited his entire family and had prepared a feast fit for royalty, with course after course of mysterious, delicious food.

Touched, Sandy said, "Oh my goodness! You live so far away yet you came every day to see my child and take care of him. How can I ever thank you?"

"Yes, yes," was all the doctor would say, embarrassed by Sandy's effusiveness.

They ate, drank, talked, laughed, and at the end of the night, took photographs to capture the occasion.

On their last night in Vietnam, the hotel staff prepared a lavish meal for them and secretly invited the doctor and his family to surprise them once again. They celebrated in grand fashion and expressed their continued gratitude to both the doctor and the hotel staff for their help during the difficult three weeks they spent in Saigon. Then, they began the long journey home.

* * *

The interview with Mark in Bangkok went well, although Sandy couldn't help but secretly glower at the man who had given her so much angst, the man who chose not to help in her time of confusion and need. But, with the adoption process finally completed, they flew home. Their flights were booked from Bangkok to Seoul, Seoul to Chicago, and Chicago to Philly. By now Le Xuan looked hideous. His rash had spread to his hands, feet, and even to his face, as oozing pustules and raw, peeling skin covered his entire body.

At the Seoul Airport, a man walked up to Sandy with a squirt bottle and said, "Your baby looks awful. Spray this on him. It will help."

Sandy thought, "Who are you and what the heck is this stuff?" She threw the bottle in the trash. But he wasn't the only one with advice. During the first three hours of their flight, the baby cried continuously and people kept crowding around Sandy, offering suggestions on how to take care of him. Sandy, nerves ragged, wished they would all just mind their own business and leave her alone.

On their flight to Chicago, another woman with a baby in a bulkhead bassinette sat opposite Sandy. When she peeked in to look at Sandy's baby, she moved away in revulsion. "Eeew, what's wrong with your kid? Is he contagious? I don't want my baby catching anything!"

"I don't know. I'm sorry. I'll keep him over here, but I have to get home. If you want to change your seat, go ahead."

The flight was long. Sandy tended to the baby's needs as Paul entertained Hannah, who made a game out of collecting everyone's sickness bags from their seat pockets. As they neared Chicago a thunderstorm rolled into the area, typical for a summer afternoon in the Midwest. Dark clouds encircled the plane and jags of lightning pinged by their windows. Just as the pilot banked the plane and started to circle, the plane suddenly dropped. Cargo and people flew into the air. Everyone was terrified. Sandy, sitting in the bulkhead holding the baby, braced her feet against the wall. Hannah thought she was on an amusement ride and yelled out, "This is fun!" Many travelers reached for their missing sickness bags, which Hannah had confiscated earlier.

There was chaos. Some people screamed and cried while others gagged and retched from the heavy turbulence. Sandy prayed and lashed out in fury at God. "You look here. I didn't go through all this crap to lose my son in a plane crash. I went through hell to get this child and now you're going to let us die? This is freakin' unbelievable! Don't you dare let this plane crash!" God must have listened to her angry tirade because the plane didn't fall from the sky, but certainly gave its crew and passengers a terrible fright as it dove for the runway and bumped along for what seemed like forever. In the end, Sandy, Paul, and the kids arrived home safely, now a proud family of four.

* * *

Despite the terrifying landing, jetlag, and all of Le Xuan Hung's problems, Sandy couldn't wait to show him off. She rushed into Adoptions From The Heart the very next day, beaming with pride at her son and the fact that she had successfully completed his adoption. Sandy put his bouncy seat on the conference room table as Maxine, Fran, and the other social workers filed in to see him. Sandy noticed that after their first glances they all stepped back several feet.

Glowing, Sandy said to no one in particular, "Do you want to hold him?"

"No! What's wrong with him?" was the chorus from everyone in the room. The baby, although lovingly dressed in his best outfit, looked worse than before. His rash was rampant; every part of his body, an open sore.

Maxine cut to the chase. "He looks terrible, just terrible. If all the kids are going to come home looking like this, you can forget it."

"No, the other babies aren't going to look like this. It's temporary; he has some kind of rash and I'm sure it will clear up with medicine. I'm going to the doctor today. Everything will be fine, you'll see."

Maxine looked at her skeptically. "Let me know what it is."

Later that day Sandy and Paul discovered that the baby had the worst case of scabies the doctor had ever seen. Scabies, an infestation of the skin caused by microscopic mites, spreads rapidly in crowded conditions (like an orphanage) where there's frequent skin-to-skin contact. The mites burrow into the skin and create intense itching; the subsequent scratching only exacerbates the rash and leads to oozing, open sores. Fortunately, scabies is treatable with prescription creams and lotions which Sandy applied to Le Xuan Hung's skin over the course of the next several weeks. Amazingly, no one else in the family caught the baby's scabies, despite their close contact with him.

Scabies, however, was the least of the baby's problems. The doctor discovered he had been born prematurely and his lungs were underdeveloped. He was underweight and malnourished, so Sandy was required to feed him almost continuously. He still needed antibiotics to fight off the pneumonia and required nebulizer treatments four times a day for the next two months to combat his asthmatic condition. Their so-called healthy baby was a special needs child who required round-the-clock attention.

Sandy, who had such an easy time with Hannah when she was a baby, was overwhelmed with his care. Paul went back to work at the greenhouse while she juggled the baby's demanding physical needs and Hannah's emotional ones. Sleep deprivation and exhaustion became the normal state of affairs as Sandy dragged herself through each endless day.

Before long, Sandy and Paul turned their attention to Vietnam again, as the Hackmans and the Bye-Dickersons prepared for their adoptions. Maxine, who saw the baby after his scabies healed, decided to go ahead with the program. By October it was time for them to travel again, this time as adoption facilitators. Sandy, who had barely recovered from her last trip, worried about the upcoming trip and the problems they might encounter this time.

CHAPTER 13

Surprises

Surprises are foolish things.
The pleasure is not enhanced and
The inconvenience is often considerable.

Jane Austen

P aul was in transition. Although single and divorced he was essentially a husband to Sandy and finally, at fifty-years-old, a father to two small children. Disheartened by his struggling greenhouse business, he was embarking upon a career as an adoption facilitator. He'd ended his search for POWs and MIAs some time ago, but his single-minded obsession with helping those who were abandoned and forgotten had never diminished. Only now, the abandoned and forgotten were Vietnamese orphans instead of POWs and MIAs. Accordingly, he placed an enormous picture of Le Xuan Hung (renamed Isaiah) on the side of his greenhouse truck, along with the slogan, "Adoptions from Vietnam."

Isaiah was a name he and Sandy had picked out earlier—a Biblical name they were both drawn to—a name that means "salvation." He felt Isaiah was his redemption, a child who partially relieved him of the sins he'd committed during the war. But in his heart, he secretly believed he'd never be totally absolved from all that he had done. He loved Hannah dearly, but Isaiah was "their" child and special because of his Vietnamese roots.

Paul's siblings watched from the sidelines with both admiration and mirth as he went down the uneven path of parenthood. Their children were grown and now it was Paul's turn to experience not only the joys, but the trials and tribulations of fatherhood. However, when it came to

Isaiah, no one was laughing. Everyone was genuinely concerned about this sick infant whom they feared would never lead a normal life.

They all rallied around Paul; even Martha, who still had minor quarrels with him over various greenhouse issues and had not fully accepted Sandy into the family circle. Martha was the one person whose approval Sandy couldn't secure. Paul was upset over the situation, but felt he didn't have the time or energy to resolve their differences. He spent his days at the greenhouse and in the delivery truck; his nights were spent with Sandy and the kids. Weekends were split between work, Sandy and the kids, and relatives. Sometimes his siblings wandered over on Saturdays to catch up on the news and receive a haircut, which Paul willingly provided.

In the course of haircutting chatter, Paul learned that Pat was dating; an update he was genuinely happy to hear. His family members loved Pat and remained friends with her after the divorce. It was through this connection that Pat heard news about Paul too. She didn't begrudge him his new life, but wondered what might have happened if she had decided to have children. However, it was too late to second guess her choices and she braced herself for the likelihood that she would eventually run into Paul and his kids. In a town as small as Manheim, it was simply inevitable.

Paul's parents and siblings were a big part of his support system. Before each trip to Vietnam, they all shared a meal together. Paul's father tracked Paul's itinerary from takeoff to landing. After all, you couldn't be too careful when your son was halfway around the globe. His brother Jim provided transportation to and from the airport, and Marty managed the greenhouse. Paul's siblings offered to babysit the children when they were in town, but Sandy and Paul politely refused. Isaiah was a clinging vine who shrieked in terror when others attempted to hold him, which left Sandy little choice but to provide him the 24/7 care he demanded.

Sandy was also in a state of flux, as she juggled a number of demands on her time and energy. Hannah was now a busy preschooler who still resented her baby brother, while Isaiah required the time and care of multiple children with his far-reaching physical and emotional needs. Still dissatisfied with Miss Kim's explanation for his surgical scar, she took him to the Hershey Medical Center for evaluation. There were no concrete answers. The doctors said that, short of opening him up, they would never know what had happened. It was not an option she wished to pursue. It seemed that Isaiah's life, much like her own, would contain some unsolved mysteries.

Proud of the new addition to her family, Sandy went to see her old friend, Donna Culberson, to show off baby Isaiah. Donna, whose children were grown, was happy for Sandy and her expanding family, but couldn't resist teasing her before her next trip to Vietnam. "So Sandy, are you bringing home another baby this time?" Donna was half-serious, knowing Sandy's soft spot for babies and Vietnamese orphans in particular.

"No, no, I'm done. My family's big enough. I'm done!" Sandy laughed. "Besides, I'll be sitting in a wheelchair by the time Isaiah graduates from high school!" Sandy felt old in comparison to Donna as she struggled with sleep deprivation, Isaiah's medical problems, and her own anxieties about the upcoming trip to Vietnam. She was dreading the endless coach flight with two squirmy children.

Before she left for Vietnam, Sandy took time from her busy schedule to visit Angel. Although the illusion of a close father-daughter relationship was gone, she loved him out of a sense of duty and respect. He was, after all, her biological father and the one who had given her life. But, instead of naming the things she liked about him (because there weren't all that many), she recognized that she couldn't change him and tried to find something positive to say: "Poppy, I love you. I'm glad you met Mommy and came to America."

Angel owned a home in Kennett Square but, struggling to make ends meet on his meager social security, rented out rooms to illegal immigrants who worked in the mushroom canneries. He had turned his home into a flophouse. Sandy had always picked up Angel by herself, but now Paul insisted on accompanying her. He wouldn't allow her to enter this house of squalor by herself. Sandy was anxious for Angel to meet Isaiah so they drove to Kennett Square and Paul ran inside Angel's house to retrieve him.

Sitting down to lunch, Sandy proudly presented the baby to Angel.

"He's Chinese," Angel remarked unenthusiastically, as he peered at the child.

"No, dad, he's Vietnamese. I adopted him in Vietnam."

"Same difference—Chinese, Vietnamese, whatever."

"How can you say that? They're not the same. He's Vietnamese. What if I said Mexican, Puerto Rican, it's all the same?"

"That's entirely different, you can't even compare the two ..." Angel started.

Sandy didn't respond; it was pointless to argue. She let his remarks slide, as she had done so many times in the past as she silently vented her frustration.

* * *

Excitement and nervous energy filled the air in August of 1997. Adoptions From The Heart launched its Vietnamese adoption program and Sandy and Paul tentatively began their careers as adoption facilitators. The Bye-Dickersons and the Hackmans waited anxiously to be matched with their babies; their anticipation building with each passing day.

Paul and Sandy held another meeting at the agency for the two couples, along with other prospective parents who were looking into the possibility of adopting from Vietnam. Armed with experience and information gleaned from Isaiah's adoption, they were now prepared to answer almost any question thrown their way. And, this time, Sandy was dressed properly.

Many prospective parents in the room had switched from the China program and had their hearts set on adopting girls. However, Sandy and Paul encouraged people to reconsider their choices; more boys than girls currently needed homes. The Hackmans, who originally requested a girl decided that gender didn't matter, while the Bye-Dickersons, who already had a boy, stayed with their request for a girl.

Within days, both couples were assigned babies and received pictures from Miss Kim. The Hackmans received a referral of a baby boy they named Dominic and the Bye-Dickersons received a referral of a little girl they named Tess. With a travel date just two months away, there was a flurry of activity as everyone prepared for the trip.

In early October the families flew to Vietnam together: Sandy, Paul, Isaiah, and Hannah; Jan Bye and Paul Dickerson; Loretta and Tom Hackman, and their daughter Emily. During the long flight Hannah and Emily were passed around and entertained by whoever was not asleep at the moment while Isaiah clung to Sandy. Loretta and Jan compared notes on their children and were startled to learn that both Dominic and Tess had the same exact birth date of June 12. How ironic! Both babies were just a few days shy of being four months old.

They arrived in Ho Chi Minh City around midnight. Paul whisked them out of the airport and took them to the Huong Sen Hotel downtown where they collapsed into bed. The next morning as they met for breakfast, Sandy advised them to be ready to leave for the orphanage by mid-morning. The couples were exhausted and jetlagged, but quickly forgot about their physical discomfort as they prepared to meet their babies for the first time.

Soon the van arrived. Miss Kim sat up front with the driver, while Sandy and Paul occupied the next two seats, and the Bye-Dickersons and Hackmans sat in the back of the van. As they made their way to the Tam Binh Orphanage, Miss Kim turned to Sandy and Paul and allegedly whispered, "Oh, the Bye-Dickersons ... they will be very surprised when they get to orphanage." Paul asked what she meant, but she shook her head and refused to answer. Paul thought, "I don't like surprises. I don't like the sound of this."

Sister Hai greeted them warmly at the orphanage entrance and walked them to the back building where babies were housed on the second floor. They removed their shoes and went up the stairs to a clean, bright room filled with images of Mickey Mouse, Donald Duck, and Winnie-the-Pooh. The babies were in two adjacent cribs, one with a sleeping Dominic, the other with a wide-awake and active Tess.

As everyone peered into the cribs it was immediately obvious something was wrong. Dominic was a tiny little thing, weighing less than ten pounds while Tess was bigger, more developed, and clearly much older than four months. Sandy and Paul now knew the surprise. Loretta and Tom, although concerned for the Bye-Dickersons, were immersed in their own happiness and joy as they held their precious child for the first time and introduced three-year-old Emily to her baby brother.

The Bye-Dickersons were confused, not only by the size and age of their child, but also by the name on her crib, which was not the same as her referral name. Although the child looked like the baby in the referral picture, they needed reassurance that this was the right child. Both Sister Hai and Miss Kim confirmed that yes, this was their child.

Eventually, Loretta walked over and placed a hand on Jan's shoulder. "Is everything okay?"

"It will be," Jan replied.

"Is the baby okay?"

"I think so, but she's not as young as we thought." Jan's voice was slightly melancholy.

"But is that all right?"

"It will be," Jan said softly.

Sandy and Paul pulled Miss Kim out of the room and grilled her about the baby's circumstances. Apparently baby Tess had been placed in the orphanage after birth and a bureaucrat had named her. On her birth certificate, he had written not her actual birth date, but the date when she was available for adoption (approximately four months later). For some unknown reason, the caretakers at the orphanage had started to call her "Lu" instead of her given name and had placed that name over her crib. So while it was confusing, she was the same child that had been referred.

Sandy and Paul learned an important lesson that day: they needed to see the babies with their own eyes before referrals were given out to avoid any discrepancies. Leaving the details to Miss Kim was perhaps not the best idea. They felt angry and disappointed with Kim and told her that the situation could never happen again. She had unwittingly jeopardized the integrity of their program before it was even off the ground.

Luckily, Jan and Paul were easygoing people who took everything in stride. They already loved this baby whose picture they had adored for the last two months. The fact that Sandy and Paul had been as surprised as they were, made them secure in the knowledge that nothing deceitful had taken place. The explanation given seemed logical and Jan and Paul knew in their hearts that ultimately, it didn't matter whether the child was eight-months-old or four-months-old; she was still their child. However, cameras don't lie and pictures taken of them as they held their baby for the first time showed both the joy and the surprise they felt that day.

As the news sank in, their more immediate concern turned to baby clothes. They had packed clothes for a four-month-old and had nothing for Tess to wear! Thankfully, the Hackmans had overestimated the size of their baby, so the couples simply switched wardrobes. Problem solved.

The three couples and their children were inseparable. They ate, shopped, toured, and of course, went through the adoption process together, all orchestrated by Sandy and Paul. The couples had many similarities; they were all approximately the same age and were experiencing parenthood a second time around. The trip was enjoyable and low-key as they adjusted to their babies and became immersed in Vietnamese culture, often comparing notes over both their cultural surprises and faux pas.

The Hackmans stood out in Vietnam. Tom, with his thin, six foot five inch frame, fair skin, blue eyes, and blonde hair, towered over Loretta, who was a full foot shorter with short, dark curly hair, an olive complexion, and a ready smile. Emily was somewhat of an oddity to the Vietnamese because of her pageboy haircut, which they scolded, made her look like a boy. The Bye-Dickersons, with dark hair and average stature, blended into Vietnamese culture slightly better than the Hackmans except for the fact that they were also Americans and were caught kissing their baby in public, a definite faux pas. Both couples good-naturedly laughed off their foibles as they felt the genuine warmth and acceptance of the Vietnamese people.

Problems, of course, were inevitable. Initially, Tess was unhappy and cried frequently. As the older of the two, she was more aware of what was happening around her and was naturally fearful of her separation from her orphanage caretakers. Firmly entrenched in her rigid orphanage routines, she fell asleep by 6:00 p.m. each evening which curtailed any socializing by the Bye-Dickersons after that witching hour. Sandy and Paul offered sympathy and whatever help they could, which sometimes was nothing more than providing a listening ear.

During the trip, both babies required medical attention. Dominic suffered from a respiratory tract infection and Tess's eardrum burst after a day of sightseeing. Sandy and Paul secured the aid of Dr. Nguyen Cong Vien, a young pediatrician who happened to be Miss Kim's neighborhood friend. When Sandy and Paul met him, they immediately liked him. He was quiet and self-assured as he patiently explained everything in broken, but understandable English. Dr. Vien had studied in France as well as in

Vietnam, and was fluent in both languages, although Sandy and Paul were not. Dr. Vien had treated numerous adopted children and knew what to expect from both the children and their anxious parents.

Although American adoptions were relatively new to Vietnam, people from European countries such as France, Germany, and Italy, had been adopting there for some time. Additionally, the Children's Home Society in Minnesota had started working at Tam Binh in 1996 just prior to the program launched by Adoptions From The Heart. Other American agencies were pursuing Vietnamese adoptions as well.

* * *

Tam Binh was a Catholic orphanage established before the Vietnam War. Sister Hai began working there in 1972. When the orphanage came under the administration of the Vietnamese Department of Labor in 1975, she stayed on as the orphanage director. In its early days the orphanage was described as a bleak place without air conditioning or any amenities. In the early 1990s only two or three American agencies ventured into Vietnam, solely by invitation from the Vietnamese Government. But by 1996 and 1997, when agencies explored this new land of adoption opportunity, a renovated and modernized Tam Binh was considered to be the premiere orphanage in Saigon.

Initially the children at Tam Binh were war orphans. Later, they were children with medical problems or babies abandoned by birthmothers who could not care for them, for whatever reason. According to Dr. Vien, many of the birthmothers were very young and extremely poor. Furthermore, it was a shameful thing for young, single Vietnamese women to have babies; it virtually eliminated their chances for marriage. In a few cases, older women in rural areas, who were uneducated about birth control or couldn't afford it, had numerous children. But, when the burden of a large family became overwhelming, they gave away their smallest or youngest child, or the child with the most medical problems.

Abortion, although legal in Vietnam, was expensive and many women simply could not afford it. Others were morally opposed to abortion, while still others were uneducated about the specific details and waited too long for it to be an option. The culminating result was that the women who abandoned their babies were typically the mothers who had not received prenatal care, resulting in underweight, pre-term babies with medical problems.

Most Vietnamese people understood the plight of orphans and were happy to see foreigners adopt them. Adoption was deemed a positive action, not just for the adopted children, but for society as a whole. Children who remained in the orphanage stayed there until they turned eighteen, when they returned to the streets to face an uncertain future. Men generally became low paid workers or laborers who were often shunned by potential mates as unsuitable marriage material. Women frequently stayed on at the orphanage as caretakers.

Most of the babies arriving at Tam Binh in the mid to late 1990s were born in Tu Du Hospital, the largest maternity hospital in Ho Chi Minh City. Mothers came from within the city limits or outlying rural areas to give birth in the hospital and voluntarily relinquished their babies. During Sandy's first trip to Vietnam, she visited Tu Du and was shocked by the lamentable conditions. She found women lined up on gurneys in various stages of labor and childbirth. It was a horror show of blood and pain; women screaming in agony (or others suffering silently) without privacy, support, or pain medication. Normally, birthmothers stayed for two weeks to recover, but many, after giving birth, slipped out into the night.

Sister Hai and Miss Kim worked primarily with Tu Du Hospital. When babies were relinquished, they were assigned and transported to Tam Binh as well as to various other orphanages in the area. Miss Kim matched infants to prospective adoptive parents working with Lutheran or AFTH. Other agencies, like Children's Home Society, had their own facilitator. It was baby economics of supply and demand: birthmothers, hospitals, and orphanages were the suppliers; adoption agencies and prospective parents were the demand. As crass as it sounds, it was a system that worked and ultimately resulted in children being placed in loving homes with their forever families.

***

Miss Kim matched Tess and Dominic to their respective parents, the Bye-Dickersons and the Hackmans. Fortunately the paperwork nightmare that Sandy and Paul experienced with Isaiah's adoption was not an issue on this trip. The Vietnamese officials required that an abandonment report be completed for each child, thus eliminating any doubt about the mother's relinquishment or the child's status as a legitimate orphan.

This trip, for the most part, was a success. It was both an adventure and a memorable vacation as the couples became parents for the second time. Sandy and Paul were disturbed by the surprise, but were relieved it was not a major problem. After spending a few days in Bangkok to complete the adoption process, the three couples and their children flew home. The couples, who had forged strong bonds of friendship, made plans to spend Christmas Eve together. The Hackmans and the Bye-Dickersons traveled home and adjusted to the new additions to their families, while Sandy and Paul prepared for their next trip to Vietnam, only two short months away.

In November, Lutheran invited Miss Kim and two Vietnamese officials to visit the United States. They arrived in Connecticut and stayed for a week. They visited the agency and LSS families who had previously adopted, like Tom and Mary Fulton and Jane and John Steele. Then they traveled to Pennsylvania to meet Maxine Chalker, visit Adoptions From The Heart, and spend time with Sandy and Paul. Maxine, satisfied that Vietnamese adoptions were running smoothly, continued to promote the program.

Once home, Sandy and Paul attempted to establish some sense of normalcy. They visited their respective families, returned to work, and cared for their children. It was during this time that Sandy began to notice some peculiarities about Isaiah, who was now approaching his first birthday. Whenever Sandy gave him finger food, he picked it up, brought it up to his eyes, and examined it intently. She didn't give this habit too much thought until he began to walk. Like any toddler, he was unsteady on his feet, but unlike other toddlers, he bumped into walls and furniture, tumbled down stairs, and tripped over toys. Concerned, she scheduled an eye exam.

Isaiah was examined and pronounced legally blind. Possibly (although it wasn't confirmed), the cause was Retinopathy of Prematurity (ROP), an eye problem associated with premature and low birth weight babies, which is common in Vietnam. The condition is usually treatable if caught early enough (generally within three to six weeks after birth), with various surgical procedures conducted by the hands of a skilled ophthalmologist. However, because Isaiah was in an orphanage, nothing had been done to correct his problems. The baby, who was just starting to recover from his other medical issues, was now a permanent special needs child.

It was through this heartache that Sandy and Paul learned the grim truth about international adoption: it's fraught with risk, there are no guarantees of anything, and virtually everything is out of your control. It was a terrible lesson to learn but one that they, and the social workers at the agency, tried to communicate to prospective adoptive parents.

Sandy struggled with her feelings of sadness and helplessness when she realized that her son's future was compromised. He no longer had the opportunities in life she once imagined. She tortured herself by creating a long list of impossibilities: Isaiah would never drive a car, pilot an aircraft, perform a surgery, and so forth. It didn't help the situation, but she couldn't stop thinking about the negatives. She also worried for his immediate safety and questioned her ability to parent a blind child. How exactly would she manage?

Paul, on the other hand, was furious. Although there was no particular person to direct his anger towards, he was mad as hell about the fact that orphans existed in the world, that they didn't receive the best medical care, and that there was absolutely nothing he could do about it. Like Sandy, he felt weak and powerless.

However, there was little time to dwell on Isaiah's problems. The greenhouse work was demanding and now that the weather was cold it was necessary for the family to sleep at the little apartment on the greenhouse property every night. Paul couldn't risk a furnace malfunction because he'd lose not only his plants and flowers, but his entire business as well. With another travel group scheduled for early December, he and Sandy conducted more travel and information meetings and prepared for the upcoming trip. And this time, they had to ensure there were no more surprises.

When December rolled around they were ready to go. Maneuvering luggage and children through the airports was challenging, but somehow they managed. They flew Korean Airlines and a few of the workers recognizing them from two months earlier, nodded a friendly hello. On this trip there were both married couples and singles. They traveled as a group, flying out of JFK in New York, arriving in Seoul, and flying on to Vietnam.

Unlike the previous trip there were no surprises from Miss Kim, but there were plenty of other issues with which to contend. One man was scared, so he spent the majority of the trip locked in his room with his child, watching endless hours of television. After persistent coaxing and cajoling by Paul, he finally came out, only to discover a little too late that he actually liked Vietnam. The group was still quite small so Sandy and Paul spent time with them, as they had with the Hackmans and the Bye-Dickersons. They introduced them to Miss Hoa's silk shop and escorted them on a Mekong Delta tour. However, this was when a little trouble—which had been simmering just beneath the surface—turned into a serious problem.

Apparently, two men in the group didn't get along with each other. On the way back from the Mekong one of them made a comment about the war, a statement the other man vehemently disagreed with. The discussion turned explosive as the two men screamed and yelled at each other in an ugly confrontation. It was just the beginning. During the remainder of the trip they argued about everything: politics, religion, the war, and virtually every topic imaginable. Sandy worried the men would come to blows, which nearly happened both in Vietnam and in Bangkok.

Even leaving the country with this group proved problematic for Sandy and Paul. Waiting in line at the airport in Vietnam, one of the men discovered he had left his luggage back at the hotel and one woman couldn't find her airplane ticket. Scrambling, the man dumped his baby with Sandy and Paul and rushed back to the hotel to retrieve his suitcase which was still sitting in the lobby. The woman purchased another ticket, only to find the missing one stuck in the bottom of her purse. However, compared to the fighting that had taken place, those incidents seemed minor. Sandy and Paul were once again caught off guard by what could transpire during a simple two-week trip.

Back home Sandy voiced her frustration. "This isn't going to work. If every group is like that one, I can't do this. That was terrible! We can't have people fighting and arguing."

"Yeah, I know. Maybe we need to make up some ground rules or something," Paul replied.

"That's a great idea. Let's make up a sheet of do's and don'ts ... and let's make a page of restaurants and shops too. I don't necessarily want to go out with the families every time we're in Vietnam. They can go by themselves—especially the ones we don't want to spend time with!" Sandy added emphatically.

As a result of their conversation the travel booklet was born. At each travel meeting going forward, Sandy and Paul gave the same speech as they reviewed the behavior expected of families: "No political conversations. No religious conversations. No conversations on controversial topics. We want this to be a good experience for everyone. You're all going for the same wonderful purpose. You should unite and rejoice with each other over your children and not argue over your personal viewpoints about religion or politics or whatever." Problem solved.

***

Paul had never proposed to Sandy, at least not formally. They were committed to each other, deeply in love, and knew that at some point they would marry; but, it simply wasn't a priority in their hectic lives. However, a new year makes for new beginnings, so in early 1998 they began the discussion of when and where and how they might like to make their relationship legal. Their conversation was like a tennis ball being volleyed back and forth across the court.

"Do you want to get married in a church?" Paul ventured.

"No, I don't. I had a big church wedding the first time and I was married in a chapel the second time, but now we have kids. It's not the right thing to do. Do you want to go to the courthouse?"

"No, that's too impersonal."

"Vegas?"

"That's a definite no. I don't want a drive-through wedding!"

"Well," Sandy teased, "how about a cruise ship wedding in Puerto Rico?" She had been reading pamphlets and discovered you could get married on a cruise ship, although she hadn't seriously considered it as an option.

"That's a great idea! Your dad and your family could come and I know Jim and Joanne would come. We could get married and go on a cruise. It'll be a wedding, honeymoon, and vacation all rolled into one and we can take the kids!"

The idea resonated with both of them so they booked a cruise ship wedding for the first weekend in July. Meanwhile it was back to business as they tended the greenhouse, cared for the children, and conducted more information meetings, as interest in the adoption program continued to grow. Sandy had one more item on her plate: kindergarten. By September Hannah would be five and ready to start kindergarten. It was fairly obvious that public school wouldn't work with their erratic travel schedule, so she explored home schooling, an appealing option. She loved teaching Hannah and was certainly capable of teaching kindergarten. The only downside was that it was one more thing to add to her already overbooked schedule.

* * *

Although Sandy's mind was on kindergarten, September was several months away. It was now April of 1998 and they were set to travel with their third group of families. This group consisted of both couples and a single woman and, as always they traveled together. While some, both in this group and the last, didn't want to travel as a group, Paul insisted. He understood their desire to make their own arrangements and fly independently, but he also knew that they might require assistance once they arrived in Vietnam. The airport in Ho Chi Minh City, the Tan Son Nhat International Airport, was still rather crude and difficult to navigate. All Paul needed was for some unsuspecting family to be robbed by a pickpocket or to be taken to the wrong hotel in the middle of the night to shatter the growing stability of their program. So everyone complied; some more willingly than others.

One man in this group, Tony Wood, was a professional photographer. AFTH requested that he take a short video of the couples as they arrived at Tam Binh and received their babies, to use for marketing and informational purposes at their meetings. Tony became friendly with Spanky and, like Paul, felt protective of him. He gave Spanky his first camera which started him on a career in photography.

Spanky was an integral part of Sandy and Paul's collective family when they were in Vietnam. Spanky enjoyed spending time with Paul and asked his advice on a number of topics including how to manage his younger siblings and how to make more money. In addition to seeking Paul's guidance, Spanky continued to look to him for financial support. Although it was sometimes a financial burden, Paul complied and maintained a symbiotic relationship with Spanky by asking him to run errands. He knew that if he gave Spanky money for an errand across town, Spanky would return with the specified items, the proper change, and a receipt. Spanky was trustworthy and loyal.

Spanky liked meeting families and helping them when he could, knowing they'd throw a few extra dollars his way. He often accompanied families during the trips required to complete the adoption process and on sightseeing trips when Sandy and Paul needed all hands on deck.

The April trip went fairly well, but they barely had time to unpack before it was time to fly to Vietnam again in May. Paul and Sandy were regulars at Korean Air and the frequent flyer miles were building up; soon they'd have enough miles for an upgrade or a free ticket.

While the perks were nice, the tension between Paul and Miss Kim was increasing with each subsequent trip. In these early days the international adoption fee, which went to Miss Kim, was hand-carried by the families, a nerve-wracking exercise of hiding bills in purses, wallets, and even bras, until they arrived in Vietnam. Upon arrival, Miss Kim was quick to ask for her fee because she had bills to cover. This annoyed Paul, who felt uncomfortable with the money exchange. Paul often thought back to the time that his father woke up everyone in the family to examine the hundred dollar bills that Charlie Rickert had stuffed in his mattress. But, unlike his father's dour prediction, he now regularly dealt with substantial sums of money, much to his displeasure.

However, money wasn't the only touchy subject between Kim and Paul. Paul was still angry about Isaiah's condition at the time they received him and the surprise with the Bye-Dickersons. He and Kim were often at odds, and Kim's priorities had changed. She had married in December and was five months pregnant. In the past she'd spent time with Sandy and Paul and the adoptive families, but now she turned her focus to her own family. Plus, the groups were becoming larger—it was no longer practical to invite the entire group into her home for intimate dinners.

Underlying it all was a fundamental personality conflict between Kim and Paul. Miss Kim was an astute businesswoman, accustomed to doing things her own way. She was on her own turf and fully expected to run the show. Likewise, Paul expected to be in charge. Not surprisingly, they didn't always see eye-to-eye.

Despite the underlying tension, the May trip was the last trip to Vietnam for the rest of the year and uneventful in all regards. Sandy and Paul returned home and turned their attention to their upcoming wedding, now only a few short weeks away. Although the wedding was small and the bulk of the work fell to the cruise ship staff, there were still details to manage and arrangements to finalize.

* * *

Early in July Sandy and Paul prepared to leave for the airport to take the short flight to Puerto Rico. The wedding and cruise clothing were packed and Hannah happily twirled around her little brother in dizzying circles. The phone rang just as they were ready to depart. Sandy's face, glowing with a bride's nervous energy, turned ashen as she listened to the speaker on the other end of the line. Angel was dead. He had suffered a heart attack and one of the men with whom he shared his house found him lying dead on the floor. Sandy burst into tears as she broke the news to Paul.

Angel would be buried in Puerto Rico. Both their wedding day and Angel's wake were scheduled for July 4. Everyone was flying in early to prepare for the wedding, but now they would also be preparing for Angel's funeral.

Sandy was mired in emotional conflict, almost bipolar in her mood swings. One moment she was a distraught and grieving daughter, the next, a giddy bride-to-be. Stress was written all over her face and produced blemishes and lines that even heavy duty makeup couldn't hide. The morning of the wedding Sandy attended her father's wake with Paul at her side while Paul's brother, Jim, and his wife, Joanne, watched the children.

Jim and Joanne helped with the kids so that Sandy could pull herself together for the wedding. Distracted, Jim and Joanne had a comedy of errors which added to their own stress level. The night before they entered the ship they stayed at a hotel in Puerto Rico. Joanne pulled out their wedding clothes and pressed them, but when they arrived on board ship and unpacked, Jim's pants were mysteriously missing, most likely still in their hotel closet. Joanne swung into action and called the porter for help. They were directed to the kitchen where extra pairs of black pants were stored for the workers. Fortunately, there was a pair in Jim's size which they rented for the ceremony.

Sandy and Paul boarded the ship and stood on deck as the ship pulled away from shore. Sandy watched Puerto Rico disappear from view, tears streaming down her face. Although she attended the wake, she would miss her father's funeral. Angel was the last of the parents; all four were gone: Hazel, Blanche, Senter, and now Angel. She knew she was supposed to be happy on her wedding day, but it was beyond her comprehension.

Paul squeezed her tightly. "I'm so sorry everything worked out this way." There was nothing to he could say to make it better, so he just held her and let her cry until she finally stopped. She glanced at her watch, took his hand, and together they walked inside to their cabin. It was time to get married.

White was the color of the day. Sandy wore a long white dress, Hannah wore a little frilly one, and Isaiah wore a white shirt, white shorts, and white shoes. Paul and Jim wore matching outfits: a white shirt, black pants, and vests from Vietnam. It was too hot to bother with tuxedos or even suits. Strangely, the minister looked like Uncle Jim.

As the ceremony started, Paul held Isaiah in his arms, but before long he was overcome with emotion and handed the child to Jim so he could say his vows. Paul held Sandy's face in both his hands and looked into her big brown eyes as he repeated his vows, choking up as he said them. Then Hannah started to cry.

"Wait, wait, we have to stop," said Sandy. "What's the matter honey?"

"If you marry Daddy Paul, then your name is going to change, and I'll have to go live with someone else. Someone else will have to adopt me," Hannah cried.

Both Sandy and Paul got on their knees and told Hannah how much they loved her. "Hannah just because I'm marrying Daddy Paul doesn't mean you have to live somewhere else. You're going to live with us. We're all going to live together forever: you, me, Daddy Paul, and Isaiah."

"Oh, okay," Hannah brightened.

They started again as both Sandy and Paul cried through their vows, this time not even attempting to stop. When the minister asked, "Do you Sandy, take Paul …?" Sandy blurted out, "I've been waiting for this for a very long time. I DO! I DO! I DO!" Paul continued to cry as he kissed his bride and received congratulatory hugs and kisses from Jim and Joanne.

When the bride and groom regained their composure, they had their pictures taken and celebrated with cake and champagne. Beaming with happiness, Sandy finally felt like a bride for the first time all day. During the next few days of their cruise, Sandy alternated between sublime happiness and aching sadness. Hannah went to kid's camp and Jim and Joanne entertained Isaiah so the couple could enjoy their honeymoon.

But soon the honeymoon was over and they flew home, back to a normal life—whatever normal now meant.

CHAPTER 14

Divine Fate

*Where your talents and
The needs of the world cross,
Lies your calling.*

Aristotle

*P*aul felt that facilitating adoptions was his real calling. However, the adoption business was neither lucrative nor consistent yet so, after the honeymoon, he returned to his job at the greenhouse. But as much as he loved working in adoptions, it wasn't without its pitfalls either. He and Kim were sometimes at odds and the agency provided its own set of challenges. Families frequently called him or Sandy for help, instead of their social worker which resulted in extra work for them and hurt feelings for her. Maxine urged families to go through the proper channels, but when they didn't, it created an awkward situation for everyone.

Paul was undeterred. Finding homes for orphans was worth any amount of aggravation in his estimation. There were no more trips scheduled for the remainder of 1998, but with parents in various stages of the paperwork process, he and Sandy conducted a steady stream of information meetings throughout Pennsylvania and Delaware.

As the year wore on several changes occurred. The social worker assigned to the Vietnam program left, which eased the building tension, but there was friction on the home front as Paul's father frequently complained that his wife was ignoring him. It didn't take long to discover the problem was more serious than a married couple's squabbles. Paul's mother had become forgetful and repetitive and, when she saw a doctor, the unfortunate diagnosis was Alzheimer's disease. Before long, his parents were forced to move out of their home and into a cottage at Luther Acres, an elder care facility.

Changes were in the works for Sandy too. In August Miss Kim gave birth to a baby girl, an event that ultimately altered their working relationship. In the fall Sandy started to home school Hannah, which placed an extra burden on her time and energy. It was also September when Sandy heard that Jan Bye, who had adopted baby Tess just a year earlier, was pregnant. It was wonderful news, but Jan was soon hospitalized, the pregnancy in danger. Sandy and Loretta became frequent visitors to provide moral support and laughter, and Sandy found she needed the visits as much as Jan, with Isaiah's blindness and Angel's recent death never far from her thoughts.

Even Christmas was a mixed emotional bag. Much to Sandy and Paul's surprise, cards and gifts flowed in from appreciative adoptive families. The letters of gratitude and pictures of adopted children moved them to tears. Sandy reconnected with her own family and invited her six half-brothers and sisters for a holiday celebration. They all agreed to come, so Paul spent several days preparing an elaborate feast, but when the day arrived, only one sibling showed. Dejected once again, Sandy turned to her favorite movie, *It's a Wonderful Life*, to remind herself why she had been placed on earth.

By January of 1999 the Vietnam program at AFTH had taken off in a big way. There were several reasons for its success. In Vietnam, infants could be adopted at three or four months of age, their health was generally good, the trip took less than three weeks to complete, and singles could adopt. AFTH marketed the program to various groups and, while the Vietnamese didn't allow gays to adopt per se, they did allow singles. However, as long as no one outwardly professed to be gay, he or she could adopt as a single person with no one the wiser. Plus, Sandy and Paul had earned a good reputation in the local adoption community and word spread quickly.

The couple worked relentlessly to make trips as seamless and enjoyable as possible, although each trip was still on their learning curve and each stumble was another opportunity for improvement. There was never a trip without a problem. Some difficulties were minor inconveniences, while others caused sleepless nights, worry, heartache, and fear. Sometimes, just maintaining the ordinary routine of life was a struggle.

Well-meaning families sent orphanage donations to Sandy and Paul, filling their basement with diapers, toys, clothing, and gifts. Although thankful for the generosity of the families, they found it difficult to manage the contributions along with everything else. They packed up plastic bins and hand-carried the items to Vietnam themselves, which taught them an important lesson in the process: plastic bins were sturdy. After destroying several pieces of luggage, they finally resorted to plastic bins for their clothing and personal items as well, wrapping tissue paper around the perimeters to conceal their contents.

Paul worried before each trip. He scrutinized their packing lists over and over again and allowed extra time to reach the airport, just in case. The international flights required that they leave their house around 4:00 a.m. The kids went to the airport dressed in their pajamas and slept in the car, but upon arrival were awakened and dressed. These early morning routines were what Paul aptly described as a "total mess," as they dragged sluggish children and plastic bins through the airports before dawn, navigated security, and dealt with airline personnel who were sometimes surly. Before each flight, Sandy and Paul turned to each other and asked, "What's going to happen this time?" knowing full well that something (bad) usually did.

Sometimes Paul had passport or visa problems. On one of the early trips as everyone left Saigon to head for Bangkok he checked in last, as usual. This time, however, the ticket agent looked at his passport and exclaimed, "You cannot go!"

"What do you mean I can't go?"

"You don't have six months left on your passport." Paul knew his passport was almost ready to expire, but thought he had enough time to renew it when he returned home.

"I still have time left on my passport! I'm only spending four days in Bangkok, for crying out loud!"

"No. The law says you cannot go." Paul's mind raced. It was eleven o'clock at night, too late to go to the embassy. He refused to be separated from his family.

"How was I supposed to know I can't travel with less than six months on my passport?"

"It's in the airline book. I show you. Unless you have six months left on passport, you cannot enter Thailand. If you go, they fine the airlines $4,000."

"All right, all right, but I'm not leaving my family. You need to let them come back, change our tickets, and stop our luggage."

The man reconsidered and, at the last minute, pulled out a release form from under the counter that would hold Paul responsible for the fine. As Paul signed it, he noticed a faint smirk on the man's face. He'd been playing him all along.

When they arrived in Bangkok, Paul felt anxious. He could easily be out four grand if caught. Fortunately, some of the babies began to cry— noise the officers couldn't tolerate. They moved the families into the shortest line and Paul planted himself in the middle of the group. The officer furiously stamped passports, processing the women and howling babies as quickly as possible. As Paul came forward, the officer put his passport aside and made him wait. Finally, when he was the last person in line, the officer picked up his passport, gave it a quick glance, stamped it, and allowed him through immigration. He had survived another close call!

On another occasion, Isaiah's passport was problematic. Although Isaiah had a Vietnamese passport, each time he entered Thailand he needed a visa. Before long, his passport was filled to capacity with stamps and visas. Sandy took the families to the Thai consulate to apply for their visas, along with Isaiah's application, but the officer threw Isaiah's passport back at her. "No, you cannot get a Thai visa. There's no room in his passport for visa."

"Can't you put it on a separate piece of paper?"

"No. It has to be in the passport!"

Sandy returned to the hotel and consulted with Paul. She called Kim for advice, but the answer was still the same: Isaiah simply couldn't go to Bangkok until he had a new passport. Everyone was scheduled to leave Vietnam the next day and there was no time to obtain a new passport. Paul made a decision about what had to be done.

The next day, passport in hand, Paul approached the consulate. Suffice it to say that everyone left Vietnam as a group.

*　*　*

More often than not, problems were encountered behind-the-scenes and involved only one family or a single individual—and Sandy. Much of what happened during the course of any given trip was hidden from other families and purposely so. Paul and Sandy wanted everyone's memories of Vietnam to be as close to perfect as possible. The more they could shield them from, the better.

Sandy and Paul's division of labor within the adoption process had evolved naturally. Because Paul and Kim didn't hit it off, Sandy ended up with the Vietnamese side of the process dealing with Kim, Sister Hai, and the orphanage. Paul handled the American side. Because of this division of responsibilities, Sandy often saw more disturbing situations than Paul.

Sandy spent a great deal of time at Tam Binh interacting with Miss Kim and Sister Hai, coordinating upcoming referrals, and taking baby pictures for the families. She loved being at the orphanage, feeding and holding babies while surreptitiously checking on their care and well-being. Although the caretaking provided by the orphanage was generally quite good, it was always disturbing to see the numbers of children with problems: premature babies, babies with pneumonia, and babies born with severe disabilities or other dire conditions. Sandy frequently became attached to the babies with serious problems and sometimes they died.

When infants died, she was depressed for days, inconsolable in her grief. She took each death personally; each death was a personal failure in her mind, because she had been unsuccessful in finding a family for the child, or finding one quickly enough. Often these were the babies with unspecified heart conditions or babies who weren't thriving—the babies that no one wanted. Sandy had pictures of each of them and, when they died, she reluctantly threw their pictures into the trash. But she may as well have thrown her own heart away because she cried for days on end, grieving each child as if it were her own. Paul was sympathetic, but felt she needed to be more detached, while Sandy couldn't imagine such a thing. She had also heard that when babies died they were buried on the grounds of Tam Binh, but without a proper funeral. This knowledge kept her awake in the middle of the night as everyone else slept.

But Sandy wasn't the only person with emotional ties to the babies. Caregivers sometimes fell in love with particular children and, when the children were adopted, they were filled with resentment and grief. Once, when a family came to adopt a toddler, her caregiver was so overcome with emotion she burst into angry tears. The baby started to cry, aware of her impending separation from her caregiver, the only mother she had ever known. Subsequently, the adoptive parents felt rejected by the toddler. Sandy, desperate, pulled Miss Kim aside. "You need to talk to the caregiver. Tell her she must walk away *now*! I promise the baby will be okay, but she needs to leave. Tell her that."

Miss Kim spoke to her and eventually the caregiver placed the distraught child in the mother's arms, kissed her goodbye, and ran out of the room sobbing. The toddler screamed and cried the entire ride back to the hotel in the cramped van, making everyone extremely uncomfortable. Sandy worried about the family all night but, by the next morning, the baby was on the mother's hip and wouldn't get down. The toddler was still upset, but appeared to be bonding with her adoptive mother. In the end, the family worked through the situation and all was well for everyone except, perhaps, the caregiver who had lost her favorite child forever.

Behind-the-scene incidents happened frequently. Whether it was an argument with Kim or a family in distress or even a personal issue involving Paul or one of the children, Sandy had to rise above it all, putting on what she called her "family face." It wasn't uncommon to have a screaming match with Kim one minute and the next, to meet families in the lobby seemingly composed and calm, smiling and exchanging pleasantries: "How did you sleep? How's the baby? Did you like the restaurant last night?"

Once, however, it was just too much for Sandy to overcome. It was impossible to hide the effects of the life-altering experience that had occurred earlier that morning. The day had started simply enough. Miss

Kim and a group of nuns had invited her to go for a drive to District 7 to see a birthing center. District 7 was a very poor section of town where only the Vietnamese lived. When they arrived, the nuns showed Sandy two factories where pregnant girls worked. The girls ranged in age from fourteen to seventeen and were in their second trimester of pregnancy. In one factory the girls made rice mats, car seat covers, and embroidered goods. The conditions were deplorable. The factory was sweltering hot, filthy, and reeked of glue. As they walked to the second factory, rats scurried about underfoot. Sandy, who was terrified of the vermin, rolled her long skirt into a ball and ran. The second factory was equally grim. It was a lacquer ware factory filled with noxious fumes.

As if the sickening smells and sights weren't enough, the next building—a shack—was the worst of all. Housed inside were little girls ready to give birth. They were lying on the floor and on a wooden bed without a mattress, waiting to go into labor. When they did, the nuns took them to the hospital and some of their babies became Kim's to transport to Tam Binh.

Sandy looked at the girls and thought, "Oh my God, one of them could be Isaiah's mother." Sick to her stomach, she ran outside for air. Leaning against the car door for support, she felt lightheaded. Miss Kim and one of the nuns followed her outside.

"What's wrong Miss Sandy?" Kim asked, puzzled.

"I have to go home. I'm sorry. I can't handle this."

Kim and the nun looked at each other, perplexed. What was this woman so upset about? Annoyed, they gathered the other nuns and headed back into the city. Sandy's head pounded as she continued to think about the girls and their babies: "Why are they here, alone and pregnant, working in horrible conditions, and giving birth without their parent's support? How can we take their babies? We can't keep taking their babies! But how will they care for them?" Her mind kept twisting the facts around and around, like a young girl twirling a strand of hair. None of it made any sense—there were no answers to be found.

Later that same day she escorted a family to a jewelry store. After looking over the merchandise, the family couldn't decide which piece of expensive jewelry to buy and asked Sandy for advice. But Sandy couldn't focus. She couldn't stop thinking about the young girls. They had nothing. They had no families to help them. Many had come from the countryside to work and give birth to babies that adoptive families—perhaps even this family—would take home with them. But here we are buying expensive jewelry ... The contrast was too much to bear and Sandy left the store weeping, leaving the family baffled by her strange behavior.

The memory continued to haunt her until eventually she came to terms with the fact that the girls were incapable of keeping their babies and that she and Paul could at least place them into loving homes. She just wished there was something she could do for these young girls. They hit a raw nerve. She saw herself in them—unloved and unwanted—or as Paul viewed it, abandoned and forgotten.

* * *

The vast majority of families were wonderful; they were caring, loving individuals who simply wanted to become parents. Occasionally there were individuals (or families) in the group who created problems for Sandy and Paul. They were the complainers who were never satisfied with anything, or the people whose expectations hadn't been met, or simply families under stress who acted out during the trip. But whatever the cause, the result was generally the same and neither Sandy nor Paul had much patience to deal with them.

Over time Sandy heard a number of complaints: the baby is too old, the baby's skin is too dark, the baby is bowlegged, the baby's eyes aren't right; comments she labeled petty and ridiculous. She didn't understand why people couldn't just be happy and accept things the way they were, especially when minor issues were involved. Childbirth, after all, is not a perfect science either and the concept that adoption somehow entitled one to expect a perfect baby was repulsive. As she had personally discovered with Isaiah, international adoption was inherently risky; one needed to accept that fact and deal with the consequences. It was because of these complaints that Sandy, along with Sister Hai, decided to keep some information private.

Early on, Sister Hai and Miss Kim matched the babies to their adoptive parents. However, after the surprise incident with the Bye-Dickersons, it became necessary for Sandy and Paul to see the babies with their own eyes before they were referred. As the program evolved and more families came into the process, it made more sense for Sandy to match babies to their families. She knew most of the families personally, she had their dossiers, and she knew what they were willing to accept. The dossier spelled out what gender the family preferred, the age of the baby requested, whether the adoptive parents were open to twins or siblings, if they were receptive to special needs children, and so forth. However, knowing how demanding and unrealistic some families were in their requests, she didn't want them to know that she was the one making the decisions about their children. So when, and if, they asked, they were told that referrals were made in the orphanage by Sister Hai. It was an arrangement Sister Hai agreed to and a little secret they shared.

However, the job of matching babies to families was not one that Sandy took lightly and it was the one task she dreaded most of all. When the time came to make the referrals, she waited until Paul and the children were sound asleep. Sitting at the little desk in the dimly lit hotel room she pulled the pictures, medical reports, and dossiers together. Taking a deep breath, she bowed her head in prayer: "Dear Lord, please let me pick the right baby for the right family. I don't know what I'm doing and you know how I hate this responsibility. I don't want to play God, so please help me to do what's right and best for the babies and the families. Amen."

The first dossier came off the pile: they want a healthy girl less than six months old. Okay, here's their girl. Next, a boy and so on and so forth until the job was done. Emotionally spent, she collapsed into bed, still seeing the faces of the babies in her sleep. She knew that as soon as the families received their referrals (consisting of a picture and a sketchy medical report) the calls would start coming into her: "Sandy I didn't want a baby quite this old; I was hoping for a four-month-old." Sandy sympathized, but thought to herself, "I'm sorry, but I didn't have any more babies available. She's two months older than you wanted, but you'll get over it. You really will; you'll see."

The calls were both annoying and discouraging, planting seeds of self-doubt in her mind. Had she done the right thing? Were these the right children for these particular parents? She worried until the parents arrived at the orphanage to meet their babies for the first time. It was a scene that replayed over and over again, but one she never tired of, loving every single minute of it. Excited parents came to the orphanage and received their babies, one-by-one as their names were called. Sandy stood to the side and anxiously watched as families held their babies for the first time, shedding tears of happiness, hugging spouses (or partners or parents or friends), and snapping those all-important, first moment pictures. When the excitement died down a bit, families made their way over to Sister Hai, who was beaming.

"Sister Hai! Look at my baby. She's so sweet, thank you so much! She's so precious and I love her so much already. Thank you, thank you!"

"Oh, oh you're welcome," Sister Hai responded, uneasy with the exuberant displays of joy.

"How did you know that this was the right child for me?"

"It wasn't me—it was divine fate!" And coming from a Catholic nun, everyone knew it to be true, especially Sandy, who felt she had received divine intervention through her late-night prayers.

Later they approached Sandy. "Isn't Sister Hai great? I can't believe she picked the perfect baby for me!"

"I know. It's remarkable isn't it? She picked Isaiah too." She was thankful that the families were happy and blissfully unaware of her role in selecting their children.

* * *

Most families were generally not privy to the sticky situations that Sandy and Paul handled, but one person who caught a glimpse into their private world was Beth Dewson, a single woman traveling in an early group. Their group was small and consisted of Beth, a married couple, and a woman accompanied by her teenage daughter.

The Pinkertons, Beth, and the married couple arrived at JFK, but the woman and her daughter were nowhere to be found. Sandy and Paul were frantic with worry as it became apparent the two would miss their flight to Seoul. Sandy called the social worker to find out what had happened to them.

"They left for the airport and should be there soon," the social worker reported.

"But they're not here and we're boarding! We have to go!"

"Call me from Seoul and we'll figure something out ..."

When they arrived in South Korea, Sandy called the social worker again.

"Sandy, I don't know where they are and they won't answer the phone. I'll be in touch."

The group arrived in Vietnam and still there was no word about the woman and her daughter. Sandy called Kim to report the family wasn't there, but was expected the next day, a little lie to buy some time while they figured out what to do. She asked Kim to tell Sister Hai about the situation so their baby wouldn't be brought out with the other two.

The next day the social worker called Sandy with bad news. "Sandy, you're not going to believe this. I kept calling, but no one answered the phone so finally I drove over to their house to see what was wrong. Apparently, when the mother was driving to the airport with her daughter, she decided against the adoption. I'm not sure what's going to happen. Obviously this isn't a good situation."

"That's terrible. I hope she's okay ... I talked to Kim about the fact she might not show, but Kim's not willing to give her a refund."

"Okay, I'll handle it," the social worker sighed.

Sandy and Paul were sympathetic for the woman, but their bigger concern was the child who would be placed back into the system with little or no chance for future adoption. Although it wasn't fair to penalize the child, it was generally what happened when people backed out of an adoption.

Beth caught wind of the situation and overheard Paul arguing with Sister Hai and Miss Kim about referring the child again, which seemed like an uphill battle. Paul refused to give up and, by the end of the trip they reluctantly placed the baby for adoption again.

Beth had her own issues to contend with including paperwork problems and a sick baby. Luckily, Paul and Sandy stepped in to remedy the situation with the INS, and Dr. Vien treated her daughter who suffered from malnutrition, scabies, and an upper respiratory infection. With Beth's most pressing concerns resolved, she was able to relax and enjoy her time in Vietnam.

Sandy and Paul set up a complete itinerary of sightseeing and cultural immersion that included the Cu Chi Tunnels, Cao Dai Temple, Mekong Delta cruise, the War Remnants Museum, and a water puppet show. The effort put forth to show families a good time went far beyond Beth's expectations, but what impressed her most was their willingness to go the extra mile for virtually anyone.

One day in the course of completing an adoption meeting, Paul and Sandy's group ran into a young woman traveling with her mother. The young woman was attempting to adopt a child, but wasn't receiving adequate support from her own facilitator and had no idea what to do next. Paul sat down with her, went over her paperwork, and invited her to join their group. Beth watched Paul and Sandy guide her; they gave her as much time and attention as their AFTH families. Beth knew then, that this was an amazing couple with big hearts.

Unknown to Beth, this wasn't an isolated incident for Sandy and Paul who believed if someone needed help, you provided it. Once they ran into a family seeking medical advice. The family worried that the child they planned to adopt was sick and they wanted more information before the adoption occurred. The Pinkertons called in Dr. Vien to help. He diagnosed the child with a heart problem, but the family decided to go ahead anyway. Years later, the couple called Sandy and Paul to thank them for Dr. Vien's help and to let them know that despite heart surgery, their daughter was now fine.

Another time a married couple saw Sandy and Paul with their group of families and begged them for help. They were invited into the group and given assistance with their paperwork. The wife's parents, who lived in Vermont, sent Sandy and Paul several cases of maple syrup that Christmas. Sandy was astonished when the package arrived because she had totally forgotten about the incident. Helping families was just something they did; it was no big deal.

While the appreciation of the families was a definite perk of the job, the fact of the matter was that adoption work was tiring and stressful and took its toll on almost every aspect of their lives. In 1999 when the program was in full swing, they traveled to Vietnam nearly every month with their two young children. Their coach flights were miserable and jetlag was a killer. Sandy found herself home schooling Hannah at three in the morning when they were both awake enough to concentrate. As soon as they adjusted to the jetlag, it was time to turn around and fly home again.

Sandy also found she ate too much and exercised too little during these trips, and eventually she put on weight. It was hard to exercise when you were tired and she was almost always tired, either from flying, parenting, or helping families through the adoption process. When she wasn't tired, she often ate due to stress or boredom. Subsequently, she received unkind comments from the Vietnamese about her full and curvy figure. According to them, she was both old and fat.

With a foot in each country Sandy didn't fit into either one which often made for an uneasy existence. While she was in Vietnam she spent most of her time with Paul and the children or the adoptive families; she had few other friends. At home she resumed contact with her siblings and friends like Jan, Loretta, and Donna, but her life was hectic and her days filled with home schooling and maintaining the house in Manheim. There was little time left over for socializing. She also had to shop for bare essentials during her brief stints at home. Although Miss Hoa made clothing for her, she needed basic items like underwear which couldn't be found in Vietnam. The Vietnamese women were tiny and Sandy joked that their underwear was the size of a dime.

Paul suffered his share of hardships too, primarily a lack of money. He hadn't signed on to be a facilitator for big money, but he did need to make a living. The greenhouse was a floundering money pit and most of the money made in adoptions was spent on airfare, hotels, and food. He knew he could make significantly more money if he facilitated adoptions alone, but he wouldn't even entertain that notion. He'd waited fifty years to become a parent, why would he leave his family behind? Family was his priority and he wasn't about to spend his time away from Sandy and the kids, no matter what the cost.

Juggling the responsibilities in his life was difficult and when he was in Vietnam, Paul relied heavily upon his siblings for support. Marty still ran the greenhouse and Dave checked the house to make sure nothing was awry. Paul stopped the mail during each trip, but he learned a hard lesson once when he returned home to find that his health insurance had been cancelled for non-payment while he'd been out of the country. The insurance company wouldn't negotiate even though Paul had his airline tickets as proof of his absence. After the incident, Dave forwarded their mail to Vietnam.

Paul felt his biggest challenge was dealing with Kim. When he and Kim disagreed, Kim went directly to Sandy and stated, "You do what I say or I will not work with you!" Sandy begged Paul to give into Kim's demands, but often he refused, placing Sandy directly in the middle of Paul's conflict with Kim. In turn, this set the stage for many fights between Paul and Sandy. Paul refused to comply with Kim's mandates, while Sandy feared that if they didn't, families would suffer and their program would end. Usually, but not always, Kim won.

For Sandy, being caught in the middle between Paul and Kim was a losing proposition. However, Sandy's biggest complaints about Kim were when something negatively impacted families. Kim set the timetable for when families went to the orphanage, the Ministry of Justice, and Immigration. On any given day she instructed Sandy to have families ready to go to the orphanage at a certain time, say ten o'clock. Sandy called the families and, by 9:15, they were assembled in the hotel lobby, anxious to leave. Invariably, Sandy's cell phone would ring at the last minute and it would be Kim calling to tell her the meeting was postponed, sometimes for hours at a time. Families, frustrated and angry, often assumed that Sandy didn't know what she was doing, causing her to "lose face." But Sandy didn't have any control over the situation. It was Kim and, more accurately, the officials in the various offices or sometimes Sister Hai, who ran the show.

Conversely, Kim became upset if she felt she was the one losing face, which happened occasionally. Sandy had very little power in their relationship, but she was not completely passive either. Kim, like many Vietnamese, took a nap each day. Generally, she was up early in the morning and returned to her home midday for lunch and a couple hours of sleep. Later, she returned to work and retired late in the evening. If Kim had been particularly difficult, Sandy made a point to call her during nap time to ask inane questions or confirm appointments.

Once, however, Sandy was so furious with Kim that she almost ended their working relationship altogether. Sandy had made the referral of Baby A to a particular family. However, shortly after the referral was made, Baby A became extremely ill and was hospitalized. Kim suggested referring Baby B for the family because she was uncertain when, or if, Baby A would recover and be able to travel. With a heavy heart, Sandy called the family and explained the conundrum. It was a difficult situation because once a baby was referred and the family had a picture, they considered the child theirs and began the bonding process. The family reluctantly agreed to the change and a second referral picture was mailed to them.

Weeks passed, but finally the families arrived in Vietnam. On the way to the orphanage, Miss Kim reportedly announced to Sandy: "That second baby got sick so we're giving them the first baby now."

"What?" the word exploded out of Sandy's mouth. She felt nauseous as the babies were brought out, one at a time, at the orphanage. When Baby A was handed to the mother, the mother didn't say a word or indicate that anything was wrong. Sandy thought that perhaps she was so caught up in the emotion of the moment she didn't notice the switch.

Later that day Sandy escorted the mothers to the Immigration Office to apply for the babies' passports. The mother was in line when she suddenly noticed Baby A's picture on her documents and started crying. Sandy rushed over, assuming the worst.

"It's not the right baby!" the mother cried.

"I know," Sandy whispered, barely breathing, trying to be discreet so the other families wouldn't hear.

"What happened to the other baby?"

"The other baby got really sick and this baby, the first baby, got well. Look, I know this is traumatic and emotional and ... wrong. I don't know what to say. I swear, I didn't know about this before today. I feel terrible, but we're in the Immigration Office and if you want to go home with a baby, this baby, you need to apply the documents right now. I'm so sorry to put you in this situation, but you need to decide."

"Okay, okay, I'll do it," the woman said, tears streaming down her face as the other families wondered about the commotion.

Sandy returned to her hotel room, slammed the door, and burst into angry tears. "I can't do this anymore," she yelled at Paul. "I'm done, I am so fucking done!" Before Paul had a chance to respond, he stood, open-mouthed as she called Kim.

"I am so fucking mad at you!! I can't believe you did this to me. You don't know what you've done. Our whole program is down the tubes. No one's going to trust me and no one is going to trust you or Sister Hai. You have to be truthful with me. You have to stop doing shit like this or I WILL NOT WORK WITH YOU!!!" Sandy screamed at the top of her lungs.

"Calm down Miss Sandy, it's not that bad," soothed Kim, who honestly did not understand the ramifications of what she had done. (Allegedly, she had saved the initial paperwork which was then presented that day at the Immigration Office, although it's not entirely clear how the paperwork processing was completed.)

"Yeah, it's not bad for you because you're not the one traveling back and forth and getting jetlagged and stressed and taking care of families who put their trust in you. You sit back and watch everything unfold and now you're doing stupid shit like switching babies! Don't you dare tell me, it's not so fucking bad!" Sandy yelled.

"It's okay, Miss Sandy, it's okay," Kim patronized.

For the remainder of the trip Sandy was on pins and needles, worried that everyone would hear about the situation and think that she and Paul were disreputable. It was a scenario that jeopardized not only their futures, but AFTH's as well. Thankfully, no one found out and there were no words to express her gratitude for the family's silence. To Sandy's knowledge, the family never told their story. Later, she knew that the couple fell completely in love with their child and went on to have a wonderful life together. But, at the time, Sandy returned home furious and ready to quit.

* * *

Trips came in rapid succession now. They had been to Vietnam repeatedly that year, with several more trips on the horizon. As they traveled to Philly to conduct yet another travel meeting, Sandy turned to Paul and said, "You know, at some point soon you'll have to give up the greenhouse."

"Do you really think so?" Paul hoped that was the case.

"Yeah, I think there'll be a lot of families going to Vietnam in the future and this is going to be our full-time job. There are tons of families who want to adopt children, I know there are." By now her anger had dissipated, although she still didn't entirely trust Kim.

It was the green light Paul had been waiting for. His heart was no longer in the flower business, but he wasn't sure if Sandy was on board to sell the greenhouse and commit to facilitating adoptions full-time. He was thrilled to hear her say it out loud because now he could take the necessary steps to rid himself of his albatross.

* * *

By May of 1999, AFTH's Vietnam program was going strong. There were increasingly larger travel groups and trips occurred almost every month. Lutheran's program had gained popularity too, although they had smaller numbers than AFTH. The primary focus of Kim's life was now her daughter, who was eight months old. Although she continued to work with Tu Du, Tam Binh, the Ministry of Justice, and Immigration, she no longer had the time or energy to devote to her Lutheran families. So she called upon Sandy and Paul to integrate those families into their group and escort them to the various meetings.

For Sandy and Paul it really didn't matter. What was one more family? But eventually, it became a sticky situation for everyone. Kim, unknown to Lutheran, told families to go with Sandy and Paul to the adoption meetings. The Lutheran families, who didn't know or trust Sandy and Paul, called LSS for guidance. But LSS, unaware of Kim's instructions, told the families that they should only go with Kim. Confusion prevailed. From Kim's perspective it made perfect sense. Families were families were families. It shouldn't make any difference who went with whom, where.

At first, it made sense to Sandy and Paul too. Adding a family here or there didn't significantly add to their workload, but as the numbers of Lutheran families grew, it placed an extra burden on them as they spent time (and sometimes money) on the families without appropriate recompense. Initially, LSS was not in favor of the arrangement nor was AFTH. Sandy and Paul were caught in the middle.

This was the state of affairs when the May 1999 group arrived in Vietnam, a group that included several AFTH families and one Lutheran family. When Kim called upon Sandy and Paul to help the Lutheran family, they were surprised to see Tom and Mary Fulton, the couple who adopted a child at the same time they adopted Isaiah. The Fultons were equally surprised to see the Pinkertons, the couple they remembered as being greatly distressed and completely mired in problems. So, when the Fultons were instructed to follow Sandy and Paul's directions, they were hesitant and reluctant to do so. They had confidence in Kim and Lutheran to be competent and detail oriented, but they hadn't seen those same qualities exhibited by Sandy and Paul.

The Fultons stayed in the same hotel as the AFTH families and were included in the group for dinners, sightseeing, and the various adoption meetings. As the two weeks progressed, their confidence in the Pinkertons gradually improved.

By now, the process to exit the country had changed. Although families still needed a visa from Bangkok, Paul could go alone, file the paperwork for the families, obtain the visas, and fly the families out of Vietnam, sparing them the expense and inconvenience of spending four days in Bangkok. The baby's exam and the final interview were now completed in Ho Chi Minh City, eliminating the need to go to Thailand. Paul gave families the option. If they wanted to go to Bangkok, they were welcome to come along, but it wasn't necessary. Early on, all the families, with the exception of the Fultons, chose to let Paul fly to Bangkok alone. The Fultons held out, but decided at the last minute that he was up to the task. In the end, they were genuinely relieved and grateful they didn't have to make the journey to Bangkok for a second time.

The Fultons, like the other families, saw the dedication and hard work Sandy and Paul put into the trip and came away with wonderful memories of their adoption experience. They concluded that Sandy and Paul, like their counterparts at Lutheran and Miss Kim, were competent and caring individuals.

After the trip with the Fultons, the Pinkertons returned to Vietnam two months later with a large group consisting of couples and singles, both from AFTH and Lutheran. The new social worker from AFTH, Elizabeth Norris, accompanied them, both to learn about the program and to help a married couple adopting twins.

Elizabeth had been with AFTH for nearly a year and had a great working relationship with the Pinkertons. She also had a good understanding of families and their trials and tribulations. Typically, what she

saw were older heterosexual couples who had gone down the path of
failed infertility treatments, gay singles (or couples), married couples who
were too young to adopt from China, and people who already had biological children, but now chose to adopt for a variety of reasons.

Generally speaking, there was an uneasy balance between parents,
social workers, and the agency, all of whom had slightly conflicting goals.
The agency was a business. It needed clients and it needed to make money.
By its very nature, there was competition among agencies to secure clients.
However, from the social worker's perspective, dealing with families was an
intimate and intense process and they openly encouraged families to check
out other agencies to make sure they were selecting the best one for their
needs. Families, in turn, chose agencies based upon various factors including
geographic location, reputation, cost, programs, or sometimes just a gut feeling about the agency, its staff, or even a particular social worker.

Through her work, Elizabeth found commonalities among the families.
People generally felt uncomfortable with the concept of spending money on
an adoption, sometimes construing it as "buying a baby," which was never
the case. She spent a great deal of time educating families about the fact that
the money spent on an adoption was for services provided both by the
agency and within the country of origin. Across the board, families found
the home study to be the most stressful part of the process as every aspect of
their lives came under a microscope. Vietnam had become popular with families because of the young age of the children being placed and the short
adoption process, which could take six months or less.

Within married couples, mothers generally drove the adoption process
and, as such, requested girls far more than boys. This was an interesting,
yet troubling, phenomenon. Women frequently fantasized about outfit-
ting little girls in frilly dresses and having a close mother-daughter relationship, unrealistically assuming girls are easier to parent than boys.
Although not overt, the underlying decision was sometimes clouded by
stereotypes about boys exhibiting aggressive behavior, along with touches
of racism. Some people, whether they were willing to admit it or not, felt
uncomfortable handing over the family surname and legacy to an Asian
boy. Plus there was the concern that when it came time for an Asian son
to date, he might have a tough time. Not every father would be thrilled to
have his Caucasian daughter date an Asian boy while, conversely, an
Asian girl might easily date a Caucasian boy. (I use this example only
because the vast majority of adoptive parents were Caucasian.)

Thrown into the mix were the stereotypes of the beautiful and obedient Asian doll and the idea that Asian boys turned into violent gang members or evil kung-fu masters. Some parents worried that an Asian boy,
generally shorter and thinner than his American counterpart, might be
teased, while a petite girl would be looked upon favorably and would

integrate into American society more easily. Whatever a family's reasoning, the fact remained that, regardless of the country of origin, people adopting internationally chose girls over boys nearly two to one (with approximately 64% choosing girls and 36% choosing boys).

Elizabeth, Sandy, and Paul felt uncomfortable with these statistics, knowing that boys were often left behind, while girls were quickly placed into loving homes. It was another behind-the-scenes reality that made everyone concerned.

AFTH was an agency that allowed adoptive parents to choose gender while some other agencies did not. Lutheran had a policy that allowed parents to choose gender only on their second adoption. Initially, Children's Home Society let parents choose gender, but reversed its policy when the vast majority selected girls, resulting in longer and longer waiting periods for referrals. Fortunately, the requests for boys and girls were pretty evenly split on this particular trip.

The trip provided new insights for Elizabeth as she observed the process through the eyes of the adoptive parents. She was particularly struck by their commitment and courage and the grace with which they conducted themselves. She couldn't imagine the leap of faith it took to get on a plane, fly to the other side of the world, and bring home a child that someone else had decided was yours. In fact, the whole adoption process required that families give up control and be the passenger, not the driver; difficult in any situation but particularly in one so fraught with emotion.

Elizabeth's other observation was about Sandy and Paul. She had received positive feedback about them across the board, but had never seen them in action. As she participated in the process, she marveled at how smoothly everything went along, as if by magic. Elizabeth felt that facilitating adoptions was not a job for Sandy and Paul so much as a calling, much as a priest or nun is called to their vocation, requiring a unique level of commitment.

One family on the trip, Baz (Richard) and Lisa McRell heartily agreed with her assessment. They were a young couple from a small mill town in Massachusetts and were one of the Lutheran families. They couldn't say enough good things about Paul and Sandy, who helped them throughout the trip and whom they regarded as their heroes. The four became close friends and spent lazy afternoons, discussing the war and Vietnam veterans, over drinks at the pool.

Paul was extremely proud of his work in Vietnam and viewed it as repayment of a long-standing debt to the Vietnamese people. He was convinced that this was the reason he had been called to serve in the war. He had suffered, but had survived. It was his divine fate to go to war so that now he could return to save the children of Vietnam, his new mission in life.

CHAPTER 15

Gratitude

We make a living by what we get,
But we make a life by what we give.
Winston Churchill

Paul wasn't shy about telling his story to whoever would listen. Most adoptive parents knew he was a Vietnam vet and some even knew about his MIA discovery and other tales from his past. As a vet, he received attention, media coverage, and credit for his humanitarian work, while Sandy's contributions were sometimes overlooked or forgotten. However, when Paul told animated adoption stories to his siblings, they realized that Sandy was an equal partner in the couples' success, their work a fifty-fifty proposition.

Sandy was, in fact, a catalyst and often the one who initiated changes and improvements to the program. During their August trip she decided she was tired of staying in cramped, inconvenient hotels and urged Paul to look at some of the newly-built apartments in Ho Chi Minh City. He generally resisted change, but she persisted, and before the end of the trip they booked Norfolk Mansion, a modern apartment complex for expatriates and tourists, for their September group.

It was a wise decision families appreciated. Norfolk Mansion offered comfortable two bedroom, two bathroom apartments, with a restaurant, store, and swimming pool on the premises. The September group included nine couples—seven from AFTH and two from LSS. The prior confusion and discord with LSS families had now been eliminated (everyone knew they were part of Sandy and Paul's contingency) and apartment living made everyone's life considerably easier. But, there was still plenty of drama to go around.

Just as Sandy wore her "family face," parents also put on a good face in public, while privately dealing with the stress of first-time parenthood, sick babies, sleep deprivation, the oppressive heat, and various other problems, behind closed doors. Brenda and Lee Rath, a couple in their late 30s, adopted an infant boy they named Zachary. When they received him, Zachary had a multitude of ailments including an upper respiratory infection, a hernia, ear infections, and scabies. He was tiny, weighing just three and a half pounds at birth and Brenda, a first-time mother, worried about every detail: his cough, his formula consumption, his reaction to the heat, and the fact that one side of his head seemed strangely flat.

One day as she hurried into the apartment, she inadvertently bumped Zachary's head on the doorframe. Panicked, she called Sandy and Paul for help, convinced she'd given her baby a concussion or perhaps something even worse. Although unspoken, her underlying fear was that Zachary would be taken away from her. Adoption was such a tenuous and unpredictable process, that parents frequently had overblown fears of losing their children over minor incidents. Paul checked the baby and felt confident there was nothing wrong; there was barely a bump on his head. Brenda was relieved, but didn't forgive herself for the accident for quite some time.

When Brenda and Lee returned home, they couldn't say enough good things about Paul and Sandy. They felt a profound sense of gratitude for their help and kindness and strongly believed it was the couple, not the agency, who had made their adoption journey a success. Maxine, while pleased with the positive feedback, felt most adoptive parents gave the Pinkertons undue credit simply because they were present at the time they received their children. It was as though adoptive parents went to Vietnam and totally forgot about the work that the staff at AFTH had performed to help them obtain their children; a sticking point with her.

Sandy and Paul were happy to help parents in need when the requests were reasonable and the cries for help genuine. But there were times when parents crossed the line into the irrational and the absurd. In one instance, a woman asked them to babysit so she could go shopping; in another, a family repeatedly called them in the middle of the night for basic help. There was also a couple who planned a side trip to Hanoi without telling them and a family who randomly selected a doctor out of the phone book because they were unhappy with the medical options available. These were the types of unsettling incidents that occurred on almost every trip. Some situations were simply annoying while others sent them into a tailspin of worry over parents, babies, and even the stability of their program. After each trip, they added new do's and don'ts to their ever-growing list of appropriate behaviors, continually amazed at how far some people pushed the envelope.

On rare occasions, parents returned babies after spending only a few hours with them, in fear that they had special needs they were ill-equipped to handle. Generally everything worked out well, but when children were returned, it broke Paul's heart. However, Sandy felt it was better for parents to be truthful upfront and admit their shortcomings rather than embark upon a difficult life they couldn't handle emotionally, physically, or financially. She, of all people, knew what it took to parent a special needs child.

Troubling, too, were the times when parents adopted children, only to divorce later. Although divorce was a fact of life, Sandy knew all too well the ramifications for children in these circumstances as she shuttled Hannah between her house and Richard's. Granted, a child was still better off than living in an orphanage, but their future wasn't quite as rosy as everyone had initially anticipated.

Sandy, more than Paul, continued to learn more about the seamy underbelly of adoption and Vietnamese life in general. Sandy knew a schoolteacher at the international school in Ho Chi Minh City and they became casual friends. One Saturday, the schoolteacher invited Sandy to accompany her and her colleague to visit an orphanage in the Go Vap District, where the two women helped out on weekends. Sandy was incredulous at the entrance: a huge shrine resplendent with a waterfall, colored lights, and carvings that gave it a Disney-like appearance. But the orphanage itself, run by monks, was hidden behind the ornate structure and was a repulsive hut of despair. The outside was filthy and rundown; the inside was filled with sick children, special needs children, and worst of all, children being mistreated. Sandy watched in horror as two older boys were repeatedly hit by a monk attempting to feed them.

She spent the day helping, only to learn that the children who lived there were not available for adoption. Deeply concerned, she urged Paul to go with her the next weekend, but he wasn't available. She returned several times with her friends, bringing donations and support; extremely frustrated by her small contributions. Eventually, the women secured the aid of a number of agencies. By the time Paul finally saw the orphanage it was a totally different place with clean facilities, new cribs and mattresses, and a sparkling swimming pool. Even the monks had received training and no longer mistreated the children.

Sandy cultivated a few friendships, mainly in the community of expatriates who lived and worked in Ho Chi Minh City, people with whom she had something in common. One day as she gathered families in the lobby at Norfolk Mansion she ran into one of the immigration officers who lived there. The woman recognized Sandy from her frequent visits to the office and invited her to stop by later for a drink.

When Sandy stepped into her apartment, it was apparent the woman was a world traveler. Her home was decorated with beautiful vases, artwork, and collectibles from many different countries which she proudly showed Sandy as she rattled off the locations from which they came.

"So," Sandy asked brightly, "how do you like Vietnam?"

"I hate it! The shopping's good, but these people are horrible. They'd stab their mother in the heart for a penny," she allegedly stated. "Why do you keep coming here?"

"We're trying to find homes for children and children for parents who can't have their own children," Sandy replied proudly, taking a sip of her drink.

"Well, let me tell you something ... you'll never save everybody!"

"I know I can't save everybody, but I can save one child at a time. Just one at a time, that's all I'm trying to do. And who knows, maybe some of these children will become successful and return to Vietnam someday to make things better."

"That's both ridiculous and futile," the woman snorted.

Sandy knew she wouldn't win her over and dropped the conversation, finishing her drink a bit too quickly so she could leave. The women were pleasant to each other, but never developed a close friendship.

The one person Sandy absolutely loved was Miss Hoa. Sandy had met her on her first trip to Vietnam and saw her during each subsequent trip. She made a point to take adoptive families to her shop where they could buy custom or off-the-rack silk clothing. Women enjoyed spending money in the beautiful shop and Miss Hoa was truly grateful for Sandy's support. In return, Miss Hoa made clothing for Sandy and her children, a situation that made Sandy more than a little uncomfortable. She didn't feel right accepting gifts from this struggling businesswoman who barely made ends meet, but Miss Hoa insisted. She was a true friend, a rarity in Vietnam.

* * *

Like Sandy, Paul had very few Vietnamese friends. His life revolved around Sandy and the kids, the adoptive families in Vietnam, and his own family in Manheim. He was still friendly with Spanky, but Spanky was more like a third child than an adult friend. Spanky continually needed advice and money, which Paul reluctantly supplied. In return, Spanky ran errands and escorted adoptive families on sightseeing trips. When they moved to a different apartment complex, the Stamford Court, Paul befriended the sales manager, a Canadian-Vietnamese man named Allen.

Allen became Paul's sounding board. Angry with Kim, Paul sought his advice, knowing that Allen understood Vietnamese culture. Allen urged him to try different approaches with Kim; strategies that might appeal to her. Some approaches worked, many did not. Frustrated, Paul told Allen he wanted to find another orphanage to work with, both to forge a relationship elsewhere and to move away from their dependence on Kim. Through Allen's contacts, Paul found his way to Go Vap, an orphanage filled primarily with special needs children. With Allen as his interpreter, Paul asked the director if she would work with him. She agreed, but it took years to facilitate adoptions at Go Vap—everything moved slowly in Vietnam.

In the meantime, Kim continued to be a thorn in Paul's side with their battles stemming from both cultural differences and a fundamental personality clash. Kim was a powerful and astute businesswoman who was accustomed to being in command. She expected compliance from Sandy and Paul, who often found her requests unreasonable and sometimes demeaning.

Once, Kim and her husband Quang came to Sandy and Paul's apartment to announce an increase in her fee. Paul tried to reason with Quang alone, stepping outside on the balcony so they could talk privately, out of earshot of Kim.

"What are the expenses here in Vietnam to do an adoption? I'd like to know."

"I'm not sure ..." Quang hedged.

"Well, are expenses increasing so much that the cost has to go up by this much?"

"No. Miss Kim, her expenses are pretty much the same. They haven't increased too much," Quang allegedly stated. Paul felt his face burning; his cheeks turned red.

Kim and Quang departed and Sandy and Paul discussed their options. First, they called Maxine and broke the news. She instructed them to find someone else with whom to work. But, after an extensive search, they found no one else available. In the process, they also discovered that all of the Vietnamese facilitators charged the same or more; Kim was actually on the low end of the spectrum. In the end, Maxine decided to continue working with Kim.

But it was more than money that put Paul over the edge when he dealt with Kim; it was her lack of urgency. Although Sandy made the referrals, she often needed Kim to send her paperwork and pictures from Vietnam, when she was back in Manheim. When the materials didn't arrive on schedule, Sandy was forced to pick up the phone and call her.

"Hello, Miss Kim, it's Miss Sandy. I'm calling about the paperwork and photos. When can you send them to me?"

"Ohhh, Miss Sandy. I give them to you when you arrive in Vietnam."

"No, that's too late. I need them now. The families are waiting for their referrals and they need time to plan their trips to Vietnam. Please, you must send them to me now."

"Miss Sandy, I don't know. You call me later, one hour from now." Kim promptly signed off, not giving Sandy a chance to respond.

Sandy called back at the appointed time, only to be told once again to call back later. The game continued until finally Miss Kim relented, but not before Sandy and Paul were furious with her. Culturally, Miss Kim needed the upper hand in order to save face. Disgusted with her need for control, Paul angrily remarked, "She saves her face while ripping ours off!"

For several months the adoption process had been relatively calm, with no major surprises from Kim, but soon she shook their trust and confidence once again. Sandy had finished the torturous process of matching babies to parents for an upcoming group and had already mailed out the referrals, when Kim came to her with the unpleasant fact that one of the babies had a heart problem of unknown severity.

"Why didn't you tell me this before? I've already mailed the referral! I need to know this up front; you can't tell me this now!" Sandy protested in disbelief.

"It's okay Miss Sandy. Just give them another baby." To Kim, it was a simple problem, with a simple solution. Unfortunately, it wasn't that easy. Sandy knew exactly what would happen next. She'd call the family, who had already started to bond with the baby's picture, tell them that she didn't know how serious the problem was, and admit that she had virtually no information to give them. The orphanage wouldn't pay for testing so there was no way to find out accurate health information and, to top it off, the family had to decide immediately whether they wished to retain the referral and continue the adoption process, or begin new paperwork with a different child. What a mess!

With a heavy heart Sandy called the family and gave them the bad news. Within hours, they turned down the child. Sandy retreated to her bedroom and wept. She felt terrible for rejected children although she understood parents' reluctance to take on the unknown. It was a tragedy for all concerned. Later, the child died, and she agonized over whether or not the problem could have been fixed had there been enough time, resources, or help available. It was a question for which there was no answer.

* * *

By October of 1999, Sandy and Paul had two years of experience behind them and their work was running pretty smoothly. They stayed in apartments rather than hotels and found the change to be easier for families, as well as for themselves. They crafted a two-week agenda of adoption meetings and sightseeing tours and knew which shops and restaurants the families enjoyed the most. Furthermore, they had established their roles as a married couple with two young children. Sandy was in charge of home schooling and general childcare, while Paul handled laundry and ironing. Spanky ran their errands, apartment staff performed their housecleaning, and restaurants provided most of their meals. Staff members at the apartment complex often babysat Hannah and Isaiah who were now six and three, respectively. Surprisingly, life in Vietnam was sometimes easier than life in Manheim, where all the responsibilities fell to them; plus Vietnam was cheap. They could dine in the finest restaurants in Ho Chi Minh City (HCMC), either on their own dime or as a treat from appreciative families. Life was pretty good.

Paul loved nearly every aspect of facilitating adoptions. Granted, the long flight was difficult, but there was something exciting and energizing about getting on international flights every few weeks, especially when there were enough frequent flyer miles to sit in business class. The Pinkertons were well-known by the staff at Korean Airlines and they rewarded their loyalty with perks whenever they could.

Frequently, as the plane headed into Vietnamese airspace, Paul closed his eyes and tried to re-create the first time he had entered this foreign land; a trip that now seemed a lifetime ago. Thankfully, the terror was gone, but so, too, was the amazing adrenaline rush—the intoxicating feeling he had attempted, unsuccessfully, to duplicate ever since.

Paul, at six feet two inches tall with a heavy frame, was an imposing figure. As he took command of the families at the airport, he envisioned himself as a shepherd with his obedient sheep. Arriving in Vietnam, he herded the group from the airport to the van to their apartments, never missing a step. He enjoyed the initial shock on peoples' faces when they first arrived, and he purposely stayed close enough to listen to their comments and observations. It was still a thrill and a reminder of what he felt the first time he'd stepped on Vietnamese soil, decades earlier.

During the beginning of the trip, Sandy accompanied families to the orphanage, to the signing ceremony at the Ministry of Justice, and to apply for passports at the Immigration Office. Paul took charge during the second week when families took their babies for their visa pictures, to Cho Ray Hospital for their exams, and to the American consulate for their final interview. He also brought families to the Korean Air desk to make the final arrangements to fly home. He exuded confidence and families knew that when Paul spoke, you'd better listen. However, where babies were concerned, he was a total marshmallow. He could appear stern and serious with parents one minute, but break into a ready grin the next, tickling and holding babies or playing games with their older siblings who sometimes came along on the trips.

Nearly everyone came away from Vietnam with a good feeling about Paul and Sandy, although there were exceptions. Supposedly, one family adopted a baby in Vietnam, but upon returning home they felt there was a problem with their child. They saw numerous doctors in the States until one finally diagnosed the baby with cerebral palsy. The parents were irate and claimed that Dr. Vien knew about the condition all along but didn't tell them. They demanded a free adoption *and* a different child. Maxine suggested that Sandy and Paul take families to the international clinic in the future. However, Sandy and Paul trusted Dr. Vien implicitly, so they decided to give families the option to either see him or go to the international clinic.

As the disgruntled family began talking about a lawsuit, Sandy and Paul realized they needed malpractice insurance to safeguard themselves from future incidents. But, apparently, it had been their responsibility to secure the insurance from the beginning and they had been remiss in doing so. In the end, the family put the child up for adoption, the agency was placed in a precarious position, and Sandy and Paul paid huge sums of money to avoid litigation. It was an unfortunate situation for everyone involved.

* * *

As 2000 rolled around, Sandy and Paul went to LSS to discuss their working relationship. They were more than willing to help Lutheran families, but they wanted to formalize their alliance with LSS and create agreeable terms for everyone. Although Maxine wanted an exclusive working arrangement with the Pinkertons, she understood that they had been maneuvered into their current situation by Kim.

Meanwhile, Paul was still waiting to facilitate adoptions at Go Vap. He wanted to circumvent Kim by developing a relationship there but, more importantly, he had a passion for special needs children. He and Sandy felt strongly about helping special needs kids and improving their prospects in life. Paul likened the kids' situation to used cars, sold at a dealership. Everyone wanted the shiny new model in the front of the lot and didn't give a second thought to the used car with the dents in the back. But these were children, not cars, and Paul felt every child deserved a home and the opportunity to thrive. It disheartened him to see so many children left behind, particularly when some of the special needs, like cleft palates, were minor and could easily be remedied in the States.

He often argued the point with Maxine and urged her to promote special needs adoptions, but he couldn't make his case with her. Maxine was reluctant to handle special needs adoptions at AFTH for a number of logical, valid reasons. The vast majority of families specifically requested healthy babies and were not interested in adopting special needs children. Furthermore, the agency was not geared up to accommodate a large number of special needs adoptions, which required more education and preparation on the part of adoptive parents. Plus, special needs adoptions were risky. Parents often forgot what the social workers at the agency told them. Maxine feared that parents would come back later claiming they hadn't been adequately advised on all the potential problems or associated costs, that come with raising a special needs child, setting the agency up for lawsuits and liability cases. Plus, if a parent decided after the fact, that he or she wasn't equipped to handle a special needs child, the agency was then responsible for finding the child another home. Paul promoted special needs adoptions whenever he could, to whomever he could, but placing them proved to be an uphill battle. It was a reality that often broke his spirit.

Paul's first visit to Go Vap had been a shock. Go Vap, unlike Tam Binh, was in a bad section of town in the Go Vap District. It was dirty, poorly maintained, and located down a little alleyway off a very busy street. The four-story buildings formed a square, with a courtyard in the middle. Parts of one building had not been used for some time and sat vacant. A pathetic playground sat in the middle of the courtyard on the ground level and an occasional rat could be seen scurrying into the scraggly foliage nearby. Baby laundry hung on clotheslines outside some of the upper rooms and offered clues about their inhabitants.

In one darkened room there were two parallel rows of metal beds covered with thin sleeping mats. Older children and their caretakers napped there during the day and slept there at night. Some tossed and turned while others were actually tied, hands and feet, to the bed frame. The vast majority of the children had special needs. Paul observed all types: children with missing limbs, children with cleft palates, children with Down's syndrome, children in wheelchairs with cerebral palsy, and at least two rooms filled with children who had hydrocephalus—the most disturbing condition of all.

The children with hydrocephalus were not infants, but older children virtually waiting to die. Although Paul didn't know the medical details, hydrocephalus comes in two forms: communicating and non-communicating. Communicating hydrocephalus occurs when the cerebrospinal fluid (CSF) surrounding the brain and spinal cord is either being over-produced or is not absorbed quickly enough into the bloodstream. In the non-communicating type, some form of blockage prevents the fluid from circulating properly within the narrow pathways that connect the spaces in the brain, called ventricles.

Hydrocephalus can be caused by a number of things. It may result from inherited genetic abnormalities (such as aqueductal stenosis) or from developmental disorders such as those associated with neural tube defects, like spina bifida. Some studies show a correlation between exposure to Agent Orange and spina bifida, and the most severe forms of spina bifada are often accompanied by hydrocephalus. Spina bifida has also been linked to insufficient folic acid levels during pregnancy. Furthermore, hydrocephalus can occur during complications of premature birth, or from meningitis, tumors, traumatic head injury, or hemorrhaging. It can also be caused by TORCH (toxoplasmosis, rubella, cytomegalovirus, and herpes simplex) infections during pregnancy that can lead to congenital abnormalities. It's easy to see how, in a developing country like Vietnam, any number of factors could increase the chances that a child might be born with hydrocephalus.

With hydrocephalus, early diagnosis and treatment are key factors in preventing the pressure of cerebrospinal fluid from damaging the brain. If left untreated, brain damage and cellular injury can occur within twenty-four hours in severe cases and within two to three weeks if the pressure builds more slowly. Over time, children left untreated can suffer significant motor and cognitive impairment, lack of growth, possible blindness, and a host of other problems, resulting in a low quality of life and ultimately, a shortened life span.

The children with hydrocephalus at Go Vap had not received treatment. Their heads were enormous—the size of watermelons—and they lay in oversized cribs, clothed in adult diapers, staring at the ceiling. It was a gut-wrenching sight. But, unlike most visitors who were repulsed and sickened by these children and left the room as quickly as they entered it, Paul spent time walking from crib to crib, talking to each child, and touching or tickling them to provide some human contact and elicit a response. For the majority of these children, it may have been the most extensive rehab they'd received in years.

There is no cure for hydrocephalus. Standard treatment involves a surgical procedure that drains the cerebrospinal fluid with a catheter or a shunt. Technically speaking, the surgery is not particularly difficult, but there are inherent risks. More importantly, the surgery is not a one-time fix. Ongoing care and monitoring of the shunt and fluid pressure are essential and most children require multiple surgeries and shunts over the course of a lifetime. In an orphanage setting, hydrocephalus has been a death sentence simply because orphanages have not had the resources for the surgery and ongoing care necessary to treat the children. Furthermore, early diagnosis requires an ultrasound or MRI, equipment generally unavailable to orphans.

At Go Vap, Paul noticed a board of numbers in the front lobby. When he inquired about it, he found that it included the number of children received from hospitals, the children available for adoption, and sadly, the children who died each month. It was startling to see that in any given month there were two, three or more children who died. Most likely, some of these numbers reflected the deaths of the children with hydrocephalus.

* * *

In April of 2000 there were eighteen families from LSS and AFTH traveling together; the largest group the Pinkertons had ever taken to Vietnam. Paul and Sandy knew before they left Manheim that something would go wrong. With so many people, it was inevitable. Simply keeping track of everyone and moving them from place to place was a huge challenge. They hired a bus to take the families to the various Government meetings and they put Spanky on call for sightseeing and general help because, with eighteen families and numerous babies and children, they needed all the help they could get.

Like every trip, there were the anticipated problems and challenges: sick babies, first-time nervous parents, and parents who bent the rules. Without fail, some parents showed up late for appointments. But the officials didn't want to be kept waiting, which put Sandy in an embarrassing and compromised position. Furthermore, it made for bad feelings among the families. Most adhered to the schedule and resented the fact that some people were perpetually late.

Sometimes parents blatantly disregarded the rules. The officials at the Ministry of Justice where the Giving and Receiving ceremony (the actual adoption) took place were stern and serious. Sandy warned families against taking pictures, but one or two always pulled out their cameras and snapped away, much to the consternation of the officials. Sometimes the officials smiled and played along, but Sandy often learned about the incidents later when she received a dressing down from the men who were displeased by this blatant disregard for protocol. Although Sandy understood the desire by families to document this important moment in their lives, rules were rules, and unfortunately, she paid the price when they were broken.

Sandy and Paul often slipped behind the scenes to repair damages made by families, to protect families from the unseemly side of adoption, and to bear the brunt of things gone wrong. Sandy, who knew too much of the inner workings of adoption, often wished she didn't.

Adoptions From The Heart and LSS only completed adoptions that were considered abandonments. It was for this reason that Sister Hai, the orphanage director, attended the signing ceremony at the Ministry of Justice to relinquish the baby from the control of the orphanage to the care and responsibility of the adoptive parents during the adoption ceremony. However, some American agencies and many Europeans engaged in direct adoptions in which the birthmother relinquished her rights to her child in the presence of the child's adoptive parents.

Sandy saw many direct adoptions over the years and it was emotionally crushing, each and every time. It looked something like this: The adoptive family came to the Ministry of Justice dressed in their Sunday best with the baby decked out in beautiful new clothing, while the birthmother arrived downtrodden and miserable. They all sat down and each party signed the papers in a quick relinquishment of parental rights. They walked out the door and the birthmother hugged the baby for what she knew was the last time in her life. The family rode off in a taxi with their baby, all smiles and joy, as the birthmother fell to the ground, head in her hands, sobbing uncontrollably. A few Vietnamese passersby came to her aid and tried to console her, but there was no consolation to be found— she had just given up her precious child.

Sandy, as a party to this scene, always thought back to the day Mary and Doug gave up Hannah and their parting looks as she drove away with Hannah in her car. But unlike the poor Vietnamese mothers, Mary and Doug knew where Hannah was and how she was being raised. And, they had the option to come back into her life at any time. Sandy realized that she gave Mary and Doug every opportunity to change their minds and back out of the adoption; there was no way she could simply take Hannah away from them. But remembering those facts was small, cold comfort when she saw a Vietnamese birthmother fall to the ground in grief and despair.

* * *

Paul and Sandy distilled the adoption process down to a science, timing the various events to occur precisely according to schedule. There was no cushion and every appointment needed to run smoothly in order to move the families through the process in the allotted timeframe. All of the steps in the adoption process were carefully orchestrated to occur on a particular day and time and, until now, everything had worked perfectly. The April group would be different.

Sandy and Paul had been told the passports would be ready on Tuesday, but when Tuesday arrived, they weren't available. Sandy told Kim to call her contact at the Immigration Office to tell him they were on a timeline; they needed the passports today.

Kim called, while Sandy and Paul checked the airlines to investigate their options. Panic set in as they discovered there were no more plane seats available for several days. If the passports weren't obtained today, families would be required to stay an extra week. Families counted on the fact that the trip was allotted a specified number of days. They planned their schedules and budgets accordingly. Extra days meant lost time at work, angry bosses, child care arrangements for siblings, extra expenses, and a host of other logistical tangles. Some babies were sick and parents were anxious to bring them home to their own pediatricians. For everyone, adding extra days to the trip was more than a simple inconvenience—it was a nightmare.

The phone lines buzzed with calls flying back and forth between Sandy and Kim. "Isn't there any way you can hurry it up?" Sandy implored. "Please, we need to get these families home."

"I'll check again," Kim replied, finally understanding Sandy's urgency.

Kim called back. "Give him $100 and he can get them today. He needs $100 ... each."

Sandy relayed the news and Paul became furious. "This is fucking bullshit! You know what he's doing, don't you? He knows we have eighteen families and he's seeing dollar signs. That's $1,800 extra, probably going directly into his pocket! He's sitting there with the passports ready to go, waiting for his money. Damn it!" If Paul was assessing the situation correctly, his anger was justified. At the time, the gross national income in Vietnam was less than $500 per person, per year.

Unfortunately, Sandy and Paul knew what they had to do. They secured babysitting for the kids, withdrew $1,800 of their own money from the bank, and delivered the money to Kim for the exchange. A short time later the phone rang. Their contact at Immigration was ready to see the families and give them their passports. It was a tough lesson they would never forget. You couldn't time things to the minute in Vietnam, because you never knew what would happen.

As they prepared to leave the country, Sandy finally verbalized the feelings she'd held inside for two long weeks. In angry sputters she declared to Paul, "I'm staying home next time. I can't take this anymore. This is your dream and you need to live it, but I'm staying home with the kids. This is too difficult: the travel, the jetlag, the home schooling, the aggravation from everybody. It's all too much and I can't do it anymore! I'm sorry, but I just can't do it!"

Paul gave her a hug. "I know, I know. We'll talk about it later. Right now we need to get going." They met families in the lobby, lined up the babies on the sofa, and took group pictures as the parents beamed with pride. It was Paul's version of Anne Geddes (the famous photographer who took pictures of babies in flowerpots). Parents laughed as the row of babies moved this way and that, some leaning, some slumping, some smiling, and, invariably, one crying. The photo shoot over, they loaded into vans and headed for the airport. It was nearly midnight. Everyone felt exhausted and dreaded the torturous flight home. Families juggled fussy babies and luggage, while Sandy and Paul went to each of them to ensure they were okay and ready to board.

Families were demonstrative in their expressions of gratitude to Sandy and Paul. Many wept as they proclaimed, "You've changed my life and I can never thank you enough for my child!" Hugs, kisses, tears, and promises to keep in touch were exchanged as parents boarded the plane. Families were surprised to see Paul wipe his eyes with a fresh, white handkerchief. Paul, Sandy, and the kids boarded last and, when they finally settled into their seats, Paul looked over at Sandy questioningly. With tear-stained eyes she looked at Paul. "Okay, one more time. That's it. I'll do this just one more time, but then I'm done."

Paul bent over to pick up his water bottle and smiled to himself. He knew he'd hear the same litany from Sandy on the next trip. But, when all was said and done, she wasn't going to stop facilitating adoptions despite her frustrations. They both had a passion for their work and, in it, found vast rewards. Truly, it was their calling; a crazy kind of fate that kept bringing them back to Vietnam, over and over again. How could he—or Sandy—turn it down?

* * *

Sandy barely had time to catch her breath. They returned to Manheim in April and by the end of May it was time to board a plane and head to Ho Chi Minh City again. They had another large group of twelve families and, once again, Paul was determined to return to GoVap to check on special needs adoptions. While Sandy worked with Kim and Sister Hai at Tam Binh, Go Vap was strictly his domain. He had formed the relationship with the orphanage and he went there alone.

Whenever he went to Go Vap, the children formed a circle around him. Some did so because of the donations of candy or dolls he distributed, while others were simply in awe of the big man they called "papa." He loved to spend time with the children, who desperately craved his attention. But he felt sad and slightly repulsed by the fact that whenever he handed out toys or treats, they turned into greedy, vicious little animals, who furiously grabbed for whatever he had, as they pushed others out of their path. It was survival of the fittest. The children, who didn't understand there was enough to go around, stepped over each other to ensure their own share.

Paul savored his relationships at Go Vap, particularly because he didn't visit Tam Binh very often. He loved Sister Hai and the children at Tam Binh, but because of his strained relationship with Kim, he couldn't go there when she was present, which was the majority of the time. Therefore, whenever he had a chance, he spent time at Go Vap or the hospitals, simply because he loved to be around the children.

On this particular trip, Sandy found out en route to Vietnam that one family's child had contracted pneumonia and was hospitalized. So, while everyone else went to the orphanage to receive their babies, this unfortunate family went to the hospital to visit their sick infant. Paul accompanied them, while Sandy and Kim took the rest of the families to Tam Binh.

At the hospital Paul tried to reassure and comfort the family as he questioned the staff about the baby's condition. He was relieved to learn the baby's illness was not life-threatening. As the family spent private time with their new baby, Paul strolled down the row of cribs. Four cribs away was a tiny pathetic-looking infant. The little child,

who was severely malnourished, had IVs sprouting from his head and a
feeding tube threaded down his throat. Paul stopped and stared at the
child for a long time; he finally reached down to caress him. The infant
smiled up at him instantly, which took him by surprise. Paul and the family left the hospital with the promise to return the next day.

Paul burst through the apartment door, filled with excitement.
"Sandy, you have to come to the hospital with me to see the little boy I
saw today! Oh my gosh, he's so cute!" Paul went on to describe his physical condition and urged Sandy to return with him the following day.

The next afternoon the family saw their baby again, comforted by the
fact that she was slightly better than the day before. Paul rushed Sandy
over to see the baby boy, four cribs down the row. Sandy took it all in: the
tubes, the emaciation, and the fact that the child was near death. But there
was also something else she noticed. "I don't think this baby is a boy,
Paul."

"Well, there's only one way to find out!" Paul chuckled as he reached
for the diaper. He was surprised to find that the boy was, in fact, a girl.
They both laughed over the mistake, but then they looked more seriously
into each others' eyes and, without saying a word, knew in their hearts
they were going to adopt this child.

The little girl had been born in a hospital outside of HCMC, brought
into the city, and left at Tam Binh. She was so ill Sister Hai had moved her
to the hospital. The little girl was now seven months old, but she only
weighed seven pounds. Paul and Sandy didn't know exactly what was
wrong with her, but knew that she was malnourished, had chronic pneumonia, and was receiving a number of antibiotics through the IVs in her
head. Mainly they knew that if they didn't adopt her, she would die.

They approached Sister Hai to see if they could begin the adoption
process. Sister Hai adamantly refused. "Miss Sandy, the baby is too sick.
I will get you healthy baby. You don't need to take a sick baby." Sandy
and Paul were well aware of that fact, but that wasn't really the point.
They told her they didn't want a healthy baby, they wanted *this* baby.

Miss Kim became involved in the conversations and, like Sister Hai,
tried to dissuade them from adopting the child. "This girl is not very
beautiful or healthy. We can get you a more beautiful baby." Sandy and
Paul couldn't be swayed and continued to press the issue.

At the hospital they talked to the doctor and asked her if the baby girl
would die.

"I don't know for sure, but she's been here for seven months and she's
not any better. Most likely, she will die." Dissatisfied with the answer,
they called in Dr. Vien for his opinion.

When Dr. Vien saw the child, he tried in the strongest manner possible to discourage them from even entertaining the idea of adoption.

"When you walk streets of Saigon, you take risks, right? It is easy to be hit in Saigon. But walking on street is necessity. You take many risks in life because you must. But why take such a risk with baby? You don't have to do it. You can have other baby. This baby is not healthy, not strong, maybe not even live. Don't adopt this baby."

Dr. Vien's other concern, which he didn't verbalize, was the fact that Sandy and Paul were not young. In Vietnamese culture, Sandy and Paul were considered old and Dr. Vien's philosophy was that old parents should adopt healthy babies because soon they would have their own health problems to worry about. Dr. Vien had noticed that American parents who came to Vietnam to adopt babies were old, which worried him. Even Spanky, who had seen the child briefly, discouraged them from the adoption.

Sandy and Paul were undeterred. They continued to visit the girl—whom they had named Deborah—every day. They also took pictures of her, although that was not allowed in the hospital. While one kept guard, the other clicked away. They wanted pictures of this precious child for two reasons: one, to carry her spirit with them when they left the country and two, to document her health for a pediatrician at home.

Before leaving, Sandy arranged to move Deborah to another facility located at 38 Tu Xuan Street, a facility for children with special needs. There, Deborah could receive the one-on-one care she required. Sandy was friendly with Dr. Thanh at 38, a woman she greatly admired and trusted. They had used the facility in the past when a measles epidemic had swept through the orphanage. Babies, who were up for adoption, were moved to 38 so they wouldn't contract the measles before their adoptions. In another case, when they were already too late, the babies with measles had been moved to 38 for special care. Sandy was extremely grateful to Dr. Thanh for taking Deborah and pressed money on her for her services. The doctor refused her money and insisted Sandy give it to her staff instead.

Reluctantly Sandy and Paul flew home, leaving Deborah in Dr. Thanh's care. Once home, they consulted with two doctors, their pediatrician and an international adoption doctor in Pittsburgh. Their pediatrician was blunt. "You better have good health insurance because you don't know what's wrong with this child and you don't know what medical expenses you're going to incur. This could devastate your family."

The international adoption doctor was equally discouraging and went to great lengths to explain to Sandy and Paul that it was highly possible the child would never walk, talk, or feed herself. Most likely she would be severely mentally challenged and require total care by Sandy and Paul. Overall, adopting the child was a huge risk. The doctor warned them to be prepared for the worst possible outcome.

After hearing everyone's case against Deborah, Sandy and Paul decided in her favor. They wouldn't let her die in Vietnam. Sandy began adoption paperwork while Deborah, under Dr. Thanh's care, improved to the point where she could be returned to the orphanage. Sister Hai arranged for foster care, believing she would receive more individual attention and better care than at Tam Binh. But Sandy, not knowing the foster family, became concerned and asked Dr. Vien to check in on them. When he did, he found that the conditions were deplorable, and he moved Deborah back to Tam Binh. She was only there a couple of days before she was sent back to the hospital, seriously ill once again.

Sandy and Paul, now back in Manheim, were frantic with worry as Deborah was bounced from place to place. Fortunately they didn't have to wait long to see her because in late July another travel group of six families was ready to travel to Vietnam. Sandy and Paul brought clothing, toys, and diapers and spent every free moment with Deborah during this trip. Unfortunately, at the end of two weeks it was time to fly home again and they had a long six weeks before they could return. They wondered if she would even live that long.

CHAPTER 16

Heroes

A hero is an ordinary individual
Who finds the strength to persevere and endure
In spite of overwhelming obstacles.
They are the real heroes
And so are the families and friends
Who have stood by them.

Christopher Reeve

My first encounter with Paul Pinkerton was in late summer of 2000, and frankly, not such a positive one. I had spent a long, tiring day researching travel options on the Internet for our upcoming trip to Vietnam, when the phone rang. It was my social worker from Lutheran Social Services of New England, the person my husband, David, and I were working with on our adoption. She gave me three startling bits of information: LSS partnered with an adoption agency out of Pennsylvania (AFTH), some people named Pinkerton were our chaperones, and we were required to travel as a group.

"Are you kidding me?" I responded. "We specifically asked during our last meeting if we could make our own travel arrangements and we were told that we could. I've spent all day planning our itinerary. What do you mean you partner with another agency? And who are the Pinkertons? Why can't we go on our own?"

"I'll have Paul Pinkerton call you, but you need to call the travel desk in Pennsylvania to book your flights. Here's the number …" she pressed, ignoring my protests.

I zoned out as she continued. I felt duped. This was the first I'd heard about partnerships, chaperones, and group travel—I wasn't happy. But, before I could call David, the phone rang again. Annoyed, I grabbed it on the first ring.

A man with a deep, slow drawl identified himself as Paul Pinkerton. "Great," I thought, "who *is* this guy anyway?" He droned on and I cut him off, expressing my displeasure at being informed at this late date of the need to travel with a group of strangers and instructed to fly on a carrier for which we had no frequent flyer miles. I wasn't sure of Paul's qualifications or what role he played in the adoption process. Why, exactly, did we need chaperones? We weren't children, after all.

Paul listened and, when I finished, he started in on some monotonous scare tactics: "Well, you could travel on your own, but when you arrive at the airport, it's very crowded and confusing with mobs of Vietnamese people and pickpockets and people hounding you for taxi rides and ..." he went on and on. I bristled at his patronizing manner, but jotted down some notes, just in case. "You think it over and call me back tomorrow," he finished.

"Yeah, whatever," I thought as we said goodbye, "there's no way I'm traveling with your group."

I promptly called David and broke the unpleasant news, peppered with a couple of expletives, just to let him know how I really felt about the situation. David was equally irate, but became a little uneasy when I relayed what Paul had said. "We'll talk about it when I get home," he promised.

Hours later I was still unwilling to give in; my stubborn Norwegian roots had kicked into high gear. David decided we should join the group, if for no other reason than to be construed as team players rather than rebels. Our conversations continued through dinner and into the evening. By the next morning, I reluctantly conceded our independence, still fuming over the final outcome. When I called Paul, he was pleased with our decision and more than a little smug, which didn't exactly endear him to me.

* * *

I was the stereotypical woman adopting through Sandy and Paul: married, forty-something, and craving a child. I'd gone down the traumatic and painful (in all senses of the word) path of failed infertility treatments. It had been a long and torturous process and, in the end, my body had betrayed me.

Unwilling to give up on the possibility of becoming a parent, my thoughts turned to adoption. I recalled my mother's excitement decades earlier when someone in our small Minnesota town had adopted two Korean children. Perhaps my mother was guiding me from the great beyond, towards a similar experience.

For a multitude of reasons my husband and I signed on to LSS of New England and entered their China program, requesting an infant less than six months of age. Our decision had less to do with a desire to parent a girl than the need to enter a well-established adoption program in an Asian country. But, one day during a casual conversation, my social worker informed me that because of my advanced age (gee, thanks), I could only adopt a toddler. I was shocked! As a first-time mother I wanted to experience as much baby time as possible and I had concerns about the issues associated with adopting an older child: attachment disorders, institutional effects, the possibility of more severe medical problems, not to mention communication issues, since I didn't speak a word of Chinese. Yes, I had read all the books; I knew exactly what could happen. I was unwilling to go further into the process, so she suggested I switch to their Vietnam program.

The very utterance of the word "Vietnam" caused goose bumps to rise on my skin. I recalled in vivid detail the war scenes I'd witnessed on television as a teen, the death of a young man in my hometown, and my aunt's concern when her son refused to talk about his tour of duty. Was she crazy? Maybe I wasn't meant to be a parent after all. Following a sleepless night I called her the next morning and fired a barrage of questions at her until, finally, I felt satisfied that the program was a viable alternative. Then I came on board and became busy, very busy.

My paper pregnancy lasted nearly nine months until finally we received a referral of a gorgeous baby boy in oversized clothing with bright, longing eyes: our son Nguyen Hoang Viet (names are backwards in Vietnam, Viet is his first name). With picture in hand, there was no turning back and we accepted the referral without hesitation. The trip to Vietnam loomed just a few short weeks away. As the travel date approached we had schemed to combine our adoption trip with a vacation in Hong Kong not only to see the sights, but to acclimate ourselves to the Asian time difference before embarking upon first-time parenthood. Someone at the agency had mistakenly told us that we could make our own travel arrangements and I had spent endless hours on the Internet coming up with an itinerary. But now, here I was, stuck traveling with a group. Generally speaking—I hate groups.

Days of nervous preparation followed until finally it was time to travel. The night before our trip we went to our local Italian restaurant for dinner to commemorate our last night alone as a married couple, sans children. We ran into our next-door neighbors, the Kaplans, who looked knowingly at their three kids and teased us that we better savor the peace and quiet of our meal because it would be a long time before we'd enjoy it again. Somehow we knew they were right.

Exhilarated, we returned home and began shutting off the downstairs lights, preparing to go upstairs to bed. Suddenly, there was a loud knock on the door, followed by a man yelling, "Police! Come out with your hands up!" I cautiously opened the front door as a policeman, reaching for his gun, yelled from behind the bushes, "Hands up!"

"But I live here!" I protested. Then it dawned on me that the police may have confused the date of our departure. I had enlisted their help a few days earlier, requesting that they check our house while we were away. Now it was my job to convince him that I wasn't an intruder!

David and I stepped outside the house, arms in the air, rattling off our names, the situation, and our travel plans for the next day. The policeman took his hand away from his holster, but continued to question us, demanding to see identification. Finally, convinced that we were the legitimate residents, he apologized and sheepishly wished us a good trip.

A bit shaken, I turned to David, "Well, at least we know he'll do his job while we're away!" We burst out laughing, but had to calm ourselves so we could get some sleep for the next morning, a task that proved nearly impossible. I worried about every possible scenario that might unfold in Vietnam, en route, and at our home, during our two-week odyssey. Would we die in a plane crash? Would our cat, Gordon, be okay at the vet? Would lightning strike our house? And, most importantly, would the adoption actually occur? Those were only a few of the thoughts that swirled through my head during that restless night.

The next day at JFK Airport it didn't take long to spot Paul. In the middle of an unlikely swarm of nervous parents and noisy kids, stood a tall, heavy-set man with dark-rimmed glasses and a crew cut so short he looked bald. He appeared stern and unapproachable, oddly mismatched to the calm voice at the end of the phone line the other day. We exchanged pleasantries and he promised to talk to us at some later point, while his wife chased after their two active children.

The people in our group were scattered throughout the plane with the majority flying in coach. David and I and another couple, Steve and Ellen Passage, sat up front. We rationalized that the twenty-plus hours of flying time warranted some creature comforts and, with any luck, the ability to sleep. As we boarded the plane, I randomly grabbed a couple of magazines from the stack provided by the flight attendant. As I sat down I discovered that the headlines on both magazines pertained to the twenty-fifth anniversary of the end of the Vietnam War. "Oh that's just great!" I thought to myself, "I wonder how we'll be treated ... the Vietnamese must hate Americans."

We filled the first hours of our Friday afternoon flight eating lunch, getting to know the Passages, and settling down. I was too preoccupied to read or watch a movie. I was about to become a mother and felt ill-prepared and inadequate to the task as every possible fear and doubt crept into my brain. My friend, Carla, had asked me about my worries and, aside from my midnight musings, I had three major concerns: (1) the baby would be sick, (2) I would get sick, and (3) I would arrive without essential paperwork. The hours passed slowly. I wrote in a journal while David slept. I was envious of his ability to slumber away so easily, but I finally fell into my own fitful sleep brought on by sheer exhaustion and boredom.

After fourteen hours, we landed in Seoul; the plane parked in the middle of nowhere on the tarmac. We walked down a long flight of skinny airplane stairs and took a bus to the terminal building. The airport had a carnival atmosphere with multicolored lights adorning duty-free shops, loud raucous noise, and a putrid fog of cigarette smoke. We sat inside a crowded lounge, in thick blue smoke, for the next three hours. I was nauseous. I felt as though I was still moving, I couldn't breathe, and my stomach hurt from all the stale coffee I'd ingested. Everyone was miserable and tired and we still had another long flight ahead of us. The only people who appeared to be fine were the Pinkertons, who chatted with families as they trailed their children around the crowded room. Finally we were back on the bus, back up the stairs, and seated in a smaller and less luxurious plane headed to Vietnam.

During the flight Paul came by to look at our paperwork, specifically our visa applications for Vietnam. He took them back to his seat and returned with a furrowed brow. "Why did you write 'tourism' as the purpose of your trip?" he asked rather gruffly. "It should say adoption."

"That's what the agency told me to write," I replied, "and it's in the manual they gave us." I had completed the bulk of the paperwork so David stayed out of the conversation.

"Well, that's not right. How's it going to look when you enter the country for tourism and leave it with a baby?" I didn't like his tone.

"I don't know. I understand what you're saying, but that's what they told me to do! I'm sure the other Lutheran couple did the same thing ..."

"It's going to be a problem. I'm not sure what we're going to do about it." Paul left me with that disturbing thought.

"Did you hear that? Does this mean we can't adopt Viet?" There was no way I was leaving Vietnam without our baby! (Although we had renamed our son, Alexander, we had decided to call him Viet for the duration of the trip.)

Before David could respond to my hypothetical question, the plane went into freefall; we looked at each other in sheer terror. The plane lurched and fell and shook violently and I wondered if we'd even make it to Vietnam. Eventually the pilot informed us that there was a typhoon in the area and he was rerouting us; the trip would take longer, but we would circumvent the bad weather. I gripped the seat with clenched

knuckles and more than thirty minutes passed before the turbulence subsided and we were back on track.

The plane landed in Ho Chi Minh City and we descended the stairs to
the surprising heat, humidity, and peculiar smells that characterize Vietnam. The terminal building was old and shabby, in sharp contrast to the
well-heeled, machine-gun-toting officials who kept watch over us. I was
sure something would go wrong, but eventually all the families came out
on the other side of immigration where Paul led us towards the baggage
claim area, one level below. An old ragged Vietnamese woman—blind,
diseased, and barefoot—teetered ahead of us on her way to the escalator.
I was shocked to see Steve Passage pick her up and carefully place her on
the stairs, as he steadied her shoulder. I was dumbstruck not only by his
kindness, but by his wanton disregard for his own safety since he didn't
know what diseases she might be carrying.

Bags in hand, we navigated the crush of people and piled into a waiting van. It was nearly 1:00 a.m. on a Sunday morning. Ho Chi Minh City
was bustling with honking traffic, people eating in restaurants, and Vietnamese sitting on their haunches on sidewalks. It was an exotic, but poor,
Manhattan. Paul showed us various points of interest along the way, but
everyone was too focused on their need to fall into a comfortable bed to
listen. The van pulled into a barbed wire compound that enclosed a modern apartment complex and we were home. By the time we finally settled
in and fell asleep it was past 3:00 a.m.

Sandy rang the next morning and instructed us to meet her in the
lobby at 2:15 for our trip to the orphanage—we were going to receive our
babies! At the appointed hour we gathered, pacing the lobby, taking pictures, shedding a few tears, and laughing nervously. Just as we were about
to load into vans, Sandy's cell phone rang. We were delayed an hour. Our
faces fell as we wondered what was wrong and, more importantly, what
to do with ourselves for the next torturous hour. We wanted our babies!

Somehow the time passed and Miss Kim arrived, just as we were getting into the vans. The ride seemed to take forever, but lasted only thirty-
five or forty minutes. We bobbed and weaved through chaotic traffic with
several near misses along the way. We pulled into the orphanage and were
escorted into a reception room where we sat down on folding chairs,
unsure of what to expect next. Sandy introduced Sister Hai, the energetic
and pleasant orphanage director. Because our group was small she
decided to allow us back into the orphanage. We walked through gardens,
past a kitchen, and by another building where toddlers stood in their
cribs. At the end of the grounds was the baby building. We removed our
shoes and entered. I raced up and down the rows of grim iron cribs looking for Viet and thought, at one point, that I had spotted him. However,
he'd already been taken out of his crib and was dressed and diapered. A

name tag had been pinned to his outfit and his name had been written in pen on his leg—a form of identification that I found somewhat disturbing.

Soon names were announced and babies were handed over to their parents. My name was called and Viet, looking smaller and balder than the picture I had carried around for two months, was placed into my arms. As I stared down at him, he broke into a big grin and I smiled back through tears of joy, mesmerized by his sweet smile and alert eyes. I finally looked up to see tears streaming down David's cheeks. We hugged gingerly, with our baby in the middle. The room was noisy with parents exclaiming proudly over their children, shedding tears of happiness, snapping pictures, fawning over their babies, and eventually checking out other family's babies. As I looked back at Sandy holding Deborah, her expression was something less than joyful and I wondered what she was thinking.

Only one other family in the group received a boy, while everyone else received girls. Two details seemed unusual. Unlike the babies in the cribs, who wore makeshift diapers and ragtag clothing, our babies were dressed in American clothing. Viet wore a one piece outfit with a fish pattern, which delighted David, an avid fisherman, and the other boy wore a cute blue outfit. The little girls were dressed in sweet pastel outfits, not your typical orphanage garb. Strangely, the two boys were tiny little things, while the girls, with the exception of Deborah, seemed hardier and more robust. It made me wonder if it was just coincidence or if the boys were not fed as well as the girls, a disturbing thought that I immediately rejected. In truth, Viet was a healthy weight at birth, but 9 percent of all infants born in Vietnam at the time were considered low birth weight babies.

Sandy's mind whirled. She was puzzled by Sister Hai's decision to take the group into the orphanage. It was a perk for the families, but might prove problematic if the October group caught wind of it and expected the same thing. There were no guarantees of anything in this process and decisions sometimes appeared to be made impulsively and inconsistently. There were more immediate problems to address: arranging for Dr. Vien to see the babies the next day, scheduling the Vietnamese meetings for the coming week, getting the families' paperwork in order, and dealing with Deborah's poor health, a task that would take every ounce of her time and energy in the weeks to come. As she looked around the room she felt excited for the families but also a little melancholy. Their babies were thriving; Deborah was not. Furthermore, the infants being adopted wore Deborah's clothing, clothing that Sandy had left for her at Tam Binh, weeks earlier. Her clothes had disappeared and now conveniently reappeared on the other children! She knew she shouldn't be surprised or upset by anything that happened in Vietnam but, still, it was disappointing.

Our group was an eclectic mix of overjoyed parents. Some had adopted before, while most were new parents. One couple was very young, while the Passages, whose ages we didn't know for certain, claimed to be the oldest. One woman was single and traveled with her mother, while another woman traveled with a co-worker; her husband and other children left behind. Only two families were from LSS while the others were from AFTH. But, despite our differences, today we were one big, happy group receiving our children.

We went back to the reception room and received bags containing formula, bottles, and medical reports. As we fed our babies, Sister Hai and Miss Kim came to greet each family individually. I tried to ask Sister Hai some questions about Viet's medical report, but she didn't seem to understand English. I was worried because the report indicated that Viet had previously suffered from bronchitis and had been given an ultrasound for some unknown reason.

Ellen and Steve Passage received a little girl they named Milena who, like Viet, had almost no hair. We speculated that perhaps the caregivers had recently shaved the babies' heads. Milena was dressed in a blue and white onesie which concerned Ellen a bit because her daughter's middle name was "Van Duc," typically a boy's name. Then, when she looked at Milena's medical report, the word "masculine" popped out at her. Concerned that perhaps her baby girl was actually a boy, she called Paul over for help. Paul, who had previously made the mistake with Deborah's gender, suggested they take off Milena's diaper. A quick check confirmed that the baby was, indeed, a girl, much to Ellen's relief.

Vietnamese women, presumably caregivers, handed out enormous rattles for the babies and bottles of water for the parents. Eventually we piled awkwardly into the van, with Paul giving us an extra boost in, for the trip back to the apartments. Most of the babies slept as everyone spoke in hushed voices.

For me, the first night was a rough one. I prepared bottles, using the formula provided by the orphanage and bottles I had purchased at home, but quickly discovered that the bottles had small, low-flow nipples, which Viet pushed away in angry frustration. Apparently, all of the orphanage bottles had large nipples to facilitate fast feeding. His breathing was raspy and I stayed by his side all night, too worried to sleep. By the next day he was very sick and I rode alternating waves of sleep deprivation and jetlag, with new motherhood exhilaration. Instead of the happy, smiling baby from the previous day, Viet was now a whimpering, coughing child, who was clearly miserable.

At 5:00 p.m. Paul and Dr. Vien arrived. Dr. Vien was a handsome, young doctor who swooped into the room, smiled, removed his motorcycle helmet, and grabbed his doctor's kit all in one smooth motion. He was

attentive, yet efficient, and prescribed cough medicine, saline, and Vita-
min D; items that Paul brought over later in the day. I was exhausted and
had a difficult time concentrating on the dosing directions, so Paul
patiently went over the instructions with me again. Finally, both the baby
and I caught a few hours of sleep.

On Monday, several meetings were scheduled, rescheduled, and
scheduled again. Sandy told David to be prepared to apply documents at
10:00 only to cancel the appointment later in the morning. The Giving
and Receiving (G&R) Ceremony, initially set for 3:00, was changed to
1:20, and then changed again to 2:15. I wondered if Sandy knew what she
was doing. The G&R Ceremony (the actual adoption) was solemn and
intimidating. I signed document after document, unsure of what I was
signing because everything was written in Vietnamese. Although Sandy
told us that no one was allowed to take pictures, one woman ignored
instructions and did, making the rest of us jealous. We also wanted pictures of this momentous occasion.

Later in the day all of the women (men were excluded) arrived at Vietnamese Immigration to apply for the babies' passports. The official was
late and we waited and waited. When the official looked at my documents, he frowned as he flipped pages back and forth and back again. It
was a nerve-wracking experience, to say the least.

The day ended on a very low note. Viet spent the afternoon crying,
coughing, and spitting up foul-smelling fluids. It was only day two, but
we were already running low on basic baby supplies and clothing. Each
time he spit up, I had changed him, creating a mountain of dirty laundry.
When we finally returned to our apartment at the end of the day, we discovered a huge, scary gecko climbing on our dining room wall and the
kitchen counters were covered in ants. What else could go wrong?

*For Sandy, Monday was a terrible day, punctuated by the usual jerk-
ing around by Vietnamese officials and her humiliation. The appointment
to apply documents was cancelled and the G&R was rescheduled at least
three times. She felt like an idiot in front of the families, but things were
out of her control. If only she could tell them what was really going on.
And, of course, there was the picture-taking incident at the G&R, for
which she was reprimanded, and the man at Immigration who stepped
out for a couple of drinks before their appointment, making everyone
wait. What else could go wrong?*

Tuesday was a free day without appointments. After a short nap we
ventured downtown to buy supplies and drop off pictures to be developed. Late in the afternoon Sandy called and requested that I come to
their apartment to review paperwork for the next day. I ran over, expecting that it would be a quick meeting, but the apartment was filled with
other families. I had to wait my turn. Sandy worked with the families

while Paul did housework and tended to the kids. Their household seemed chaotic to me. Deborah was crying, Hannah was trying to feed her, Sandy was talking to families, and Paul was dealing with housework, kids, and families all simultaneously. Finally, a number of families left and it was my turn.

Sandy leafed through my documents and frowned. "Some of these forms are incorrect! We need to redo them," she said with displeasure, as she pulled out replacement forms she had on hand.

"I thought I filled everything out correctly ... I don't know what happened." I was tired and discouraged and the last thing I wanted to do was fill out more forms! Plus, these were forms that the agency had helped me complete. Why were they wrong?

Sandy told me what changes to make, and when I finished, she said, "Okay, you're done with that. Let me put them in order." I could see her mind working as she thumbed through the stack of papers and reorganized them. "Where's your document from the Institute Pasteur?"

"What document is that?"

"You know; the one that states that the baby was tested for HIV and hepatitis." Sandy saw my blank stare and continued, "The form with the little picture on the top?"

"Oh God no! I didn't know we needed that form! It's at home!" My heart skipped beats as I realized the document was sitting in my office, thousands of miles away. Sandy picked up the phone and called someone to see if the authorities would accept a copy. Satisfied that they would, I ran back to my apartment, jumped on the phone, and called my next-door neighbor. I asked her to break into my house, find the document, and fax it to me. I was nearly hysterical at the possibility that this could put the adoption in jeopardy. Eventually the form was in my hands and I ran back to Sandy's apartment, choking back tears. Sandy assured me that everything was okay, but I still had my doubts. It had been another completely stressful day and again I wondered, what else could go wrong? So far I had hit two out of my three major fears.

Sandy was upset. Two families on this trip had incorrect paperwork and both were missing a document. She was tired and frustrated; she wanted to go home with her new baby and adjust to life with three children. It wasn't meant to be. Next month another group was arriving and she was already preparing for their adoptions. At least the Vietnamese side of this trip was over; now Paul could take the families to the various meetings. Tomorrow, however, she still had to finish up with the families to ensure that their paperwork was in order for their final meetings. When would this end?

Paul briefed us on our immigration meeting while Sandy quickly checked everyone's paperwork one final time. The meeting was held at the

Saigon Centre, a beautiful modern building with air conditioning, a rarity in Vietnam. The interview was conducted through a high window covered in bulletproof glass and I stood on my toes to answer the officer's questions. It seemed endless and my calves ached by the time we finished. Finally, we were free to leave and went shopping at the Saigon Centre and in downtown Ho Chi Minh City. The heat was oppressive and we dragged around, covered in sweat. Viet was overwhelmed by the stimulation, the sunshine, and the heat. Every time we left the apartment, he buried himself deep into his baby carrier, closed his eyes, and promptly fell asleep—as if he wanted to shut out the world.

By mid-afternoon it was time to leave again, first to take pictures for the babies' visas, and then to visit Cho Ray Hospital for their visa exams. Viet fell asleep and was the last one to have his picture taken; Paul's big hands held him in front of the camera, his sleepy eyes barely open. We drove through the gates of Cho Ray and I was shocked by its enormous size and sprawling, dreary buildings. It was raining and we followed Paul into an open area of the main building; a parade of Caucasians and their babies in a sea of Vietnamese. Paul led us to a covered walkway where we waited while curious Vietnamese gathered around us and tried to touch our babies. I edged away as far as possible to avoid their groping hands, afraid of germs and contagious diseases. Eventually, we moved to another building and followed Paul as he cut through a line of 300 waiting Vietnamese and placed us in a secluded hallway that served as a waiting area.

As the first baby was called in for an exam, Paul disappeared downstairs to pay the bill. Viet, second in line, was clearly not happy with the nurse who weighed and measured him. The doctor finished with the baby ahead of us and I noticed two sickening practices: the doctor didn't wash her hands between babies and she didn't change the examination sheet—all the babies were examined on the same crinkly paper sheet. The doctor asked me about Viet's eating and sleeping habits and Viet immediately coughed a terrible, rattling cough. I feigned surprise and pretended not to know anything about it, afraid of what would happen if he didn't pass the exam. However, he was pronounced healthy and we went back to the stifling waiting area until all the babies were finished. Then we retraced our steps and boarded the bus to return to the apartment.

The next three days were open and we could do what we wanted. Paul announced we might have a chance to fly home early and my spirits rose. I desperately wanted to go home although part of me felt guilty that I had experienced so little of Vietnam. Viet fell asleep early each night making it impossible to go out to restaurants. Our sightseeing had also been severely curtailed, but we decided to venture out and, with help from Paul and Spanky, we arranged for a driver and city tour the next day.

The following afternoon we met with our driver, Paux, who took us to an orchid farm outside the city. We stopped to take pictures of water buffalo along the way and ended up at a little farm off the beaten path; clearly not a tourist destination. I purchased several orchids knowing I wouldn't be able to take them home, and proceeded down the street to a Buddhist temple where Paux gained permission from the local monks to allow us to enter. Children swarmed around us and the monk harshly shooed them away, while scolding me for not covering Viet's exposed arms and legs.

Next we drove a short distance to an area with local stores and David went with Paux in search of conical hats; I waited in the car with Viet. While David and the driver were gone, a group of curious Vietnamese gathered around the car, peered in, and pointed at us, making me feel a little uncomfortable. Finally, David and Paux returned and we went off to see the sights.

Unfortunately, Viet was having another bad day. He was hot and tired, and refused to eat. However, our tour had just begun, so we returned to the city to see the War Remnants Museum, a sobering place that illustrated what the Vietnamese called the American War, as told through the eyes of the North Vietnamese. The museum was replete with photographs of Americans committing atrocities, displays of confiscated weapons, and deformed babies in jars—the devastating effect of Agent Orange. We left, and headed for Chinatown, a sprawling area with no clear beginning or end. Viet was growing more agitated so I suggested we cut the tour short. Paux pointed out the sights along the way: the Post Office, the Opera, and Ben Thanh Market. Back at the apartment we sat by the pool, but Viet was sweating profusely so we brought him inside to rest.

The next day we traveled to the Ben Thanh Market, which was filled with live chickens, fruit, and various souvenirs. Although I didn't see any, Sandy claimed the market also had its fair share of rats. She was terrified of them and sent Spanky to the market in her stead. We did a little shopping and ate a buffet lunch at the beautiful New World Hotel. But, between Viet's constant crying and my blond hair, it was a toss-up over who received more stares.

On Sunday, David departed early for a Mekong Delta tour with Spanky. I opted out because it was clearly too much for Viet; in hindsight, a wise decision. By now Viet was in real distress, growing sicker by the hour. I called Sandy and Paul and they added him to the list of babies that Dr. Vien would see that day. The endless day alternated between Viet sleeping, playing, and crying until mid-afternoon when Dr. Vien arrived. He looked in one ear and said, "Problem, oh, oh." As he cleaned out Viet's ear, the baby screamed louder than I had ever heard him scream;

crying so violently that sweat poured down his puckered red face. The doctor completed his exam and gave Viet a shot of antibiotics while I looked on anxiously.

Sandy was happy that Spanky was able to take over the sightseeing tours. How many times could she possibly go to Cu Chi Tunnels or the Mekong Delta? Paul enjoyed accompanying the families and still went on the tours now and then, but he had stayed home today to help her with the children. Spanky was more than capable of handling the tours and it benefitted everyone; it freed up their time and gave Spanky money, something he always needed. Plus, it gave Spanky the opportunity to take pictures or run errands for the families in exchange for cash. The families frequently needed help and Spanky needed their generosity. It was a good arrangement for everyone.

The next day was more of the same. Viet was very sick and the doctor appeared two hours late to clean out his infected ear and inject him with antibiotics. We were on call to pick up passports, but that didn't occur and there was no explanation why. I was disappointed. With Viet still sick, I desperately wanted to go home.

The next morning the women piled into cabs and returned to the Vietnamese Embassy to pick up the babies' passports. Sandy handed us our receipts as we entered the building. Standing in line, we were talking and chattering when suddenly, the Vietnamese woman behind the counter yelled at Sandy. She came running over to us and told us we had to be quiet. We felt like children being scolded and it seemed ridiculous, but we did as we were told and walked out with the passports, which Sandy promptly collected.

Later in the day Sandy asked me to come over to their apartment to review paperwork for the upcoming U.S. Consulate interview, the last step in the entire process. The scene in the apartment was again one of confusion: Sandy reviewed paperwork with parents, Dr. Vien took care of patients, and kids made noisy requests in the background. Luckily, everything was in order this time.

Dr. Vien arrived at our apartment some time later to give Viet his final shot. Fortunately, his temperature had gone down from its previous day's high of 103 degrees. We might actually be able to fly home as scheduled.

The next day I woke up feeling nauseous with a bad bout of diarrhea. I wanted to spend the day in bed, but I had to attend the Consulate interview. One family forgot about the meeting and showed up at the last second after frantic calls from Sandy. She was angry with the family and showed it, which was surprising since she was typically so cool and calm.

Sandy was livid. She couldn't believe the family forgot about the interview after she had just reminded them about it the night before as they reviewed paperwork. "It never ends," she thought. "This trip has been one big stress load between coping with all the problems with the Viet-namese side, adjusting to Deborah's needs, and helping these families solve their own problems. And now, I can't even go home because we have another group coming in a couple of weeks. It doesn't make sense to fly home only to turn around and fly back, but I really want to go home ..."

The process at the Consulate was lengthy. We received a ticket and waited in line to pay a cashier. Then, one by one we underwent an interview in a room so highly air conditioned that my teeth chattered. Finally, our documents were reviewed, we were sent back to the waiting room, and another woman came out to talk to all of us about the process. We paid yet another fee and were called back into a small booth where she leafed through our paperwork, asked us questions, and congratulated us on our adoption. Paul congratulated us too; our adoption process was finally over! Unfortunately, I was too sick to enjoy it.

Next, we headed over to Korean Air to finalize our airline reservations. Once there, we had some problems, as did other families. The airline wouldn't guarantee that we could actually sit with our babies, who had reservations in the bulkhead seat (the spacious first seat in the plane, with a bassinet that snapped into the wall)! It was ridiculous and maddening. Back at the apartment I discovered my temp was 102. I crawled into bed, nauseous and exhausted, with a terrible stomachache—my triad of fears had come to fruition.

* * *

Ellen and Steve Passage went back to their apartment instead of going to Korean Air, deciding they could take care of their plane reservations later in the day. Steve held Milena and got into one cyclo as Ellen, an avid photographer, got into another so she could take pictures along the way. As the cyclo neared the hotel, Ellen noticed a group of Vietnamese people sitting on the street with colorful signs all around them and started taking pictures. Within a couple of minutes, a man came over to her cyclo and made the driver pull over to the side.

"You cannot take pictures. Not allowed!"

"I didn't know that."

The man spoke to the cyclo driver in Vietnamese and the cyclo driver nodded his head as he prepared to pedal off again.

"Where are we going?" Ellen asked, as they headed in a different direction.

"To see police," he answered.

Ellen looked back to make sure Steve and Milena were behind her and shrugged her shoulders at Steve as if to say, "I don't know what's happening." After a short ride they all arrived at a small police station that housed three policemen, a desk, and a couple of chairs.

The men spoke to each other in Vietnamese until finally one said, "You can't take pictures of a demonstration."

"I'm sorry. I didn't know they were demonstrating. I didn't know I couldn't take pictures."

Ellen looked over at Milena and was relieved to see that she wore a big floppy hat. Perhaps they wouldn't notice that she was Vietnamese. Ellen wasn't worried about what the police might do to her, but she was deeply concerned about endangering the adoption.

"What's on that film?" a policeman asked, pointing to her camera.

"Sightseeing pictures ..." Ellen tried to think of what was on the film: pictures from the Consulate today, last night's pictures at the Rex Hotel, baby pictures, of course ...

The police motioned to Ellen to take the film out of the camera and she obliged.

"Where are you staying?"

"Stamford Court," Ellen answered, holding her breath as she waited for the police to ask for their names.

"Okay. You can go."

They went directly to Paul and Sandy's apartment and told them what happened. They were relieved to see that neither Sandy nor Paul seemed too upset about it. However, Ellen spent a restless night, worrying that the police would arrive at Stamford Court to search for them. She was also concerned that the police would develop the film, see the pictures of the families and their children, and purposely stop all of their adoptions. She didn't know how adoptions were viewed by the police and wondered whether they had any power to interfere with, or worse yet, stop the families from leaving the country with their children. But, by the next morning when there were no further consequences, she relaxed, confident that her punishment consisted of merely losing a roll of film and nothing more.

* * *

When the Passages left the apartment, Sandy turned to Paul. "Didn't we tell this group not to take pictures of that demonstration?"

"Yes," Paul answered.

"Then why would she take pictures?" Sandy was incredulous.

"I'm sure she just forgot, or maybe she didn't hear us. You know how families are when they get their babies. They're jetlagged and tired and not focused on what we're saying."

"Well we can't have every group coming here and getting arrested by the police! Our program will go down the tubes!" Sandy was shrill.

"I know, I know, but it's okay. Nothing happened and everyone's going home in a couple of days. It gave them a scare though, huh?" Paul chuckled.

Sandy wasn't mad so much as she was worried about the ultimate fall-out from the incident and she failed to see the humor in the situation.

* * *

The next day was a blur as I slept fitfully, still weak and feverish. David ran into Sandy while running a quick errand and told her I was sick. She called me and offered to send Dr. Vien over, but I politely refused. Dr. Vien was kind and well-meaning, but I wasn't entirely comfortable with Vietnamese medicine for myself. Dr. Vien had treated Viet effectively, and his condition had greatly improved, but we also relied upon David's brother Robert, a neonatologist (via telephone), to confirm that Dr. Vien was providing appropriate treatment. I didn't want to take any chances. Worst case basis, I decided that David and Viet could fly home together and leave me behind until I was healthy enough to travel. David flatly rejected that idea. Panicked, he called in reinforcements. The woman named Claudia and her co-worker, Janice, were both nurses. They arrived at my bedroom door with tea bags, lemon-lime soda, and words of advice and encouragement, which was greatly appreciated.

Friday was our last day in Vietnam. Still feeling miserable, I spent the day alternating between packing and resting while David watched Viet. I hadn't eaten for days and my clothes felt baggy on my haggard body. I didn't realize it at the time, but I had lost ten pounds in one week. Around 6:00 p.m. our luggage was picked up and we met the other families in the lobby. Everyone looked well-rested and ready to go; I barely had the strength to sit and watch as the babies were lined up on the couch for pictures. I wondered how I would manage during the long flight home, but I had no choice. I was flying home whether I was able to do it or not. I had prepared baby bottles in advance with pre-measured formula; all I needed was hot water from the flight attendant and I'd be set. Sandy, not understanding how sick I was, teased me about my over-the-top preparations. The diaper bag was packed to the gills and ready to go with diapers, wipes, toys, and extra clothing. There was nothing to do now but fly home.

During our time in the lobby I was shocked to learn that Sandy and Paul were not flying with us. Paul was accompanying us to the airport, while Sandy was staying behind with the children. My goodbyes with Sandy were emotional. We both wept, parting as old friends who had been through a lot together. Truly she and Paul made the adoption possible and without their hard work and ingenuity through all of our difficulties, we would not be taking Viet home. We owed them the type of debt you can't repay and, for today, they were our heroes.

For some adoptive families, the adoption trip had simply been a relaxing vacation spent sightseeing, dining, and shopping in Vietnam, taking full advantage of Sandy and Paul's recommendations, and enjoying their babies. For me, the trip was fraught with worries, problems, challenges, and difficulties; a rollercoaster of emotions that spanned the highest highs and the lowest lows. My triad of worries had come to pass. But, through it all, the most miraculous event had occurred: we had adopted our precious son! Nothing else really mattered.

One final time we loaded ourselves into a van; luggage went into another. Paul pointed out the sights that we had missed on our ride in, which now seemed so long ago. Although we were on the last flight of the night—the midnight run to Seoul—the airport teemed with people and it was nearly impossible to navigate into the terminal building. Paul saw that David and I were struggling, so he held Viet while we dealt with our luggage. Inside, he waited with us, concerned about my health. The ticket counter hadn't opened yet. Weak and exhausted, I leaned over the piled suitcases for support. Paul pushed us to the beginning of the line, helped us check in, and walked with us until we reached the security check-in point.

As with Sandy, our goodbyes were tearful; but Paul had to leave, so thankfully they were short. The woman at the checkpoint looked at Viet and remarked "lucky baby," which was a phrase we had heard over and over in Vietnam. I marveled again at the generosity of spirit of the Vietnamese people. The flight back was much the same as the flight over: long and exhausting as we anticipated our destination point which, this time, was home. Everything went according to schedule and we returned home not as two, but three jetlagged travelers ready to embark upon our new journey as a family.

CHAPTER 17

Commitment

Wherever you go,
Go with all your heart.

Confucius

By the end of 2000, the Pinkertons were back in Manheim, now a family of five. They took Deborah to their family physician; their first order of business. The doctor examined her and administered antibiotics to treat her remaining pneumonia symptoms, but felt that Deborah needed long-term care. She passed her along to a group of pediatric specialists who tested her for everything from TB to HIV. They found little wrong except that she was underweight and severely malnourished.

Months earlier, a proud and excited Paul had shown pictures of Deborah to his siblings, announcing that this was their next child. He failed to notice their facial expressions as they flipped through photos of the frail, deathly ill child, who had IVs sticking out of her head. Although they admired his courage, they worried about Deborah's long-term prognosis. Then, when they saw her in person over the holidays, they were convinced she'd never be a normal child. Nearly a one-year-old, Deborah couldn't sit up, roll over, or even play with toys. Dave looked at her and thought, "Boy, they're in over their heads this time!" He was deeply concerned that his brother's ever-increasing family now included two special needs children.

But while everyone else worried, Sandy and Paul rose to the challenge. They fed Deborah every couple of hours, played with her to provide physical therapy, and showered her with love and attention. Slowly, she flourished.

Paul and Sandy weren't home long before it was time to return to Vietnam. It was 2001 and adoption groups were lined up for February, April, and beyond. As soon as they returned to Vietnam, Spanky paid Paul a visit. Spanky, who had been agonizing over whether or not to marry the woman his mother had arranged for him to betroth, sought Paul's advice.

"Mr. Paul, what should I do? What should I do? Should I marry her?"

"How well do you know her?"

"I don't know her. We've written letters a couple of times but that's it."

"I don't know what to tell you Spanky. Why do you think you have to marry her?"

"My mother thinks I should be married and everyone in the village thinks I should marry her." According to Vietnamese custom, it was time for Spanky to have a wife and a child as well. At the age of twenty-eight, he was past due.

"But do you love her?"

"I don't know if I love her. I think so ..."

"Well, do you think you *can* love her at some point?"

"She seems like nice girl ... Mr. Paul, you are like my daddy. You're the same age as my daddy would be, so I look up to you like a daddy. I hope you don't mind that I ask questions."

"No Spanky, I don't mind, but you're an adult and you need to make your own decisions. I can't tell you what to do or who to marry. You're the one who has to live with her."

In the end, Spanky decided to marry the girl and asked Paul for a loan so he could have a proper Vietnamese wedding. Sandy and Paul missed the happy occasion because they were back in Manheim. The loan was never repaid.

* * *

Paul was often in the wrong place at the wrong time. He had missed both Spanky's wedding in Vietnam and the funeral service at Arlington National Cemetery for the members of Freight Train 053, which was held in May of 2001.

Thirty-three years earlier, on October 20, 1968, five members of the 243rd Assault Support Helicopter Company had been lost in a crash in the Central Highlands of Vietnam. Members of the company searched in vain for eight long days until the search proved futile and was terminated on October 28. Colonel Jon Beckenhauer, a pilot of another plane on the same mission, remained on duty in Vietnam nearly three years after the crash. He had hoped to catch a glimpse of the wreckage during subsequent flights, but he never did. He returned home haunted by memories of the only crew from the 243rd to disappear without a trace. Eventually the five men were declared dead and were no longer considered MIAs, according to Army protocol.

It was the summer of 1992 when Paul, through persistence and a large dose of luck, stumbled across a man in Nha Trang who gave him a dog tag and bone fragments from a crash site. Paul had turned the items over to the U.S. Government, convinced they were those of the five members of the 243rd who had gone missing. When he returned home, he looked up family members and went on a personal crusade to close the case. In reality, he was but one piece of a much larger puzzle.

Evidence (in the form of dog tag rubbings, bone fragments, and accounts of knowledge of the crash) had been turned in prior to, and after, Paul's discovery, and were submitted to the forensic lab in Hawaii. In 1994, a joint investigation team traveled to Ninh Giang Village to investigate REFNO 1306 based upon previously gathered evidence. The team interviewed first- and second-hand witnesses who turned over additional remains and led the team to a site with a large amount of wreckage. Analysis revealed the wreckage correlated to REFNO 1306 and the site was excavated in January of 1995. However, it wasn't until December of 2000 that the families were notified and the remains returned.

Each family had gone through their own misery; each man had been a story unto himself. Charles Deitsch (Pappy) was the oldest and most experienced pilot. He was close to retirement although no one thought he would actually retire unless he was forced to do so. His widow never remarried and lost her only son to illness. Charles Meldahl was single and had traded places with his friend Brian Main the day of the mission. Jerry Bridges was only twelve days into his second tour when he was killed. Ronald Stanton was one day shy of his twenty-second birthday on the day of the crash. Henry (Hank) Knight was married, with a one-year-old daughter. He had arrived in Vietnam just a short time before the crash. His widow, Shayne, learned that he was MIA on her twenty-second birthday and she later received letters from him that were delayed in the mail.

Most of the family members were unaware of the details of what had transpired the day of the crash and only gleaned bits and pieces of the story through either Jon Beckenhauer, the pilot of one of the planes on the mission, or Paul. But Jon didn't know Paul and vice versa. Strange twists of fate would eventually bring them together.

Jon posted information on a Vietnam website about the 243rd which included his name and position as a Colonel in the Company. It was purely coincidental that a young boy, conducting Internet research about his uncle, Jerry Bridges, stumbled across the information. The boy and his dad, Gene Isom, gave Jon a call. Gene was astonished to learn the series of events that had taken place on the day of the crash because the Army never communicated any of the details to him or his wife, Doris, Jerry's sister. A long and emotional phone call ensued.

In December of 2000, when Gene and Doris were notified by the Army that the case was closed and Jerry's remains would be returned to them, Gene picked up the phone and called Jon to let him know. Jon, who had been waiting for closure, swung into action. He contacted over 160 alumni of the 243rd and informed them of the resolution of the case and provided details regarding the upcoming funeral at Arlington National Cemetery. Jon lived in the D.C. area and had attended funerals at Arlington before. Since he had served three tours in Vietnam and was considered the unit historian, he was chosen to deliver the eulogy at the funeral.

Jon learned of Paul's role in the saga through Gene Isom, who had communicated with Paul since 1992. Together Jon and Gene decided that Paul should be invited to the funeral so the families could meet him. Jon began a series of communications with Paul and thought his story should be captured on videotape for use in a piece about the 243rd. He contacted a friend who was currently filming a different documentary with him for the History Channel.

Events progressed quickly. Paul traveled to D.C. and told his story on tape, Jon helped with funeral arrangements, and the families prepared to say their final goodbyes to their loved ones. Paul had every intention of attending the funeral, which was scheduled for May 25, but, like so many of his plans, it was foiled by Miss Kim. She was a strong believer in the Chinese calendar, a calendar that predicted which days were lucky and which were not. Unfortunately, the calendar indicated that the time around the 25th was good for business, so Kim insisted that Paul and Sandy return to Vietnam.

The funeral service was held as scheduled for the five members of Freight Train 053: Charles E. Deitsch, Henry C. Knight, Charles H. Meldahl, Ronald V. Stanton and Ronald Bridges. The solemn service included a missing man formation flyover by five CH-47D Chinook helicopters, a lone bagpipe player, a horse-drawn caisson, a flyover by a bald eagle named Challenger, and a heartfelt eulogy by Jon. During a dinner held in D.C., Jon recounted Paul's story for the families. The grief-stricken families finally pieced together the complete story of the crash of Freight Train 053 and its ultimate recovery, bringing closure to the thirty-three-year-old nightmare that had been their lives. All five men were posthumously promoted.

* * *

Paul was disappointed to miss the funeral, but he turned his attention to the adoption world where rumors were running rampant. Some claimed that Vietnam would soon close its doors to U.S. adoptions, while others said that Vietnamese adoption would soon entail two trips instead of one, requiring families to apply their own documents in person. A handful of corrupt facilitators had been arrested for unlawful adoption practices, setting off a firestorm of bad publicity within Vietnam. Meanwhile, Sister Hai had retired from Tam Binh under somewhat mysterious circumstances and had disappeared without a word.

Everyone was concerned about the rumors but, for now, things were pretty much status quo, which was to say hectic. Paul and Sandy facilitated groups in April, May, and June, with more groups lined up for July, August, September, October, and November. There was no shutdown and certainly no slow down either.

Many families, who were happy with their first experience, returned to adopt a second time. Baz (Richard) and Lisa McRell, who adopted a little boy, Noah, two years earlier, came back for a little girl in July. Baz and Lisa's Vietnam veteran friends made requests of them prior to their trip to Vietnam. Some were curious about the country and asked to see pictures and hear stories upon their return. Others wanted soil samples and still others inquired whether or not dog tags were still being sold on the streets of Saigon. The underlying hope was that a random dog tag might belong to one of their fallen comrades. The McRells took their friend's requests seriously and did their best to fulfill them.

Six other couples traveled with the McRells. Unlike their first trip, when families enjoyed being together, this group was much less cohesive. Baz and Lisa spent most of their time with the Pinkertons. They dined together, watched water puppet shows at the zoo, and simply sat by the pool and talked while their children played. Their four-month-old daughter was healthy and robust, so that even with two-year-old Noah in tow, the trip seemed easier and far more relaxed than their first.

They returned home with their beautiful baby girl and tales from Vietnam, including a light-hearted story from a Mekong Delta tour that Spanky orchestrated. Spanky had made the arrangements and accompanied the families, along with a tour guide and boat captain. Baz, a self-proclaimed "hairy little man" was teased by the tour guide, who called him a chimp. Baz good-naturedly shared the story as one of the more humorous moments of his trip.

Brenda and Lee Rath also returned to Vietnam for their second child, arriving in August, a month after Baz and Lisa. Brenda had conducted research on the Internet and knew about the rumors. She wanted to complete their adoption as quickly as possible to ensure its success. Sandy reassured her that, for now, everything was still on track. Lee and Brenda made the difficult decision to leave their son, Zachary, at home with his grandparents.

For many adoptive families the question of whether or not to bring siblings was problematic. The decision was most often driven by logistics, emotions, financial concerns, and an honest assessment of how well a sibling (or siblings) might handle the trip. Sandy and Paul could attest to the fact that sometimes the decision to bring siblings along, no matter how carefully considered, was often the wrong one and disastrous for everyone concerned.

Similar to Baz and Lisa, the Rath's second experience was also very different from their first. Although it was difficult to be away from Zachary, they were more relaxed and confident about parenting. Their second child, Sean, was healthier and more on target developmentally than Zachary had been, and that eased some of their earlier worries. However, their travel group was huge and most of the families wanted to do things by themselves, which eliminated the sense of fellowship they had previously enjoyed.

With such a large group to manage, Sandy and Paul had little time to spend with them, so they took advantage of the many tours Spanky ran. Lee, who felt compassionate towards Spanky, encouraged families to pay him for his services, thereby ensuring Spanky received a handsome tip at the end. Like Baz, Brenda came home with a story of her own, which was only funny in hindsight.

One day she and another mother decided to venture out to an Internet café. Brenda handed the taxi driver a business card with the address, but soon realized the driver was going in the wrong direction. Brenda and her companion tried to communicate directions, but the man insisted they were almost there. After a frightening hour of driving around aimlessly, Brenda finally convinced the driver to take them back to the hotel. Brenda relayed the story to Paul who thought perhaps the driver was new and didn't know all the streets yet. That night as Brenda and Lee stepped into a taxi to go to dinner, Brenda realized they had the same driver! Fortunately, this time he took them to their destination on the very first try.

Both the McRells and the Raths went home with their babies and lifetime memories of their trips. They were appreciative of Sandy and Paul's help and felt the couple had been instrumental in showing them a good time. For Sandy and Paul, there were the usual problems, but nothing insurmountable.

The Pinkertons overriding concern at this point was Sister Hai, whom they loved dearly. They knew that without her they couldn't have adopted Isaiah and Deborah. They even forgave her for a little game she had played with them. Early on, Sandy and Paul assumed that Sister Hai couldn't speak English very well, because Miss Kim often acted as an interpreter, relaying what they said to her, in Vietnamese. But, when they completed Deborah's adoption, Miss Kim was unavailable and Sister Hai miraculously spoke perfect English the entire day! They knew then, that it had been a carefully crafted ploy, to keep Sister Hai above the fray. It was a strategy to avoid answering questions from not only Sandy and Paul, but from the families who constantly hounded her for information about their babies. They didn't blame her for avoiding the families' questions, but wished she had been more upfront with them.

But now Sister Hai had vanished and Sandy and Paul were extremely concerned about her. Some said that she had retired and was running her own orphanage nearby. Others thought that she had been forced to resign against her will. Only a few people knew for sure what had happened.

"Miss Kim, do you know where Sister Hai is? We've heard she's running an orphanage and we really want to see her. Please tell us where she is."

"No, Miss Sandy, I don't know. She disappear. I don't know."

The questioning continued for nearly a year until finally Sandy and Paul heard through families on the Internet that Sister Hai had started a school to care for children from impoverished families whose parents needed assistance. The school, called the Xuan Phuong House of Love, was located only a few miles from Tam Binh. Eventually, Sandy and Paul tracked her down through an address posted on the web.

When Sister Hai found Sandy and Paul on her doorstep, she rushed to them, arms wide open, grinning broadly. She hugged them both with tight squeezes as tears formed in her eyes.

"I'm so happy to see you! How are you? How are the children? Come in, come in!"

"It's great to see you! We've been looking for you for such a long, long time."

Sister Hai frowned. "Really? I ask Kim all the time, 'Where are they? Do they come back to Vietnam?' Kim said you don't come back anymore."

It was a terrible revelation but not one that Sister Hai wanted to dwell on at that particular moment. She served Sandy and Paul tea, proudly showed them her school, and basked in the company of old friends.

In her absence, Tam Binh had undergone significant changes. Mr. Trung was now in charge and he ran Tam Binh quite differently from Sister Hai. She had kept a tight lid on the adoption process, controlling which agencies were allowed to work at the orphanage. But with Mr. Trung in charge, the doors had been flung open, and more and more agencies came in search of babies. This was problematic, because there were only so many babies available and demand sometimes exceeded supply. Previously, Kim (and ultimately AFTH and LSS) had supposedly taken 90 percent of the babies coming out of Tam Binh, primarily because she and Sister Hai had a long-standing and close relationship. But Mr. Trung had no such connection to Kim and children were now up for grabs, divided among the numerous agencies as he saw fit. For Sandy, the only advantage to having Mr. Trung in charge was that he insisted upon matching babies to parents, which relieved her of the task that had caused so many sleepless nights and supplications to God.

Change loomed on the horizon and everyone was worried. Families had heard the rumors about Vietnam closing for adoption and were rushing to adopt as quickly as possible. To make matters worse, AFTH was also in transition. Sandy and Paul had worked with Elizabeth Norris, the coordinator for the Vietnam program, since approximately 1999 and had a close working relationship with her. Everything was running smoothly. Elizabeth had a strong commitment to helping families and went the extra mile to patiently answer questions, relay information, or provide a sounding board for nervous parents-to-be.

The fact that she loved her job was no secret. She took her work home with her and spent sleepless nights fretting over the details of the paperwork, the families, and their babies. She also had a big picture perspective. She admired and appreciated Maxine's business acumen, she understood the huge leap of faith and courage required of adoptive parents, and she felt that Sandy and Paul were unique in their commitment to helping children.

But, as much as she loved her job, Elizabeth was now leaving the agency. She and her husband were eagerly anticipating the birth of their first child in October. For Sandy and Paul, her departure not only signaled the absence of a fine colleague and friend, it also meant they would need to establish a new working relationship with her replacement. They anticipated some growing pains as a new coordinator learned the nuances of the job. The well-oiled machine was about to become derailed once again.

* * *

Transitions were in the works back home too. The situation with the greenhouse had gone from bad to worse. A year earlier, when Paul realized he couldn't devote time to the business because of his adoption work, he put the greenhouse up for sale. It still chugged along with Marty at the helm, but it was a dying enterprise. There was little money coming in, the buildings were in disrepair, and Paul simply wanted to be rid of it. The only problem was that no one was buying. Not only was no one buying, no one was even looking. Disappointed by his realtor's results, Paul switched agencies. Still nothing happened. It was a depressing situation of waiting and hoping while the bills continued to pile up on his desk.

But tending the greenhouse was not the only reason they flew halfway across the globe nearly every month to return home. The primary reason was Hannah. Legally, Richard was Hannah's father and he had a right to see her on a regular basis. Paul understood Richard's rights and would have resigned himself to accommodate them except for the fact that his visits frequently didn't occur as planned. They often made arrangements for Hannah to spend the weekend with Richard only to have him back out at the last minute. Or, sometimes he picked her up for the weekend only to pass her off to his girlfriend while he spent time with his buddies. It was disappointing for Hannah and infuriating to Paul.

"This is bullshit Sandy! We're spending a lot of time, not to mention money, sitting on airplanes so he can take her to his girlfriend's house. Hannah's supposed to spend time with Richard, not his girlfriend!"

"I know, I know, but what can we do? He has a right to see her. I don't control what he does!" In Vietnam Sandy ran interference between Paul and Kim and at home she ran interference between Paul and Richard. Both situations were losing propositions.

* * *

While Paul and Sandy were home between trips, they received a strange request. They received a phone call from Family and Children's Agency (FCA), located in Connecticut, inquiring whether they would be willing to facilitate a few Vietnamese adoptions for them. After some discussion, the couple agreed, unaware of the fact that FCA and LSS were competitors and were located only a few miles apart.

Sandy and Paul naively believed that adoption was a noble cause for which there was no competition. What was more important than finding homes for children, after all? But agencies begged to differ and when the director at Lutheran found out, she was displeased, as was Maxine at AFTH, who maintained the position that Sandy and Paul should have an exclusive arrangement with her. But an agreement was an agreement, so in August the first FCA adoption was facilitated by Sandy and Paul.

It was during this trip when Sandy was at the orphanage taking referral pictures, that she spotted a pitiful little baby lying face down in a crib. Sandy couldn't see the child's face and didn't know if the infant was a boy or girl. All she knew was that this child was severely malnourished and extremely ill. She had seen so many of these children over the years that she knew what the ultimate outcome would be. A sense of doom filled her and, despite the heat, she shivered with goose bumps. Sandy gently pulled aside a caretaker and motioned to the baby.

"Whose child is this?"

"I don't know, but we have a family for him."

"Really, you do? Okay." Sandy was skeptical. Experience told her that sick babies were often turned down by prospective parents. The baby had not been assigned to anyone in her group of families, so she wouldn't have inside information on the outcome.

Sandy felt her maternal instincts kick into gear, although she certainly wasn't looking for another addition to her family. In fact, it was the furthest thing from her mind. She had more than enough on her plate with an eight-year-old, a five-year-old, and a two-year-old. But a baby was a baby, and a baby in distress tugged at her heartstrings more than she was willing to admit.

Thoughts of the sick baby were soon displaced as the United States was plunged into chaos on September 11, 2001. Paul, Sandy, and the children were between trips and happened to be home at the time. Their phone rang as one family panicked; they wondered what the disaster meant in terms of their upcoming travel plans a few days later. For Paul, it meant nothing. The trip was going to happen, with or without terrorists. Paul believed that the threat, at least for the time being, was over. It was highly unlikely the terrorists would be geared up to strike again. Besides, the majority of their trip consisted of international, not domestic, flights. He sincerely doubted that terrorists had much interest in Americans flying to Korea and Vietnam. Families, although afraid and shaken by the attacks on American soil, were even more determined to see their children. No one backed out.

One week later, on September 18, Paul and a group of families flew to Vietnam for the sole purpose of applying their documents in person, in compliance with new regulations that had been put in place. Making two trips to Vietnam was expensive and inconvenient, but worse, it put families in the gut-wrenching position of spending a week with their babies, only to leave them. For most families the pain of leaving their children behind was almost too much to bear but, short of staying in Vietnam for forty to sixty days, there was no alternative. Families consoled themselves by bringing suitcases filled with clothes, toys, and family pictures for their children; hoping to form some small bond before boarding the plane back to the States. Like so many aspects of the adoption process, this was yet one more step that was completely out of the control of adoptive parents, that caused considerable heartache and angst.

* * *

Sandy's life, more so than Paul's, was a difficult juggling act. As the mother of three small children she spent the bulk of her time nurturing and caring for them, as well as home schooling both Hannah and Isaiah. In Vietnam she had the responsibility of guiding families through the Vietnamese side of the adoption process, dealing with Miss Kim and Mr. Trung, and working with the new program coordinator at the agency on referrals and travel dates for the families. Constant travel left her perpetually jetlagged and tired. Still, Sandy tried to maintain contact with her relatives, that strange collection of half-brothers and half-sisters that comprised her family circle.

Angel's sons were still hurt over the fact that Angel had given Sandy and Sandra a house, even though the home had long since been sold. Only Raymond and Sandra maintained contact with her and they were far from close knit. The other side of the family wasn't much better. Karl was much older than Sandy and, although they were friendly, they simply didn't have much in common. Bobbi was the one family member that Sandy felt most connected to, but she was also the most elusive, just like their mother, Hazel, had been.

Sandy desperately wanted a relationship with Bobbi so she invited her to come to Vietnam. Sandy had two main goals for the trip. She wanted Bobbi to understand her work and see her for the person she had become, and she wanted Bobbi to appreciate Isaiah and Deborah's roots in order to feel a closer bond to her children. In truth, Bobbi did admire Sandy for the work she did and felt proud of her, but she truly didn't know what Sandy's work entailed.

Their late September/early October trip, not surprisingly, did not meet Sandy's expectations. Bobbi had never traveled to a foreign country and was ill-equipped for the difficulties of traveling such a long distance. Once she arrived in Vietnam she expressed her displeasure over everything and complained, "This place is dirty and it stinks!" Sandy thought back to her early days in Vietnam when conditions were much cruder, and felt Bobbi was being unreasonable in her assessment, especially given the fact that they stayed in a beautiful Westernized apartment and dined in the finest restaurants in town.

The clincher came halfway through the trip however, when war broke out in Afghanistan. Bobbi panicked and worried that she'd be trapped in Vietnam. She told Sandy she wanted to leave immediately and Sandy agreed that it might be for the best. Bobbi took the next available flight home and was more than happy to leave. She came away from the trip with a slightly better understanding of Sandy's work and a terrible impression of Vietnam. It was clearly not the outcome Sandy desired.

Half-sister Sandra also admired Sandy and her work although she had no desire to travel to Asia. Sandra saw how Sandy had changed over the years and marveled at how strong and self-assured she had become—so different from the woman she'd once described to others as "weak, confused, and uncertain." Sandra, who had hated Sandy for so many years, now considered her a remarkable woman, someone she aspired to emulate. Sandra felt a common bond with Sandy; both women grew up feeling unloved and unwanted. And although she couldn't articulate what she felt was her own life's purpose, she believed that Sandy was born for a specific reason: to help Vietnamese orphans.

But Sandra, like Bobbi, had her own life, her own concerns, and her own time constraints. She and Sandy talked on the phone occasionally, but they didn't have the close connection that Sandy craved. Sure, Sandy had Paul and even Dr. Vien, whom she loved, but it wasn't the same as having a female friend to compare notes with or gossip with over lunch. She searched for female friends, often in vain.

Friends did eventually enter Sandy's life, primarily in Vietnam. Miss Hoa, the owner of the silk shop, continued to be one of her dearest friends although she was very busy with her business and frequently unavailable. It was a rare and pleasant treat when the two women spent the day together shopping, eating lunch, and getting manicures.

Sandy, although hard-pressed to admit it, did, in fact, love Miss Kim. When they weren't bickering, she and Miss Kim exchanged small talk, gossiped a little, or talked about their children. Sandy was a frequent guest at her daughter's parties. And most importantly, Sandy felt enormous gratitude to Kim for her help in Isaiah's and Deborah's adoptions.

But the primary source of Sandy's new friends came from the international church in Vietnam, a church she and Paul attended. The church was designed for passport-holding foreigners and consisted primarily of American, European, and Asian expatriates trying to maintain some semblance of normal life overseas. It was through this connection that Sandy met Cindy Yarger and Grace Mischler; women who fulfilled different needs for her.

Cindy had interests similar to Sandy's. Both had adopted children whom they home schooled. Most of Sandy's visits with Cindy were family outings where the children played and the husbands talked, while Cindy and Sandy compared notes on homework requirements, parenting responsibilities, and both the joys and negative aspects of living between two cultures. Cindy, perhaps better than anyone else, understood the flavor of living overseas and the way it permeated a person's blood. Cindy loved living overseas, but readily acknowledged the difficulties she experienced when she returned to the United States, only to discover that life had gone on without her.

Cindy and Sandy enjoyed each other's company. Although they never engaged in intimate conversations about their private lives, they respected each other and had a connection that allowed them to strike up easy conversations about a number of topics, making for pleasant times together.

Grace Mischler, another friend from church, had a degree in social work and had worked on adoptions in the States. Grace had a great admiration and love for Sandy and Paul, whom she described as "totally engaged in what people rarely enter into: unconditional love, utter compassion, and a mission to take on the 'rejects of society.'" By rejects, Grace meant not only orphans, but people with special needs, like herself. Grace was blind. Grace had a special love and affinity for both Deborah and Isaiah, whom she could relate to in her own unique way.

Grace began teaching English to social workers at the National Vietnam University in Saigon as part of a church mission, but went on to develop a course that integrated persons with special needs into society. Grace's assistant, Ba Thien, had lost his eyesight one Sunday afternoon as he and his college friend cooked food on the beach unaware that a landmine lay just below the sand's surface. Grace knew about Paul's Vietnam War experiences and felt that he had been transformed from "a participant in human destruction to a participant in human construction," and found both Sandy and Paul to be extraordinary human beings. Likewise, Sandy felt inspired by Grace and often remembered Grace's strength in overcoming obstacles during those difficult times when her own problems seemed truly insurmountable.

Besides the obvious adoption and special needs connection, Sandy and Grace had other similarities too. Both had been divorced, both had navigated two cultures while never quite fitting into either one, and both shared secrets about their personal lives that they didn't easily reveal to others. It was for this reason that Grace was the first to know when Sandy confided in her that she was obsessed with the infant she had seen lying face down at the orphanage, the infant whose image she couldn't get out of her head. There was only one problem: What was she going to do about it?

CHAPTER 18

End of an Era

*I wanted a perfect ending.
Now I've learned, the hard way,
That some poems don't rhyme, and some stories
Don't have a clear beginning, middle, and end.
Life is about not knowing, having to change,
Taking the moment and making the best of it,
Without knowing what's going to happen next.*

Gilda Radner

Initially, Sandy resisted the temptation to hold the sick infant. Partly it was because everyone insisted there was a family for him and partly it was because she knew it would be a dangerous thing to bring him close to her heart, a heart that beat faster than normal whenever she saw him. But her maternal instincts were too strong. Soon she was spending more and more time with the baby, gazing into his large black eyes as she stroked his shriveled little body to provide some measure of comfort.

Sandy had learned a few things about the child by pressing Miss Kim and Mr. Trung for information. The boy's parents lived in the Mekong Delta and had another son. They were extremely poor. The baby boy was born prematurely and had serious medical problems, including a hernia that had required surgery. The mother had abandoned him because he was so ill; she couldn't take care of him. However, she did not immediately relinquish her rights. Riddled by guilt and overcome with sadness, she returned to Tam Binh repeatedly, unable to give him up, unable to keep him, and unable to decide what to do. Eventually Mother Nature made the decision for her. A tremendous flood hit the Mekong, destroying her home and all of the family's possessions in its wake, making it financially and logistically impossible to keep him. She returned to the orphanage one last time to say an anguished goodbye to her son.

After the relinquishment, the child was made available for adoption. When Sandy first saw him in the summer of 2001, there was a family ready to adopt him, but they backed out a short time later. The next time Sandy saw the child, she was told once again that there was a family ready to adopt him. They, too, declined. Sandy was desperate. She knew that if someone didn't adopt him soon he would die; he was simply too ill to survive much longer. She implored Mr. Trung to let her and Paul adopt the child. Mr. Trung refused on the grounds that they already had three children, which was more than enough in his opinion. Plus, there was yet another couple lined up to adopt the child.

The baby was transferred from Tam Binh to another facility in the city for special care. Sandy and Paul spent the day with him; they took pictures, held him, and assisted with his care, which was difficult, at best. The child cried incessantly and refused to eat. The caregivers, like many in Vietnam, resorted to hitting him on the forehead to force him to eat. The technique sickened the couple, but it worked, and the child wouldn't eat without being slapped. The caregivers, exhausted and exasperated, told Sandy, "He lazy. He don't eat. He cry all the time." Sandy and Paul loved the little boy and once again tried to convince Trung to allow them to adopt him.

Trung held firm; the answer was no. A short time later the prospective adoptive parents, a couple in their 50s, arrived from Washington. They spent a week with the infant and took him out of the facility for medical evaluation. By the end of the week they decided not to adopt him. This was their first child, they were older parents, and they felt ill-equipped to deal with his special needs. Furthermore, the doctor at the international clinic strongly advised them against taking him. For the third time, the child was rejected.

Sandy and Paul, now home in Manheim, were unaware of what had transpired. Mr. Trung finally came to the conclusion that the child, now eight months old, was never going to be adopted. He instructed Kim to call Sandy.

"Hello Miss Sandy. You know that baby you really like? Will you take him?"

"Miss Kim? What are you talking about? Didn't that family take him? What happened?"

"No, they don't want him. He's too sick. Do you still want him?"

"Oh my God, yes! Yes, of course we do!" Sandy was joyful beyond belief. She knew she was meant to be his mother. She felt it every time she looked at the pitiful little boy whose huge eyes reached out to her from his emaciated body, his skin so transparent it revealed nearly every vein and bone in his being.

"Then you need to start paperwork," Miss Kim stated simply.

"I will!" Sandy had already planned how to complete the tedious paperwork, convinced the only thing the child needed was love, attention, and food to get him back on track. It had worked for Deborah, why not for this little boy? Deborah had turned out to be an easy child and had responded quickly and efficiently to her nurturing care. It would happen for this child, too; this child they had named Noah.

* * *

The rumors that had swirled for so long finally became reality. Two trips were now required to apply documents, as the Vietnamese Government attempted to take back some of the control it had lost and put an end to the corruption that had permeated adoption. But everyone who knew what was happening knew it was too late. A shutdown was imminent. Sandy and Paul heard the news from U.S. Immigration Officers and, of course, from Trung and Kim. The agencies knew, and so did families, who followed the news on the Internet, desperate in their desire to complete their paperwork before the country shut down.

Sandy and Paul were frantically busy. Not only were they taking two trips for each group, the groups were larger than ever. In March they facilitated a huge group comprised of adoptive parents from AFTH, LSS, and FCA, all rushing to get in under the wire. By April, the last family from FCA adopted a child, and in May, the shutdown was officially announced. Agencies were told to stop taking new applications although any adoptions in progress would, with luck, be completed.

Sandy and Paul felt concerned about the shutdown, but what it meant for them personally hadn't hit home yet. They flew back and forth to Vietnam to facilitate adoptions, worked on Noah's adoption, and home schooled and cared for their children as usual. There wasn't a spare moment to ponder what the future held.

In August they officially adopted Noah, who was now fifteen months old and still a bundle of bones. He was very sick and his care was considerably more work than Sandy anticipated. He cried nonstop and stuck to her like Velcro, refusing to let her out of his sight. He was also unable to eat solid food and gagged on virtually everything that went into his mouth, including baby formula.

When Paul's family saw Noah for the first time, they were horrified. Their first encounter with Deborah had been quite a surprise, but this went far beyond surprise—this was downright shocking! Jim described Noah as a "spindly little bird" and Joanne knew in her heart this would be their biggest challenge yet. Dave was convinced the child would never walk or talk. He worried about what Paul and Sandy had done to themselves this time, but he also felt they were elevated somewhere near sainthood. There were large numbers of healthy children available for adoption, yet they chose this child who would be a severe burden upon them for the rest of their lives, if he survived. Dave couldn't imagine taking on such a huge responsibility and was astounded by their selflessness.

To their fellow passengers on Korean Air, Sandy and Paul were about as far from saints as anyone could be. They were simply obnoxious, odious travelers with four squirmy children, one of whom cried nonstop during the fourteen-hour flight. They received a multitude of angry comments, disgusted stares, and loud sighs of frustration during their flights. The flight crew, however, did not complain (at least not so they heard). This family not only brought in a huge amount of business for them, they practically subsidized their airline. In 2002 alone, the Pinkertons supposedly spent over $175,000 on Korean Airline tickets; a figure that would have been double but for the fact that they often used frequent flyer miles.

Given these travel expenditures it was no surprise they had financial worries. The adoption business paid the bills, but it certainly wasn't lucrative. The greenhouse was a money pit, Noah's special care was expensive, and Spanky continued to beg them for funds. Amazingly, neither Sandy nor Paul spent much time worrying about money, adopting the attitude that they had struggled before and would struggle again. This was just one of those times to endure.

However, Paul did eventually put the brakes on handouts to Spanky. The young man spoke to Paul privately about a medical condition that he wanted to correct with some expensive, elective procedures. Spanky wanted to have the medical treatments, but Paul was skeptical.

"I don't know Spanky," Paul hesitated. "That's a lot of money."

"I pay you back Mr. Paul."

"Maybe you will, but it's still a lot of money. What if these treatments don't work?"

"Then there are other things I can do, other treatments. The doctor can try many things." That was exactly what Paul feared.

"But Spanky, how will you ever be able to pay me back? If I give you a thousand this trip and a thousand the next trip, how can you afford to pay me? The medical expenses will add up over time and you'll be further and further behind on the bills. It doesn't make common sense."

Spanky had no response but looked at Paul with pleading eyes. "I'm sorry Spanky, I can't do it. We have more groups coming and you can give tours, but I can't loan you any more money right now." Paul felt he had made the right decision while Spanky stormed off, angry at Mr. Paul and his stupid common sense.

* * *

Between trips, Paul finally received the news he had been waiting for, sort of. He had just arrived home from Vietnam, jetlagged and barely coherent, when his realtor called.

"Paul, we need to talk. I have an offer on the greenhouse. There's a community action group that wants to put housing on the property. They're offering 'x'."

"That's too low," Paul replied, discouraged by the offer.

"I know it may seem low, but consider the kind of response we've had. No one has even looked at this property for months. Frankly, I think we're running out of time to sell it. If I were in your shoes, I'd take the offer—if you still want to sell it, that is."

Paul thought for a moment and reluctantly agreed. If nothing else, the sale would be a breakeven proposition. It wasn't a great offer, but it would free him of his ball and chain. Later, however, he discovered that his math was all wrong. He was actually going to lose money on the deal and owe the bank money. Then he found out the worst news of all. It seemed that the community action group wasn't just planning to build housing; they planned to build low-income, subsidized housing. Paul suspected that building low-income housing in downtown Manheim wasn't going to sit well with some members of the community, and he was right.

No one spoke to him directly, but when word spread about the property's future use, angry comments and questions were flung at Sandy.

"What's this we hear about you selling the greenhouse for low-income housing?" a woman asked, cornering Sandy in the grocery store. "We don't want that kind of riff-raff in Manheim!"

"I'm sorry. We didn't know it at the time. We didn't know what they planned to do with the property and they weren't honest with us. But now we're stuck in this contract."

Stuck was the operative word. Not only was the group dishonest with Sandy and Paul, they led the building council astray as well. After the initial plans were filed, they kept making changes, adding more and more units to the project, altering the specifications for the job. Meanwhile, the realtor failed to write an end clause into the contract. Although the property technically belonged to the community action group and the down payment was in escrow, there was no end date to specify when the deal was final. So, while the building council and the community action group hammered out the details, Paul continued to insure the property—a property now abandoned and being ransacked by juveniles.

But with everything else going on, Paul had virtually no time to focus on his real estate problem. Travel groups were becoming smaller, but they still made constant trips as the final families in process rushed to complete their adoptions. During 2002, Paul and Sandy took thirteen trips back and forth to Vietnam; it was almost impossible to recover from jetlag.

Because of the impending shutdown, Paul implored his siblings and his nieces and nephews to come to Vietnam with him. He wanted to share his love of the land and the children with them, since he feared that once the shutdown occurred, he might not have an opportunity to return to Vietnam for quite some time, if ever.

Sister Carol didn't like to travel, Rosemary couldn't get away from her job as a health care provider, Jim and Joanne owned their own business, and Marty had time constraints. The nieces and nephews were busy, disinterested, or didn't have the money to go. Only Dave expressed some interest in going. Paul immediately jumped on it and secured a plane ticket for him before he could change his mind.

Dave's trip began the morning of September 11, 2002, on the one year anniversary of the terrorist attacks on American soil. However, Dave was less worried about terrorist attacks than he was about being apart from his wife of twenty years. The trip was planned for two weeks, the longest period of time the couple had ever been separated. The endless flight gave Dave plenty of opportunities to reflect on his situation. From Chicago to Seoul, he thought: "I can't go on. I have to turn around and go home! I can't do this. How am I going to tell Paul?" But, by the time he reached Seoul, he decided to continue on to Vietnam, stay for a couple of days, make up an excuse to leave, and fly home. It wouldn't hurt to see the country for one or two days and he didn't think he could handle any more flying time; he was already exhausted.

Dave's flight, although stressful, was also eye-opening. He, Paul, Deborah, and Isaiah flew in business class while Sandy, Hannah, and Noah flew in first, all lucky recipients of upgrades. When they arrived in Seoul, Dave learned that Noah had screamed the entire flight. Angry Korean businessmen, incensed by the commotion, kicked Sandy's seat and made nasty remarks to her for the duration of the flight. Granted, it was extremely unpleasant for everyone concerned, but there was little she could do. Noah was simply an extremely difficult child.

Once they arrived in Vietnam, Dave quickly changed his mind about leaving. He couldn't believe his good fortune as all of his senses took in the wonder of Vietnam. He embraced the experience, finally understanding his older brother's infatuation with the country that had caused him so much pain.

Dave also gained a new admiration and appreciation for Sandy. He observed her transitioning from the anxiety-filled flight with Noah, to the orphanage meeting the next morning, with complete composure. He marveled at her energy level and efficiency as she worked with the families and managed both their paperwork and their concerns. He realized that Paul, as the Vietnam veteran, received most of the press and glory while Sandy stayed in the background as the unsung hero, a situation that seemed a little unfair. It was clear to him that Sandy and Paul were a team and that neither could work without the other.

Dave shadowed families on the trip. He saw them receive their children at Tam Binh, accompanied them on sightseeing tours, and had drinks with them on the rooftop at the Rex Hotel. Sipping a local Tiger brew, he reflected on the hotel's rich war history as a surreal scene played out below. Old-fashioned motor scooters and cyclos whizzed by, honking their horns loudly, in a strangely modern setting of high-rise buildings and designer stores.

He also went to Go Vap with Paul. As the two brothers stood on the second floor balcony and looked down at the children, Paul remarked, "The saddest thing for me is realizing they don't sit down to Sunday dinners with their moms and dads or celebrate Christmas morning like we did." Dave nodded, not fully understanding Paul's meaning. For Paul, his work at Go Vap had been a disappointment and a personal failure. He wanted to facilitate adoptions for special needs children, but it had been extremely slow in coming.

At the end of an exciting two weeks, Dave returned home, bursting with stories from Vietnam. He was so enthusiastic he asked Paul if he could return again, and began planning a second trip in December.

* * *

As a young child Debra Brunt had always had a very clear vision of her future. When she played "mommy" to her dolls, her pretend children were adopted just like her; and Asian, because she felt a bond to the beautiful Asian children in her neighborhood. Debra had always wanted to be a mother but, when marriage and children eluded her, she began the process of adopting a child from China. Then, plagued by a series of unfortunate life events, she was unable to complete her home study and she waited two long years before she pursued adoption again, this time through LSS in their Vietnam program. In March of 2002, Debra received a referral of a little boy she named Austin and eagerly prepared for her trip to Saigon. Six months later she received the heartbreaking news that the child was no longer available for adoption.

Debra spent an entire day and night crying over her loss, but woke up the following morning thinking that perhaps there was a logical reason for her despair: maybe there was a child who needed her more than Austin. Debra knew plenty about children in need. She was a program manager at the Crotched Mountain Rehabilitation Center in New Hampshire and worked with eight children with various special needs. She called her social worker and asked for another referral, receiving it just one week later. In September she flew to Vietnam with Paul's group to apply documents for a little boy she named Tyler. It was Paul's first adoption from Go Vap; sadly, the orphanage where Austin still resided.

Once there, Paul accompanied Debra to the orphanage each day so she could become acquainted with Tyler. Initially, Tyler didn't want to be held and wouldn't look Debra in the eye. But by the third day, he was smiling and laughing as they sat on the floor playing with toys. When it was time to leave, it was clear that Debra and Tyler had bonded, at least a little, because it was tearful parting for both of them. For Debra, it was a long and torturous forty days before she could return. She kept herself busy and finally returned with her oldest niece, Sarah, on November 3.

The day after their arrival, Sarah slept late to recuperate from the long flight while Debra arrived at Go Vap with Paul, anxious and excited to receive Tyler. Debra fed him lunch while the caregivers loaded up a backpack with diapers, outfits, cereal, and a hat. When one of the caregivers picked him up and proceeded down the stairs, Tyler cried and screamed. Debra surmised that he was attached to the caregivers and somehow knew that he was leaving them. The orphanage director was outside waiting in a car that would take them to the Ministry of Justice for the signing ceremony. As Tyler continued to cry, the director placed him on her lap and tried singing, clapping, and shaking keys to distract and calm him. Tyler didn't respond, causing Debra to worry.

Tyler cried through the entire signing ceremony and when it was over, she and the orphanage director parted ways. After applying for his passport, Debra returned to the hotel where Sarah was now wide awake. Debra didn't know if Tyler wasn't responding to her because he didn't understand English or if there was some other reason. Suspicious, she decided to conduct a little experiment. She pulled out her video camera and instructed Sarah to make loud noises. While they taped him, a door slammed next door, yet there was no response from Tyler to any of the stimuli. Debra's heart sank as she realized the truth: Tyler was deaf.

The revelation was disturbing, but Debra wasn't angry. She did think it was odd that the orphanage hadn't identified her child as being deaf, but thought perhaps it was a blessing in disguise. Had the orphanage staff known, perhaps he wouldn't have been made available for adoption. And, chances were slim that the orphanage would have been able to provide the medical care and services he required. So, instead of telling Paul about her discovery, Debra said nothing, afraid that if she mentioned the situation, her child would be taken away from her and the adoption revoked.

As the days went by, Tyler's crying decreased, although Debra felt that it had less to do with the fact that they were bonding than the fact that he was simply tolerating the events in his life more easily. Finally they went home and Debra had him evaluated. In addition to deafness, Tyler had a laundry list of special needs that included global development delays, failure to thrive, microcephaly, autism, reactive airway disease, and speech and language impairment, to name a few. Eventually Debra told Sandy and Paul about his special needs, thankful that they had helped her with his adoption. Although he was a child with severe problems, he brought so much love and joy into her life she felt nothing but gratitude for her funny, engaging little boy with his wonderful personality.

Debra, like Sandy, discovered that having a special needs child could be extremely rewarding while she readily acknowledged that parenting a special needs child wasn't for everyone. She quickly found that it required patience, a sense of humor, flexibility, and the ability to adapt to ever-changing conditions. It also required a good support system and the ability to provide a host of resources to care for the child. Fortunately, Debra had everything in place to parent Tyler and she later went on to adopt a little girl from China.

After Debra's adoption of Tyler in November, Paul completed two more adoptions at Go Vap in rapid succession. Although those children were also considered special needs, their problems were minor in comparison to Tyler's. Paul was happy he could facilitate the adoptions, but he still felt he had shortchanged himself and the children by not accomplishing more.

* * *

By January of 2003, the adoptions in progress had been completed and Vietnam closed its doors to Americans. It was time to leave. Sandy visited Miss Hoa at her silk shop and the Vietnamese woman burst into tears, hugging and kissing Sandy as her workers fidgeted nervously, uneasy with this rare display of emotions. Sister Hai also expressed her sadness with tears raining down her round face. She said goodbye to Sandy, Paul, and the children, bear hugging each of them in turn. Miss Kim and Spanky, while concerned about their friends' departure, were also concerned about their loss of incomes. Dr. Vien, Grace Mischler, and other friends vowed to stay in touch by phone and e-mail.

For Paul, leaving was bittersweet. He was convinced that adoptions would start up again soon and, for now, he looked forward to spending some much-needed time at home. He was coming off a marathon of thirteen trips in one year that had stretched not only his pocketbook but his patience as well. He longed for the time when he could sleep in his own comfortable bed and feel well-rested.

Sandy also craved normalcy in her life and a chance to recuperate from the stress she had been under for so long. She would finally have the opportunity to settle into a normal routine. The kids were another story. Deborah and Noah were too little to be aware of what was happening, but Isaiah was unhappy about leaving the place where he looked like everyone else.

Hannah was leaving a close circle of friends. She spent the majority of the flight home crying, finally running out of tears when they reached Chicago. Hannah, who had spent much of her childhood in Vietnam, often felt more Vietnamese than American. She was completely at ease in Vietnam and couldn't go for a walk in downtown Saigon without bumping into friends. Coming home was going to be a major adjustment for everyone.

Once home, Paul got his wish. He finally slept in his own bed, recovered from exhaustion, and spent time doing small projects around the house that had long been neglected. He felt confident that adoptions would resume soon, so he held off getting a job. For now it was nice to spend time with the children and he watched the two little ones, while Sandy home schooled Hannah and Isaiah. He'd put some money aside and they weren't spending much, so he wasn't too worried about finances. But then, as weeks dragged into months, he became more concerned. Worse than that, he sorely missed Vietnam. He missed the families, the children, the Saturday night dinners at the New World Hotel, authentic pho (noodle soup), and the excitement of getting on an airplane. He missed it all and became bored and edgy.

But while Paul was bored, Sandy was depressed. She was devastated over the loss of her job and mourned its ending like a death. She worried about the children who had been left behind in the orphanages and, unlike Paul, had no confidence that Vietnam would reopen for adoption any time soon. She worried about their finances and what they would do with their lives. Maxine felt their pain, but had no other job opportunities available for them. The future looked grim.

Sandy was also dealing with culture shock. She had grown accustomed to having someone else cook, clean, do laundry, and grocery shop for her. But now, she was responsible for housekeeping duties, in addition to home schooling and childcare. Paul helped with the chores, but sometimes everything seemed overwhelming. Furthermore, she and Paul had often been treated to expensive dinners in Saigon's best restaurants by appreciative families, with babysitting services only a phone call away. Now they rarely went out to dinner and then, only to kid-friendly restaurants, with the entire family in tow. Reality had set in.

Isaiah and Hannah cried frequently because they missed their friends, and complained that things were not the same as they were back in Vietnam. In an attempt to make friends, Sandy joined a home schooling co-op where mothers home schooled their children together once a week. The intention was good; the results disastrous. Most of the families in the group were very conservative and Sandy felt they didn't accept her or her Asian children. Sandy was miserable by the time she finally picked up the phone and called her old friend Cindy Yarger, who had returned to the States and was living in Florida.

"Cindy, I am so lost. I'm here in my house, where I'm supposed to be comfortable, but I don't have any friends and I don't know anybody. I don't know what I'm going to do. I just don't know what to do." Sandy went on to explain her situation in dramatic terms while Cindy listened patiently.

Cindy, never one to mince words, said, "Well, the first thing you need to do is get out of that co-op! I can tell you that!"

Sandy burst out laughing. She knew her friend was right and followed her advice. Eventually the situation for the children improved as they reconnected with old friends, found new ones, spent time with family members, and began new hobbies. Isaiah started karate and Hannah took art classes, new-found loves for each of them.

Meanwhile, Paul explored the possibility of starting an adoption program in another country. He researched possibilities on the Internet and flew to Mongolia only to find out that establishing a program there, wouldn't work. Mongolia had only a few children available and three American agencies had already taken over the area. Undaunted, he went on to Nepal where he quickly established a relationship with an orphanage director by asking for special needs children. He reasoned that if he asked for "unwanted children" and showed the orphanage that he really cared, they might eventually allow him to facilitate adoptions for healthy children, as well. His strategy worked and he came home with a referral of a blind child.

It was May of 2003 when Paul returned home, weary from his trip to Nepal. Sandy and Paul had been invited to a friend's home in Philadelphia for an adoption reunion. Realizing how tired he was from his trip, Sandy said, "You know, we really don't have to go to this party if you don't want to."

"I know, but let's just go and see some families. I can sit and talk even if I'm tired." Paul didn't want to give up the opportunity to see families and their children. Although they frequently went to adoption reunions, picnics, and parties, he didn't like to miss them. It was an opportunity for adults to maintain their friendships and it gave the kids a chance to spend time with other Vietnamese children.

As soon as they arrived at the party, Paul and Sandy ran into Beth Wetterskog. Beth and her partner, Nancy Ferguson, had adopted their daughter, Chloe, in September of 2001 with Sandy and Paul's help. They were anxious to adopt another child.

Beth met Paul at the door with a question and a smile. "So, when is Vietnam going to reopen? We're ready for a little sister for Chloe."

Paul shook his head. "It doesn't look good ... I just got back from Nepal. I'm going to set up a new adoption program there. Would you consider a little brother? There's a little boy who's about seven or eight months old; he's considered special needs because of his eye problems. He's been diagnosed as blind, but I'm not sure I believe it. When I held him, I could swear he made eye contact with me. But, he may be blind or have some eye problems, I'm not really sure."

"Yes!" Beth responded.

Paul looked at her quizzically. "Don't you want to talk it over with Nancy?"

Beth laughed. "Oh, yeah, that. I guess that might be a good idea!"

They walked together into the home where the reunion was being held. Paul saw Nancy and said, "So, I hear you want to adopt again." He went on to explain that he had been in Nepal and found a child, but before he could finish, Nancy interrupted him.

"Yes!"

"Wait, Nancy," Beth cautioned, "this child might be blind. Paul's not sure."

Paul repeated what he had relayed to Beth and added that he didn't know all the facts about the boy; there could be other problems as well. "Why don't you two think about it and call me later," he suggested. "Give it some serious thought."

Nancy and Beth drove home chatting about the reunion, but not about the little boy. They returned home and went about the business of life and still didn't mention the boy. Finally, Nancy turned to Beth, "Should I call Paul now?"

"Sure!" Beth grinned, knowing that enough time had passed for Paul to think they had discussed everything in great detail. Both absolutely knew they wanted the child; there was really nothing to discuss as far as they were concerned.

Paul was elated; he was back in business. Nancy prepared the paperwork and by the end of November she and Paul flew to Nepal on separate flights while Beth stayed home with Chloe. The trip contained its usual series of mishaps and problems, but Paul was used to surprises. Plus, Nancy was an emergency medicine and family practice doctor and was more than capable of dealing with her son's medical problems. They returned home after two weeks in Nepal. Nancy and Beth were overjoyed with their son, Deven, whom they discovered was not blind. Meanwhile Paul realized he wouldn't be able to do more Nepalese adoptions, much to his bitter disappointment. It was time to figure out a new strategy once again.

* * *

Sandy was thoroughly disgusted with herself. She'd spent more than a year depressed and grief-stricken over the loss of her job, but nothing had changed. Paul had moved on; she hadn't. While she was in Vietnam, she often wished that she was home and had fantasized about the activities she wanted to do, the tasks she wanted to complete. But now that she was home, she hadn't done any of them. One morning as she stirred to the sounds of her children in the kitchen, she felt as if she was waking up from a bad dream. She sat straight up in bed and thought, "Oh my gosh! I've been home for over a year. I haven't done anything—I haven't lost any weight, I haven't enrolled in an exercise program, and I haven't done anything for the children of Vietnam for an entire year. What have I been thinking about? I've wasted a whole year!"

Sandy ran downstairs determined that today her life would be different. She called Isaiah's karate school, inquired about adult classes, and signed up for one that very evening. It was the beginning of a two-year process in which she earned her black belt and became an instructor. Next she looked at Paul and said, "We have to talk. Do you realize we've been home for over a year and we haven't done a single, solitary thing for the children of Vietnam?"

Paul sadly realized she was right. That night as the children slept, they sat at the kitchen table brainstorming and before long had a few ideas in place for fundraising. The next day they presented their ideas to Maxine. Paul felt that AFTH was better positioned to raise funds than they were as individuals. As a non-profit organization, contributors could receive tax deductions for their donations to AFTH, and would be more likely to contribute significant dollars. Maxine liked their ideas, but she wanted a say in how the money was spent. Obviously, helping orphanages was good PR and made good business sense, in addition to benefitting the children, but she wanted the money in her general fund to be allocated as she saw fit. Paul didn't agree and dug in his heels until they reached a compromise.

In the end, Sandy and Paul wrote the fundraising letter; Maxine placed it on AFTH letterhead and mailed it to adoptive families. Checks, made out to AFTH, were sent directly to Paul, so that he could monitor the amounts coming in and send personal letters of thanks to each donor. And, Paul was in charge of determining how the money would be spent and would oversee its execution, provided it was reasonable in Maxine's eyes.

To everyone's amazement nearly $30,000 was donated, with the money to be divided fairly between Go Vap and Tam Binh. Both orphanages were asked to provide a list of viable projects and Paul could decide which projects were most needed. Go Vap had a large number of worthy projects, while Tam Binh simply wanted the cash, indicating they needed the money to support their growing numbers of children.

At the end of September, Paul and Sandy returned to Go Vap where the most urgent need was installing toilets for toddlers. Until then, the toddlers had been placed on crude plastic buckets, a situation that was both unsanitary and pathetic. Paul worked with a contractor to design a modern bathroom, complete with child-size toilets. Then, they fixed a decaying room below the bathroom where children had been eating peeling paint chips, installed a new septic system, and provided a dozen oversized cribs and mattresses. They also installed a car park to help load and unload handicapped children who needed to be transported by van.

When Tam Binh administrators got wind of the renovations, particularly the installation of the toilets, they were jealous. Paul reminded them that they had selected cash over projects; they had the resources to install the toilets for themselves. But the Tam Binh administrators insisted, so when the Go Vap projects came in under budget, Paul installed toilets at Tam Binh, as well. The projects were a success and, in the end, everyone was happy, especially the children who could now use real toilets for the first time in their lives.

* * *

Despite the success at the orphanages and the excitement of traveling back to Vietnam, the latter half of 2003 proved to be a difficult time. The fights over the greenhouse between the community action group and the town council had turned so ugly that the group finally gave up and turned the albatross back to Paul. Paul knew he couldn't sell the property with ramshackle buildings on it, so he inquired about how much it would cost for demolition. The estimates, which ranged from $20,000 to $100,000, were way too high. Finally, he found someone who came in at $10,000 and he immediately hired him. Within four days everything was gone. As soon as the land was cleared calls poured in nonstop. One and a half acres in the middle of Manheim was prime real estate. A bidding war ensued and within a short time Paul received three times his asking price. But then, realizing he'd be stuck with capital gains tax, he spent the money on a new dump truck. Paul was back to a career of driving a truck. In the end, everything turned out okay, but it was a stressful time that had taken its toll on him.

The sale of the land was minor in the overall scheme of things. Paul's father was ill and had been admitted and released from hospitals for quite some time. First, he had surgery to put in a pacemaker. Then he had a blood clot that required another surgery. He was living at Luther Acres with his wife who had dementia, but as the months wore on he became increasingly frail and weak. Doctors diagnosed him with asbestosis, possibly due to exposure to asbestos in the brake lining plant where he worked for forty years. With fluid on his lungs and severe breathing problems, the end was near. Paul spent a considerable amount of time with his father, but wasn't at his bedside when the end finally came.

The elder Pinkerton died on September 6, 2004 and Paul, perhaps more than anyone else, had a difficult time accepting his father's passing. His siblings thought that as the eldest son he would be the one to take charge and make funeral arrangements, but it was simply too much for him. He stood back, consumed by grief, while others in the family completed the unhappy tasks. For many in the family, the passing was somewhat of a relief; their father had suffered a great deal and had been miserable for a long time. But for Paul, it wasn't yet time to let go. He had spent a lifetime of guilt trying to apologize to his parents for the follies of his youth. He regretted some of the wrongs he felt he had committed and felt he hadn't atoned properly. But even worse, he now faced his own immortality. He was over fifty and was among the older siblings of the next generation—he was next in line.

Paul's feelings of foreboding at the time of his father's death were fortuitous. Just two months later, Paul was diagnosed with prostate cancer. It came as a terrible blow. Both Sandy and Paul asked themselves: "How could this happen? We haven't been married that long. We have four lovely children. How can this be right?" One minute they asked God for help; the next minute they cursed Him for allowing Paul to have cancer.

The day he received the news, Paul forgot that his brother Jim and his wife, Joanne, were coming over that evening. They noticed he was strangely quiet as he cut Joanne's hair. Finally he told them the truth, expressing his uncertainty about what to do next or how to feel about the doctor's advice to act swiftly and aggressively. After they left, Sandy and Paul continued the discussion. Hannah, who was drying the dishes, caught snippets of their conversation.

Casually she asked, "What are you guys talking about? Who's sick?"

Paul looked at her and said quietly, "I've got cancer."

Hannah started to cry and the three stood in the kitchen in a group hug, as they wondered what the future held.

In the coming days, family and friends rallied around Paul. Everyone came to offer support and help him through the difficult decision-making process as he sorted through his treatment options. Paul stopped at Pat's flower shop and gave her the news. Although the circumstances of their divorce were difficult, they had remained friends. Pat had celebrated his parent's 50th wedding anniversary with him and, more recently, had attended his father's funeral; she was still part of the Pinkerton family. When she heard the news, she felt terrible and offered to help in whatever way she could. Other friends jumped in to provide babysitting support to allow Sandy to go with Paul to his medical appointments. Maxine worried about Paul and called frequently to see how he was faring.

Despite all the help and encouragement, Paul shut down emotionally. He was depressed and scared; powerless against the evil forces working inside his body. And, he felt angry, convinced that his cancer was the result of being exposed to Agent Orange during the war. Everyone offered advice, but the more advice he received, the more confused, depressed, and frustrated, he became. Even his doctor provided conflicting information. He told Paul there was a possibility that he only had six months to live, yet he also wanted him to wait six weeks before operating. None of it made any sense.

The family called in Uncle Jim, the kindly pastor who had been Paul's confidante during his divorce. Uncle Jim became Paul's personal chaplain and prayed with him each evening. Uncle Jim also told him flat out, "Your surgeon might be good, but he's not the only one around. You can fire him, you know. Call him on Monday and tell him you have concerns about the timeline and see what he says. Work with him, get another opinion, or fire him, and start fresh with someone new. Remember that you're in charge of your own health and you make the decisions."

It was the empowerment Paul needed. He came out of his depression and went into fighting mode, undergoing surgery at the end of the month. However, his prognosis wasn't good, the cancer was aggressive, and his doctor had no plan for long-term treatment. Paul, however, did. He contacted a support group, found specialists in the field, and began a series of treatments elsewhere.

Throughout the ordeal Sandy bounced back and forth between putting on a good face for friends and family and feeling utterly terrified. When she spoke to her old friend, Donna Culberson, she appeared upbeat as she talked about how they would conquer the cancer and get through the ordeal. But privately she went through days of severe depression when she considered the prospect of losing her husband. The one positive outcome was that Sandy and Paul grew closer together. They had always been in love but now, facing illness and death, they knew that what they felt for each other went far beyond physical attraction or romantic ideals.

Once word got out that Paul had cancer, the Pinkertons received an outpouring of love from adoptive families they never imagined possible. Cards, phone calls, e-mails, and baskets of food poured in, in record numbers. One woman, wondering if this would be Paul's last Christmas, decided to forego her own family's gift-giving in order to provide Christmas for Sandy and Paul and the kids. She gave them all gifts, invited them for dinner, and took the girls to The Nutcracker Ballet in Philadelphia, a truly unexpected surprise.

Brenda Rath, editor of the Vietnam Fellowship newsletter for adoptive families, thought about ways to help the couple. As e-mails flew back and forth among the families, Brenda and one of the LSS families decided to put on a fundraising dinner and silent auction to aid the couple with their ever-increasing medical bills. Maxine helped with the publicity by urging families to support the Pinkertons. An invitation was mailed to all the adoptive families, including those from LSS and FCA, and a dinner was held in King of Prussia, Pennsylvania, in March, 2005. Some families, like the McRells, traveled long distances to attend. Others, who were unable to attend the dinner, provided items for the silent auction or sent cash donations. The generosity of families spoke volumes about their feelings towards Sandy and Paul as thousands of dollars were raised.

But, the fact remained: Paul still had to fight his cancer. In June, the family temporarily moved to Florida to allow him to receive treatments at the Dattoli Cancer Center and Brachytherapy Research Institute in Sarasota, Florida. One of the adoptive families arranged for housing that allowed them to be together during this painful time. It was stressful and difficult, made only slightly better by visits from friends.

By late fall, Paul's health situation looked more hopeful and Paul prayed that the treatments had done their job. The Pinkertons returned home to resume a lifestyle of home schooling and working. Although Paul suffered from aches and pains, he used his truck to haul various items, in order to provide an income for his family. Paul was optimistic about his future, especially when he heard that adoptions in Vietnam might resume. Outside of surviving his cancer, his one wish in life was to step foot on Vietnamese soil at least once more.

Epilogue

Paul's wish to return to Vietnam came true sooner than he expected. Early in 2006 the Pinkertons applied for a license with the Vietnamese Department for International Adoptions (DIA) in Hanoi and made logistical arrangements in Ho Chi Minh City for the upcoming adoptive families. By July, adoptions resumed. Paul and Sandy reconnected with old friends and began their careers for a second time, delighted to be back.

Initially, the adoption process went well, but within a very short period of time, problems cropped up, even worse than before. Paperwork complications resulted in public humiliation by the Vietnamese officials. Families were upset and frustrated by the new procedures. Not only did the families have lengthy stays in Ho Chi Minh City, they now had to travel to Hanoi and back, turning the adoption process into an expensive three-week marathon. There were still sick babies to contend with and Miss Kim's demands to meet. The Pinkerton children, initially thrilled to be back, quickly became bored and wanted to fly home. In Vietnam there were few activities for children, so the kids spent most of their time swimming in the pool, missing Manheim.

By the end of the year, Kim informed AFTH that she didn't want to work with the Pinkertons anymore. The feeling was mutual. Sandy and Paul returned home for Christmas, disillusioned and frustrated. Sandy swore she wouldn't go back while Paul worried about his health and his ability to continue the grueling schedule. They decided to investigate the possibility of starting a foundation—perhaps a more productive way of helping Vietnamese children than continuing their facilitation work.

Paul didn't remember, but after returning from his first trip back to Vietnam in 1990, he had stated in an article published by *The Patriot News* in Harrisburg, that he planned to start a foundation to deliver medical supplies to the Vietnamese. Maybe that idea had been in his subconscious, all along. But before they could fully research the idea, they were called back to Vietnam to facilitate an adoption for a special client. In mid-January of 2007, Miss Kim and Sandy spent the day with Angelina Jolie. They brought Pax to her hotel room so she could play with him and discuss his upcoming adoption, out of the spotlight of the press.

In February they returned home so that Paul could receive additional medical treatments. By early March they flew back to Vietnam. Angelina came back to complete her adoption and Paul accompanied her to Hanoi on her private jet. Although it was interesting and exciting to spend time with this famous celebrity, it was also disconcerting due to of all the media attention. Eventually, life went back to normal.

With the celebrity adoption completed and on their resumé, Paul and Sandy launched a charitable organization called Paul's Kids and began working on fundraising projects aimed at helping children left behind in orphanages. It was the beginning of the end of their adoption career. In October their working relationship with AFTH came to a close. Maxine put a new team in place that included neither the Pinkertons nor Miss Kim, and turned the program over to a man named Mr. Binh in Vietnam.

Paul and Sandy focused their attention on their foundation and Miss Kim quickly landed another position. But, once again, an adoption shutdown loomed on the horizon. Early in 2008, word went out that the 2005 Memorandum of Agreement (required by Vietnamese law to authorize U.S. adoptions) would expire in September and would not be renewed. In April a warning was issued to adoption providers to stop initiating new adoptions; by September, the program was finished.

Sandy and Paul, now released from the pressures of constant travel, felt liberated as they selected projects for the foundation and made their own schedules. Many of their foundation's officers and board members, like Brenda Rath, were adoptive parents eager to help. Spanky helped launch one of their first projects: Spanky Scholarships. In Spanky's native village of Tho Thanh many children couldn't attend school because parents didn't have the requisite funds. Paul's Kids provided scholarships to children for tuition, uniforms, books, and supplies.

Between projects, Paul used his truck for hauling and Sandy taught karate and exercise classes. The kids continued to be home schooled. Paul maintained strong relationships with his siblings while Sandy continued to struggle with her half-brothers and sisters. Paul reconnected with his old high school friends, including Jimmy Thomas and Steve Bucher, who returned to Manheim occasionally to see his mother. As a result of researching and writing this book, I restored communications between Paul and two of his Army buddies: Mike Hardin and Lewis Page. Paul also reconnected with Ron Murray, the man who had attended POW/MIA meetings and who was rumored to have shot Marty Sauble, Paul's closest high school friend. Through their conversations and my interviews, Paul finally learned that Ron was not the man who shot Marty.

The adoption agencies mentioned throughout this book continue to help clients by forming families through both domestic and international adoptions. AFTH now focuses exclusively on domestic, open adoptions. LSS of New England continues to work in both domestic and international adoptions and has formed partnerships with several other agencies. FCA works domestically and in China, Korea, and Taiwan. Children's Home Society & Family Services works domestically and in eleven countries abroad. The Pearl S. Buck Foundation works domestically and in four international countries. All of the agencies maintain strong standards of excellence, while proudly serving their clients and communities.

Although Vietnam is closed to American adoptions, families throughout the world (primarily from Canada, Australia, and Europe) continue to adopt children from Tam Binh, Go Vap, and other Vietnamese orphanages. Americans continue to support and help these orphanages through their humanitarian efforts. I was recently surprised and excited to stumble across a story about New York Rotarians and Vietnam veterans in Rockland and Orange Counties (NY), who in late 2007 organized a three-week trip to Vietnam in conjunction with Kids Without Borders, from Seattle. They delivered clothing, toiletries, and supplies to 1,000 children in orphanages, schools, and poor villages. But the most heart-warming fact was that they delivered life-saving brain shunts for the children with hydrocephalus living in three orphanages, one being Go Vap.

Unfortunately, a number of people mentioned in this book are now deceased. Betty and Earl Smith, who tried to get into Laos to search for their son, died in 1998 and 1999, respectively. Their son Lewis is still missing, although legally considered dead. Lewis Smith was the Air Force Major who was shot down in Laos. Paul, although unsuccessful, spent considerable amount of time, money, and energy trying to get the Smiths into Laos to look for their son's remains, but access to Laos was eventually denied because of the age and health of the elder Smiths. Paul regrets that he was unable to help them.

J.C. Campbell, who was married to Hazel and gave Sandy her surname, died in 2005. Martin Sauble Sr., Marty's father, died in February of 2007 and Jane Sauble, his mother, died in October of 2011. The beloved Sister Hai, orphanage director at Tam Binh, died in early 2008.

In Paul's family, a number of his closest relatives have died. Paul's Uncle Jim, who was both his confidante and his personal chaplain, died in April of 2006. Paul's father died on September 6, 2004 and Paul's mother, Deborah Singer Pinkerton, died on February 1, 2010 at the age of 90.

For Paul, each death is a reminder of his own mortality as he struggles against the cancer that has pervaded his body so insidiously. He continues to fight, still optimistic about new projects and trips to Vietnam while knowing deep down that each journey to Vietnam could potentially be his last.

Paul reflects on his life frequently these days. He has few regrets, although he wishes he could remove some of the pain he's caused others, and is disappointed that he never took the time to learn more about his parents. However, when he thinks about Vietnam he's emphatic that there are no regrets; there's nothing he'd do differently. He feels only immense pride in the fact that he's helped the abandoned and the forgotten—POWs, MIAs, and orphans—who never had a voice of their own.

Paul has received many awards and accolades over the years, but what remains most important to him is family. His children are a constant source of both strength and worry for him. Deborah was diagnosed with idiopathic juvenile arthritis and Noah continues to suffer from a number of serious problems, including autism.

As Steve Bucher, Paul's friend from high school, once said, "All of us pass through this life and die, and when everyone you know dies, you'll be forgotten. But Paul, doing what he's doing, he will be remembered for a long, long time. There are advantages to leading the kind of life that he does." It's likely that the 400-plus adoptive parents and their children would agree, as would the relatives of Freight Train 053, and the children he continues to help through his foundation.

Both Paul and Sandy readily admit to leading unconventional yet rich lives, perhaps summed up best by a Vietnamese proverb:

Venture all, see what fate brings.

THE END

Acknowledgments

My heartfelt thanks and gratitude go to Paul and Sandy Pinkerton, who opened their lives, hearts, and memories to me. I spent countless hours interviewing them in Westchester, New York; Manheim, Pennsylvania; Sarasota, Florida; Ho Chi Minh City, Vietnam; and by telephone and Internet. Paul graciously shared his personal journals, photographs, personal letters, opinion papers, newspaper articles, and files on Freight Train 053.

Sandy granted me interview time even when it was clearly inconvenient for her, as evidenced by the frequency of children's voices on my audiotapes! Thank you for your patience and candor; I know how courageous it was for you to share your story.

Many thanks to the Pinkerton children (Hannah, Isaiah, Deborah, and Noah) who let me borrow their parents and participate in their family time; especially Hannah, who granted me an interview and gave me her teenage perspective on growing up in Vietnam.

My gratitude to the Pinkerton siblings who provided insights into the "real" Paul: David Pinkerton, James and Joanne Pinkerton, and Rosemary Pinkerton Young. Heartfelt appreciation goes to Patricia Schaumberg for her honesty and bravery in sharing her side of the story.

I'm indebted to all those who helped me understand the life of a soldier, the Vietnam War, the POW/MIA issue, and the story of Freight Train 053: Jon Beckenhauer, Steven Bucher, Ann Mills Griffiths, Mike Hardin, Shayne Henderson, Charles Humm, Bob Jones, Don Luce, Earl Martin, Ronald Murray, Everett Lewis Page, Roger Rumpf, Jane Sauble, Keith Short, Bettie Stanton, James Thomas, and the Van Schaemelhouts: Andy, Elaine, Liz, and Martin. Special thanks to Terry Derr for his humor and support (you always make me laugh!) and Robert J. Destatte for his fascinating personal stories, research assistance, and thoughtful advice.

I'm grateful for the help of Sandy's friends and relatives: Donna Culberson, Grace Mischler, Sandra O'Connell, Vicki Robinson, and Cindy Yarger.

I'm forever indebted to those who not only contributed to this book, but also helped me adopt my son Alexander: Adoptions From The Heart, Maxine Chalker, Lutheran Social Services of New England, and the late

Sister Hai. Sincere thanks and appreciation go to Julie Hessler, Elizabeth Kendrick, Elizabeth Norris, and Jennifer Yang-Kwait for their unique perspectives on adoption and Vietnamese culture.

Special thanks to Mr. Trung for allowing me to return to Tam Binh Orphanage and to Miss Loan for her gracious hospitality at Go Vap Orphanage.

I appreciate the interviews granted to me in Vietnam by Miss Hoa, Spanky, and Tran Ba Thien. Special thanks and sincere gratitude goes to Dr. Vien for treating Alexander when he was an infant, and for contributing to this book.

Thanks and appreciation to the many adoptive parents who shared their stories; you continually amaze me with your compassion, unconditional love, and unfailing sense of humor: Debra Brunt, Jan Bye, Beth Dewson, Nancy Ferguson, Tom Fulton, Christine Grimshaw, Loretta and Tom Hackman, Baz and Lisa McRell, Ellen and Steve Passage, Brenda and Lee Rath, and especially John Steele, who paved the way for the rest of us.

I'm grateful for the medical information and guidance provided by Dr. Jane Aronson, orphan doctor, and Dr. Robert Insoft, Medical Director of NICU and Neonatal Respiratory Services at Brigham & Women's Hospital. Special thanks to those who helped with my research on hydrocephalus: Dory Kranz and Pip Marks, Hydrocephalus Association; Dr. Katrina Gwinn-Hardy, National Institutes of Health; and Dr. James (Pat) McAllister, University of Utah School of Medicine. Pat spent countless hours patiently answering my questions and educating me on hydrocephalus. Pat, your kindness is only surpassed by your wisdom.

Many people helped me with the research of this book. I'd like to single out the following: Sherie Brown, Andrew Fasnacht, Tony Garbo, Cheri Goldner, Cynthia Marquet, Keith Short, and Kitty Wunderly. Not only did they go above and beyond the call of duty in assisting me, they did so with remarkable speed and professionalism. A special shout-out goes to Rachel (Rae) Phillips at the Joint POW/MIA Accounting Command (JPAC), Hawaii who always went the extra mile and diligently sought the truth. I miss our weekly e-mails. I'd also like to thank Corinne Hagan, Team Chief of the U.S. Army Human Resources Command in Fort Knox for her persistence, patience, and wry sense of humor.

I'd like to thank my readers who gave me sound advice and made me a better writer: Jeannie and Andrew Beresin, Pam Harney, Lorraine Love, and Larry Mondi. Not only were you readers at one time or another, you have all been my long-time friends and supporters and I couldn't have done it without you! Thanks also to Ken Swensen, a recent reader and acquaintance, for his comments. I'm grateful to Lewis Page for his keen military review and his continuing friendship. On the legal front, I'd like to thank Joseph Leightner and Eric Osterberg for their sound and intelligent advice.

Special thanks to Robert Kurson (author of *Shadow Divers* and *Crashing Through*) for his guidance and encouragement throughout the years. You truly inspire me.

Words cannot adequately express my gratitude for the many friends who have stood by me and believed in me during this long process: the moms at PRES, the Equitable/AXA gang, my dear friends at St. Mark's Church, my new friends at St. Luke's School, and so many others in my local community—you know who you are! I'm so lucky to have you in my life.

I'm deeply indebted to my friends at the Hiram Halle Library, especially Marilyn Tinter who has seen me through both Alexander's adoption and the writing of this book. Your love, support, and enthusiasm have sustained me over the years; I'm so happy you still save your special hugs for Alexander! Special thanks to Alan Ramsay, Deborah Kivisalu, and the late (and much loved) Arlene Stein. They all encouraged me to persevere. One couldn't ask for better friends and advocates.

In my own family, I'd like to thank my (late) parents: Dad for giving me the love of reading, and Mom for teaching me to not give up and always do my best. I hope I made you proud! Much love to my sister Bev who kept me grounded, always had time to lend a sympathetic ear, and provided some humor during our frequent phone calls. To my other family members, thank you for your support—you never stopped believing in me.

To my editor and long-time friend, Steph Winter, I thank you for pushing me intellectually and for making me a better writer. I would have missed many "things" without your help!

To Dog Ear Publishing and their competent staff (especially Matt Murry), thank you for your guidance and attention to detail.

And finally, it's with overflowing love and eternal gratitude that I thank my son, Alexander, whose curiosity, sweet nature, and sense of humor always puts a smile on my face; and my husband, David, my biggest cheerleader, fan, and best friend. I know I'm not the best writer you've ever read, but thanks for saying so anyway! I couldn't have done it without your patience, love, and support.

BOOK SOURCES

Chapters 1, 2, and 3 – Paul:
Interviews:
Steven Bucher, Mike Hardin, Ronald Murray, Everett Lewis Page, David Pinkerton, James Pinkerton, Joanne Pinkerton, Paul Pinkerton, Jane Sauble, Patricia Schaumberg, Keith Short, James Thomas, and Rosemary Pinkerton Young

Articles:
Gnerlich, Captain Charles H. "A Vet Looks Back." *Newsweek*, December 5, 1994.

Kuharski, Mary Ann. "Thanks for Our Memories." *Newsweek*, November 7, 1994.

Books:
Ebert, James R. *A Life in a Year: The American Infantryman in Vietnam, 1965-1972.* Novato, California: Presidio Press, 1993.

Kaufman, Deborah. *Fodor's Vietnam, 3rd Edition, Fodor's Travel Publications.* New York, NY: Random House, Inc., 2003.

Murray, Ron. *Memories Never Die.* Mechanicsburg, PA: Waveline Direct Inc., 1987.

Short, Keith B. *1st Infantry Brigade (Red Devils), 5th Infantry Division (Mechanized): South Vietnam.* Colorado: Roshtiek, 2003.

Singer Family History

Letters:
Reverend Raymond Foellner (deceased), Mike Hardin, Everett Lewis Page, Mr. and Mrs. Paul E. Pinkerton (deceased), Paul N. Pinkerton, Martin G. Sauble, Jr. (deceased), and Mrs. Martin (Jane) Sauble (deceased)

Other Resources:

Buch Funeral Home, Manheim, PA – Memorial for Paul E. Pinkerton

Carl Hiestand, Editor, Society of the 5th Division

Christopher Raab, Archives & Special Collections Librarian, Franklin & Marshall College, Lancaster, PA

Everett Lewis Page – Explanations of MOS; military extract for the Combat Infantryman Badge

Indochina Cultural Tours

Intelligencer Journal (Lancaster, PA) – Obituaries for Paul E. Pinkerton (9/8/04), Rodger Singer (6/1/02)

LancasterOnline – Obituary for Deborah S. Pinkerton

Lancaster Public Library

Manheim Central High School

Manheim Community Library

Mike Hardin – Copies of citations and awards

Obituary for Mary Sachs Pinkerton – From Paul Pinkerton

Paul Pinkerton – Opinion papers on the war

Raymond Mendola, B Company, 1/61st

Ronald Rice, Illinois – Information about the infusion program

Vietnam Veteran Oral History Project, Franklin & Marshall College, Paul N. Pinkerton Interview Transcript (12/1/93) Conducted by Melinda Sue Freshman

Photographs:

Mike Hardin, Everett Lewis Page, and Paul Pinkerton

Websites:

(Over 30 websites were used)

Chapters 4, 6, and 8 - Sandy:
Interviews:
Donna Culberson, Sandra O'Connell, Sandy Pinkerton, and Vicki Robinson

Other Resources:
Chester County Historical Society, West Chester, PA
Obituary of Cecil Fletcher

Danny Layne, Network & Publications Administrator, Julian Samora Research Institute, Michigan State University

Garcia, Victor Q. (Ph.D) *Mexican Enclaves in the U.S. Northeast: Immigrant and Migrant Mushroom Workers in Southern Chester County, Pennsylvania*, JSRI Research Report #27, The Julian Samora Research Institute, Michigan State University, East Lansing, Michigan, 1997.

Home Study prepared by Welcome House Social Services of The Pearl S. Buck Foundation, Inc., Perkasie, PA. May 28, 1993.

Oxford Public Library:
Obituaries for Hazel Fletcher Osborne, Angel Silva, William Senter Robinson, Blanche Fletcher and J.C. Campbell

Chapters 5 and 7 – Paul:
Interviews:
Steve Bucher, Robert J. Destatte, Ann Mills Griffiths (conversation only), Mike Hardin, Don Luce, Earl Martin, Ronald Murray, Everett Lewis Page, David Pinkerton, James Pinkerton, Joanne Pinkerton, Paul Pinkerton, Mrs. Martin (Jane) Sauble, Patricia Schaumberg, Tran Van Thanh (Spanky), and Rosemary Pinkerton Young

Articles:
"Final Rites Sunday For Two Syracuse Youths Killed in Auto Accident." *The Syracuse- Wawasee Journal (Syracuse, IN)*, July 16, 1969. (Floyd Rensberger)

Holland, W. Thompson. "Returning to 'Nam on Mission for Missing/Vietnam Veteran Heads Back to Press the POW/MIA Issue." *Intelligencer Journal (Lancaster, PA)*, January 23, 1990.

Kaufman, Leslie. "After War, Love is a Battlefield." *The New York Times*, April 6, 2008.

Luce, Don. "We've Been Here Before: The Tiger Cages of Vietnam." *History News Network*, April 4, 2005. (web)

Rutter, John. "The Final Days." *Sunday News (Lancaster, PA)*, April 30, 1995.

Shanker, Thom. "Army is Worried by Rising Stress of Return Tours." *The New York Times*, April 6, 2008.

Other Resources:
Andrew H. Fasnacht, Editor, Lancaster County Weeklies, Ephrata Review and Lititz Record Express, PA

Cynthia Marquet, Historical Society of the Cocalico Valley, Ephrata, PA

"Lament of a Warrior's Wife" videotape by Bob Kane Productions, Asia Resource Center

Library of Congress - Ly Nam De Street

Matthew Nute, Coordinator of Membership Marketing, Veterans of Foreign Wars National Headquarters (Vietnam Veterans eligibility in the VFW)

Paul Pinkerton's Travel Journals

U.S. Department of Health and Human Services, National Institutes of Health, *Post-Traumatic Stress Disorder (PTSD): A Real Illness*. (booklet)

Websites:
(Over 10 websites were used)

Chapter 9 – Paul:
Interviews:
Jon Beckenhauer, Robert J. Destatte, Ann Mills Griffiths (conversation only), Shayne Henderson, Bob Jones, Don Luce, Earl Martin, Paul Pinkerton, Roger Rumpf, Patricia Schaumberg, and Bettie Stanton

Articles:
Anthony, Ted. "Centre County Mom Vows to Comb Laos for MIA Son." *The Patriot News (Harrisburg, PA)*, August 13, 1991.

Anthony, Ted. "Mock-Up of a Viet Jungle Prison Shows Plight of American POWs." *The Patriot News (Harrisburg, PA)*, September 21, 1991.

Byard, Katie. "Glimmer of Hope Massillon Woman's Brother Missing in Action in Vietnam for 25 Years, But Vet She Didn't Know Has Found His Dog Tags and is Trying to Locate the Crash Site." *The Akron Beacon Journal (Akron, OH)*, July 18, 1993.

"Citizens Group Helps Account for POW/MIAs." *The Patriot News (Harrisburg, PA)*, September 28, 1993.

Kiner, Deb. "Veteran Changes Beliefs on Viet MIAs." *The Patriot News (Harrisburg, PA)*, August 7, 1990.

Knox, David. "Long Vigil for MIA May Be Over, Pennsylvania Man Believes He's Discovered the Remains of Massillon Man Missing in Vietnam Since 1968." *The Akron Beacon Journal (Akron, OH)*, September 19, 1992.

McCrary, Lacy. "Activists Are Relentless in Battle for POW Details to Close Vietnam Book, They Seek an Accounting." *The Inquirer (Philadelphia, PA)*, October 25, 1992.

Naylor, Romayne. "Fed Help at Last for Smiths." *Keystone Gazette (Bellefonte, PA)*, October 17, 1991.

Naylor, Romayne. "Smiths' Laos Trip Still Up in the Air." *Keystone Gazette (Bellefonte, PA)*, November 14, 1991.

Niquette, Mark. "Closure for Vet's Family/Military Funeral for Vietnam Soldier from Massillon Ends 'Mission'/Remains of MIAs Discovered in 1994." *The Akron Beacon Journal (Akron, OH)*, April 7, 2001.

Warner, Mary. "Midstater Spotlights MIA-Embargo Link." *The Patriot News (Harrisburg, PA)*, February 11, 1990.

Yoshioka, Wayne. "MIA Remains On Verge of Disappearing Forever." *National Public Radio*, March 28, 2010.

Letters and Memorandums:
Letter from Roger Rumpf to Linthong Phetsavan, dated September 16, 1991

Memo from Ann Mills-Griffiths to Linthong Phetsavan, dated October 16, 1991
Letter from Betty and Earl Smith to Linthong Phetsavan, dated November 11, 1991
Letter from Scot Marciel to Audrey Insoft, dated March 26, 2010

Other Resources:
Arlington National Cemetery

Cheri Goldner, Librarian, Akron-Summit County Public Library, Akron, OH

Chris Fetner – Information on the videotape of Freight Train 053

Corinne Hagan, Team Chief, SEA/WWII, U.S. Army Human Resources Command Past Conflict Repatriations Branch, Ft. Knox, TN

Johnie E. Webb, Jr. Deputy to the Commander for Public Relations & Legislative Affairs
Joint POW/MIA Accounting Command Hawaii (Hickam AFB)

Kitty Wunderly, PA Room Supervisor/Curator, Centre County Library and Historical Museum, Bellefonte, PA

Library of Congress – Information on Ly Nam De Street
Jeannie Sanash for RVN: Status of the Accession Turned Over by Mr. Paul Pinkerton to JTF-FA, Reel 164, Pages 238-239.

Martha Moorehead (relative of Charles Deitsch)

Murray Hiebert, Sr. Director, Asia
U.S. Chamber of Commerce

Nellie Stinson
CBS21, Harrisburg, PA

Norma Hill, *The Akron Beacon Journal*

Notes from Gene and Doris Isom and documents from the Army addressed to Ora Bridges

Official Report on REFNO 1306
U.S. Army, Central Identification Laboratory
Hickam AFB, Hawaii

Paul Pinkerton's Journals: Dated October 4, 1991 through November 13, 1991; June 16, 1992

Rachel (Rae) Phillips Freedom of Information Act Officer and Correspondence Specialist, External Relations
Joint POW/MIA Accounting Command Hawaii (Hickam AFB) Reports Dated June 7, 2010 and September 16, 2010 and countless e-mails

Rhiannon McClintock, Program Coordinator, Centre County Historical Society, State College, PA

Sherie Brown, Head of Reference Services, Massillon Public Library

Tony Garbo, Managing Editor
WJW Fox 8, Cleveland, OH

Websites:
(Over 15 websites were used)

Chapter 10:
Interviews:
Donna Culbertson, Terry Derr, Charles Humm, Sandra O'Connell, David Pinkerton, Paul Pinkerton, Sandy Pinkerton, Vicki Robinson, Andy Van Schaemelhout, Elaine Van Schaemelhout, Liz Van Schaemelhout, Martin Van Schaemelhout, and Patricia Schaumberg

Other Resources:
Luna County Clerk's Office, Deming, NM - Obituary of Guy Van Schaemelhout

Chapter 11:
Interviews:
Donna Culberson, Vo Ngoc Huyhn Hoa (Miss Hoa), Elizabeth Kendrick, David Pinkerton, James Pinkerton, Joanne Pinkerton, Paul Pinkerton, Sandy Pinkerton, Patricia Schaumberg, John Steele, Tran Van Thanh (Spanky), and Rosemary Pinkerton Young

Other Resources:
Betty Wilson, Public Relations, Boston Gift Show

It's a Wonderful Life, Frank Capra, Liberty Films II, 1946. (Movie)

Mason, Margie. "Instant Gratification for these Pennsylvanians, Viet Adoption Quick, Easy." *The Patriot News (Harrisburg, PA),* June 18, 2000, Page F-01.

Chapter 12:
Interviews:
Jan Bye, Maxine Chalker, Tom Fulton, Loretta Hackman, Tom Hackman, Elizabeth Kendrick, Hannah Pinkerton, Paul Pinkerton, Sandy Pinkerton, John Steele, and Dr. Nguyen Cong Vien (Dr. Vien)

Other Resources:
Home Study, Prepared by Adoptions From The Heart, September 30, 1996

Chapter 13:
Interviews:
Jan Bye, Maxine Chalker, Donna Culberson, Dawn Degenhardt (conversation only),

Tom Fulton, Loretta Hackman, Tom Hackman, Julie Hessler, Sandra O'Connell, David Pinkerton, James Pinkerton, Joanne Pinkerton, Paul Pinkerton, Sandy Pinkerton, John Steele, Tran Van Thanh (Spanky), Dr. Nguyen Cong Vien (Dr. Vien), Tracy and Anthony Wood (e-mail only), and Rosemary Pinkerton Young

Articles:
Birtley, Tony. "Vietnam's Abandoned Children." *Aljazeera,* December 4, 2007. (web)

Brody, Jane E. "Personal Health; Adoptions from Afar: Rewards and Challenges. *The New York Times,* July 22, 2003. (web)

Carroll, Julia, Renee Slobodzian and Deborah K. Steward. "Extremely Low Birthweight Infants." *MCN,* 30:5, September/October 2005.

Corbett, Sara. "Where Do Babies Come From?" *The New York Times,* June 16, 2002. (web)

Gross, Jane. "Seeking Doctors' Advice in Adoptions From Afar. *The New York Times*, July 22, 2003. (web)

Hack, Maureen, et al. "Chronic Conditions, Functional Limitations and Special Health Care Needs of School-aged Children Born with Extremely Low Birth Weight in the 1990's." *JAMA*, 294:3, July 20, 2005.

Jobe, Alan H. "Predictors of Outcomes in Preterm Infants: Which Ones and When?" *Journal of Pediatrics*, 138, 2001.

Johnson, Dana. "Adopting an Institutionalized Child: What Are the Risks?" (web)

Raju, Tonse N.K., et al. "Optimizing Care and Outcome for Late-Preterm Infants." *Pediatrics*, 118:3, September 2006.

Tuller, David. "Adoption Medicine Brings New Parents Answers and Advice." *The New York Times*, September 4, 2001. (web)

United Nations Children's Fund (UNICEF) and World Health Organization (WHO). "Low Birthweight: Country, Regional and Global Estimates." *UNICEF*, New York, 2004.

United Nations Children's Fund (UNICEF) and World Health Organization, "Immunization Summary." *UNICEF*, New York, 2005.

UNICEF, The Joint United Nations Programme on HIV/AIDS & U.S. Agency for International Development. "Children on the Brink." *UNICEF*, New York, 2004.

Other Resources:
Vietnam Travel Information (prepared by Sandy & Paul Pinkerton, AFTH)
Step-by-Step in Vietnam (prepared by Sandy & Paul Pinkerton, AFTH)

Websites:
(Various)

Chapter 14:
Interviews:
Dr. Jane Aronson, Jan Bye, Maxine Chalker, Beth Dewson, Tom Fulton, Loretta Hackman, Julie Hessler, Dr. Robert M. Insoft, Baz (Richard)

McRell, Lisa McRell, Elizabeth Norris, David Pinkerton, James Pinkerton, Joanne Pinkerton, Paul Pinkerton, Sandy Pinkerton, and Rosemary Pinkerton Young

Articles:
"Baby Mo: A Letter From Vietnam." *JAMA* 292: 2, July 14, 2005, pgs. 153-154.

Juffer, Femmie and Marinus H. van Uzendoorn, "Behavior Problems and Mental Health Referrals of International Adoptees." *JAMA* 293: 20, May 25, 2005, pgs. 2501-2515.

Miller, Laurie C. and Nancy W. Hendrie, "Health of Children Adopted from China." *Pediatrics*, 105: 6, June 2000.

Miller, Laurie C. "Caring for Internationally Adopted Children." *NEJM* 341: 1539-1540, No. 20, November 11, 1999.

Miller, Laurie C., "International Adoption, Behavior and Mental Health." *JAMA* 293:20, May 25, 2005, pgs. 2533 – 2535.

Murray, Thomas S., et al. "Epidemiology and Management of Infectious Diseases in International Adoptees." *Clinical Microbiology Reviews*, 18: 3, July 2005, pgs. 510-520.

Onis, Mercedes de, et al. "Estimates of Global Prevalence of Childhood Underweight in 1990 and 2015." *JAMA* 291: 21, June 2, 2004, pgs. 2600-2606.

Pomerleau, Andree, et al. "Health status, cognitive and motor development of young children adopted from China, East Asia, and Russia across the first 6 months after adoption." *International Journal of Behavioral Development* 29: 5, 2005, pgs 445-457.

Saiman, Lisa, et al. "Prevalence of Infectious Diseases Among Internationally Adopted Children." *Pediatrics* 108: 608-612, 2001.

Other Resources:
U.S. Citizenship & Immigration Services, Yearbook of Immigration Statistics, Immigrant Orphans Adopted by U.S. Citizens by Gender, Age, Religion & Country of Birth, 2003

Websites
(Various)

Chapter 15:
Interviews:
Maxine Chalker, Dr. Katrina Gwinn-Hardy, Vo Ngoc Huyhn Hoa (Miss Hoa), Elizabeth Kendrick, Dory Kranz, Pip Marks, Dr. Pat McAllister, Grace Mischler, Paul Pinkerton, Sandy Pinkerton, Brenda Rath, Lee Rath, Tran Van Thanh (Spanky), and Dr. Nguyen Cong Vien (Dr. Vien)

Articles:
Brooke, Jill. "Close Encounters With a Home Barely Known." *The New York Times*, July 22, 2004. (web)

Clemetson, Lynette. "Adopted in China, Seeking Identity in America." *The New York Times*, March 23, 2006.

Fitzenrider, Ellen. "Personal Thoughts on Ethics in International Adoption." (web) (www.internationaladoptionnew.com/archives)

Lang, Anne Adams. "Identity; When Parents Adopt a Child and a Whole Other Culture." *The New York Times*, March 8, 2000. (web)

National Adoption Information Clearinghouse Articles:
"Adopting Children With Developmental Disabilities." July 1999.
"Adoption and School Issues." 1993.
"Adoption and the Stages of Development." 1990.
"How Many Children Were Adopted in 2000 and 2001?" 2004.
"Persons Seeking to Adopt: Numbers and Trends.: March, 2005.
"Voluntary Relinquishment for Adoption: Numbers and Trends." March, 2005.

Sember, Brette McWhorter. "*The Complete Adoption & Fertility Legal Guide.*" Naperville, IL: Sphinx Publishing, 2004.

Other Resources:
Adoptive Families Magazine

Brochures from Tam Binh, Go Vap and the "Monk Orphanage"

Brochures from the U.S. Department of Health and Human Services, NIH: Cephalic Disorders, Hydrocephalus, Publications List

Carol D. Rowan, Chief, Public Inquiries, Office of Communications and Public Liaison, U.S. Department of Health and Human Services, NIH, NINDS

Chao Ban Newsletter – Allison and Rick Martin

Dr. Katrina A. Gwinn, NINDS-NIH

Dory Kranz, Executive Director, Hydrocephalus Association, San Francisco, CA

Information on Shunts provided by the Hydrocephalus Association, San Francisco, CA

James P. (Pat) McAllister II, PhD, Professor of Neurosurgery and Director of Basic Hydrocephalus Research, University of Utah School of Medicine

Margo Warren, Chief Public Liaison Section, National Institute of Neurological Disorders and Stroke, National Institutes of Health (NIH)

Pip Marks, Outreach Director, Hydrocephalus Association, San Francisco, CA

Websites:
(Various)

Chapter 16:
Interviews:
Ellen Passage, Paul Pinkerton, and Sandy Pinkerton

Other Resources:
American Society for Reproductive Medicine, Copyright 2003, Booklet: Age & Fertility, Adoption, Assisted Reproductive Technologies

Audrey M. Insoft - Personal journals

Binder provided by LSS of NE

CDC- Fertility, Family Planning and Reproductive Health of U.S. Women: Data from the 2002 National Survey of Family Growth

CDC – 2003 Assisted Reproductive Technology Success Rates, National Summary and Fertility Clinic Reports

Pham, Andrew X. *Catfish and Mandala*. New York: Picador, 1999. Farrar, Straus & Giroux.

United Nations Children's Fund and World Health Organization. *Low Birthweight: Country, Regional and Global Estimates*. UNICEF, New York, 2004.

Chapter 17:
Interviews:
Jon Beckenhauer, Shayne Henderson, Bob Jones, Richard (Baz) McRell, Lisa McRell, Grace Mischler, David Pinkerton, James Pinkerton, Joanne Pinkerton, Paul Pinkerton, Sandy Pinkerton, Brenda Rath, Bettie Stanton, Tran Van Thanh (Spanky), Jennifer Yang-Kwait, Cindy Yarger, and Rosemary Pinkerton Young

Articles:
Venella, Meghan. "Manheim Man Helps Families Adopt Orphans from Vietnam." *Lancaster New Era (Lancaster, PA)*, October 20, 2001.

Other Resources:
Arlington National Cemetery
(All information previously listed under Chapter 9 pertaining to Freight Train 053)

Chapter 18:
Interviews:
Debra Brunt, Maxine Chalker, Nancy Ferguson, Christine Grimshaw, Sister Hugynh Thi Kim Hai (Sister Hai) – conversation only, Grace Mischler, David Pinkerton, Hannah Pinkerton, James Pinkerton, Joanne Pinkerton, Paul Pinkerton, Sandy Pinkerton, Brenda Rath, Rosemary Pinkerton Young, and Cindy Yarger

Articles:
Kopfinger, Stephen. "Finding the Peace Amid the Battles." *Sunday News (Lancaster, PA)*, May 8, 2005.

McCarthy, Harriet. "Sensory Integration Disorder in Children Adopted from Institutions." 1998. (www.childrensdisabilities.info)

Strock, Margaret. "Autism Spectrum Disorders (Pervasive Development Disorders)." *National Institute of Health*, U.S. Department of Health & Human Services, 2004.

Epilogue:

Interviews:
Maxine Chalker, Hannah Pinkerton, Paul Pinkerton, and Sandy Pinkerton

Articles:
"Adopted Children Immigrant Visa Unit – Warning Concerning Adoptions in Vietnam." U.S. Embassy, April 2008. (web)

"Angelina Jolie Chose Adoptions From The Heart to Handle Vietnamese Adoption." *The Seattle Times*, March 16, 2007. (web)

"Angelina's Viet Man." *The New York Post*, March 22, 2007.

Bernstein, Elizabeth. "Rules Set to Change on Foreign Adoptions." *The Wall Street Journal*, November 2, 2006.

"Brad and Angelina: Another Baby." *In Touch Weekly*, December 11, 2006.

Bromley, Melanie, et al. "It's a Boy!" *US Weekly*, March 9, 2007.

Brummitt, Chris and Ian Demsky. "Vietnam Ends Adoption Agreement with U.S. Following Fraud Allegations." *The News Tribune (Tacoma, WA)*, April 29, 2008. (web)

Brummitt, Chris. "Vietnam to Halt American Adoptions After Damning U.S. Report." *The Seattle Times*, April 29, 2008. (web)

Fitzenrider, Ellen. "Personal Thoughts on Ethics in International Adoption." International Adoption News. (web)

Gootman, Elissa. "Investigation by INS Delays Obtaining Visas and Snarls Adoptions in Vietnam." *The New York Times*, January 29, 2002. (web)

Graff, E.J. "The Lie We Love." *Foreign Policy*, November/December 2008. (web)

Hauserman, Julie. "Alleging Fraud, State Moves to Close Adoption." *St. Petersburg Times,* November 20, 2002. (web)

Hong, Vu Tien. "U.S. Allegations Prompt Vietnam to Halt Adoption Program." *The Washington Post,* April 29, 2008. (web)

"Interview with Larry Crider, Officer in Charge, MCMC INS." October 15, 2001. Adopt Vietnam website.

Johnson, Kay. "The Tale of Angelina's New Son." *Time Magazine,* March 22, 2007.

"Jolie, Pitt Tour Vietnam Orphanage." CNN, 2006. (web)

Lynch, Jason, et al. "Coming Soon: Kid No. 4." *People Magazine,* March 29, 2007.

Roane, Kit R. "Pitfalls for Parents." *U.S. News & World Report,* June 6, 2005.

Stocking, Ben. "U.S. Alleges Baby-Selling in Vietnam." *Newsday,* April 25, 2008. (web)

"U.S., Vietnam Sign Agreement on Intercountry Adoption." June 23, 2005. (web) www.usinfo.state.gov

"Vietnam to End Adoption Program with U.S." *Forbes,* April 28, 2008. (web)

Other Resources:
Grande, Paula, Adoptive Families Magazine

Hendy, Meghan, Joint Council on International Children's Services

Neroulias, Nicole. "Rockland Rotarians Take Lifesaving Devices to Orphan Babies in Vietnam." *The Journal News (Lower Hudson Valley, NY),* November 21, 2007. Web

(Obituaries - sources stated in previous chapters)

Websites:
(Various)

CPSIA information can be obtained at www.ICGtesting.com
Printed in the USA
BVOW020133031012

301925BV00001B/3/P